I0788940

A Journey to Mouseling Hollow

A Journey to Mouseling Hollow

Book 1: The Fabled Two

Written By:
Robert C. Feol

Edited by: Matthew Ross, PhD
Illustrated by: Greg Condon

Published by Best Seller Publishing®, Pasadena, CA
Best Seller Publishing® is a registered trademark
Printed in the United States of America.
ISBN: 978-1-949535-81-5

This publication is designed to provide accurate and authoritative information
with regard to the subject matter covered. It is sold with the understanding that the
publisher is not engaged in rendering legal, accounting, or other professional advice.
If legal advice or other expert assistance is required, the services of a competent
professional should be sought. The opinions expressed by the authors in this book are
not endorsed by Best Seller Publishing® and are the sole responsibility of the author
rendering the opinion.

For more information, please write:
Best Seller Publishing®
253 N. San Gabriel Blvd, Unit B
Pasadena, CA 91ten7
or call 1(626) 765 9750

Visit us online at: www.BestSellerPublishing.org

To Shannon, Robbie, Kerrigan, and Tennessee
You are my life, my breath, and my vision.
My reason for living.
You are my Mouseling Hollow.
I love you.

And to Wilding
For Believing

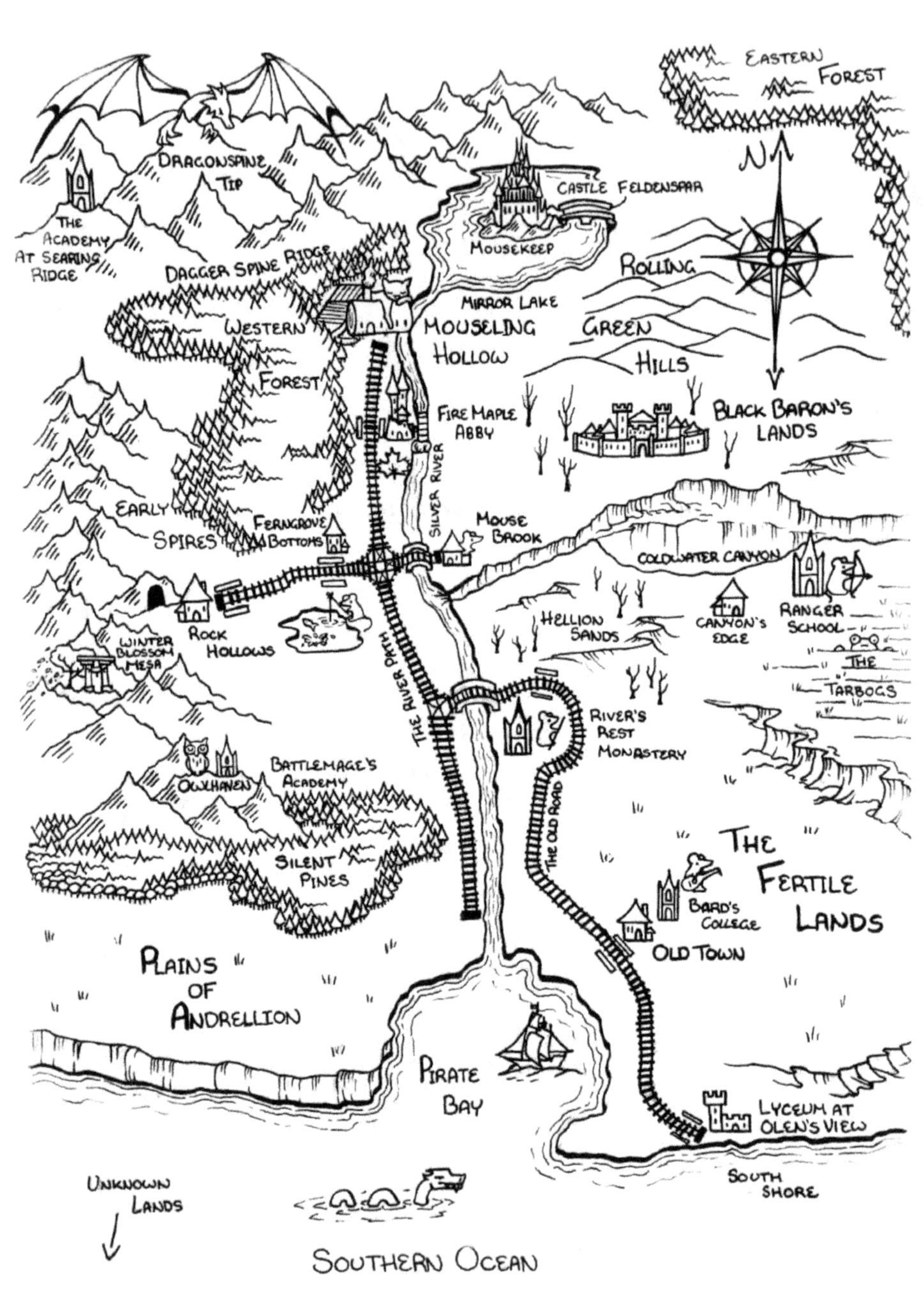

EASTERN FOREST
DRAGONSPINE TIP
THE ACADEMY AT SEARING RIDGE
CASTLE FELDENSPAR
MOUSEKEEP
DAGGER SPINE RIDGE
WESTERN FOREST
MIRROR LAKE
MOUSELING HOLLOW
ROLLING GREEN HILLS
N
FIRE MAPLE ABBY
BLACK BARON'S LANDS
SILVER RIVER
EARLY SPIRES
FERNGROVE BOTTOMS
MOUSE BROOK
COLDWATER CANYON
RANGER SCHOOL
ROCK HOLLOWS
HELLION SANDS
CANYON'S EDGE
THE TARBOGS
WINTER BLOSSOM MESA
THE RIVER PATH
RIVER'S REST MONASTERY
OWLHAVEN
BATTLEMAGE'S ACADEMY
THE FERTILE LANDS
THE OLD ROAD
SILENT PINES
BARD'S COLLEGE
OLD TOWN
PLAINS OF ANDRELLION
PIRATE BAY
LYCEUM AT OLEN'S VIEW
UNKNOWN LANDS
SOUTH SHORE
SOUTHERN OCEAN

TABLE OF CONTENTS

Part III: Returning Home

FOREWORD

There's only one word that can properly capture the experience of talking to Robert Feol about the world of Mouseling Hollow: Passion. Within the first minute of my first conversation with Robert, it was already clear to me that for Robert Feol, **The Far Collective** was not just a unique location for a fantasy story, but a living, breathing, vibrant world he was eager to bring to life. It was easy to get swept up in his enthusiasm, and to see the world through his eyes.

Robert's passion for this story and its characters instantly drew me to this project, and I believe that passion can be felt on every page you're about to read. While the story of Robert Teague and his companions is a classic 'David vs. Goliath' tale of underdogs banding together against incredible odds to fight for what they know is right, the story of its publication — ironically enough — just so happened to follow a similar arc.

By the time I met Robert, he had already run an incredible gauntlet of naysayers who only wanted to take his story and turn it into something that it wasn't. 'Adults won't want to read a story about mice,' he was told, 'The only way it'll work is if you make it a children's book.' 'Children won't want to read a story about middle-aged heroes,' others said, 'you'll have to make the protagonist one of the younger characters.' Voice after voice kept telling Robert why his story wouldn't work...but instead of giving in to doubt, Robert stuck to his guns.

He knew he wanted to tell a story of high adventure and epic scope that readers of all ages could enjoy — one that would be peopled with the bravest of heroes and deadliest of villains, feature pulse-pounding action and shocking twists, that would embrace the classic values of courage, friendship, loyalty, and teamwork — and one in which every reader could find a little bit of themselves in the characters. He wanted to tell a story that showed that anyone, young or old, large or small, could have the heart of a hero beating inside them...even the tiniest mouse.

Like the Mouseling innkeeper Robert Teague, Robert Feol trusted his instincts and went with what he knew in his gut to be right. He told the story he wanted to tell, the way he knew it had to be told, instead of compromising it to try to please others. The first time I sat down to read it, I was captivated by his story within the first few pages, and found myself slipping away from my own everyday life into the world of Mouseling Hollow.

And if we are **telling true tales,** I hope you'll find your own journey into Mouseling Hollow to be every bit as captivating as I did.

Matthew Ross, Ph.D.

EDITOR
9/16/20, Redondo Beach, CA

PROLOGUE

In front of the roaring fire, the old mouse sat comfortably dozing in his ancient wingback chair.

Outside the cozy, windowed library nook, on the western side of the log that he called home, a blizzard raged menacingly, adding even more of winter's tight grasp to the land. As the fierce wind outside blew ferociously, snow accumulated upon the frosted windowsills of the long-fallen oak log, resulting in an almost magical — yet still frigid and hostile — picture which began to form upon the landscape outside.

But for this mouse in particular — and the abundant family members who had come to visit him for the joyous holiday season — all was well, and all were cheerful, snuggly, placid, and secure as they sheltered within his stout, weathered wooden home.

Clothed in his silken night robe, with a matching tasseled cap upon his head, this mouse had just settled in for the evening, having placed his hind paws on a wooden stool carved in a 'figure 8' pattern. On his fireside table sat a small snifter of fine tawny port ready to serve a dual purpose as both a nightcap and — just as importantly — a toast to the deep sleep he looked forward to enjoying, dreams and all.

He **had** earned it, after all.

His belly was full after three helpings — three! — of the best foods that the first night of The Yuletide Feast had to offer. In his head he recounted each course and recipe, his whiskered nose twitching slightly as he recalled sniffing their delectable scents...

Roasted meat pies, their lattice crusts doused in melted herb butter and folded over countless times to yield a rich and flaky crust, the essence of rosemary still hanging on his whiskers; Mousebrook Pudding, abundantly rich and light and cooked in drippings so decadent you could make a splendid gravy out of them alone; braised, shredded beef simmered in a crock for twelve hours, tasting of red wine and fresh garlic; buttery whipped potatoes with just a touch of cream; golden goblets filled to the brim with aged red wine still cool from the cellar, saved for this feast across many seasons; and for dessert there was the rum cake — the richest, most golden and buttery sponge a baker could produce — all scratch made — combined with the finest aged spiced rum, sweet confectioner's sugar, and a decadent, sour orange glaze atop the hot, bubbling crust — oh, and lots of whipped cream on top. If you could imagine how full you'd be after three helpings of these delicacies, perhaps you'd have a notion of why this old mouse, on this particular night, was quite ready for a nap.

With his belly full and sagging, the delightful memories of the feast foremost on his mind, and the barest hint of whipped cream still smudging the corners of his whiskers, he took a nip of the decadent port. Leaning back into his chair, he closed his eyes and took a great big stretch, finally resting his hindpaws on the stool. He listened to the winter wind outside, whipping by the log in a mesmerizing yet soothing frenzy — and then, he prepared to drift off into blissful slumber.

The warmth of the embering fire lulled him, and he felt himself drifting, drifting...

Until all of a sudden, he felt the slightest tug on the pantleg of his pajamas.

It's nothing, he thought to himself. *Just the jerk of my lower paw as I drift off...*

Then, he felt another tug on his pantleg again. Actually, two tugs this time.

Reluctantly, he opened one eye and peered down, only to see at least a dozen young Mouselings at his feet, settling in on the carpet in front of the fire.

'Tell us a story, Grandpa!' said one of them. 'We want a story!'

'Yes! A story, a story!' chimed the young bucks and does. None of them were more than eight seasons, and most looked well below that.

'Now, Grandpa, now! Or sing us a song!' they chirped adamantly at him.

Sleepily, but with great pride, he slowly opened his other eye and peered around the room. All of the young mice looked wide awake and quite ready to hear a tale or two. The sight of his offspring, all gathered around a cozy fire within his home while a blizzard raged outside, suddenly awoke the bard within him. A storyteller he would always be, as well as a musician — no matter his age. And, when an audience presented itself to him, he always felt inexplicably energized.

Even if his audience was just babes.

'A story?!' he said, before closing his eyes again. 'I am far too tired for a story. Leave me be.'

He pretended to settle back into his chair and fall asleep.

'NO GRANDPA! NOOOO! TELL US A STORY!' The young Mouselings shouted almost in unison now. They knew their grandfather was a legendary storyteller, and they would not even think of hearkening to bed without hearing one of his grand tales, especially on the first night of Yuletide.

'So it's a story you want, eh?' He opened one eye again and peered around, eying each young Mouseling in turn. 'I might be able to muster up a quick tale, if only to send you pestering mice to bed.'

The young mice all laughed. They knew what a deep love their grandfather held for them all, and it was a love reciprocated by the young mice as well. They adored — no, **revered** — their grandpa.

Silently, they waited for him to begin weaving a tale.

But instead, he gave them a question.

'What story do you want to hear?' he asked. 'Do you want to hear about Princess Kerrigan Teague's ride upon the bats of the RockHollows and the reuniting of The Dragonspeaker Amulet?'

'No, no!' they cried out in protest. Some of the young mice looked at each other, shaking their heads defiantly.

'Well, then,' said the old mouse, 'perhaps you would like to hear the tale of the famous Arena in the lands of The Black Baron, where mice and all manner of other creatures came to fight for coin and glory? The Arena where some of the greatest champions were made, including the hermit of Winterblossom Mesa, who floated to The Western Lands through the sky upon a cloud from the East?'

'Boo, boo!' they continued to cry out. More head shaking and disapproving looks ensued.

'Oh, very well.' The old, wizened mouse looked up at the ceiling, and he rubbed his greying chin as he thought. 'Perhaps you would like to hear some tales of the greatest detective of Mouseling Hollow, Sir Pendleton Stormsnout? He captured many a villainous and clever foe, solving many mysteries while having the greatest of adventures! Of course, in one of the tales, he even invented an airship, which was used late in The Rat King War!'

'Hiss, hiss!' they cried out disapprovingly. The young mice chattered quietly but energetically amongst themselves, trying to ascertain a verdict of which story was to be selected, while the embers in the fireplace crackled and danced.

Finally, one of the older mice called out.

'Tell us the story of The Rat King!'

A silence suddenly befell the room.

'Yes, yes!' they all cried out. 'Tell us the story of The Rat King!'

'The Rat King?' The old bard sat up on his chair and looked around the room, suddenly animated.

'THAT,' he emphasized, 'is a story which will take days to tell. It is the story of the greatest of mice — Mouselings who sacrificed everything so that we may live freely as we do today, and fought bravely against all odds. It is the story of one of our greatest secrets, and how we allied with humans to fight an unheralded threat. And, if we are telling true tales, it is not a tale which can be told in one night. It takes many evenings for us to weave the story of The Rat King.'

He looked at the young Mouselings, eying each one of them in turn.

'And yet, I hear your families have come to this log to stay for The Yuletide, which lasts for ten days. With a fierce blizzard raging outside, we may have nothing much to do but listen to stories. And, as you older mice know, I don't tell stories to those who don't listen — I would rather nap.'

He leaned back into his chair, pretending to fall back asleep once more.

The older mice began to look at the younger mice quite sternly, telling them 'shhh! shhh!'

Opening an eye once more, he asked firmly: 'Do I have your solemn word that you will listen to this story over the course of many days, and that you will pay attention as I tell you how I witnessed these events firsthand, no matter how long it takes?'

'Yes, yes!' they cried, imploring the old mouse to begin.

'Very well,' he acquiesced, and suddenly got up and walked over to the fireplace, poking around one of the many dusty bookshelves that stood to the right of the hearth. After a few moments of searching, he finally drew out a large, thick, and very grubby leatherbound tome. Carrying it back to his wingback chair with slow steps, he sat back down, brushed a layer of accumulated soot off the worn cover, and opened up the book.

Dust continued to rise from the book as the spine creaked open in protest, and the old bard began to thumb through the pages.

Taking a drink from his glass of port, he looked up at the young Mousekin who sat in front of him, staring eagerly at him with anticipation.

He began to open his mouth as if to speak, then slyly took another drink from his port glass. With the impeccable timing of a seasoned storyteller, he let the silence of the moment continue for a beat.

Finally, he started.

'My young mice, there once was a Mouseling bard known as Ainsley Hearthseeker. And contained within this book is the true chronicle of his many journeys. But this particular journey happened to be the one in which he fell in with a party who was destined to face The Rat King, giving everything they had to try to undo his evil ways, always against nigh-impossible odds.

And so, I give you:

The Story of The Rat King

With a practiced paw, the aged mouse turned the page and began to read one of the greatest stories in the Mouseling tradition — a story of unlikely heroes and dark betrayal, which all started innocuously enough one warm autumn day on the banks of The Silver River, in a small hamlet known as Mouseling Hollow.

Part I

THE HAMLETS THAT TIME FORGOT

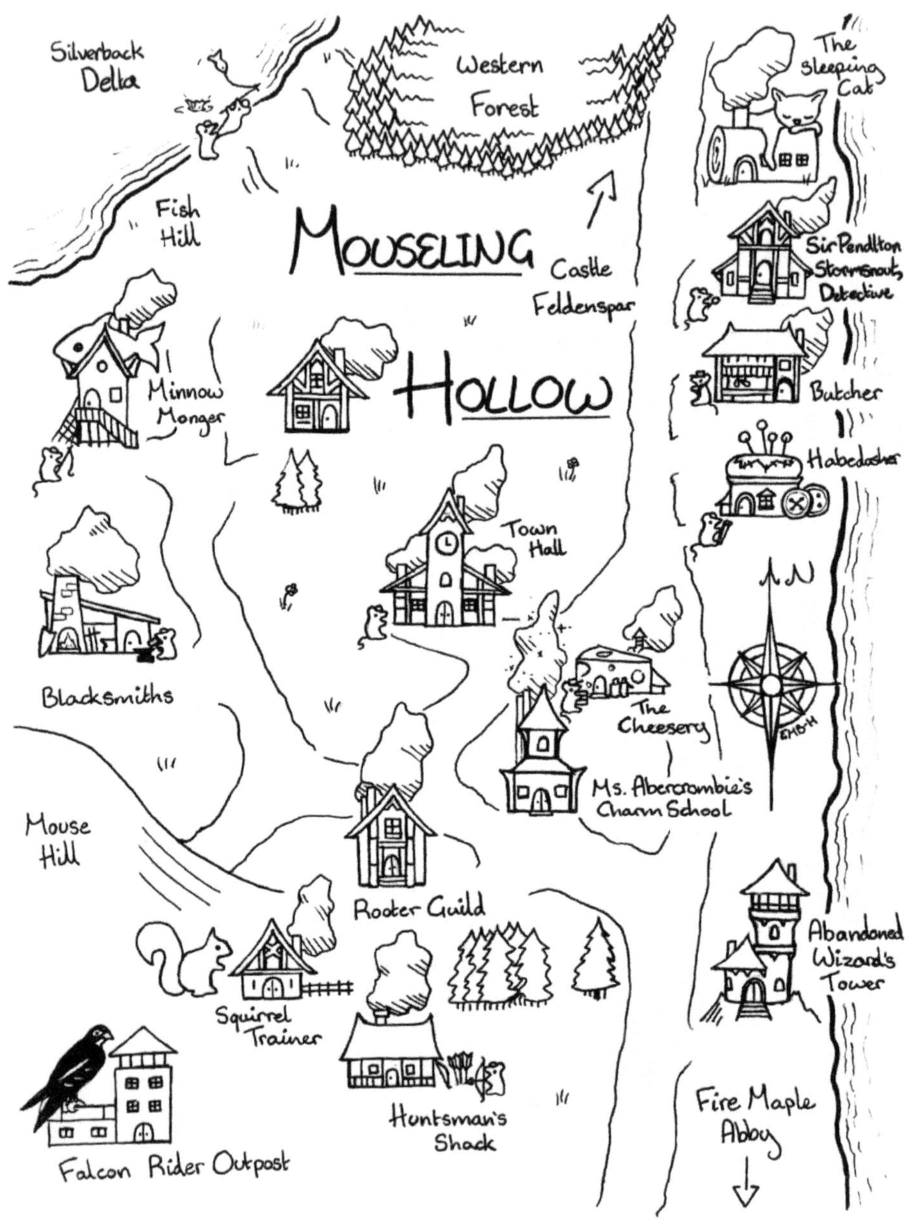

Silverback Delta
Western Forest
The Sleeping Cat
Fish Hill
MOUSELING
Castle Feldenspar
Sir Pendlton Stormsnout, Detective
HOLLOW
Minnow Monger
Butcher
Habedasher
Town Hall
Blacksmiths
The Cheesery
Mouse Hill
Ms. Abercrombie's Charm School
Rooter Guild
Squirrel Trainer
Abandoned Wizard's Tower
Huntsman's Shack
Fire Maple Abbey
Falcon Rider Outpost

Chapter 1

THE SLEEPING CAT INN AND TAVERN

R obert Teague gazed down through his spectacles at the manifest that the tall mouse, mutedly dressed in dark purple robes, had lain before him. The innkeeper brushed his long whiskers out of his sightline and, peering down his greying snout, glanced back and forth between the papers in his hand and the barrels which had been unloaded and stacked high in the wine cellar which lay below the main floor of his tavern.

In his head, he counted meticulously.

With the precision of an aged business mouse who had started with less than nothing, he browsed through the barrels of ale (and more preferably, the cold aged lagers) and checked them against the manifest. A few stouts had made their way into this shipment, which Teague nodded at with assent, but also with a slight trepidation — would his fellow Mouselings enjoy the dark, thick stout which had been brewed by the mouse who had delivered the shipment now standing in front of him?

Time would tell, he thought to himself — and finally, he spoke.

'Well, all seems correct as usual, old friend. It will be interesting to see what the guests think of the Blackhollow Stout you brought. I hope it sells well.'

The tall mouse in front of him looked down at his friend of more than thirty seasons, and then stated with his usual dry wit, 'If your previous sales over the past twenty seasons are any indication, you will be returning this entire shipment to me as dry casks by Sunday night.'

Known as 'The Professor' by most of the village, due to his unchallenged craftsmanship as brewmaster of the most desired drink in the township, Robert Teague called his old friend only by his last name, 'Wilding.' Few knew the Professor's real name, and fewer still knew its origins, though many had asked the innkeeper about it. But when asked, Teague always feigned ignorance to protect his friend's privacy.

The secret of Wilding's origin — and his unrivaled mastery of the craft of beer brewing — was something that the two close friends would take to their graves, it seemed.

'Wilding, you have always been a good friend,' the innkeeper said. 'My best, if we are telling true tales. But you know I have to take care of the people who come to this tavern. Not only their taste in food and drink, but also by making sure they have enough coin to afford what we offer. I have no doubt the stout will sell well. Shall I pay you now?'

The tall mouse peered down over his own greying snout at his best friend, through his own pair of spectacles. 'No, old friend! As per usual, you can pay me when I come to get the empty barrels on Sunday eve. And if it pleases you, could you prepare me a plate of the Sunday harvest special that I can take back with me to my river home? You know it's my favorite. Consider it a tip for an old friend.'

'Done,' said Teague. 'And by the way, don't forget that this coming Friday I need you to plan on being at the tavern early, because we need to...'

A knock at the cellar door and a voice calling down from the main hall interrupted the conversation between old friends.

'Father?' yelled a voice. 'Father, come quick, a messenger is at the door!'

Teague looked at his friend Wilding and they both wistfully embraced each other's furry paws. 'Alas my friend, duty calls — if duty is most assuredly some unimportant task relating to innkeeping! I must now take my leave, though I wish you could stay for an ale, or that we could try this stout together alongside a plate of crispy buttered bacon and herbed potatoes! My lovely Shannon just finished a batch of fresh rolls over the hearth about ten minutes ago, and I think...' — he lifted his whiskered snout to the air — '...I can smell them now. To Friday then?'

'Indeed, Robert, I would not miss it — even for one more chance at catching the great fish we know as The Silverback. But if I may ask, it is a long trip back to FireMaple Abby by squirrel cart — I was thinking, with the harvest celebration starting today, would it be possible for me to requisition a room for the evening? I was hoping to play some **Root and Field** later on, in the companionship of players whom I know are traveling from afar and will be eager for a game as well — not to mention some refreshment! I brought my gaming box with me in anticipation. Assuming you have room, that is?'

'Wilding, I would have you rest in our upstairs apartment, as you are just as much family to me as my children are. And, should you wish, feel free to unhitch your squirrel and feed and water him in the barn out back. The night promises to be an interesting one, and I am sure you will find some fellow **Root and Field** enthusiasts to challenge at the gaming tables as evening draws near. Perhaps even some friendly wagers will be made, eh?'

Embracing gently, the two friends took their leave of each other. Wilding ambled lankily up the cellar staircase and back to his wagon, drawn by a grey squirrel, to untack him and get him situated. Teague, on the other hand, made some final notes on his manifest before starting up the stairs from the cellar. When he reached the outside, he paused — was that rain he smelt on the air?

No time to worry about that now, he thought to himself as he entered a small door to the left of the cellar entrance, which led into the tavern area and great hall. The great hall was the main part of the tavern, which had been hollowed out of a log felled by a storm some twenty seasons previous. A massive piece of wood, it had been carefully hewn to preserve the structure of the exterior bark by adding a healthy amount of timber bracing on both its top and bottom. These architectural improvements had given it strength against rain and wind, prevented water from entering, and allowed the roof to support the massive weight of heavy snowfalls when winter arrived, keeping all the patrons cozy and safe within even in the harshest of conditions.

On both sides of the hollow log, timber and thatch had been intertwined with a number of windows which allowed light to come in. A knothole in the roof, which had long since been removed, provided the only skylight the inn had to offer, filled in with etched stained glass. Within the glass, the patterns formed two colorful cat paws, lending a fanciful touch to the Inn that had become known throughout The Western Lands as 'The Sleeping Cat.'

A front door had been placed in the main area of the great hall where some wood rot had begun to fester, allowing access from the small dirt road outside. And in the middle of this log, craftily hewn by mice who were, for all purposes, expert stone masons, a great hearth rose from the middle of the floor and exited near the knothole at the top, providing warmth and comfort to all of the Inn's guests. The hearth was open on all four sides and supported by stone pillars on the corners. The pillars themselves had been designed to look like the stylized faces of a rat, a cat, a hawk, and a lynx — all, historically, predators and enemies of the mouse folk. When the hearth's fire was high, flames would glow in the mouth of each animal and create a stunning and palpable visage to behold.

The residents of Mouseling Hollow who sought to dine at the Sleeping Cat Inn would often request a place according to which animal 'side' of the hearth they preferred. 'Rat table,' for instance, would be a typical reservation which came in each night. Often the small bucks and does, instead of eating the fine fare laid before them, would get lost in wonder and awe staring up at the faces of the stone rat, cat, hawk, and lynx which towered above them, 'breathing'

fire. It had been costly to construct, for sure, but had paid for itself in spades over the seasons. Robert Teague, for a Mouseling of fifty seasons, had proven himself to be quite the entrepreneur — if an enigmatic one at that.

Naturally, it was an honor to have a place by the fire, and only mice of significant stature, or those who frequented the Inn the most, got these choice tables and seats. But whether you were a wealthy business mouse or a humble rooter, the people of Mouseling Hollow knew — if it was warmth and comfort you sought, Robert Teague, Mouseling, and his family of four, would most certainly accommodate you at their Inn and do whatever was necessary to ensure your comfort. They had been doing it for so many seasons now — and doing it so right — that The Sleeping Cat Inn was the place to be after weekdays (or weekends) of toil were finished.

Whether it was an ale, lager, a plate of scrumptious victuals, or a story that you craved, the Inn had it all. Companionship was a currency traded freely at the Inn, and highly prized. And, they also had fine herbs for smoking (the finest, in fact, outside Castle Feldenspar itself) for those inclined to a pipeful every now and then.

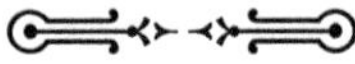

Teague entered his tavern and gazed up at the beams and rafters which had been a fixture of his log Inn for so many seasons. It was early afternoon on the edge of the fall harvest season. As an innkeeper, Teague had become accustomed to interruptions, often for the delivery of various sundries, linens, earthenware, fish, or other such necessities. Entering the great hall, he looked over at his daughter. A mouse of twelve seasons, though she was garbed in the attire of a serving mouse, there was no doubt that she was brilliant. Whether it was the sharp intelligence in her eyes, her silky brown fur, or her lean and athletic stance, she was most certainly no ordinary mouse.

No, not at all.

Kerrigan Teague, daughter of the innkeeper, was a prodigy if there ever was one. As far as Mouselings went, she was at the top of the curve, so to speak — and, for the benefit of both Kerrigan and the family business, the Teagues had tried their best not to show it. They had tried to teach her to humble herself in front of the Inn's patrons (though she was certainly more intelligent than the lot of them) in deference to her twelve seasons versus their interminable ones.

And yet, it seemed there wasn't a subject that young Kerrigan couldn't master once she put her mind to it. She could run you through mathematical tables, the positions of planets and astrological charts, which hops and in what quantity created which type of amber ale or unfiltered wheatberry ale (**and** how to age them), or which bait was best used in each season to catch fish, clams, crayfish, mollusks, or other delicacies found in Mirror Lake.

She spoke languages which the Teagues taught her from a young age, but implored her not to use openly — owl and oscelot, even human and fischer. She had done so well in her early schooling as a doe that her parents were forced to pull her out and train her themselves in between their duties at the Inn. She learned the ways of cooking, herbalism, and basic apothecary skills from her mother, and from her father she had learned, well...everything else. But most of his teachings he had asked her to keep secret. Given her gifts, she might have ended up as an outcast, had she demonstrated openly what she was capable of. Mouselings, though fine folk on the whole, could sometimes be scared by what they didn't understand — and it was all too well known that when a mouse stood out in an unusual way, sometimes the more superstitious (or jealous) types would suspect foul dealings, spread nasty rumors, or worse.

So, out of an abundance of loving caution, the Teagues had done their best to hide their daughter's brilliance and precocious gifts.

But Kerrigan loved her parents so much, and was so enamored by what they taught her, that she didn't seem to mind keeping her talents hidden. Between her thirst for knowledge and her desire to please her family, if being a serving Mouse at the Inn was what she was required to do between her lessons — well, then Kerrigan Teague was happy to help. Besides which, she still loved food, music, and tall tales — none of which were in short supply in the aged log Inn which she called home.

Robert Teague looked at his daughter and sized her up. Her frocked dress was covered in flour, a sure sign that she had been helping her mother bake the biscuits and rolls which would most certainly serve — and satisfy — this coming evening's patrons. As he looked at her, she wiped some flour from her paws and chin.

Without speaking, Kerrigan read her father's thoughts and knew that his meeting with his friend of so many seasons, the Professor, had been inadvertently cut short by her cries. She simply gestured with her paw towards the bar top, which had been hewn out of what was once a massive crooked branch, then sanded and finished with a glossy coat to make it shine — and, of course, to make it impervious to the nicks, spills, and stains which inevitably would come from the business of serving food and drinks to mice who had traveled far and wide to enjoy the hospitality of the Teagues' Sleeping Cat Inn.

'Father, a messenger for you,' she said. Kerrigan then answered his unspoken question by whispering 'I thought it was best that I call for you. He refused to say where he is from, and asked only to speak with you directly.'

Teague thought this a bit odd. But, given the fact that the harvest was nearly upon them and there was going to be an influx of traders, proprietors, adventurers — and inevitably, ne'er do wells — wending their way to the Sleeping Cat, nothing on the surface seemed too alarming to him. Teague was no stranger to, well, *strangers*, so he ordered his daughter to return to the kitchen, posthaste.

'Thank you my dear, I will attend to this unusual guest. Go help your mother prepare the fish shipment which should be arriving shortly. We need them ready to be fried for tonight's harvest special — and the potatoes as well. I want them all fresh, crispy, and golden. And don't forget the tartar sauce! I brought up some pickles from the root cellar especially for the harvest.'

'Yes, Father,' said Kerrigan, who curtsied slightly and disappeared through a split two-door exit behind the bar.

Teague silently and (almost) effortlessly slipped behind the bar top and peered down upon the visitor who had requested an audience with him. It was hard to see the face of the mouse who sat across from him, as he was still wearing a hooded traveling cloak of charcoal grey — and a thick one indeed — drawn up over his head. About all that was discernible were his whiskers and a black nose at the edge of his snout.

'Hail, friend! I am Robert Teague, innkeeper and proprietor of The Sleeping Cat. What can I offer you? Are you in need of an ale or grog after dusty travels?'

'Ale, indeed, good sir — and so much more. We can start with the drink of kings and move on to more pressing subjects.'

Teague found this reply strange and off-putting, but as an innkeeper of countless seasons, he had encountered more than his fair share of strange and off-putting mice. It was a tavern, after all, where alcohol was freely imbibed.

Grabbing a wooden stein from underneath the bar, he began to draw the ale and fill it from the tap. Golden liquid, still cold from the wine cellar from whence he had just taken leave from his friend not ten minutes prior, poured generously into the cup. When it started to froth to a creamy head, Teague capped it off and slid the mug across the table to the unusual, and still unidentified, traveler. He had become known for his hospitality like that, and prided himself on seeing the signs of a wearied traveler and providing them the 'medicine' that they needed, in whatever liquid form that took.

And, of course, the Mouselings loved him for it, and revered the innkeeper for his ability to make a mouse feel like they were at home, no matter how far away from their homes The Sleeping Cat happened to be.

'Harvestberry Ale, my friend, and some of the finest brew that can be found in the shadow of Castle Feldenspar! So fresh, too — these berries were picked this season, and crafted by our local brewmaster, whom the townsfolk reverently call 'The Professor.''

Teague nimbly handed the mug to the strange mouse across the bar top from him with a smile, and to his great surprise, the strange mouse quite suddenly knocked the mug aside.

How **rude**, Teague thought incredulously.

'I changed my mind,' the mouse across the bar said abruptly. 'Actually, I think I'd prefer some of your 'legendary' Crab Apple Frost Wine.' The strange mouse held up his fingers as if to make quotation marks when he used the word **legendary**, with some disdain.

Reluctantly, and with more than a little offense, Teague went back to the wall where the taps were and drew a fresh mug of Crab Apple Frost Wine. The Frost Wine was a limited edition drink — only available each fall — which took an entire year to age, greatly limiting the supply. It just so happened that it was the innkeeper's favorite drink too, and the fact that this rude mouse whom he had never met was bossing him around, wasting his ale and making demands was starting to give him an irksome disposition. Nonetheless, he was always a consummate professional, so he had an amicable smile on his face when he returned with a new mug in his paw and gently slid it across the table.

'This is a very special vintage,' Teague started to say as he tried to engage the strange mouse once more, 'also made by The Professor. However, what is interesting to note is that we have to wait an entire year for the drink to be ready. Due to the fermentation process, and the fact that you have to wait for the first freeze to increase the sugar content of the crabapples...'

'Yes, yes,' the strange mouse said, waving his paw in an incredibly rude gesture of dismissal.

The visitor raised the mug to his lips, though the grey tunic still masked his face. He took a long, long draught of the Frost Wine, and when he set the mug back down on the bar top, he inhaled — then exhaled — in a sigh of satisfaction. To Teague's surprise, he saw the mug was now half empty. After a moment, the strange mouse looked up at Teague.

'This Professor...' he started. He looked up at the ceiling for a moment, suddenly lost deep in thought.

'And yet you call him by a different name now, innkeeper, don't you?' said the mouse who sat across from him at the bar top. 'You and he called each other different names long ago, did you not?'

A pause fell between them, as they locked eyes in the moment.

Robert Teague now understood that this strange visitor was uninvolved with commerce or anything else related to the business dealings of the tavern. Teague looked at the stranger who raised the cup again to his lips. But before he could drink, the stranger spoke once more.

'We have much to discuss, Robert Teague. Or should I call you innkeeper? Names don't seem to matter much to you, it would seem. But know that I come on official business — so official one would find it hard to believe I was sent to meet a Mouseling who lives in a hollowed out log, serving ale to mice who come from all across The Far Collective. Yes, yes...' the mouse said, as he drew back his hooded tunic to reveal his battle scarred snout, 'you and I have a great many things to discuss beyond your tavern duties. I wonder, Robert Teague, have you ever heard of The Legend of **The Fabled Two**?'

Teague shuffled uncomfortably at the bar. This Stranger was asking questions which were very unusual, and acting oddly on top of it.

'Yes, Stranger, I have heard the tale. In this Inn we have a great deal of music, and there are no shortage of tall tales and legends to be heard — though some are told as tales, while others are told in song, as ballads. What does this have to do with your need to see me, or any other business at this Inn?'

'Everything,' he retorted. 'And let's begin with this.'

From underneath his tunic, held in a paw whose brown fur was beginning to fleck grey with age, the strange visitor brought forth an envelope with the royal seal of Castle Feldenspar on it.

Silently, he handed it to the innkeeper.

Teague stared at the mouse for a moment, and then finally took the parchment from him.

'I'm sorry, Stranger, but I didn't catch your name?' said the barkeep.

'My name is unimportant and none of your business,' the mysterious mouse snapped.

Whoever he is, nothing good can come from this rude Stranger's visit, Teague thought to himself.

In the silence that passed between them, Teague distantly heard the great Midnight Clock that sat atop the town hall chime three pm.

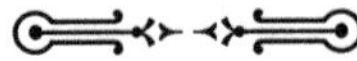

'Sniff out the cheese and make sure the cat is fast asleep!!!'

— MOUSELING HOLLOW
SLANG MEANING 'TO GET READY.'

• • • • • • • • • • •

Chapter 2

Bringing in The Harvest: A Celebration

• •

If the Harvest was the most beautiful season in the land of Feldenspar, then the greatest testament to this fact were most certainly the forests of Mirror Lake (or 'The Mirrored Lake,' as mouse folk sometimes called it). The forests were filled with trees whose leaves were brilliantly colored in red, orange, and yellow hues, cast radiantly against the grey and white background of the Daggerspine mountains off in the distance. A close second in beauty were the fields of wheatberries which dotted the outskirts of Feldenspar Castle in a rich and golden-hued yellow — where the berries, in full blossom, were so rich they almost looked like ink quills fresh from the scrivener.

In Mouseling Hollow, Harvest season was a critical one — mousefolk everywhere scurried to bring in the harvest in preparation for the coming Great Winter — and though the many different kindred families had varying jobs they performed dutifully, it was understood that **ALL** had to pull together, or all would starve in the coming season. Critical jobs, such as ploughing the mini-wheatberries which had been harvested generations ago from the human wheat fields, were given to older, more weathered mice.

The younger bucks and does, eager to learn the ways of their forefathers, were relegated to tasks more suited for their energetic physique (and short attention spans), such as gathering fruit from the fallen apples of Castle Feldenspar's orchards (a laborious task indeed, given the length of the trek across The Western Forest while bringing an apple twice the size of a mouse in tow), collecting grapes that had fallen to the ground from the castle's vineyards, or, for those who had been on their best behavior, there was the most prized assignment of all: the daily fishing assignments. The common school of the mousefolk, where the younger generations learned how to read, write, use mathematical theory, and study language, took a break during Harvest time for all the young mice to contribute. While the young ones could be counted on to try their hardest at whatever Harvest job they were given, nevertheless, all the eager bucks and does knew that getting a fishing assignment was truly a special assignment, indeed.

And what a sport it was! Stories were told in abundance, plentiful indeed, about the one which 'got away,' including the most legendary fish of all: The Silverback. The mousekin, truth be told, fished for mere minnows on the shores of The Mirrored Lake, casting a line from a stout oaken twig with a lure of grub usually, or maybe some corn kernels scavenged from the fields nearby. But even a two inch minnow, when it struck hard and deep, could drag a mouse into the depths of The Mirrored Lake, never to return. Because of the dangers, fishing was always done in pairs, and sometimes even entire teams of Mouselings. One mouse would man the fishing rod, while the other waited vigilantly, standing ready to help bring in the fish — or save a friend from taking a swim. Sometimes that meant tugging on the fishing rod, and sometimes tugging desperately at the rear paw that was the only thing preventing a terrified fishermouse from being yanked from the shore.

Naturally this proved to be a terrific bonding experience, and the young bucks who successfully managed to bring in a minnow would spend weeks proudly discussing this feat and boasting of how they

had saved each other's fur from the brink of disaster. Other mice, who came home from a fishing expedition empty handed and sopping wet, shook their heads and spoke instead of how the fish seemed a bit 'too big' for any decent mouse to handle — and if they couldn't have reeled it in, no one else could have landed the monster either, that was for certain!

It was all in good fun, anyway, and a task that was necessary before The Mirrored Lake froze. A two or three inch minnow could provide enough filet and other sundries, in the form of giblets, fish stock, and bones (which could be crafted into any number of useful items), that the truth was it didn't take too many minnows to provide the mousekin with everything they needed — and when the sun descended past the mountain top at the closing of the day, not a single mouse spent too long dwelling on the fish that had gotten away, for everyone was too thankful for what **HAD** been brought in. When one was lucky enough to draw a fishing assignment, it was never lacking in adventure — **ESPECIALLY** when a mouse had a close companion to accompany him.

Adventure, however, was not on the mind of Robert Teague that day as he watched the sun descend over the jagged peaks which backed up to Feldenspar Castle. He sniffed the air delicately, and frowned — it still smelled like rain was coming shortly, just as it had a few hours previously when he and Wilding had been finishing up their business in the wine cellar. Between his vantage point outside The Sleeping Cat and his stature, he couldn't actually see the whole castle — but he saw the spires edging above the trees, and the peaks of the Daggerspines rising high behind them. When the sun went down it would be time for him to begin to work — *really* work — and the seemingly endless procession of couriers and artisans bringing their wares to the tavern for the coming weekend feast felt more pronounced than usual.

Teague could almost imagine the cascade of dry goods and sundries being brought into the Inn's storehouses and cellars stretching the subterranean walls until they were about to burst.

There were fish, of course — silver minnows, fresh from The Mirrored Lake, with the young bucks who brought them in wheeled carts eagerly looking for a silver coin — and for some of the more mature bucks, asking for a cold ale on top — as a tip. Teague sent these boys scurrying after paying them, letting them know, in no uncertain terms, that there was no room at his Inn for underage mice gallivanting about without their parents — let alone louts who sought an ale simply for catching a fish. Naturally, Wilding and Teague had enjoyed many a pint after a day of fishing, in that very same Inn no less — but, the young bucks didn't need to know that. And besides, he barely had enough ale to cover the coming weekend influx of travelers anyways, let alone some thirsty young fishermice!

And then there was flour from the miller, fresh from the milled wheatberries which had just been brought in. Mulled and deep spiced wine from the vintner, just up the riverpath. Potatoes, golden carrots, fingerlings, pumpkins, corn and other rich bounty from the Harvest, courtesy of the gardener. Eggs from the chickens of Feldenspar Castle, painstakingly taken by cart across The Western Forest from the coops just outside the Castle. Honey from the beekeeper — also nicked from Castle Feldenspar, because what mouse had the fortitude or constitution to wrestle a colony of bees, for heaven's sake? Stealing into the castle to bring some honey back was a much more preferable way of acquiring the sweet golden nectar — not to mention safer. In the world of Mouseling Hollow, and for the proprietors of The Sleeping Cat, all of these goods and sundries collided in a tapestry of market supply, demand, and innkeeper's oversight. And always foremost on Teague's mind was the thirst and hunger of eager mice famished after a day, or week, of toil and labor — and how he could help to satiate it.

Entering from the kitchen, Teague's wife, Shannon, exuded grace with every step. Ten seasons his younger, she was nonetheless his reason for being — along with their three young children, of course.

It was obvious she had spent the entire day in the kitchen, since not long after sunup, preparing all of the baked goods and pie crusts for the evening's service — not to mention those notable items which were to be served only on the occasion of the Harvest holiday, which ran through the coming Sunday. This, of course, was when the harvest would be brought in and the mousefolk would start collecting what non-food items they would need, in earnest, to stay warm throughout the coming winter.

Teague watched his wife step from behind the bar top and point to the black slate on the wall, visible to both the patrons already seated at the bar top, as well as any who entered — presumably hungry, thirsty, and eagerly scanning the hall for an open table around the four animal stone fireplace.

'Shannon, my love...have you seen Wilding?' Teague asked. Absentmindedly, he fingered the note in his pocket, annoyed and irritated at the thought of The Stranger.

'No, Robert, not since he went upstairs for a post-lunch nap. I fed him some of the roast pork cutlets from the grill, with the raspberry chipotle glaze, which the children and I shared for lunch. Oh, and with a side salad of greens and blue cheese crumbles. Light and delicious!" Shannon sighed at the memory. 'But truly, I think he may be saving his appetite for eating and...' she paused for a moment, a frown of disapproval crossing her face, '...drinking for later this evening, when the Harvest festival opens. Why, what do you need him for?'

Teague fingered the note in his pocket once more. He felt the broken seal brush his fingertips, and his stomach churned at the thought of the message inside. But still, he feigned innocence. 'No reason,' he fibbed. 'I wanted to ask him about, um...' he thought for a second as he stammered, then quickly recovering, continued '...whether we have enough of his new stout for the evening. By the way, did you see that strange mouse at the bar?'

'Yes, he booked a room with Thistlefur and asked her to start a tab, saying that you and he had already spoken and that you knew who was going to reconcile his bill. He also told Thistlefur that you had given him permission to take our royal suite. He mentioned that he was quite looking forward to the feast tonight, and to enjoying some more Crab Apple Frost Wine. He must be a mouse with some wealth and privilege, which I hope translates into some coin for us, my dear.'

Shannon smiled at the thought. 'Imagine, such a royal mouse 'dropping in' to our 'Inn!''

The irony of the pun was not lost on Teague, who tried his best to contain himself. However, despite his self restraint, he could feel the irritation inside of him growing.

Now this Stranger has a tab? he thought to himself. *Inconceivable!*

Working to calm himself and not let his emotions show, he glanced back at his wife.

'Shannon, my darling, where were we?' He pointed back towards the clean menu slate hanging behind the bar.

His wife looked at him eagerly, excited about the Harvest festival, which was always her favorite season.

'My dear, we have loaded and stocked so many delicious items, while I have some ideas of what we should serve over the coming week, I wanted to get your opinion.'

'Show me,' said Teague, tempering his annoyance with the Stranger. 'Write them on the board and I will read them all before I dare to interject a comment!'

Teague's wife smiled, not only because of his respectful and reserved demeanor, but also because this was an exercise they had both been through countless times before. While the patrons of The Sleeping Cat all knew that Shannon Teague was the master chef behind the Inn's fine offerings each day, another little known secret was that she **and** her husband were both experts in the kitchen. Robert Teague was glad to let his wife have all the credit for the quality of the Inn's victuals. But when it came to menu making, both were equally responsible — and this disguised fact was one of many reasons why mousekin from all across The Far Collective had sought out this place for fine fare, smokes, ale, and perhaps most cherished of all, tales.

Teague's wife began to write the evening's menu on the board. Grasping a small piece of chalk in her brown furred paw, she pulled a stool over, climbed up, and began to write. When she was done, the slate was filled with flowing writing, artistic in design but easily readable by all mice. It said:

The Sleeping Cat Inn
Harvest Season Menu (Good Through Sunday)

Fried Crispy Silverback

Lemon Butter, Golden Salted Fingerlings, Fresh Herbs

Tomato Cheese Pie

Golden Lattice Crust, Mushroom Corn Filling, Honey Corn Butter Biscuits (by Robbie Teague)

Feldenspar Rarebit

Melted Aged Harvest Cheddar, Blackhollow Stout, Rosemary, Eastern Thyme, Toast Points, Served in Crock

On Tap (from 'The Professor')

Harvest Berry Wheat Ale

Frog Grog

Blackhollow Stout (seasonal selection from 'The Professor')

Crab Apple Frost Wine

Mulled Glacial Wine (red)

Lion's Mane Select Rum (from the King's private stock)

Dessert

Lion's Mane Rum Cake — Rich Grassy Butter, Orange Cognac Sugar Glaze — by Robbie Teague

Gates of Feldenspar Tawny Port (20 Year, Special Reserve for the Harvest)

Proudly, Shannon Teague turned to look at her husband. She had worked so diligently throughout the past weekend and into the midweek preparing this menu, and she knew it was a special one. The Rarebit alone was sure to be a massive hit. But when she looked expectantly at her husband in anticipation of his grandiose praise, she noticed he was staring quietly out the western window, lost in distant thought.

'Robert, what's wrong?' she queried, slightly concerned.

Teague, upon hearing her voice, looked back from the window. 'Nothing,' he said. 'The menu, as always, looks wonderful. There is no doubt all of our guests, from travelers afar to our regular patrons, will be thrilled to feast on this menu. With the new shipment of ales and other drinks from The Professor, by Her blessing, everyone will be sated before the night is finished.' Teague got up from his barstool and headed upstairs to the bedroom wing which included their personal residence. 'I've got to get cleaned up and get ready for the dinner service,' he said as he padded up the staircase.

How odd, thought his wife. Normally Robert Teague was thrilled by food: the subtle variation in recipes, the complement of side dish accoutrements, the synergy in pairing fine ales and wines with the fresh fare they complement to create perfection on a plate — it had become an artistic pursuit almost as much as a culinary one as the years had passed. While still a necessary part of the Inn's business, the couple had grown to share a great pride in the purely culinary aspect of their food service, and a love of designing dishes and menus that would delight and surprise their customers. There was no doubt in Shannon Teague's mind that something was amiss with her husband, but she hadn't a clue what it was. She felt a slight pulse of trepidation, like butterflies in her tummy — which was also growling, as thanks to the sheer amount of food preparation that she and Kerrigan had been doing all day, she'd barely had a spare moment since breakfast.

It was so busy, in fact, that they'd had Robbie, their oldest (and only) son of fourteen seasons, helping in the kitchen for the past several days as well — and he was none too happy about it. He'd been lucky enough to draw a coveted fishing assignment, only for his father to politely recuse him from the task, saying he was needed instead to stay and help at the Inn. Getting stuck baking bread at the Inn for three straight days instead of fishing with his best friend, a young buck named Tad Reedwhisker, on the shore of Mirrored Lake — ***and*** having to watch his fishing duty get reassigned to a less deserving mouse? Young Robbie nearly choked on the thought. Shannon Teague knew their son was pretty upset, but work — and family — came first. Not to mention that Robbie was quite the baker and budding pastry chef himself. Besides, they would make it up to him when they took their annual vacation down the Riverpath at Ferngrove bottoms, where he could spend the entire week fishing with his dad, if he pleased.

Shattering the silence, Shannon heard loud voices and what sounded like shouting coming from the kitchen. She blitzed behind the bar top and through the double doors which led to the kitchen, then stopped and curved an ear through the window at the upper part of the door frame and listened:

'Take that, you no good Fischer Keeper!' A piece of risen bread dough went flying across the kitchen.

'Have at you, you mangy Ratlicker! You couldn't even serve the Rat King himself!' A piece of dough, shaped vaguely like a saucer, went hurtling in the opposite direction. From out of the corner of her eye, Shannon Teague saw her son Robbie barely duck in time to avoid taking a snout full of dough. She looked back in the direction from which the dough had just been flung to see Kerrigan, a rolling pin grasped firmly in her paw, stand ready for an imminent hand to hand engagement.

Shannon burst through the double doors and yelled, 'Now you listen here you two, what exactly do you think you are do—'

But before she could finish her sentence, Robbie wound up and fired the same piece of dough which he had narrowly avoided getting smacked with by his sister's nimble throw — but instead of hitting Kerrigan, it came flying, unintentionally, right at their mother! Before the two siblings could say anything — ***SMACK*** — it struck their mother squarely, and somewhat firmly, right in the snout, and her glasses went flying. The kitchen, joyful and boisterous not but a moment ago, fell quickly into an uncomfortable stillness.

A cloud of flour raised by the melee slowly started to settle. Robbie and Kerrigan both looked at their mom, then at each other, then *back* to their mom. The tension in that pause was so thick it could have been sliced with a rapier.

Kerrigan looked at the rolling pin in her hand and lay it back down on the kneading table. The **thump** of it coming to rest on the wooden tabletop finally prompted their mother to move. She peeled the dough from her face and peered intently at both children, who looked somewhat more fuzzy than usual without her customary spectacles.

'Mom, are you mad?' Robbie asked, breaking the uncomfortable silence.

He watched as his mom ripped the dough in half, expressionless.

'We're sorry, Mom, we were just fooling around...' started Kerrigan.

'You know what I have to say about this, children?' said Shannon Teague as the furrow in her brow deepened.

The siblings looked at each other, then back to their mother.

'DOUGH IN YOUR FACE!'

With the grace and agility of one of The Lionsmane's elite guardians, she whipped the two halves of dough in her paws at her children and struck them both squarely in the snouts. After a brief moment of shock, the two younger Mouselings burst into laughter as they peeled the dough from their faces.

'Now clean this up before your father finds out that you have been playing with his food!' she humphed, before walking out of the kitchen. 'Tonight is the busiest night of the year, after all.'

Note from Teague to Wilding For a Supply Order:

Wilding,

Here is what we shall need this week for the upcoming Spring Planting festival. There are some sundries I will also need you to grab for me from Rock Hollows when you head down there on Tuesday. The ratty old vole who runs the General Store here simply refuses to carry the stuff, and if I have to march over there and ask him to order it one more time, I just know I'll end up fighting him.

- *4 Kegs Dandelion Wine*
- *6 Kegs Strawberry Bitter*
- *As many cases of the Abby's Red Chianti as you can muster (you know the ones, in those cute wicker-wrapped bottles)*
- *5 Kegs of Flaming Rock Ale*
- *Parsley bitters*
- *Orange peel*
- *Mousebrook stone ground mustard, 7 crocks*
- *That grass fed butter I like (if they don't have any, let me know and I'll check with The Rooting Guild here in Mouseling Hollow)*
- *2 wheels Feldenspar Roquefurt*
- *4 wheels Feldenspar Aged Sharp Cheddar*
- *ten wheels Feldenspar Swiss*
- *3 eggs*

I think that should be it for now. See you Thursday morning. If you happen to see that ratty vole, tell him I'll fight him the next time he even thinks about taking that rude tone with me again. I'm sick of his little games — maybe I'll open up my own store.

- *Teague*

Chapter 3

A GAME OF MICE AND KINGS

Shannon Teague had been right. It felt like never before had there been a busier night at the Inn.

From all over, the Mousekin had come for the harvest — from The Western Forest's edge clear down the Riverpath, all the way to the Rock Hollows. For many of them, it was a seasonal obligation — many of the mousekin sought work in the fields, which was never more needed (or more pressing) than when the harvest was ready to be brought in. These laboring mice had come to complete the harvest gathering and had done so for years, with many long-lasting friendships having been formed in the process. The end of the harvest was completed with a multi-day celebration that was always held at Mouseling Hollow — with Robert Teague's Inn being, at any given time, the unofficial center of all harvest activity.

Mouseling Hollow and the surrounding plains were some of the most fertile land in all of Feldenspar. And for the mousekin, harvesting came in two forms — the first form was the actual bringing in of crops and other goods through farming and crafting. The second, and somewhat more dangerous form was the art of scavenging the mousekin referred to as ***Rooting***. Rooting might cover anything from the simple collection of small, easily totable items, like crab apples fallen to the ground in an orchard, to the riskier task of pilfering items from unsuspecting human farmers, such as nicking eggs from human coops, to the most dangerous of all tasks — infiltrating Castle Feldenspar and other human enclaves to seek out those goods which were otherwise unobtainable for mice due to excessive peril. The collection of honey, for example, was much more easily performed by discreetly drawing it out of a jar in a human kitchen in the dead of night, rather than taking on the undesirable task of trying to collect it from an active beehive — where multiple stings could mean permanent injury — or far worse — for an unlucky Mouseling.

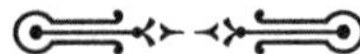

The faces of hardworking mousefolk, both new and familiar, overflowed the Inn that evening. And while Robert Teague had sometimes had difficulties matching a name with a face, he could most certainly match a weary face with a good heart.

'Tavernkeep Robert, my good friend,' one mouse started, 'it is such a pleasure to see you again. My crew and I have been bringing the berries up all the way from The Dark Caverns to The Western Forest's edge. It is good tidings, indeed, to see your face and know another successful season is upon us.'

A seasoned housekeeper, innkeeper, and greeter, Teague met his guest with a graceful hospitality and an impressive remembrance of detail.

'I have been wondering about you and your crew since the last harvest, as it were. What a relief to see you all here and intact once again! And know that it makes my heart happy to see your whiskers still as full and dark as they were three seasons ago. Please, make yourself at home. If it may please you and your hardworking kin, I think you will find the Golden Silverback to be beyond your expectations — especially if washed down with a fine mug of Frog

Grog. Finish it off with some of my young Robbie's cake, and you may find yourself ready for a hay bed in short order!'

'Thank you, kind Robert!' the crew chief said, nimbly extending a work-worn paw. 'My crew and I are thrilled to have been able to book a room for the next few nights at this very Inn, so we can look forward to more of this wonderful hospitality of yours!' The crew chief turned back to his colleagues and raised his mug. 'A toast,' he cried, 'to Robert Teague of The Sleeping Cat! The greatest innkeep all the way from the Daggerspine Tip to Mouseling Hollow! Huzzah!'

'Huzzah!' the tavern erupted in an excited chorus.

Teague smiled and nodded, but as a humble mouse, he certainly wasn't one to give a speech — especially about himself. Besides, there were many more customers to be taken care of, and evening had only just fallen — which meant many more mousefolk would need to be fed and entertained before Teague's family saw their beds. Overall, as Teague glanced around, he couldn't help but be pleased at the turnout, and at the tavern that had become his livelihood for so many seasons. It all impressed him — the way the food was flowing, the fantastic menu that his wife had designed specifically for the evening, The Professor's ale and grog (and stout — indeed, his friend had been right about the stout) flowing freely from the taps and complementing their fine cuisine while people parted freely with their coin, issuing rave reviews all the while as the dinner service continued.

It is a work of art in motion, really, thought Teague. Then he glanced down at the whiskered faces of those who sat at his bar top until he noticed who was sitting in the very last barstool, and his smile slowly faded. 'Well, almost,' he muttered.

Teague glanced back in the kitchen and saw his wife Shannon, as well as Robbie and Kerrigan, busily ferrying food to and fro, bussing plates and tables, and taking orders while he kept the bar and tried to provide a general sense of steadiness in this packed and somewhat chaotic environment. Yet for all of his pride and happiness in that moment, he couldn't help but be aware of a rising feeling of dread in his gut — especially as he looked to the end of his bar, where the

Stranger had handed him the envelope with the King's seal on it earlier that day. The Stranger sat quietly and ate, with a surprising amount of grace, his plate of Feldenspar Rarebit — a delicacy of blended golden cheeses and Blackhollow Stout, melted in the oven in a creamery crock and served with toast points — truly a delicacy for any Mouseling if there ever was one. As he watched, he saw the Stranger chase each bite of rich, golden cheese toast with a draught of Crab Apple Frost Wine.

Something about this annoyed Teague, and he knew it irritated him far more than it should have that the Stranger had booked a room at the Inn without even telling Teague directly, instead of delivering his missive and leaving. Even more irritating was the way that, without even saying so directly, the Stranger had somehow insinuated to Teague that he expected to be treated like a VIP customer of long standing — it was extremely bothersome in its arrogant presumptions. Teague hadn't even seen the strange mouse the rest of the day, until he somehow crept into that last bar seat unnoticed and ordered food and drink from Teague's assistant barkeep, a younger mouse known by his nickname, Hawkdodger.

Hawkdodger got his name, allegedly, because of the scar on his face extending down towards his nose. The story went that on one unfortunate day, a hawk had tried to grab him and turn Hawkdodger into his evening meal. By mere chance, he turned around and spied the hawk in mid-attack — and while he was deft enough to dive out of the way of the grasping talons, the hawk's left talon, which had been reaching for him as he turned, gave Hawkdodger a pretty hefty gash on his snout. The gash eventually scarred over, and on that day Hawkdodger escaped with his life, a story to tell, and an enviable nickname to boot.

He had become indispensable to Teague during the harvest season (especially on nights like this) and helped out in the daytime when Teague was busy with the tasks required of an innkeeper beyond the mere servicing of customers — the mandatory ordering, stocking, menu planning, food and drink prep, bookkeeping, and so forth. Even with Teague's family of four all working at the Inn they still needed the additional help, especially with the baby of three seasons up in the nursery. Hawkdodger was a pretty charismatic mouse, as well, which left him perfectly suited for the position of barkeep. A speedy hand behind the bar, he was equally adept at serving out lore and mousetales as he was Frog Grog and Harvest Berry Ale. He really was a legendary storyteller, and a great listener as well — which was the first prerequisite for anyone seeking to be well liked behind a bar top.

Teague went up to Hawkdodger, who was, with some notable agility, washing, drying, and sanitizing a massive stack of wooden mugs underneath the bar top in a makeshift sink.

'Dodger — did you happen to serve that mouse at the end of the bar, the one in the tunic?'

'Aye sir,' replied Hawkdodger. 'And a strange fellow he was, that one. He ordered the Rarebit and a cup o' the Frost Wine, then told me you would be picking up his tab. When I tried to ask him how he came to be at The Sleeping Cat during this harvest season, he rather curtly told me to mind my own business and said any questions I had for him would be better directed to you, and that I could kindly leave him be. I didn't mean to pry, as it were, I was asking more to be hospitable than anything, y'see. I found his manners — if you go by the standards of those of us who live here in the Hollow, that is — to be rather short and, if I may say sir, lacking.'

Teague's annoyance, if mild a moment ago, began to deepen. He felt himself get hot under his whiskers. 'Don't mind him. But take care of him, and if he does anything strange, come get me.'

'Strange, sir?' Hawkdodger said quizzically. "Such as...'

'Well, I don't know,' sputtered Teague, sensing the silliness of his statement. 'If he does anything, well, odd. Like, if he gets up, for instance.'

'What if he has to relieve himself sir? Should I come get you then?' Hawdodger failed to suppress a grin on his face as he asked this seemingly benign question.

'Well, WHATEVER!' said Teague crossly. 'You know what I mean!'

'Aye, sir. Will do.' Hawkdodger noted a customer calling for him at the bar and excused himself to refill a mug of stout.

Teague sensed, with Hawkdodger steadily in control of the bar patrons and his family taking care of those seated at the tables, that now was a good time to meander over and say hello to the Mousekin who were in the smaller restaurant area of the Inn, seated by the large fireplace in the middle. Teague began to make his rounds, clasping paws heartily with the older mice, gently patting the shoulders of their young bucks and does, telling stories, and ambling about.

Yes, if it wasn't for that stranger who came to the bar, thought Teague as he moved from tabletop to tabletop, greeting honored guests who begged him to sit for a moment and tell them a story, *tonight would be a rather spectacular evening in the history of the Inn.* But every time Teague was asked to join the families and workers sitting at the tables, he nimbly excused himself, citing the sheer volume of patrons at the Inn that night. Though the families accepted Teague's excuses graciously, many found it a bit strange. Robert Teague was a mouse known to sit down with the families who dined at The Sleeping Cat and tell them a tale, however short, on any given night.

But tonight, it seemed, was **not** that night.

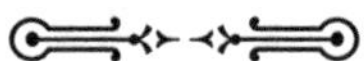

In the corner of the hollowed-out log, just past the small service side of the bar top where drinks were made for table patrons, stood a separate set of tables. These tables, however, were **NOT** for eating and drinking — though many of the mice seated at these unique tables were certainly doing their share of both. These tables were reserved for a popular game that the mice inhabitants across The Far Collective called **Root and Field.**

And this game, for those who played it, was truly revered as a game of mice — and kings.

Teague always ended his rounds at the Root and Field tables because he loved watching the masters of the game play. It was fascinating to watch, and even the artistry of the board and the cards (not to mention the carved models that stood on the tabletop) made for a fascinating representation of mouselife in The Far Collective in its most exquisitely detailed artistic miniature. And, since no two games were ever quite the same, watching the tables on any given evening treated Robert Teague to new and dynamically varied renderings of the game, as well as new — and sometimes brilliant — tactical strategies. It was a geographically accurate miniature-scale overview of The Far Collective — rendered always in varying stages of invasion and conflict.

The game itself was simple, taking only a few moments to learn, but a lifetime of study to truly master. Two mice sat across from each other with a flat wooden board — that would soon become three dimensional 'terrain' — in front of them. Each mouse had a deck of cards, and in that deck were any of a near-endless variety of creatures representing different factions of the animal and human kingdoms, as well as building resources which would allow the player to place intricately carved pieces representing the cards in their deck onto the game board.

For example, one locally renowned master of Root and Field liked to play a deck called 'felines.' He would, on any given turn, play a 'cat resource,' denoted by a Lynx paw — and when he had enough of these 'resource cards' in play, he could then 'pay' to place a particular cat piece on the board. Once on the board, each piece had certain movements, magical abilities, and statistics which could be used in turn to move a rapidly growing army of miniatures and building constructs towards an opponent's keep — while at the same time, his opponent's army would be rapidly growing and moving towards HIS castle in turn. Skirmishes, incursions, and the removal of an opponent's pieces (called 'material') all contributed to a player's chance of victory. The ultimate victory came when you 'captured' an opponent's most powerful piece — known as his 'Sovereign' — in his castle. This was considered the most devastating, brilliant, and desirable type of win, called an 'Ultimate' because it didn't get any better than that!

It was a game of both incredible simplicity and astonishing complexity, and cherished by those who played it.

The most interesting thing about Root and Field, however, is that no one really knows who first invented the game or where it came from — the origin of the game was quite a mystery. The first Root and Field cards had all been found accidentally, serendipitously, or by happenstance, and all in random places — from inside the corridors of Castle Feldenspar, to abandoned and rotting tree hollows picked seemingly at random across The Far Collective. It was almost as if they had been left intentionally for other mice to find. Though the creator of the game had never been found, the distinctive artistic style found across all cards indicated that they had all been illustrated by the same artist — and the general theory held that this person (a mouse, obviously) was also the game designer. Yet no identifying markings or signatures could be found hinting at even a trace of the original author.

The general consensus was that the designer had wanted to remain hidden by, well — design. If he (or she) was even still alive after all these seasons. But still, the question lingered: what mouse would create such a brilliant game, design so many cards, and illustrate them so beautifully, and then journey throughout The Far Collective scattering them in desolate ruins for other mice to find — all without recompense? It was a mystery many mice had spent long hours discussing until late into the night, indeed.

And there were a few specific rules surrounding these Root and Field cards which players would not stand to see broken, as well. You were not allowed to 'make' your own cards, but could only play if you had access to a collection of the 'real,' official cards. As long as they had legitimate Root and Field cards, players were welcome to fashion their own pieces for the board game aspect of play, however. And it was through this rule that the intricate carvings of wood representing miniature castles, keeps, towers, elves, humans, mice, lynxes, and so forth really came to shine. Some of the top masters were prized for their wood carving ability almost as much as for their game play. Other players would, at times, pay these master craftsmen to fashion pieces for them — assuming, of course, that they had the 'official' game cards in hand. Cards could be traded between players, and once made, trades were always final — though they could always be re-traded, if the two mice were so inclined.

The cards were so prized, in fact, that some mice had spent entire seasons looking for them — and on rare occasions, finding them and selling them at a profit. And while some cards were considered common in their known 'count,' it had been rumored that some mice had obtained rare or unique cards in spectacularly hidden ruins — cards that were truly 'one of a kind.' Some players claimed to have seen such cards used in other inns by traveling mice who passed through the Western Kingdoms on their way to elsewhere within The Far Collective. But when you got right down to it, these stories seemed to be but the stuff of rumors and myth, as no mouse (or at least, no mouse in Mouseling Hollow) had actually seen a verifiably Rare or Unique card for Root and Field.

Teague, for his part, was a pretty good player of the game, although with his tavernkeeping duties he rarely had the time to get his collection out. He preferred to watch the more practiced masters in the corner waging their siege campaigns in perfect miniature, while making sure things went smoothly in the rest of the Inn — that was *his* real game board.

Teague looked over the tables and was somewhat surprised to see his best friend, The Professor, sitting across from another mouse, deep in a strategic assault on his opponent's keep.

'Robert!' Wilding called out cheerfully. 'Come and watch me bring in a game-changing construct that is sure to be immortalized in legend, and sung by bards at this Inn for seasons to come!' Wilding took a sip from his mug.

'What are you drinking there, Professor?' asked Teague. He already knew the answer.

'Blackhollow Stout, of course! And the master players here seem to have taken quite a liking to it as well!' Teague looked at the six mice spread across the three tables and noticed they all had stout in their mugs. Whether Wilding had actually come to play Root and Field, he certainly had a secondary mission for the evening, which was to help sell his experimental stout — and based on the fact that Teague spotted Hawkdodger disappearing into the basement to change out a keg of it from the corner of his eye, Wilding's plan seemed to be working.

Teague looked at Wilding and said, 'Show me this move which will soon be a legend.' He watched as Wilding drew a card from his deck and proceeded to put a piece on the board.

'Not so fast, Professor,' smiled his opponent, a Mouseling named Oakpaw who, by the look of him, was some ten seasons younger. 'I'll play Dragon Assault!' After revealing a card from his hand, the younger mouse produced an intricately carved red dragon, placed it on the board, and 'flew' it into Wilding's keep. 'An ultimate victory!' The young mouse started to clap excitedly.

Wilding's face wrinkled as he examined the board. He then smiled and burst out laughing. 'Excellent, my young friend! Well done, well done!' He clasped the young mouse's paw and heartily said 'Shall we drink another round of stout to celebrate your victory?'

'Absolutely, Professor! The next round is on me, of course!'

Wilding winked at Teague as the two sidled off to the bar to draw another mug of what seemed to be shaping up as the most popular drink of the night. Before he left the gaming tables to return behind the bar, however, Teague picked up the pile of cards his friend had laid face down when his young opponent declared victory. Teague

45

was surprised to see one of the unplayed cards his friend had in his hand was called 'Repel Dragon Assault' — a card which would have allowed Wilding to deny his opponent's previous play and, in doing so, win the game.

Teague glanced back at the bar and watched the younger mouse slide some coin into Hawkdodger's paw as two fresh mugs of Blackhollow Stout crossed the bar top and went into the eager, waiting paws of the two thirsty players.

That sneaky mouse, thought Teague to himself, and chuckled.

Both farming and rooting were considered highly noble professions that were absolutely indispensable in Mouseling society. The Rooters, revered by the mouse folk for their bravery and daring, were quite honorable in their own right. They had an unwritten code of only taking what they needed when it came to 'borrowing' from humans, never leaving a mess, and usually leaving something in return as recompense for their scavenging, whether it be a small gift or a lost item extracted from some inaccessible place.

On a recent expedition to Castle Feldenspar, one of the most well-renowned and experienced Rooters — a Mouseling by the name of Leafcatcher McGuinn — had, when drawing honey from a crock in the King's pantry, noticed a small golden ring lying in an inaccessible corner under a large oaken pantry, where humans would never have been able to find it. On the inner band of the ring he read an inscription: **'to my precious daughter, Imogen, on her 8th birthday — Love Father.'** *McGuinn had recognized the importance of this lost treasure, and remembered having heard 'mousetales' (Mouselings' slang for 'gossip') that the King's youngest daughter had been so upset and forlorn after losing the precious gift from her father that she'd even begun losing sleep in her distress! But McGuinn, as the tale was told, returned it to the young girl's bedside, ambling up the tower stairs encumbered with the heavy golden ring in his mouth, then placing it gently on her bedside nightstand without a sound whilst she lay tossing and turning in a fitful slumber.*

He then returned to the kitchen and, with the help of his experienced Rooting colleagues, ferried several mouse-sized crocks of the precious honey into the waiting squirrel cart hidden outside the Castle's basement. They then made their way to the shores of Mirrored Lake, where their flat skiff — designed specifically for carting sundries from the Castle — carried them back across to the shores of The Western Forest. The skiff was then stored discreetly under a tree where it would be barely noticeable to any human eyes on the lake's eastern bank, indiscernible from the pieces of driftwood and flotsam that washed up on the shore. The Rooters were experts at this 'trash on the shore' ruse, and had used it effectively to keep their presence a secret from humans for generations...

— TAKEN FROM **HOW TO STEAL AN EGG: CHRONICLES AND LEGENDS OF THE ROOTERS**

Chapter 4

MOUSETALES FOR A RAINY NIGHT

As the night progressed, Robert Teague went from feeling elated by the size of the crowd pressing in through the door (save for the rude stranger at the end of the bar) to becoming concerned about his ability to fill the needs of his customers. Mice from all along The Riverpath were crowding the entrance trying to get some food or a cold taste of ale after a hard day of the hot, tiring harvest work. And being the astute business mouse that he was, Teague couldn't help but notice as his family and staff struggled to keep up with the enormous crowd. He saw Hawkdodger, now pressed by the line at the bar standing three deep, continually running down to the cellar to change kegs. There was his daughter Kerrigan, her fur moist with sweat as she scurried to fill customer orders, and his wife, normally so cool under the pressure of a tavern filled to the brim with Mouselings, beginning to look overwhelmed.

He heard Robbie in the kitchen, frantically trying to put plates of food together, yelling 'No more Silverback! Take it off the menu, we are out of the fish!'

Teague listened to a groan emit from the bar patrons who were within earshot of the kitchen. Crispy golden fish, fried to perfection with a side of creamy tartar sauce, was considered a harvest delicacy. Could they really be out already? Teague pulled out his timepiece from his pocket and looked at it — 8 P.M. The night was still young. He nabbed his wife as she attempted to pass by with a pawful of plates.

'Are we out of the fish so soon?' he asked, somewhat frantically.

'We have served over one hundred orders already, and there are fifteen more behind!' she said, breaking free of his grip to offload the plates at a nearby table. Teague raced towards the bar to cross out the Crispy Silverback dinner entree written on the menu slate. On his way there, he glanced out the side window of the bar and noticed the harvest moon being consumed by impending storm clouds. Sniffing, he could smell moisture in the air. He thought back to earlier in the day, in the wine cellar with Wilding, when he smelled the same distinctive scent of rain setting in, and turned the whiskers of his soft, moist nose down. Glancing back at the open front door of his bar, what had started as a moderate trepidation at filling his customers' orders now became a feeling of impending doom. He knew that in a short time it would begin to rain, and dozens of mice would be stuck outside the Inn, hungry and thirsty, without a seat to be found. Teague pondered in passing how the day had gone from bad to great, and now seemed poised to end disastrously. Then, he happened to look back and spy the stranger at the bar. *Just not my day,* thought Teague, until he was interrupted from his reverie by his front hostess, a young friend of his daughter's named Thistlefur.

A tiny mouse of eleven seasons who was as cute as a GlassWing Fly in pupae, Thistlefur leaned up to whisper in Teague's ear, obviously concerned about the crowd still waiting at the front to be seated.

'Sir,' she said hesitantly, 'there's a mouse here who says he is a minstrel. He'd like to speak with you about entertaining the crowd. He says he needs to talk with you posthaste.'

If ever I was in need of a miracle, Teague thought to himself, *one might have just shown up.*

'Send him to me behind the bar, right away.'

'Aye sir,' said Thistlefur, as she scurried back towards the front of the Inn.

Teague continued on his way to the slate behind the bar and started to erase the Crispy Silverback from the menu. Within a few seconds he was interrupted by the sound of a light, nearly feminine voice which called out his name.

'Tavernkeep Teague, I would speak with you if you have but a moment!'

Teague turned around and was greeted by a mouse of some stature with brown fur which featured streaks of blonde running down from his ears to the back of his tail. He was a handsome one, to be certain, though somewhat lean in build. On his back Teague spied a framed pack which held a bedroll at the top of it, a blanket at the bottom, many small, indiscernible pouches hanging in between, and that seemed stuffed with whatever sundry items might be needed by a wandering minstrel. Wearing a bright green travel tunic and brown leggings, as well as a small vest of leather armor around his torso, he seemed like a mouse who had 'seen some action,' as Teague would recall it to his friend Wilding later in the night. Teague could see a small short sword with a worn leather-laced wrapping strapped to one side of his pack and a bow with a quiver of colorful arrows strapped to the other. And hanging from the pack, just under his right paw, was a lute of polished golden wood, which shone brightly in the candlelight of the tavern as the dwindling vestiges of moonlight began to slip behind the encroaching storm clouds.

Teague liked him immediately.

'My hostess told me that a minstrel wished to speak with me, but I suspect you are far more than that. Are you a bard?' Teague started.

'Innkeep, some may know me as a bard, and others have called me a ranger of the wood, but all who have known me call me by my given name, Ainsley Hearthseeker. If it pleases you, you may call me Ainsley for short.'

'And why do they call you that, Hearthseeker?' said Teague. The directness of the question, as well as the pointed use of his formal last name, were not lost on the bard, who retorted:

'Sir, I would be very glad, dare I say inclined with great pleasure, to discuss this with you over a cup of your soon to be legendary Blackhollow stout. But at this moment it seems you have more pressing concerns, which, if I might be so bold to say, look to require immediate attention. The crowd of your unfed Mousekin at the door and the distant clapping thunder which tells us a fable of the rain soon to come, when added together, paint a picture of some greatly dissatisfied customers in this Inn's future — and perhaps even of greater troubles to follow. If you would find me a space near the fire, or clear me one where I can sit and play my instrument, for but the small and modest fee of my order from your menu, drinks as I need them, and a warm bed for the night, I believe I can calm the hungry crowd — and bring a great deal of ambiance to your already spectacular hospitality. In addition, sir, you could have some of the waiting mice gather round me and have your hostess provide them with drinks from the bar while they wait for a table to clear. If nothing else, it would be an amazing distraction to draw the attention of the hungry Mousefolk who are standing outside from their — and your — most pressing problem: seeking shelter in what is soon to be a torrential downpour.'

Teague scratched his chin thoughtfully...perhaps a miracle **had** arrived?

He shot back, 'You can set up by the fire and start immediately. The terms of this minstrel agreement are as follows: you eat after we close with whatever is left over, but may eat as much as you like, and may drink freely throughout the evening. We have no rooms left, but do have a hay bed in the wine cellar with some woolen blankets and other accoutrements which will make your night warm and keep you free from the elements. In the morning, if you do as you say and perform to our guests' liking, you may join my family and I for breakfast before you take your leave. What say you?'

Ainsley Hearthseeker extended an eager and relieved paw towards Teague in what was known as an 'embrace of coin,' which by Mouseling custom was considered a binding business agreement. As they clasped paws, Teague wondered if the bard's eagerness to seal the deal came from getting a business contract which included food and shelter for the night, or, as Teague thought more on it, from being able to help the innkeeper avoid a disaster unfolding.

The bard, with surprising deftness, headed towards the fire after leaning in to whisper something in the ear of young Thistlefur, who immediately departed from the bar. Within minutes, he had taken a wooden chair and backed it up to the fire, having asked some of the mice dining nearby 'if they would be so gracious' as to move their tables back a few feet to make way for the mice who had not been on the reservation docket for the evening. With the sounds of thunder getting closer, the frequenters of The Sleeping Cat were gracious and sensitive to the plight of the mice who risked being caught out in the rain. Room by the fire was made in short order. Glancing around, Ainsley the Hearthseeker began to speak:

'My good Mousekin! From all along The Riverpath — from Rock Hollows to the shadows of Castle Feldenspar! I want to welcome you,' he paused, and gestured magnanimously with his left paw, 'TO THE FINEST INN IN ALL OF THE WESTERN LANDS...THE SLEEPING CAT, HOSTED BY ROBERT TEAGUE AND HIS FAMILY!'

The crowd erupted into a massive cheer. Teague, while humbled, also recognized that the bard was doing a bit of grandstanding, and rolled his eyes behind his spectacles.

'Huzzah! Huzzah!' the bar patrons cried in unison.

'Now, my friends,' continued the bard, 'I want you all to know there is more than enough food and drink to satisfy every one of us here tonight! I have spoken with Robert Teague personally, and he and his family are working hard to get everyone's orders filled! Of course, they have run out of fish, but you mice know how popular that Silverback harvest special is each year...'

The mice in the Inn laughed good-naturedly, and the bard waited for the chuckling to die down before continuing.

'And I know you all have been looking to try the seasonal stout crafted by your brilliant 'Professor' of Mouseling Hollow, of whom I have heard many tales as I have traveled The Riverpath. In fact, I have heard that not only is he the greatest brewmaster in all The Far Collective, but he is a master player of Root and Field to boot — and is here at this Inn THIS VERY NIGHT!'

Hearthseeker gestured to the gaming tables where the Professor, caught in the midst of eagerly consuming another cup of his experimental stout, almost choked when he heard his name. He always tried to keep a low profile, which was seemingly impossible at that moment.

The crowd erupted into a thunderous applause. 'The Professor! The Professor!' they chanted in unison. 'Professor, Professor!'

Teague started to worry they might mob Wilding's gaming table — and if that happened he knew he would never hear the end of it from his best friend. Fortunately there was an exit right by the gaming tables in case of emergency.

The bard continued, gesturing for the crowd to quiet.

'But now my friends, as we make way for our fellow mice who have been waiting so patiently outside this Inn for a bit of ale to quench their thirst and a bit of The Sleeping Cat's marvelous food to sate their rumbling bellies, as the rain begins to set upon us in this cozy log...'

As if on demand, or called down by a mouse trained at the Battlemage academy, the rain began to fall torrentially outside the Inn.

'I now give you an epic tale. The *only* tale you will need to hear all night...'

All the mice in the Inn looked in anticipation at the bard. They were absolutely captivated.

The only one who wasn't entranced was Teague, who could only shake his head in admission that this Hearthseeker truly was a master of his craft. He watched as Thistlefur, with adoring eyes, came up and handed Hearthseeker a cup of something from the tap. Teague wondered briefly what it was.

After a hearty sip, the bard continued.

'I give you the story...of THE RAT KING!!!'

A chorus of clapping and 'oohs' was emitted by the patrons of The Sleeping Cat. The legend of The Rat King, now long since dead, was a wonderful one, and something they looked forward to.

The bard began to strum his lute, using a skilled fingerstyle pattern to create melody and harmony which engaged the mice whose eyes all lay expectantly on him. To say he had the attention of the entire Inn would be an understatement. Even Teague's family — Robbie, in the kitchen, Kerrigan, bussing dirty dishes, and Shannon, who had been taking orders, all paused in their duties as the bard began to weave his tale. It was a musical tribute to an enemy that all mice were told as they grew up, having heard the tale over and over from their forefathers.

Hearthseeker began to sing:

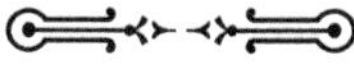

Up Upon a Massive Mountaintop

Above the Pumpkin Farms

The was a dark black force

We need a hero

Is there a hero

Who will shatter his reign to dust?

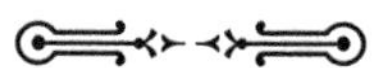

The Rat King
In his towered perch
With the fischers and their crew
Now I'm telling you
Well they worked
To bring the Mouselings to the end
Up The Riverpath and down to Hollows End
When all seemed lost one mouse appeared
And well
The rest was history
He rode a squirrel into the Rat King's castle and then
Slew his black heart and
The heart of The Fischer King too
Will you, do you, believe what I am telling you?

Up Upon a Massive Mountaintop
Above the Pumpkin Farms
The was a dark black force
We need a hero
Is there a hero
Who will shatter his reign to dust?

The bard finished his song and after a moment of silence, bowed his head. The mice in the Inn promptly went crazy with applause. 'Again, again!' the mice chorused.

Hearthseeker started another song which similarly entranced the mice, and this gave Robert Teague's team time to fill orders, clean, bus, and prepare some additional dishes from the foodstuffs which they happened to have on hand. Periodically, Teague saw Thistlefur get a cup of something from Hawkdodger and take it back to the bard between songs, who would start another tune after a healthy draught from his new mug. Things were calming at the Inn and it was almost serene — although the sheer volume of drinks being served was almost certainly in record numbers.

Teague started to feel at ease again, and he knew in his heart the bard couldn't have shown up at a better time. In fact, during the lull that had been created from Ainsley Hearthseeker's masterful entertainment, young Robbie Teague came out of the kitchen and said 'Father, we have some strawberries and cream, and I just baked some crusts from leftover dough into small shortcake pies with a fresh honey drizzle. We could serve about twenty five orders of this — do you want to write it on the board? The crusts are still hot and I believe this will be quite a complement to this evening's meals.'

Teague's heart swelled with pride and he hugged his son. 'Well done Robbie! Way to think on your feet! Those are skills that will serve you well as you get older and begin to face the challenges that life in The Far Collective will most certainly bring you. I will get them on the board, posthaste! Get the kitchen ready to send these out, as I know they will be greedily consumed in short order.'

Teague glanced down the bar and once again saw the Stranger as he prepared to climb his footstool and add to the slate under the **Dessert** section:

Strawberry of the Glade — Fresh Western Forest Strawberry, Cream, Served in Cookie Crust with Honey Glaze

While eying the Stranger at the end of the bar, still in his cups and not seeming to have lost any steam, for a moment Teague enjoyed a wonderful sense of security and thought to himself, *Maybe this day isn't that bad. Maybe it will all be ok in the end.*

However, when he had gotten this far in his writing:

Strawberry of the Glade - Fresh Western Forest Straw-

He was absolutely unprepared for the cataclysm that came next.

With a massively loud **CRASH** through the double oaken doors at the front of the Inn, Teague heard the entire crowd of Mouselings let out an enormous 'gasp' — almost a collective inhale, as Teague would come to describe it the next day. Though he could not see the door through the crowd of patrons blocking his view, it was evident that several of the Inn's guests had been knocked down by some powerful force.

Hawkdodger, Thistlefur, and Ainsley Hearthseeker, as well as Shannon and Kerrigan Teague, had already raced to the door and were staring at something that lay on the ground amidst the crowded group of mice that had formed a circle around them. Teague saw his wife's face as she stood by the entrance, noting with great concern that she had turned white with a look of horror. Meanwhile, Kerrigan stood next to her mother, her face blank and expressionless, as a strange silence seemed to befall the Inn. Those who had not gotten to their feet to see what was going on were craning their necks from the tables to see what all the fuss was about. As Teague began to climb down his stool, his pace quickened when he heard his friend Wilding break the silence:

'Robert! Come here — quickly!'

Teague practically toppled the stool over as he hastily made his way to the front entrance. He pawed his way through the crowd, politely but forcefully, and his murmurs of 'excuse me' and 'pardon me' echoed through the silent Inn. When he finally reached the innermost circle of mice, he looked down and spied a Mouseling with an unfamiliar visage dressed in the garb of a woodland ranger. Teague could see that on his back he carried twin hand axes trimmed in leather, with a small gold accent around the hilt, and Teague knew what this meant even before he spied the small patch on the mouse's shoulder — an outline of Castle Feldenspar's northern spire with a falcon under it, and a small nose and whiskers right in the center of the keep: this mouse was one of the venerated, but highly secretive, Falcon Riders of MouseKeep.

He lay on the floor in an awkward position — neither completely on his back nor on his side, but somewhat between the two — as he struggled to lean forward and sit up, obviously in pain. Wilding was already on the floor trying to render aid. Gently, he turned the poor mouse over to reveal that his back had three arrows in it — all with broken shafts — which prevented him from lying flat. Dark stains of blood ran down his back and onto the floor, staining Wilding's purple tunic as he knelt to examine the arrow shafts. The mouse had crashed through the Inn's heavy oaken door and onto the floor in what seemed to be a last ditch effort to complete some unknown mission.

Amidst the deafening silence, he looked searchingly through the crowd until he spied Teague, then reached his paw towards him and started to speak.

'Captain...' he coughed up violently, and tried to breathe in deeply to regain his composure as best as he could.

He started again.

'Captai...Captain Teague...'

Teague knelt down and grasped the wounded mouse's paw with a sense of respect and great sadness. He looked at Wilding, who locked his gaze and shook his head, indicating that the mouse was mortally wounded and little hope remained.

Teague spoke soothingly and stroked the wounded mouse's shoulder where he knelt. 'Shhh, don't talk, Falconrider...it is going to be ok. We will take care of you. You...' he choked a second, then continued, 'You are safe here.'

Teague looked up at Hawkdodger and said 'Get a wine flask — *immediately* — and some bandages.' Hawkdodger had never heard Teague sound so...***commanding***, and immediately started towards the bar.

The Falconrider continued, sensing that his time grew short.

'Captain Teague, I knew not where else to turn. We were ambushed by fischers just outside of the Early Peaks — a massive volley of arrows struck down most of the Falconriders. My falcon was killed in flight and we crashed far south of Mouseling Hollow, near the Ferngrove Bottoms. The fischers pursued me as their quarry. While I had taken an arrow in the back in flight, their hunters sent two more into me as I fled. Finally, I managed to make it to The Riverpath, where they gave up the chase...'

'Captai...' He coughed again, harder this time. 'Captain, I need you to take this to the King...'

Out of his tattered garb he produced a small, bloody scroll, which was torn and covered in mud, still damp from the torrential rain that raged outside.

'Captain Teague...'

The mouse coughed again and closed his eyes for the last time. But with his final breath, he pulled Teague down and whispered in his ear.

'The Rat King...'

Teague felt the strength in the mouse's paw slip, though he still clasped it tightly.

'...The Rat King lives.'

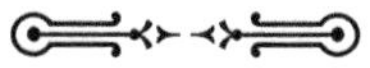

On The Legend of The Silverback:

It is well known that one of the top leisurely pursuits among Mouselings is fishing. For these diminutive mice, fishing is an endeavor that both requires and celebrates partnership — although if we are speaking truly, it is no more than the catching of mere minnows, or the occasional tadpole or bullhead that has recently emerged from its yolk sac. That being said, there is one fish spoken of within Mouseling arcana that deserves mention: The Legendary Silverback. On the shores of the Silverback Delta, located near the western shore of The Mirrored Lake, it is said that a large minnow has been pursued by anglers spanning many generations. 'The Silverback,' as it is called colloquially, has been known to grant one wish to whomever is lucky enough to catch it — and generous enough to release it afterwards.

While no modern day Mouseling anglers have been lucky enough to catch this elusive fish (or should I say, no anglers willing to go on record), it has been said that one Mouseling did: the wizard who once inhabited the ancient wizard's tower on the shore of The Silver River, at the southeastern corner of Mouseling Hollow. It has been said that, one golden harvest afternoon, he went out for a day of angling on a skiff made of reeds that he'd constructed. After several hours with nary a nibble, he miraculously caught The Silverback and was granted a wish in exchange for granting the fish its freedom. What that wish was, we shall never know — it is said that he disappeared immediately and his tower fell into abandonment, eventually becoming the ruins that still stand today.

None have tried to purchase this property since, nor attempted to restore it, for fear of invoking the wizard's wrath. It is said this tower is cursed or haunted or somesuch. Even the mayor of Mouseling Hollow has forbidden trespassing on that property...

— Taken from **Sir Pendleton Stormsnout's Book of River Travels, Volume 1: Feldenspar Castle to Mouseling Hollow**

....

Chapter 5

SILENCE AND SPECULATION

....

Four hours later, the Inn's Great Hall was practically deserted. Behind the bar, an exhausted Hawkdodger sat bussing plates, cups, and other serving items while Thistlefur was busy cleaning the front of the house — wiping tables, sweeping the floor, and generally moving tables back into their original positions. In the kitchen, behind the double door which led into the bar and restaurant area, the clanging of baking sheets and pots and pans being put away could be heard as Robbie, Kerrigan, and Shannon Teague tidied their kitchen in anticipation of tomorrow's lunch service. Wilding and Teague had disappeared into the cellar, where they had reverently taken the body of the fallen Falconrider of MouseKeep, and the pair had been gone for at least an hour. Only the Stranger remained at the end of the bar, still in his same seat, nursing a final pint of Crab Apple Frost Wine.

Ainsley Hearthseeker — who had never had a more challenging performance in his lifetime than one where a mouse crashed into an inn and subsequently died — also sat at the bar a few stools down, looking at the food on his plate. He pushed it around with his fork, seemingly having lost his legendary appetite. He was fortunate

63

enough to have gotten a full serving of the Tomato Cheese Pie, and Hawkdodger had drawn him a hefty cup of the Blackhollow Stout right before it ran out, but neither of these highly satisfying items held his interest as he sat quietly at the bar top. It was silent in the Inn, other than the routine sounds of cleaning — cups and plates clanging together, a corn husk broom scratching the worn wooden floors of the hollowed out log, and the continuous sound of the rain which kept falling, though the thunder and lightning seemed to have moved on an hour earlier.

Shortly after the mouse had whispered his last words into Teague's ear, Wilding announced that he had 'passed out,' and he and Teague quickly prepared to move him to the cellar. Teague caught Hearthseeker's eye as he was still holding the Falconrider's paw, and as he rose to his feet, muttered 'For the Lady's sake keep playing, let them know everything is alright!' just loudly enough for the bard to hear.

With a nearly imperceptible nod, Hearthseeker had done just that, turning to the crowd and brightly saying 'My fellow Mouselings, all is ok! Our injured friend here is now in the care of the great Professor! Make way now, make way, give our hosts some room to attend to the poor fellow in private!'

Upon hearing this, the mice clapped in a subdued way — the way they might have clapped for a player who falls down at a sporting event but eventually gets back up — and shuffled back to give Teague and the Professor some room. The two carried the Falconrider's body away as Ainsley began to play an upbeat tune. As they walked past his wife, Teague whispered to her 'Keep serving! We have to get these customers fed and out of the bar.' And, as sharp as the day he married her, she called Kerrigan and Robbie to her side and they began to go from table to table, reassuring the patrons that all was well.

Teague and Wilding had acted so quickly that many mice never had a clear view of what had happened, and for most of the Inn's patrons the incident was soon forgotten. Some of the more snooty mice even began to discuss how it was in poor taste 'For a mouse to come through the door already drunk and interrupt everyone's harvest celebration.'

As the night progressed, the story of what had happened that night got passed around and changed, then altered and altered again, until no one had any idea that a rider of MouseKeep's legendary FalconGuard had just come tumbling through the doors of The Sleeping Cat with three arrows in his back, a gang of fischers in hot pursuit seeking him as their quarry.

Had that knowledge been passed around, the Inn would have emptied in short order, its patrons transformed into a terrified rabble of mice panicking and rioting, turning over tables for shelter and preparing for an incoming onslaught of unknown size, magnified to frightening proportions by their own fears.

None of that took place, however, thanks to Teague and Wilding's quick thinking and their staff's quick wit and hospitable demeanor. Now, with the bar empty and most of the cleaning duties completed, an exhausted Shannon Teague emerged from the bar with two tomato pies in hand and drew three mugs of Frog Grog for herself and her kitchen staff.

Hawkdodger, finishing his duties under the bartop, smiled at Shannon Teague and said 'I'll take one of those too, m'lady!' Shannon grabbed a clean wooden mug to fill the order of the mouse who had filled nigh-on five hundred drink orders that night alone. *He deserves this*, thought Shannon. She slid the four mugs across the bar top and then left the back of the bar to sit in a stool on the other side, next to the bard. Kerrigan filled in the empty stool next to her, then Robbie, and then Hawkdodger.

Thistlefur, who had finished her duties, quietly came up to Shannon and said, 'I'm finished, Mrs. Teague, and with your permission, I will return home now.'

Shannon smiled at her young hostess.

'Thistlefur, darling, it is much too dangerous in this rain.'

The truth was, it wasn't the rain that Shannon Tegaue was worried about, but the incident with the Falconrider that had her on edge. She'd seen the three arrows in his back, and while she heard very little of what the rider had said to Teague, she had heard enough. *'Fischers'* had been one of the things she'd heard, as had *'pursued me as their quarry.'* With this limited knowledge, she wasn't about to let the young doe venture home alone. No, she would keep her safe — or as safe as she could. Deep in her heart, Shannon Teague wasn't quite sure now how safe that was, given the night's unsettling events.

'Thistlefur, you can stay with us tonight in our upstairs den. Take this to the nanny and let her know we will be up soon. And here is one for you as well...' She handed Thistlefur the two tomato pies, then returned behind the bar to draw two more mugs of the Frog Grog to give to Thistlefur. The hungry young mouse's eyes grew wide as they set upon the pie and the Grog, and she happily hugged Shannon Teague. She then made her way upstairs, stepping lightly so as not to spill a morsel of the food she had most certainly earned on her night shift as a hostess. Her footsteps on the wooden landing echoed until she reached the top step — the only sound that could be heard in the ever-increasing uncomfortable stillness that had now settled over the bar of The Sleeping Cat Inn. Wilding and Teague had not yet returned from the basement, but when they did, Shannon Teague had some **VERY** pressing questions for the pair.

Especially for her husband. *'Captain,'* the Falconrider had called Teague. But Shannon Teague had never known her husband to have had any military experience. What did the Rider mean? And why had he come to The Sleeping Cat? The legends said that the MouseKeep was hidden deep within Castle Feldenspar, but those were children's stories really, more akin to fairy tales than to real life. A Falconrider at The Sleeping Cat, looking for *her* husband? Furthermore, she now recalled that her husband's best friend, Wilding, did not seem to have been shocked or bemused by a Falconrider showing up and calling her husband 'Captain Teague.'

Oh yes, questions she had aplenty.

But answers, now those weren't quite as forthcoming, since the two Mousekin of the evening who had answers were either hiding in the wine cellar or attending to more pressing matters down there — though Shannon Teague wasn't quite sure which. So, she drew the mug of Frog Grog to her lips, and wiping the sweat from her brow, took a deep drink — the well-earned kind, the kind of drink you take when you are tired and dehydrated after a long, long day — and immediately began to feel a pleasant refreshment and a slight 'buzz.' She went to set the mug down, but instead took another deep draught. The two Mouselings on her left, she noted with some interest, were doing the same.

It **had** been a long night.

The six mice at the bar, while filled with pressing questions, dared not break the silence. It was a full silence, rich to the point of being oversweet. It was more than a pause, but a space in between heartbeats, if Mouseling Hollow had a heart that pulsed regularly. With so many questions inevitably arising as a result of the night's events, and with no immediate information available to resolve the curiosity of the six mice left in the bar area, they just continued to drink in silence. That was, until Ainsley spoke.

'You know, I always thought the Falcon Riders of MouseKeep were just a myth designed to keep us behaving as small bucks and does!' the bard said. 'My da used to tell me the most fantastic stories of the Falcon Riders and each and every one of their adventures. The Siege of Castle Feldenspar, The Raid on The Rat King's Black Citadel, The Aerial Assault on Dragon Perch, The Daring Escape from Rock Hollows — and now, to find out they are real? Absolutely fantastic!'

Ainsley couldn't have said anything more poignant or appropriate in the midst of this pregnant pause full of unshared questions, because every other mouse (except the Stranger, who remained silent) burst out talking at almost exactly the same time. The older mice said things like 'I know, that's exactly what I was thinking!' while young Kerrigan and Robbie were excitedly blurting out 'I thought those were just bedtime stories!'

It was if a pressure valve had been released. Bards are required by their trade to become exceptional conversationalists with impeccable timing, and Hearthseeker's decision to break the silence couldn't have come at a better moment. It clearly placed all the mice at ease and a flowing conversation soon followed. Young and old, the mice discussed the stories, fables and tales of their childhoods, and how this actual Falconrider showing up at The Sleeping Cat had suddenly brought the long-ago, half-forgotten tales of the legendary Falcon Riders alive, right into the midst of their present lives. Wondering what to make of the Falconrider's appearance made for exciting, if scary and somewhat anxious, speculation.

Hearthseeker took out his lute and began to regale the mice seated at the bar with The Silent Song of MouseKeep. It was a song about how MouseKeep couldn't really exist, almost certainly doesn't exist, but the last line of the song's tag indicated that it *might* actually exist, if mice could keep alive their belief in what the MouseKeep stood for. The mice, now ensconced in their Frog Grog and speculative conversations,found it to be a particularly poignant and appropriate song to choose for that moment. Tensions had begun to ease. *Although,* Shannon Teague thought as she glanced back at the end of the bar towards the Stranger, *HE certainly doesn't say much.*

Though the conversation had become somewhat livelier, it quieted once the six mice heard distantly the pad of mouse paws coming up the cellar stairs. Two mice, to be precise, headed up to what was about to become an interrogation. The staff of The Sleeping Cat had questions — lots of questions — and Shannon Teague found herself glancing back once more to the end of the bar. *This stranger might have to answer some questions as well,* she thought.

And so it was that Robert Teague and Professor Wilding turned the corner from the cellar entrance and reentered the bar area of the tavern. Teague, looking beleaguered, went to the taps, grabbed two wooden cups from under the sink, and drew some Crab Apple Frost Wine. Topping it off, he slid one mug to Wilding, who had taken an empty stool next to Hawkdodger, and then lovingly placed the other mug in front of his wife's cup of Frog Grog and went to stand behind it. He and Wilding looked at each other while the rest of the mice stared at them in silence, then raised their mugs up. As the others watched them, Wilding suddenly said 'To The Riders of Mousekeep.'

'The Riders of MouseKeep,' echoed Teague.

Teague distantly heard the midnight clock chime.

Teague and Wilding both silently drank from their mugs. Not wanting to break the now-awkward silence, the other mice took smaller sips from their mugs. The silence seemed set to continue — but Shannon Teague wasn't having any of it.

'Robert — why did that Falconrider call you Captain?' she said.

It was the foremost question on most of their minds. But before Robert could answer, the Stranger drew back his hood and began to speak, as if to answer Teague's wife's question.

'Taverness Teague, ask not why the Falconrider came seeking aid at The Sleeping Cat, or why he called your husband by his military rank. The more important question — the more important question by far — is who are these two Mouselings, these best friends standing together at the bar — my very reason for being here — who have been summoned to Castle Feldenspar with great expediency and even greater secrecy? What is the pressing nature of their summons? And why are you, his wife, completely unaware of both of their heroic acts, now spoken of in song and tale? Do you know, **exactly**, who you have been living with for the past twenty seasons?' His tone bordered on accusatory.

The eyes of the gathered Mouslings looked at Teague, then down the left side of the bar at Wilding, then swung back to Teague again. Hawkdodger stared at Teague like he had been suddenly placed on a marble pedestal.

'Dad, were you a Falconrider of MouseKeep?' Kerrigan asked incredulously.

The Stranger answered on Teague's behalf. 'A Falconrider? Nay my young mouse, Captain Teague was not a Falconrider, though a skilled rider he most certainly is. Captain Teague was much more than a mere Falconrider, as was this 'Professor' who sits beside you at this bar top. Teague and 'The Professor,' as he is now called, served King Teegan's father in the First Incursion of The Western Lands — or what Mouselings in this region refer to as 'The First Rat King War.' Captains Teague and Wilding were instrumental in the Defense of the Outcropping at Owlhaven, and once *that* incursion was stemmed, it was Captain Teague and Professor Wilding themselves who rallied the White Owls of Frost Grove in the counter attack which routed the Rat King's forces, and dispelled them from Owlhaven forever.'

'Father, you served in The First Rat King War?' said Robbie and Kerrigan, almost simultaneously.

The Stranger continued before Teague could answer.

'The Professor himself personally saw the transfer of the Decoding Stones from OwlGrove to The Lyceum at Ocean's View in the midst of the onslaught, while Teague intentionally remained behind and fought valiantly alongside a tiny group of dreadfully outnumbered Mousekin who were forced to engage in paw to paw combat high upon the steep cliffs. They defended Owlhaven from what was most certain to be the doom of the White Owls. Their failure would have meant the placement of a garrison of The Rat King's Bat Riders on the OwlGrove Cliffs. Had that happened, it would have been the precursor for what would have inevitably come next: an aerial assault on The Early Spires, followed by a move north up The Riverpath, and eventually the capture of Mouseling Hollow to serve as the final staging area for an assault on Castle Feldenspar itself. Both of these mice here, though called 'Captain' by the Falconrider, are not really 'Captains' in the strict sense of the word. They were both given a promotion by King Teegan's Father, whom you know as 'The Heaven's King,' to nothing less than *General of The Mousekeep.* After the Rat King was defeated, both were asked to stay on in defense of the MouseKeep and Castle Feldenspar as a personal favor to the King.'

'General of the MouseKeep?' Hawkdodger looked like he was about to pass out in adoration as he eyed Teague, then Wilding, then Teague again.

Looking annoyed at the interruption, The Stranger pressed on.

'Yet, both refused. As The First Rat King War came to a close, **BOTH** asked for a decommission from the elder King Teegan, to be released from His Majesty's service. King Teegan the First, born from Heaven as they say, could not do anything but grant their wish based on their merit and service. And so, *The Fabled Two* who saved Owlhaven — and in doing so, safely transported the Decoding Stones which allow animals and humans to understand each other, AND...'

He paused for extra emphasis here.

'...in all likelihood, prevented the occupation of Mouseling Hollow and the fall of Castle Feldenspar itself...intentionally faded into obscurity, myth, and legend...right here on the shores of Mirrored Lake.' He gestured to Teague and Wilding, then settled back to take another drink.

Shannon Teague was dumbfounded, and looked over at her husband, who was staring at the wooden floor behind the bar. *The Fabled Two? HER* husband? Yes, of course, he was eloquent and well versed, certainly a jack of all trades, a fantastic storyteller — but never once in their twenty seasons together had he ever spoken to her about the military, combat, heroics, or violence of any sort. He was so kind and gentle — so giving in all aspects of his life, and adoring of their children, not to mention a speaker to animals whom he cared for and would never harm.

In fact, whenever they had bards in the bar singing tales of Mouseling heroics, he often dismissed them as being 'tales for coin,' or 'grand fantasies.' Glancing at him again, she noticed that his cheeks were getting flushed and his whiskers had started to straighten out. His nose looked dry. Turning towards the end of the bar while trying to sneak a glance at Wilding, he continued to seem as if he was inspecting something fascinating on the floor. The irony of her being in the presence of **The Fabled Two** while they both stared humbly at the floor was not lost on her by any stretch of a Mouseling's imagination.

Could this Stranger's fantastical story really be — well — **real?**

Ainsley Hearthseeker could have asked any number of questions at this point in the conversation, or burst into joyful song for being in the (alleged) presence of two of the greatest heroes of Mouseling mythos. But as Shannon Teague meditatively reviewed her entire marriage in retrospect, he asked the only question that was actually right to ask under the circumstances. He looked directly at the Stranger, who had now removed his hood completely, revealing a nasty scar from his nose up to his eye, which was missing. He wore no patch, but his eye appeared 'closed' through a combination of scar tissue and dark black fur grown long in its absence. Still, it was rather nasty to look at, which presumably was why he had kept his tunic hood drawn up all afternoon and evening.

'Stranger...you come here, telling tales of these mice whom I have just met. There is no doubt these are humble and noble mice who are, if only in acts of work and servitude to others, simply trying to earn a living. I watched you sit here drinking all night and yet not speak to anyone, save to Hawkdodger when you needed a fresh draught. You paid for nothing, at least from what I could see. A mouse of the FalconGuard crashed through the Inn in the middle of dinner, yet you seem unsurprised by this — by all of this. So, I think the question that sits on all our minds is, why are *YOU* here?'

Without missing a beat, the Stranger retorted with some annoyance, 'Perhaps you should ask 'Captain' Teague himself.'

All eyes turned towards Teague, standing behind the bar alone, and he suddenly felt himself get hot under the whiskers. He had just wanted to be a tavernkeeper, after all. A simple tavernkeeper, husband, and father, and nothing else.

After a moment of silence, his wife spoke.

'Well, Robert? Why is this Stranger here?'

Teague almost spoke, then cleared his throat, then started to speak again. But when he realized he couldn't find the words, he simply took out a scroll from the pocket of his bar apron and handed it to his wife. She noticed it had a red wax seal of the Royal Castle of Feldenspar on it. The seal had been broken, the message obviously having been read by Teague. It made her tremble to see it, and she trembled a bit more when she saw her husband's paw shake — just for a moment — when he handed it to her.

She unfolded it and began to read silently.

'Well, what's it say?' Hawkdodger asked, in a slight accent which betrayed his upbringing at FernGrove Bottoms.

When she finished reading it, she took a deep breath, but found her throat was suddenly dry. She took a sip of her Frog Grog, swallowed a big lump in her throat, and as she prepared to read the message aloud, she wondered to herself, again, *'Is this all really happening?'*

Somehow, between the grog and her throat-clearing, she found a voice to read the summons:

General Teague

Growing up as a young prince, I was told voluminous tales about your valiant defense of Owlhaven during The First Rat King War. My father would regale me with stories of your many adventures with your best friend Wilding, and how you and he, armed simply with hand axes and wizard's staff, ran missions in the defense of our kingdom while assuming such danger to yourselves. He also shared with me, with an exceptional sense of sadness, tales of the tremendous sacrifices the two of you made, including General Wilding's great and personal loss, in service to our Great Kingdom and Keep, which rests peacefully on the quiet, glassy shores of The Mirrored Lake.

That it continues to rest peacefully today is due, in no small part, to the both of your substantial contributions in the past which still echo amongst us today.

General Teague — my prayer is that you will forgive me, and my boldness, in sending an emissary from MouseKeep to summon you back to Castle Feldenspar — and to summon you with great expediency. The Falcon Riders have gone missing on a mission of critical importance. I had to call in a favor from MouseKeep's Thief's Guild just to get someone willing to cross the shore and speak with you, given our mutual desire for secrecy.

*However, it is imperative that you know that I have lost faith in many of my human court — and troublingly, my Mouseling court as well. I believe my council has been infiltrated by those I cannot trust, and I seek — daresay, I **NEED** — the counsel of those whom I can. The Kingdom of Feldenspar faces a grave threat, one which is still unknown to me. Many of my scouts (those who have survived to report back, that is) have reported that strange groups of humans and animals are amassing on the edges of our Western Lands with hostile intentions. Skirmishes have been reported taking place to the East and South. The size, force, and disposition of these invaders still remains unknown.*

However, there is to be no doubt — war is most certainly descending upon us, and I fear that it may be a war which dwarfs the First War of The Rat King.

*Upon my father's deathbed, the very last words which he whispered in my ear were **'if you need help, find Robert Teague, the Mouseling. Ask him and Wilding for help.'** And so it is, following the wisdom of my father, amidst the uncertainty of a likely invasion, that I would ask you, as Your King, to come to Castle Feldenspar. Come with the greatest of speed, and grant me an audience at the MouseKeep, in The King's Pedestal. I will meet you all there, alone, tomorrow at noon.*

Your King and Great Friend,
King Lionsmane Teegan

P.S.: The Western Shore of Mirrored Lake is the fastest way here, and the safest. I have set archers on the Western Spire to spy on the forest as you cross, should you encounter trouble. My emissary has made the arrangements for the arrival of the two of you.

'Three of you,' said Wilding.

The gathered Mouselings all jumped slightly as Wilding's voice startled them out of their reverie.

'What do you mean?' said Shannon Teague.

'We are taking the Rider's body back to the Keep for a proper burial,' said Wilding.

There was a moment of silence among the bar.

'I think you mean the four of you,' added Ainsley Hearthseeker.

Wilding and Teague looked at Ainsley, then took another draught of their cups. When Teague set his mug down, he thought about Hearthseeker's great contributions to the evening, as well as his fascinating charisma. Given the circumstances, he would almost certainly be an asset — plus Teague really liked him. And besides, Teague wondered about the equipment Hearthseeker carried. He looked like he had seen some — as Teague would put it later, to Wilding — *not inconsiderable action.*

'I'll be on the boat with you as well,' said the Stranger.

'That makes five, with Hearthseeker,' said Teague.

Hearthseeker lifted his cup of Frost Wine and winked at Teague and Wilding. Teague knew, in his heart, that this mouse had more to offer them than just tales and song.

And in that moment, Teague also knew he made an invaluable friend.

Part II

A Journey to MouseKeep

Chapter 6

A King's Summons

Early the next morning, before the dawn arrived, Teague roused himself from what could have only been described as a fitful sleep in his bedchamber upstairs at The Sleeping Cat, and headed down to the wine cellar with a small candle lantern in his paw. He couldn't help but have an eerie feeling as he descended the stairs, knowing the Falconrider's corpse was also being stored down there, and that save for the small lamp in his paw, the cellar was pitch black. Teague went directly to a dusty cask in the corner and pushed it away from the wall. While these casks were traditionally very heavy and required several mice to move them around, this one was so light Teague was able to maneuver it on his own with ease.

Kneeling down and placing his lantern on the dirt floor of the cellar, Teague popped out a false backing and started maneuvering items around inside the cask searching for...something. Finally, he was able to grab what he was looking for and pulled out a small wooden chest. The bronze bindings were weathered with age, and the handle of the chest was clearly battered, nearly falling off its hinges. Yet the sturdy oak construction of the case had held over all these years, and its solid construction had prevented the elements from permeating the precious interior, keeping the treasured contents inside intact. On the top of the chest was inlaid a small plaque which read:

Robert Teague, Captain of MouseKeep.

Opening the case, Teague took a quick look at the items within. He exhaled in the chill of the morning, which was even cooler in the below ground cellar. *Yes, all was accounted for after so many seasons,* he thought, though these were items he had never expected to see again. But there was no time for reminiscing or nostalgia now. Even arising this early, they would be hard pressed to make Castle Feldenspar by their noontime appointment — and this was assuming they had no encounters of any kind.

Pulling items from the case, Teague went to make a full inventory of its contents. He saw:

— Two hand axes of MouseKeep issue, with the hilts wrapped in leather and trimmed in gold at the edge of the binding. Their blades, still sharp after all these years, shone in the dim light of the cellar, accented by the glow of the candle within the lantern. These were housed in a set of leather sheaths designed to be carried on a mouse's back, for quick access in combat and maximum comfort out of it.

— A laced leather vest; light armor by any means, but standard issue for mice who battled in woodland and field and needed to prioritize mobility and speed above all else for particularly dangerous missions or tasks, including combat.

— A chain coif; a head covering of linked metal rings with an opening for a mouse's face, allowing the snout and ears to protrude while still protecting the neck and skull of the warrior. Inside the coif was a satin lining for comfort, which was removable. Teague's lining was black.

— A small set of three throwing daggers in a leather pouch, which were attached to a sturdy leather belt which had seen a great deal of wear.

— A green 'hunter's tunic;' a hooded cloak which could double as a blanket or sleeping pad and was quite thick.

— Leather boots which laced up above the ankle.

— An embroidered insignia of MouseKeep indicating a Captain's rank.

— A leather journal, which Teague had kept faithfully as a chronicle of his journeys in The First Rat King War

— A small necklace with an engraved falcon on it, holding a small ruby gem in its beak.

— A short Yew bow with a quiver of arrows, fletched with owl feathers and tipped with 'frog's legs' arrowheads.

With a quiet sigh, Teague began to dress in his battle garb which he had so caringly stored — for what he'd thought would be the last time — so many seasons ago. The night had been a whirlwind, to be sure — the whole day, really, from the moment the Stranger had first delivered the King's summons. But between the massive number of Mousekin in town for the harvest, the Falconrider's appearance, and the sheer volume of work that had taken place the day before, Teague had been utterly exhausted. And now, here he was: donning his twin hand axes, sheathing them with the practiced hand of a battle-scarred veteran upon his back, lacing up his leather boots, placing his necklace around the ruffled ridge of fur on his neck, and fastening his leather combat belt, like it was just another day in the service of the King.

Except it wasn't.

Teague had retired years ago, had given this all up, and intentionally kept his experiences a secret — all with the King's blessing. He'd thought he would never see combat again. He'd never wanted to — he had no desire to see humans or animals writhe in the agony and pain inflicted on one another for senseless material gains, or in the name of country, King, or cause, all of which seemed so empty to him now as he reflected on it. He owed the King nothing. He had done his duty — he and Wilding had gone far beyond their duty, Wilding especially. Yet between the Falconrider's missive (which Teague had not yet shared with anyone but Wilding) and the King's summons, Teague felt in his heart that Mouseling Hollow was in grave danger. And this threat, whatever it was, could not be allowed to exist. No matter how much he wanted to live quietly in his happy retirement, Teague knew he could not passively sit by playing the innkeeper and watch this new threat come to pass, in whatever form it might come to be. He had left his military service to the King. No one disputed that, not even the Stranger — but he would not disrespect the crown, or the service he and so many Mousekin had given willingly in seasons past, by ignoring the desperate call of the King of Feldenspar. Were he to do so, the sacrifices of so many young mice under his command would have hence been for nothing — and Teague, a mouse of integrity, was not about to let such a sacrifice go unheeded.

But besides his sense of duty, the very fact that his family, his Inn, his whole life might be in danger necessitated a response. Robert Teague, for one, was not likely to back down from a fight — ever. And any creature, be they man or animal, who threatened the safety of his family, would regret the day they pulled Robert Teague, Captain of MouseKeep, from retirement.

After Teague finished gearing up, he started up the stairs of the wine cellar. As he ascended up the steps, he heard the creaking of wooden wheels come up the path to the Inn and turn off by the cellar side of the log. He knew it had to be Wilding's squirrel cart. He saw Wilding as he crested the top of the stairs and the two locked gazes and looked each other up and down. Wilding observed Teague's battle dress, a sight he had not seen in a long time, nearly twenty seasons. And Teague, by his own measure, was somewhat surprised to see that Wilding had donned his own battle dress, that of a Sorcerer Captain of MouseKeep.

His grey flowing robes, tall, gaunt figure, and wide brimmed hat made it clear to anyone who observed him that he was a Mousling

Battlemage. He carried a sheathed shortsword at his side, and in the back of his cart, a gnarled staff with a ruby gem inlaid at the top completed his ensemble.

Next to him, in the wooden seat of his squirrel-drawn cart, Wilding also carried a leather-bound tome with some occult symbols on it.

A spellbook, Teague thought to himself, *of Combat Spells. A book a battlemage carries into war.*

An awkward silence passed, then Wilding spoke.

'Well old friend, I never thought we would find ourselves in a position to don combat dress again.'

Teague smiled wistfully.

'Nor I, Wilding, nor I. I must thank you — truly — for accompanying me to Castle Feldenspar. If we're telling true tales, I wasn't really looking forward to doing this alone.'

'I wouldn't have let you, my friend. Though had the events of last night not transpired, and had I not been privy to the King's summons, my gut instinct is that you would have insisted on doing this alone anyway.'

Teague didn't need to answer, because Wilding was right. When he had first read the summons from the Stranger, he had planned to go alone and not inform anyone. But in a sense, he was glad things had worked out this way.

'Shall we get the Falconrider?' asked Wilding.

Teague sighed sadly. 'Let's get to it.'

Together, the pair descended back down the cellar steps. Teague, with his lamp in his paw, made a left turn at the bottom of the steps and shined the light at where the Falconrider's broken body lay, wrapped in a soft linen that Teague's wife had sewn years earlier. Wilding brought forth a wool blanket and spread it on the ground next to the Rider. Heaving together, the duo picked the body up and laid it carefully in the center of the heavy woolen fabric. With Teague taking the front end, Wilding grabbed the back, and together they silently carried the body up the stairs and placed it into the back of the squirrel cart. Teague readjusted the soft linen that his wife had sewn so as to discreetly cover the Rider. Then, brushing his hands to get the dirt off, he turned back to Wilding.

'It should be just about time for us to embark on our journey. Where are our traveling companions?'

Wilding closed his graying eyes and sniffed the air. 'It would seem our friends have been delayed by a sumptuous breakfast, courtesy of The Sleeping Cat!'

Teague smelled it, too. Sizzling, crispy bacon, fried eggs, the citrus accent of the fresh squeezed juice of oranges from the southern tropics (presumably having been 'borrowed' by Rooters on a recent raid of Castle Feldenspar). Teague also smelled fresh baked bread slathered with herbed butter after being toasted in a seasoned oak fire, whose wood smoke aroma emanated delicately from the side door. Leftover Rarebit for the toast, also. Teague's wife, it seems, had been quite busy since shortly after he arose preparing food to fortify them before the day's journey.

The pair went inside. Teague was ready to be off, knowing what lay ahead for all of them. Still, he hoped to be back in his bed at The Sleeping Cat before midnight. As he and Wilding emerged into the great hall and bar area, they were met with a joyous but muffled cry by Ainsley Hearthseeker, whose mouth was not only full of hot breakfast food, but whose attempts to butter his freshly toasted bread had resulted in a butter stain sliding down his woodsman tunic of brown and green.

'Good morning, my friends!' said Hearthseeker, eager to see his new companions in a more sedate environment than the previous night's excitement. 'The lovely Missus Teague has been kind enough to prepare us a most delicious repast, so we may fill ourselves properly before our day of travels!'

Next to Hearthseeker sat the Stranger, whose mouth was also full. He turned an eye towards the pair, and with a barely noticeable head motion, nodded.

How rude, thought Teague.

Shannon Teague came out of the kitchen with two more wooden plates of food practically heaping over the sides. Teague looked hungrily at the fixings on the plate — fresh eggs from the local woodland chickens, fried over easy, their yolks dark orange and runny. Thick cut bacon which was dripping with grease. Crusty toast from the oak fire slathered in butter and topped with fresh green herbs, and more. It was only at that moment that he realized he had not eaten a crumb since his mid-afternoon meal the previous day. His stomach rumbled. To his left, he noticed Wilding's gaze was transfixed on the plates, too.

His wife, trying to remain stoic, yet sensing the imperative nature of the task at hand, intimated the need to prepare themselves for the journey ahead.

"Come now, boys,' she said, 'you *certainly* can't be planning on crossing The Mirrored Lake to go see King Teegan, the Lionsmane himself, on an empty stomach.' Without missing a beat, she started filling clean wooden mugs with freshly pressed juice. She gestured with the mugs to two empty stools next to Hearthseeker, beckoning her husband and Wilding to sit down. The Stranger, as per usual, had retained his stool in the corner of the bar. With a practiced glance at each other, the two old friends sat down at the bar and tucked in with great eagerness.

'You know,' said Ainsley, glad that his compatriots had chosen to join him in his insatiable appetite for breakfast rather than chastising him for it, 'I've been thinking about this summons of yours. It all seems rather odd, doesn't it?'

'Odd?' said Teague's wife. 'Whatever do you mean? It carries the royal seal of Castle Feldenspar on it. I've never seen anything more official in all my seasons!'

'That's exactly my point,' said Ainsley, in between mouthfuls of crispy sausage patties, which he swirled in the egg yolk pooling across his plate before deftly using his fork to deliver them to his mouth. 'Other than the Rooters' usual incursions into Castle Feldenspar for supplies, no one has reported anything amiss. There's been no talk about incursions on The Western Forest's edge, which our lookouts would have most certainly reported. Nothing about the Falcon Riders being missing. There has been no interruption in supply, the harvest is being brought in as usual, and no mice or day laborers are missing in their migration up The Riverpath. Yet King Teegan summons **The Fabled Two**, through a stranger no one has ever seen before, to come with expedience to Castle Feldenspar.

'**The Fabled Two** have faded into myth and legend long before we learned of their existence in disguise at Mouseling Hollow. The Lionsmane's need of them particularly, or might I say, peculiarly, and in such pressing matters, seems unusual to me. Does he not have an entire hierarchy of staff at the MouseKeep from which he could draw wisdom?'

Silence set across the tavern, which surprised Ainsley. Was he the only one who had these thoughts? *Maybe these mice know a lot more than me and I sound like an utter fool,* was the exact thought that crossed the bard's mind.

For a second, all that could be heard was the sound of food scraping across wooden plates. A few of the mice stared at the fire in the wood oven which bridged the kitchen and bar, the same fire which so recently had cooked their breakfast to perfection. The flame in the hearth danced around the stone masonry work, mesmerizing them and resigning them all to their own thoughts. Then, Wilding spoke.

'Hearthseeker, you are right. It is extremely odd. And that, my friend, is even more reason why we need to go with great haste to Castle Feldenspar and assess the situation. Only one of two things can be possible in this situation, and I daresay the Stranger here at the end of the bar may already know the answer.'

The Stranger continued his breakfast, seemingly ignoring Wilding's words, but Wilding continued.

'Either the court of the MouseKeep and Castle Feldenspar, humans and mice both, have been compromised with spies, or else

King Teegan, The Lionsmane, is dead. Assuming either of these scenarios is correct, we have been summoned into a trap. Both bode a terrible fate for our lands and the reign of the line of Teegan. But this — this is why we must go. And before the sun sets over the spires of Castle Feldenspar this day, we will most certainly have our answer.'

Shannon Teague put a kitchen towel to her eye and pretended to wipe something from it.

Wilding looked without emotion at the Stranger and called directly to him.

'What say you, Stranger? What intelligence do you have that might shine Her heavenly light on such a dark and pressing matter? One which would seem to concern **ALL OF OUR FURS?'** He could feel the anger rising under his whiskers.

The eyes of each mouse at the bar turned towards him. The Stranger swallowed his food and took a sip of juice, then spoke, somewhat indignantly.

'You of all people, *Professor*,' he said condescendingly, 'should know how this works. Did you not run missives and use The Thief's Guild of MouseKeep for reconnaissance and intelligence gathering operations back in your day? I know you did, and *YOU* know you did, and the first — and might I add, *lifesaving* — rule of using The Thief's Guild of Mousekeep is this: the less a thief knows about his mission, the better — and safer — for everyone. These rules have been in place for generations to prevent mice from asking unnecessary questions when they are ordered to do something by their superiors. And more importantly, to prevent critical intelligence from being spilled, should they be captured, under the duress of their captors — information which might compromise hundreds, or even thousands of troops who would have benefitted had their task been successful. Any knowledge that we don't need in order to complete our missions is forbidden for us to know for safety purposes. The fact that you seem to have forgotten *these very basic rules* indicates to me just how long the two of you have been out of service.'

Wilding looked down. The Stranger was right, and Wilding flushed under his whiskers at the realization that he'd just openly asked a member of the Thief's Guild to share compromising information which could jeopardize his mission — *their* mission — or get them all killed. He knew how it all worked, and why the Guild took the precautions that it did. But still, it all seemed so, well...*strange.*

The Stranger then continued.

'I, myself, am not a high-ranking mouse in the Guild. I am but a humble thief of low ranking, who lives at the foot of Castle Feldenspar in the tunnels below the outlying village. My superior, a mouse whose name is unimportant, summoned me, brought me this task and handed me the Royal Summons himself, with the wax seal intact. He told me to find the tavernkeeper Robert Teague at the Sleeping Cat in Mouseling Hollow, and gave me some backstory on Teague and Wilding's service to the Keep during The First Rat King War that I was told may be needed to secure their cooperation. Granted, I *had* heard the legends, of course, like everybody has growing up. My job was...' he corrected himself, '*is*...to find Teague, and bring him to King Teegan. At that point my task is done and I can rejoin my family — until another mission is given. I will say it is rare to be given any mission at all in peacetime, especially for a lower ranking member of the Guild like myself. My last mission was almost four seasons ago, merely a simple courier task.'

Ainsley Hearthseeker rubbed his chin thoughtfully.

'It would make sense, then, that perhaps the court of the MouseKeep has been infiltrated, for a lower ranking mouse of the Guild to have been trusted with such an important task,' conjectured Hearthseeker. 'One thing is certain...something is amiss in the court of the Lionsmane.'

Teague, having finished his breakfast, pushed back his stool and stood up. For the first time in her life, Shannon Teague saw her husband in his woodland battledress, his sheathed twin hand axes protruding behind his back. The sight scared her, yet also made her swell with pride. She had so many questions, but between the events of the previous evening and the party's imminent departure for the shores of The Mirrored Lake, the two had really not had any time to talk.

After a moment, Teague spoke.

'It matters not whether we walk towards a mission of mercy or a devious trap, we must make haste for the Castle. Wilding's cart stands outside with the Falconrider's body in it, and it will take us to the Western Shore of the lake. It is two hours across, assuming no trouble, and then we will need to ascend to MouseKeep itself through the city tunnels. With luck, we can have a noon audience and be on our way home by three. With the harvest moon full above the trees, we should be able to navigate the Western Woodpaths back to Mouseling Hollow with ease.'

Shannon Teague sensed he was being optimistic. He looked at his wife and stared into her beautiful hazel eyes.

'Come back to me in one piece,' she said, reaching her arms across the bar to him.

He smiled and grasped her paws firmly with his. Then he drew the hood of his woodsman cloak above his head, covering his chain coif. Throwing his bow and quiver of arrows on his back, he, Wilding, Hearthseeker, and the Stranger made their way to the door and climbed upon the squirrel cart, setting off for what would be the first adventure for **The Fabled Two** in nigh-on twenty seasons.

As she went to wave to the cart of adventurers riding slowly away from The Sleeping Cat, Shannon Teague saw Ainsley Hearthseeker draw his lute out and begin to sing a traveling song as they disappeared off into the forest.

Distantly, she heard Teague and his companions start to sing along, which comforted her heart...if only a little bit.

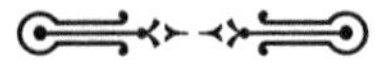

On The Fabled Two's Defeat of The Rat King:

*No one really knows what happened when **The Fabled Two** descended into the Black Citadel after the Falcon Riders reclaimed the Bat Rider's Perch. It is said, in legends and songs, that while the army of The Heaven's King ferreted out the human mercenaries loyal to The Rat King at the base of the tower, a small invasion party of Mousekin began the arduous process of clearing out the tower's animal denizens from the top down. And, as the story goes, the Wizard and the Ranger agreed to part ways at some point midway down the tower — the Ranger knowing that the Wizard was a better match for The Rat King and recognizing that the unspoken (and unsettled) business between the two took precedence. It is said that the Wizard defeated The Rat King on that day, but at a great personal cost — his family being killed in an insidious trap laid by The Rat King to bait the Wizard into mortal combat.*

After that day, no one ever saw the Ranger or the Wizard again. They disappeared into history — it is possible they died in the tower, or went missing in action shortly thereafter. Or, as some speculate, they may still be alive even now, walking the shores of The Mirrored Lake as its ever-vigilant silent guardians, keeping watch in case the evil minions of The Rat King should ever return.

Whatever their true fates might have been, only one thing remains certain: no living soul has seen either of those two heroes since The Rat King was defeated...

— Taken from **The Fabled Two: Heroes Who Disappeared into the Mists of Legend**

Chapter 7

CROSSING THE MIRRORED LAKE

The trip through The Forest Path to the shores of Mirrored Lake was uneventful. Both Teague and Wilding, their bellies full of delicious food, had been able to find some sleep in the cart as Ainsley Hearthseeker took over the reins of Wilding's squirrel, a companion beast Wilding had kept for many years and treated like his own child. Of course, most days, Wilding and his squirrel, whom he affectionately called 'Ducky,' spent their time delivering kegs of his homebrew up and down The Riverpath, where daring adventures were distant thoughts best left to afternoon naps. Ainsley had offered to take the reins so Teague and his best friend could get some rest, knowing what a night the pair had had, and the gracious offer had been accepted immediately. The longtime friends climbed into the back of the cart among the storage racks that normally held wooden casks, but now held the gently placed body of the Falconrider, and promptly fell asleep on some hay bales.

Before he dozed off, Wilding said to the bard 'Let me know if you have any trouble with Ducky, and I will come to take back the reins.'

'Why do you call him Ducky?' Hearthseeker replied.

Half asleep, in what sounded to Hearthseeker almost like a baby voice, Wilding murmured 'Because he is so sweet and cute like a little baby ducky, oh he's such a special lil guy...'

Then, Hearthseeker heard a loud snore, and Wilding was out. It was hard to believe someone who was that enamored with a squirrel could be a Battlemage of some notoriety.

But looks can be deceiving, thought Hearthseeker.

Of course, the tradeoff was that Hearthseeker, now stuck with the Stranger sitting by his side on the driving bench of the squirrel cart, could not have asked for a worse possible conversationalist. Ainsley tried to make some casual conversation with his one companion who remained awake, but the Stranger was having none of it. He just scribbled some notes in a journal and nodded along to Hearthseeker's jovial questions, grunting 'umm hmms' and clearing his throat in the midst of a few mumbled 'yes's' and 'nope's.' After a half dozen such failed attempts to strike up a conversation, Hearthseeker realized the squirrel, who was unable to talk, would be a much better traveling companion. Of course, after a while spent talking to 'Ducky' without receiving a response, Hearthseeker remembered that even if 'Ducky' was capable of speech, he had never learned any of the animal languages in his bardic training other than local mice dialects, as well as some passable human. Once that thought occurred to him, he made sure that his words to Ducky were only uplifting and encouraging. He didn't want to risk alienating a potentially new animal friend. Hearthseeker was a friend to all, as his reputation was known — and squirrels were no exception.

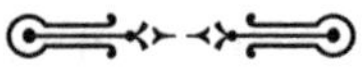

After two hours spent going down The Riverpath, Hearthseeker could see the sun's reflection on The Mirrored Lake, but no sign of the castle just yet. Finally, after traversing some more ground, the Western Spires of Castle Feldenspar could begin to be seen rising up off the island which jutted out of the lake. It was an awe-inducing sight, indeed, and Hearthseeker gently reached back to give a brief shake to the shoulders of Teague and Wilding, who started awake.

'Milords, the spires of Feldenspar are near.'

Wilding hopped up from his hay bales and climbed back onto the driver's bench to take over the squirrel reins, yawning and opening his eyes wide to try to invigorate himself and shake the sleep from his lids. Teague remained in the back as the three mice in the front of the cart all stared silently at the gleaming white stone spires and the standards, brightly colored in purple and royal blue, which flew high above them. These jutted out over the citadel and seemed almost to pierce the sky, which in turn rose above the outlying city at the castle's base. This sight was impressive for any human, to be sure, but when you are the size of a small mouse, seeing such a grand human establishment was humbling indeed.

Of course, very few mice ever encountered humans — it was meant to stay that way, too. This is why the mice who worked as Rooters were so well respected, as it were. The energy, effort, and courage required to go into human establishments and effectively steal items twice the size of a small mouse — or larger — and to do so over and over again on a daily basis as a way of making one's living was truly inspiring.

But the companions were not Rooters, stealing stealthily into the castle in the dead of night under cover of darkness. This was a daytime summons, the most dangerous time of all for any mouse to go traipsing about in human spaces, whether they were experienced or not.

Up ahead, Teague spied the Stranger's rowboat stored under some walnuts and leaves, cleverly hidden to look like a piece of deadwood washed upon the shore.

'One thing is for sure,' he said. 'Either we are crossing The Mirrored Lake by day because no one knows we are coming, or because *everyone* knows we are coming and we are expected.'

The three companions looked at the Stranger, who seemed to want to make an effort to reassure them.

'My orders, as all orders that come from the Thief's Guild of MouseKeep, were given in secrecy — and I have not betrayed that trust. Unless someone else has betrayed my mission, I can assure you, with a great deal of confidence, that we should encounter no trouble while crossing to the Eastern Shore.'

As Teague and Hearthseeker worked to remove the cover and debris camouflaging the rowboat, Wilding produced a spyglass and peered across at the shores of the Castle's base and the rest of the lake's landings. High up on the citadel's spires, he was just able to make out three human archers staring watchfully towards the Western Shore.

'The archers are in place, as the missive stated,' said the wizard. 'I see no other signs of disturbance.'

'Then let's hope it stays that way,' said Teague, who was busy loading the Falconrider's body into the rowboat.

When they were ready to shove off, Hearthseeker took his place in the middle of the rowboat, assuming the oars with selfless assertion. The Stranger chose to sit in the front of the craft, positioning himself sideways on the seat so he could watch the castle as they moved towards it while still keeping a close eye on his three companions. Wilding and Teague sat in the rear. As Hearthseeker manned the oars to start maneuvering them across the lake, Teague pulled his bow out and nocked an arrow, just in case.

And so, the tiny rowboat drifted its way across the water. Unless one was a trained observer, this small floating raft carrying four mice would have appeared — to human eyes — as nothing more than a piece of driftwood shambling and ambling its way across The Mirrored Lake, caught in a tiny undercurrent which beckoned it, ever so slowly, to the Eastern side. But if that same observer was patient enough, they would have seen that this small vessel moved in one direction, and with great — albeit agonizingly slow — purpose. With a good and practiced stroke, Hearthseeker took them closer and closer to their destination with each pull of the oars, keeping them steadily moving towards the opposing shore.

When they had made it about halfway across the lake, Teague turned to Wilding and said flatly, 'So, what's our agenda? The closer we come to our destination, the farther I seem to be from wrapping my head around what, exactly, we are dealing with.'

Wilding closed his gray eyes and lifted his nose up, sniffing the wind. He meditated for a second, then spoke.

'Nothing good, I am afraid. We have to proceed with caution, as if our very lives depend on it. Do you have a plan?'

Wilding looked at Teague without expression.

Teague smiled back at his old friend. 'Do you?'

Wilding retorted, 'I was never the one known for tactical planning, Robert. As I recall, that falls under your skillset. And besides, my instinct tells me you formed one yesterday afternoon.'

Teague burst out laughing.

'You know me too well, Professor. My plan is simple. When we reach landfall on the Eastern Shore, we stow the rowboat, leave the Falconrider's body with it, and enter the tunnels to MouseKeep through the City Sewer entrance. You know, the one that cuts directly up to the ground floor of the castle, and then several lengths upward. As I recall, there is an entrance in the kitchen to the inner sanctum of MouseKeep, and then, with any luck and Heaven's blessing, we can go through the 'official' MouseKeep channels from there. Ideally, we will get escorted up to The King's Pedestal in the safety and presence of old friends — or at the very least, mice pledged to the service of the King. Based on our reception at the entrance of MouseKeep, we should be able to infer what we are dealing with and assess the situation further from there.'

Teague paused, then lowered his voice, and with an enigmatic smile, said 'Plus, we have an asset with us that no one realizes, one which may offer us some additional...protection.'

Both Wilding and Teague looked at the Stranger, then back to each other.

'For insurance purposes,' Teague continued, and Wilding nodded without interrupting. 'Either he is oblivious to what is happening via Thief's Guild protocol, as he's claimed, in which case we will all discover what's going on together. Or else he is part of something...more...'

Teague paused here to find the right word.

'...nefarious.'

Hearthseeker, who had overheard the entire conversation despite Teague's attempts at subtlety, stared up at the blue sky. His muscles rippled and strained beneath his leather doublet, struggling to keep the boat moving steadily and smoothly under the weight of five fully loaded and equipped mice.

Someday, I could write a really good song about this, he thought silently to himself. *Or perhaps even write it down as a tale...*

Wilding looked towards the bow of the boat, and after a moment's thought addressed the Stranger.

'Stranger, what is the plan once we make landfall? I'm assuming there is no welcoming party waiting to greet us due to the secret nature of this summons?'

The Stranger didn't even look up at Wilding, but kept his stance, half looking forward towards the castle, half using his peripheral vision to keep an eye on the back of the boat. Without emotion, he answered.

'My instructions were to take you to the MouseKeep grounds through the western entrance to MouseKeep, in the hope that we will still have some shadows from the rising sun over the western walls to screen our approach and help keep us hidden. Once you have entered the western gate of the MouseKeep, my mission will be complete. I will not be traveling with you further from there, but will be returning to my home at the bottom of the hill near the island shore to rejoin my family. In all likelihood, after my mission is over, we shall never meet again.'

An awkward silence ensued as Teague and Wilding silently pondered what this may mean. The Stranger's tone could be interpreted many ways, but no one would deny it was *ominous*. Mice of the Thief's Guild may have been known for their silence, but never for their tact. However, Ainsley soon broke the silence with a well-timed question.

'All my life I grew up hearing tales of MouseKeep, but they were always used interchangeably with Castle Feldenspar. Not to sound like an ignorant vole, but, well — what exactly *is* the MouseKeep, and how is it different from Castle Feldenspar — if at all?'

Wilding, a true sorcerer and antiquarian, as well as a bibliophile and historian, smiled expansively and eagerly went to answer Hearthseeker's questions.

'Well, Hearthseeker,' Wilding began, 'most mice incorrectly assume that Castle Feldenspar and the MouseKeep are, in fact, one and the same, their names and descriptions being so often used interchangeably. However, as you will soon learn, MouseKeep is, in fact, *a castle within a castle...*' he paused here for effect, 'and is related to Castle Feldenspar only in the sense that it shares, in essence, an identical location in space and time as the larger castle itself.'

'What do you mean, exactly?' queried Ainsley. 'How can there be a separate castle within a castle? Is it underground? Certainly MouseKeep did not exist before the construction of Castle Feldenspar several hundred years ago...did it?'

Teague broke in and added, 'Well, it is *kind* of underground...'

Wilding snorted at his history lesson being so rudely interrupted. Playfully, he shot a faux-nasty look at Teague, cleared his throat audibly, then continued.

'In the precursor and lead up to the The First Rat King War, a small group of Mousekin had been assisting with reconnaissance and intelligence gathering for The Heaven's King. But the King insisted that even his own trusted advisers, as it were, remain ignorant of the fact that thanks to the existence of the decoding stones, the dialects of mice and humans could be mutually understood by each other.

Indeed, The Heaven's King understood how imperative it was to keep the secret that mice can learn to speak and understand the human dialect, while The Heaven's King himself — a scholar of no small measure on his own credit — had also worked diligently in secret to learn Mousespeak. In his heart, The One from Heaven knew that should this knowledge fall into the wrong hands, it could be used for something far more...sinister.'

Pausing for a moment like the great storyteller he was, Wilding then continued.

'Before the first skirmish at The Andrellion Plains between the King's forces and his adversaries, he had begun to commission more and more mice into his service to bolster his defensive ranks. The One From Heaven was wise enough to deploy the Mousekin strategically — in matters of intelligence, aerial reconnaissance, and other delicate missions which could be performed by skilled mice behind enemy lines and without the knowledge of the enemy. The Falcon Riders were formally established, and the King had his human Falconeers train falcons to carry small payloads of rocks on their backs in makeshift saddles to accustom them to the weight of a mouse — which was brilliant in and of itself. But, the King couldn't simultaneously stage the Falcon Riders on the spires of the Eastern Wall and keep human archers stationed there as well, lest the secret of the force leak out, or the brave mice themselves be put at risk from the humans who were unaware of their existence and special role within the King's forces.'

Ainsley was becoming transfixed by the tale. He asked impatiently, 'Well, what did he do? What was his answer to this problem?'

'His answer,' offered Wilding as he looked down his greying snout at the bard, 'was MouseKeep. Privately, and away from the castle grounds, he gathered the most accomplished master stonemasons in the land and their apprentices. There were three pairs in all, Master plus apprentice, and the King shared with them — and them alone — the secret knowledge of the existence of Mouseling Hollow and the assets that the Mousekin were becoming — nay, *had become*, to the crown. Swearing them to secrecy, he commissioned them to build unnoticeable false walls which hid within them a mouse-sized citadel, complete with staircases and tunnels for mice to easily navigate without being noticed by their human counterparts. These spaces were fully ventilated and tactical in nature, and even found room to include the occasional, barely noticeable window, which...' Wilding smiled here '...were cleverly designed to look like small fractures in the stone, allowing mice to peer out into the interior of Castle Feldenspar. And the best part of all, young Hearthseeker, is that the residents of the castle were none the wiser.'

He paused a moment to let this sink in, then continued.

'So you see, my young bard, The Citadel at MouseKeep is truly **a castle within a castle**. The master masons used their craftsmanship and skills in such a way that the guardians of MouseKeep were able to effectively continue to do their jobs, all while being safely hidden from the unknowing eyes of Castle Feldenspar's human population.'

'On the Eastern Spire of Castle Feldenspar, where the Falcon Riders are...' Wilding sniffed '...or should I say, **were**, stationed, the masons rebuilt the spire at the King's command. While the side facing inward looks like a standard parapet to any passing human sentry, the exterior of the spire contained a cleverly disguised opening, allowing the falcons and their riders to have free entry and exit, with a smooth, cobblestone landing space. The falcons even had their housing built right into the Spire's open face, and staircases downward safely lead to the interior quarters where the Riders, their supply staff, a full kitchen, barracks, and so forth all reside. The construction of MouseKeep, the King's secrecy, and his brilliant military mind had been so successful that as the task came to completion, rumors started to fly that he had commissioned other divisions of Mousekin to supplement the Falcon Riders — divisions whom we only hear about in tales today, to be established and well supplied for critical missions throughout The First Rat King War. Tactical flight groups like The Harriers of MouseKeep, or the armored squirrel riders, the LanceGuard, were allegedly formed. Though we sometimes hear of their adventures in tales still told today, few have ever seen the soldiers of MouseKeep who bear such rarified rank as to serve in these divisions. So you see, my friend Ainsley...'

He looked at the bard in satisfaction at having finished his tale. 'MouseKeep *is* an actual castle within a castle — and most humans have no idea it exists! A veritable fortress, living and breathing in service to the King, unknown by the very residents who live above, below, and around it, and — with a great and noticeable irony – *their ordinary Mouseling counterparts are equally in the dark as to what, exactly, it is!* **Brilliant!'**

'I had no idea!' shouted Ainsley, excitedly. 'But I do see now how the presence of MouseKeep makes The Rooters' job that much easier, acting as a staging area for their furtive nighttime raiding missions.'

'Nay, the Rooters' job is still a dangerous and difficult one,' interjected Teague. 'They have to exit the safety of the MouseKeep and risk being caught by humans every time they set a paw outside its hidden walls. MouseKeep may make traversing Castle Feldenspar a bit easier, but the Rooters' open missions into human spaces are still fraught with peril. Humans are not the only denizens of the castle who view mice as pests, for example. There are many cats about as well, and we haven't even brought up the subject of rats...'

Hearthseeker's eyes widened. 'I thought cats were forbidden in Castle Feldenspar.'

Teague answered him gently. 'Yes, they are forbidden, but many of the servants keep them anyway. Mostly as private pets, and to help keep rats away — and in doing so, curb the spread of disease. But you can see the double-edged sword here, obviously,' he said as he looked back at the bard.

'Indeed,' said Ainsley, who nodded with assent. He continued rowing as he looked back up and gazed in his exertions at the cloudless blue sky. *Hopefully,* he thought to himself, *this won't be the last day I ever see it.* He had heard once of the ancient berserker warrior mice whose battle cry had been 'today is a fantastic day to die!' But thinking on the comfort of his fresh, hot breakfast at The Sleeping Cat earlier in the morning, as well as his newfound friendships with

Teague and Wilding, Ainsley couldn't help but feel that life may have a bit more to offer him — in both adventure, experience and food — and he hoped his would remain a long one. At that moment, it was hard to understand the eagerness the legendary berserker mice possessed to give their lives so easily, and with such zeal, to whatever the day's challenges presented them.

Still, he thought, as he sniffed the air and took in the scents of the cool, crisp lake water, carried by the breeze on which so many delicate scents wafted, and glanced at the sharp eyes of his companions, *I can't help but respect their resolve.*

'Landfall, my friends!' said Wilding suddenly. 'Be on your guard. There are more than rats that we have to be wary of as we embark upon this dangerous quest — if a quest it truly turns out to be.'

Teague picked his bow up and kept his arrow nocked. He looked directly at the Stranger, then pointed to a small pile of debris on the rapidly approaching shore of the castle's island soil.

'We can store the boat there, under that morass of driftwood and flotsam,' he said. 'Then, with the Stranger in the lead, we will make our way to MouseKeep's western entrance.'

'What about the Falconrider?' asked Hearthseeker.

'We will leave his body here. Once we have made contact with any of the guards at MouseKeep, they will send a party to retrieve it. Brave fellow that he was, we cannot afford to be encumbered by his weight as we traverse the castle's grounds — especially the open terrain leading up to its entrance. It would mean a death sentence for all of us, assuredly. The Rider would understand.'

Out of the corner of his eyes Teague spied the Stranger, who said nothing, looking emotionless. In that moment of silence, the rowboat gently bumped against the sandy shore. Hearthseeker hopped nimbly out of the craft and started pulling it towards the pile of debris where they would store it until they returned from their meeting with the King.

'Then our plan is decided' Teague said flatly. 'Stranger, lead the way, so that you may complete your mission and can then rejoin your family with the greatest expediency.'

Once the rowboat was stored, the Stranger headed up the beach to the dirt path lined with some worn stones. Teague followed, then Wilding, and the bard fell in behind them. As they walked, Teague held his bow, with its fletched arrow, at the ready. Wilding leaned upon his wooden staff, using it to help him walk up the gently sloping hill. Hearthseeker followed in the rear. Having taken his sword off his pack and affixed it to the belt around his waist, he placed his paw firmly on the hilt that now rested on his right side.

Teague looked back and glanced at the sword around the bard's waist and thought to himself, *So he's a leftpaw ...interesting.*

High above them, the spires of Castle Feldenspar rose so distantly into the air that the mice could no longer see its proud battle standards, gleaming in the sun and gently caressed by the wind, as they flapped high up in the sky.

Large human buildings mean quite a lot of work and effort for small mice to traverse. As young bucks and does, all mice are required to learn what are known as 'The Ten Rules' from an early age, which are a set of rules devised to keep mice safe when entering human dwellings.

These 'Ten Rules' are as follows:

1) *Don't be seen*

2) *Don't get caught*

3) *Don't EVER eat cheese off the floor, no matter how safe it looks*

4) *Never jump into bowls, especially those which have liquid in them, or you may never be able to escape them*

5) *Don't talk to humans, even if you understand their language*

6) *It takes about six times the effort to traverse a human building as a Mouseling one, so plan and prepare well.*

7) *Not all mice are friendly*

8) *All RATS ARE ENEMIES*

9) *Avoid open spaces which may contain aerial predators*

10) *Falls from a human wall or ceiling are usually deadly*

— Taken from **HOW TO STEAL AN EGG: CHRONICLES AND LEGENDS OF THE ROOTERS**

Chapter 8

EXCITEMENT IN THE VILLAGE SQUARE

If the row across The Mirrored Lake had been somewhat peaceful, the traverse to the entrance of MouseKeep was anything but. Having very little cover to screen their advance, the mice sprinted from the shore to the early outskirts of the village which lay below the castle, and had grown over the years to surround it. Though he had seemed pretty lethargic since his unexpected arrival at The Sleeping Cat the previous day, the Stranger now scurried deftly from hiding spot to hiding spot, forcing the three other mice to keep up with him. His concentration was so focused on plotting each movement that he barely even paused to check if they were still with him. Between the frenetic pace and the midday sun rising higher in the sky, all four mice were soon soaked in sweat, and found themselves short of breath.

As they got closer to the village, the Stranger paused behind a wooden barrel outside a small blacksmith's shack. Inside the mice could hear the *'tink tink tink'* of the blacksmith's hammer on steel, hear how the fire roared when he stoked the bellows, see the crimson glow of the forge emanating through the stone windows, and feel the searing heat which billowed forth even from the cracks at the base of the small building. Sweat poured down their snouts and ran into their eyes, saturating their battlegear. Teague felt the leather-wrapped grip of his bow grow slick with sweat, and realized that stowing the bow on his back would allow him to run faster. Any altercation which arose would probably be with human sized counterparts anyways, making his mouse-sized bow somewhat...unreliable.

Suddenly, the Stranger spoke. 'We must keep our pace up lest we find ourselves trapped in the market at noonday. The vast amount of people and animals there would certainly belie our presence. A horse or donkey rearing up with us underfoot is not an obstacle we need to contend with if our goal is to preserve a stealthy approach. But as you two know, there is no faster way to the Castle's gates than through the market. Come now, make haste! Stay close to me, or stray at your peril!'

With that, the Stranger darted on, leaving the safety of the nook that the blacksmith's barrel had afforded them.

They all felt fatigued, yet followed dutifully, the pace quickened even further from what it had been before.

For Teague, it was all a blur. Barrel, mouse hole, stray rock, corner of building. After an interminable time spent sprinting breathlessly from one spot to another, he saw an opening up ahead — one which was seemingly beginning to fill with humans and animals of all shapes and sizes. He could see goods of all kinds hanging from stalls — meats, cheeses, fine wines and casks of ale, baskets of fruits and vegetables, and live animals in cages, looking worried.

The Market!

But it was still far off. He glanced behind him, and for a moment thought he spied a black cat pursuing them. But a passing wagon cut the cat off from his (admittedly peripheral) view, and they labored on at a frenetic pace.

Finally, at the edge of the market, the Stranger stopped. After scanning the crowd ahead, he glanced back at the party and stated flatly:

'Assuming we can keep stealth on our side, once we pass the marketplace, it is only a few short paces to MouseKeep's hidden exits within the village. Any of those entry points will take us to the western gate, where I will then take my leave. Hurry now! With me!'

Having barely had a moment to catch their breath, the companions trailed quickly after the Stranger — and 'daring' was the only word which could properly describe the route that the thief had chosen for them. He ran directly into stalls and between the legs of horses and donkeys, pausing only before they would have directly crossed the path of any human.

'I thought he said we needed to keep stealth on our side!' blurted Hearthseeker breathlessly as he strove to keep up with the group.

'Not far now!' remarked Teague as he sprinted in close pursuit of their guide. The town surrounding Castle Feldenspar had changed a great deal since Teague had served the Heaven's King, almost twenty seasons previous. It was so much busier now, more full, more... congested. What had been easily traversed so many moons ago was now a route brimming with human activities — all of which were highly dangerous to Mouselings.

Whatever happened next, Ainsley Hearthseeker couldn't quite put his paw on, try as he might to retrace the events in retrospect. All he knew was this: while running at the end of the line behind his companions, staring up to admire the cheeses and sausages handily dangling for display from strings tied to the roof of the stall they were darting through, he suddenly heard a horse whinny. It was not the kind of whinny which you hear when a horse is placidly grazing in a pasture, but rather, the whinny a horse makes when something has placed him into a state of absolute terror — a whinny that said a horse was preparing to buck riders and stampede with his (or her) equine compatriots. Ainsley had traveled far and wide, and knew what that sound meant. So, part of him wasn't surprised when he turned his gaze away from the cheeses and sausages to check how far ahead his companions were in front of him, and spied the front hooves of a grayish-white horse (when he was trying to piece it all together later, he thought that perhaps the horse had been white, but incredibly dirty and unwashed) about to land directly on top of him.

Out of the corner of his eye, he could see escaped chickens flying everywhere after the cart that had been carrying them was knocked over, spilling their cages to the ground with a crash. A basket of fresh red and gold apples had also been overturned, and Hearthseeker saw the rest of his companions disappear ahead into an onslaught of fruit, now rolling and bouncing its way down the gentle slope that they had been running up in their now-impeded ascent to the Castle's entrance. He saw Wilding's staff go flying into the air, having been hit directly by a rolling red harvest apple. He nimbly caught the Battlemage's runaway staff in flight as the cascade of apples surged forward to envelop him. Using a bard's dexterity, he tried to deftly dodge each apple as it bounced towards him, but they were so profuse that after avoiding the initial rush, one knocked his bottom paws out from under him. Though he managed to hold onto Wilding's staff, the collision flung him skywards, spinning him upside down in the air. He hit the ground with a loud and painful *THUD* — while in the midst of the chaotic fray, he just prayed that nothing was broken.

The sheer impact of his tumble, and subsequent return to earth, sent his pouches crashing out onto the dirt outside the stall — pouches which were filled with some coin he had made the previous evening (wisely, he'd stashed most of it back at The Sleeping Cat) as well as small spiked metal traps, often carried by bards to ward off pursuers, called caltrops.

The horse, now in a state of utter panic thanks to the mice running underneath it, attempted to gallop away, but was almost immediately made lame when it landed on one of the caltrops that Hearthseeker had spilled in his fall. After a heart-rending scream of pain, it stopped frenzying and began to nurse its tender hoof as humans everywhere rushed to restrain and calm the injured animal. The villagers all yelled to each other as animals everywhere were baying, caawing,

clucking, and screeching, and food and other human wares intended for the market now lay scattered everywhere. It was a complete and utter mess.

Suddenly, in the midst of the ruckus, he heard the Stranger cry out 'To the cart!'

Ahead, Ainsley saw the Stranger mounting a four wheeled horse-drawn cart which had a small leather braid hanging from the back of it. It was almost comical, watching the old thief spin around as he climbed the twirling braid, all while the cart continued its uphill ascent to the castle. With Wilding's staff in hand, he kept running towards what he now realized was their only option for escape before the market stalls became completely overrun with human onlookers.

As Teague ran forward in his own pursuit of the cart, he reached and grabbed an arrow out of his quiver, swiftly tying a small rope to it from his shoulder satchel. He yelled 'Go Wilding!' at his old friend as the wizard loped past him.

After taking a precise aim, he let his roped arrow loose and it squarely pierced the tail end of the cart with a *THUNK*. Wilding grabbed the rope and, with surprising fleetness, climbed up to the safety of the cart. The Stranger had reached the top of the cart at about the same time, and now the two were beckoning to their companions to make haste amidst the frenzy that was rapidly overtaking the marketplace.

Teague kept sprinting forward, but refused to grab the rope until he was sure the bard was safely with them. 'Now Hearthseeker! With your life!' He pointed urgently towards the rope.

Ainsley had never run so fast — run desperately 'for his life,' which is what he thought Teague had meant. With a mighty leap he hopped aboard the tail of the rope, which was now dragging on the ground, and scurried up it.

Halfway up the rope, he looked behind him. Teague was still chasing after the rope, laboring to get his paws on it as the horse drawing the cart had begun to pick up speed.

'Let's go, Teague!' yelled the bard. He could see Teague struggling to keep up, still unable to get a firm grip on the rope. Hearthseeker wasn't about to give up on his new friend, though. He scampered back down the rope, until his paws were nearly scraping in the dirt, and extended Wilding's staff out towards Teague.

'COME ON, YOU ROGUE!' he screamed, and the sound of his cry reenergized Teague, who found a small burst of speed and was just barely able to grab the end of the staff with a flying leap.

However, while he was securing the end of the staff with his paws, his acrobatics landed him face down in the dirt, holding onto the staff for dear life as he was dragged bumping and thumping along behind the cart. Rocks and pebbles flew into his furred face. But Ainsley refused to give up.

'CLIMB, YOU FOOL!'

And climb he did. Paw over paw, Robert Teague worked his way to the end of the staff and latched onto the rope, after which Hearthseeker retracted the staff and began to climb back up himself. Looking back every few moments to check on Teague's progress, he made it to the top of the cart and extended his paws to an exhausted Teague as he finally approached the top edge of the cart.

Once Teague was safely over the side, Hearthseeker handed the staff back to Wilding and slyly said 'I think you may have dropped this, Professor. Just another day's work for a humble bard, you know.' He pretended to yawn and stretch his paws. He smiled at Wilding, but was interrupted by the Stranger.

'You fools! Now half the kingdom is in an uproar over a mass frenzy in the marketplace! With no other clear cause to blame for this disturbance, our adversaries will surely know something is amiss — something like a group of Mousekin secretly attempting to infiltrate the castle!' The thief looked genuinely upset, as if he was caught between the warring impulses to rage and to weep.

'What 'adversaries,' exactly, do you speak of?' queried Ainsley. 'I thought you said no one knew we were coming except the King?'

The Stranger cleared his throat audibly.

'Well, yes, but…'

'But what, thief?' said Wilding, with sudden hostility. He pointed his staff at the Stranger, who looked fearful as he stared at the ruby gem perched at the end of Wilding's staff. 'What exactly is so alarming about our presence? You said no one knows we are coming. Wasn't that your mission…to make sure we arrived without the knowledge of others?'

Silence fell across the party. The only sound they heard were the wooden wheels of the horse-drawn goods cart gently *clickety-clacking* up the cobblestone streets as it wound its way to some unknown destination high in the village, or perhaps to the gates of the castle itself.

But still, no one spoke.

That was, until the bard suddenly had an epiphany of sorts.

'It looks like this Stranger is more than just a pawn in this game.' He drew his short sword and pointed it at the thief. 'I'd say he is playing for high stakes — but whether he's playing voluntarily or against his will…now, *that* is the question.'

All eyes fell on the thief, who was sitting on a small stack of hay in the middle of the cart. A long, pregnant silence befell the party as the companions waited for some elucidation as to what, exactly, was the Stranger's real mission. Staring at the pointed end of the bard's sword, he choked back a lump in his throat, then whispered.

'They have my family. If I don't deliver you to MouseKeep as promised, my life — and the lives of my wife and child — will be forfeit.'

'Who is this 'they,' exactly?' asked Teague. He sounded impatient.

'I don't know,' said the Stranger. 'I don't know if you will believe me, but I will tell you all I know, for now I see that the fate of my family rests not in the hands of those who took them, but in yours.'

He paused for a moment, then continued.

'A few days before I arrived in Mouseling Hollow, I received a summons to MouseKeep. As I told you before, it is very unusual for lower ranking members of the Thief's Guild to be given assignments, especially tasks of such importance, but somehow I was 'selected.' And when I say selected, what I mean is this: when I arrived at MouseKeep, it was practically deserted. Strangely, the usual guards of MouseKeep — mice I have known for many seasons — were gone, replaced by mice I have never seen before. Mice who had a harder look to them, I would say.

'But it had been some time since I had last visited the castle, and I assumed that the guards I'd known had simply been rotated out. Yet when I went into the Keep to receive my assignment, even the superior in the Guild who awaited me there was a mouse I had never met. Perhaps not that unusual, given the desire for secrecy in these matters. But when I went to give him our secret paw embrace, he swatted my paw away, saying 'we don't have time for formalities right now.' And then he gave me the backstory on **The Fabled Two**, told me they were in Mouseling Hollow, and gave me the King's sealed missive.

'But before I left, he called to his 'guards' — if that's what they can be called — and paraded my wife and child right in front of me. They were bound, their forepaws cinched tight with ropes, and my superior, or whoever he was, made it very plain what would happen to my loved ones if I failed in this mission. He told me that my family was being held for their 'protection,' and would be treated as his 'guests.''

'Who was this strange mouse who allegedly hails from the Thief's Guild?' asked Teague.

'I am not sure, Teague.' The Stranger shook his head mournfully. 'I wish that I were, but I am not sure. But all of the mice that I saw that day wore strange new clothing — black tunics with a high-backed collar, and on the chest of their tunics they wore a small gold medallion with a black and red ribboned trim. The sigil of MouseKeep was not visible, which I thought was odd. And they all carried strange weapons, like a...' He paused for a second as he closed his eyes. 'A crescent blade attached to a straight blade, which was fixed to a wooden shaft and wielded with both paws. Somewhat like a halberd, only shorter and more...nasty looking.'

Wilding rubbed his chin thoughtfully, then spoke.

'So this, then, is what we know: it would seem the mice who have traditionally guarded MouseKeep have been either replaced or killed. Even your Thief's Guild superior is unknown, and prone to using extortion tactics, like snatching your family as a function of your mission's success — or rather, should I say, as an impetus to its success. Stranger, tell me — when was the last time you saw the King?'

The Stranger thought about it for a moment. 'Not since a few weeks ago, as I ponder it. He was in his daughter's bed chamber trying to console her about her lost ring.'

'The ring that Leafcatcher McGuinn found, as I recall,' said Teague.

'Who?' said the Stranger.

'Never mind that,' said Teague. 'It would seem all of our fears and trepidations are about to come true. We are most certainly about to walk into a trap, and it would seem the King has gone missing — or worse — along with our Mouseling brethren. The Falcon Riders have been sent on a mission — one which we do not know the purpose of — which resulted in significant casualties, possibly even a total loss of the division. Now we have been summoned out of hiding, which means someone has either betrayed our trust — or been forced to betray it.'

'For all we know, we may be the last of the MouseGuard leadership,' said Wilding.

'As it may be. Though that doesn't matter much at the moment,' said Teague. 'Right now, we need to make a plan. The most important element that we have on our side right now is the element of surprise.'

'Surprise?!' said Hearthseeker. 'But they know we are coming!'

'Exactly,' said Teague. 'And yet, they do not know that the Stranger has revealed to us the true nature of his mission, and that his family is being held hostage to his success. We also have an additional resource that our...hosts...remain yet unaware of.' Teague looked at the bard and grinned broadly. 'So, we must play a game superior to the strategies of the best Root and Field masters if we are to get to the bottom of this mystery.'

'I like where this is going!' said Wilding.

'Stranger, let us be clear — your orders are to deliver us to the western entrance of MouseKeep, correct?'

'Yes.'

Teague continued. 'And, although you were not told *specifically* to accompany us all the way to The King's Pedestal, presumably, with your family being held hostage, you would want to make sure that we arrived safely and securely to the end point of your mission, if only to ensure their safety — correct? To prove that your mission had been completed successfully?'

The Stranger thought about this. 'Yes, absolutely. In fact, when I left the castle I distinctly remember thinking, 'I will bring these mice directly to the Pedestal, to make sure there is no confusion about my mission being completed.' At that point my plan was to take my family and flee the castle — forever.'

'Good, good,' said Teague as he stared up at the blue sky, thinking about their next moves and what was awaiting them inside the castle.

'The entrance to MouseKeep is rapidly approaching,' said Wilding. 'We need to finalize a plan, with haste!'

Teague looked at Hearthseeker and asked him quite bluntly, 'Ainsley, you are an accomplished musician. But how good is your acting?'

The bard smiled broadly. 'I was actually employed in my younger years by the Actor's Guild, having been cast for the role of Leftpaw in the popular play *Mouse on a Hilltop*. To quite good reviews, I might add!' The bard puffed his chest out a bit, proudly.

'Good,' said Teague. 'Come here and I will give you your, well... special task. Your stop is coming up quite soon.'

Teague leaned over and began to whisper in Ainsley's ear. The bard smiled and nodded, and then suddenly, with a deft leap, jumped off the moving cart and into an oak barrel near a horse stall on the rising cobblestoned hill which led towards the castle. The three remaining companions looked back at him, and watched as the barrel was covered in a cloud of dust kicked up by the passage of the cart on its final ascent up the hill.

The Stranger pointed to a small hole at the base of the upcoming castle, where the cobblestone road met the Keep's base. 'There!' said the Stranger. 'The western entrance to MouseKeep!'

Teague had recovered his roped arrow and now nocked it again, letting it fly from his perch on the cart. He watched as it struck firmly in an old wooden signpost along the roadside.

'Time to go!' shouted Teague. He tightened his hold on the line as Wilding, placing his staff over the rope and gripping it tightly, nimbly zipped down the rope towards the sign, dropping down at the last moment into the soft, green grass beneath the signpost.

'Your turn!' said Teague to the Stranger.

The Stranger grabbed the rope with his thick leather gloves and slid down with some level of finesse, landing lightly next to Wilding.

Wilding looked back at his best friend and yelled, 'COME ON, TEAGUE!'

From his vantage point on the cart, Teague could see that his rope was already starting to run out of slack. The window in which he would be able to rejoin his companions was rapidly closing. So, taking a firm grasp on the quickly-tightening rope, Teague swung off the cart with the agility of an acrobat and, climbing the rope in mid swing, let the rope's curve pendulum him mid-air into the soft grass by the signpost. He landed on his two rear paws, then pulled the arrow out of the sign and stowed it quickly back inside his quiver.

'That was impressive,' admitted Wilding.

'And I wouldn't even call this a good day,' retorted Teague slyly.

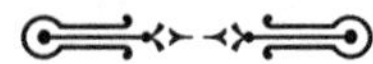

On the Game of Root and Field:

This board and card game — perhaps the favorite of Mouselings across the land — is strange and unique in that the mice themselves did not create the game, nor do they manufacture or produce its cards. No one knows who first designed this deep and strategic game. Rumors abound, of course, and given that the cards are perfectly sized for Mouselings, it is often assumed that a Mouseling was its original creator. Naturally, that has been disputed, as various other intelligent mammals have been known to play the game as well — beavers and river otters, for example — and caches of its cards and game pieces have been found stashed underwater (in dry waterproof wrappings, naturally) as well as in hollowed out logs, knotholes in trees, and so forth.

*The mystery of who created these unique cards and figurines remains just that — a mysterious and unsolved event, but one which brings great joy to Mousekin across The Far Collective. And, its players have come to understand that the cards themselves vary in uniqueness — some cards can be easily found across the land, while for other cards, there is only one known copy. These are known as **legendary cards**. These rare and powerful cards bestow unique abilities upon the player (or field state) which makes them very enviable, indeed. If and when they come up for sale, they fetch a very handsome price.*

While many have made a life's pursuit out of attempting to locate the original creator of these cards, none so far have succeeded.

Some claim that the wizard who once lived in the old abandoned tower in Mouseling Hollow was involved in the game's creation, but the mayor of that hamlet has dismissed such claims as 'baseless rubbish.'

Others claim to have seen a Mouseling carrying a pack full of cards and figurines into a secret door at the caverns near Rock Hollows — but who knows? Mouselings who have disappeared into Rock Hollows are often never seen from again...

— Taken from **Stormsnout's Guide to Gambling -
A Strategy Guide**

Chapter 9

INFILTRATING MOUSEKEEP

Amidst the soft green grass that had grown up around the wooden signpost, the three mice held a vantage point where they could grab a brief respite from the excitement in the square and discuss their next move. So much had happened since yesterday, when the Stranger had first appeared — the Falconrider crashing into the Inn, the King's sealed summons for Teague, and now the Stranger's admission that he had been sent on a task by superiors whom he had never met, who either didn't know or were unwilling to engage in the usual protocol for the Thief's Guild, and who didn't balk at holding his family captive to ensure his cooperation. All signs pointed to things having taken a sinister turn at Castle Feldenspar, and within the MouseKeep in turn.

Neither Wilding nor Teague had any doubt that they were walking into a trap. But why? What was its purpose? Whatever the answer might be, they knew they wouldn't get very far in uncovering it if they were disarmed or captured at the western gate.

Still, no one in MouseKeep knew that *they* knew about the Stranger's family having been taken hostage, so some element of surprise remained on their side — and Robert Teague, master tactician, planned on using this element to his fullest possible advantage.

He turned to his sorcerous friend and said, 'Wilding, it's funny how old we have both gotten since last we crossed the MouseKeep's doorsteps, don't you think? No one has seen either of us in almost twenty seasons. I'd imagine they would be shocked if they knew how old we have really become!'

Wilding knew exactly where Teague was heading with this line of thought and picked up the conversation without missing a beat. 'Yes, yes, my innkeeping friend, it's funny how the ravages of time can wear a Mouseling down, making him look old and frail. I'd suppose that two old — dare I even say elderly — retired mice couldn't possibly pose a serious threat to whomever awaits us in the castle! The so-called **Fabled Two**, looking as decrepit as a pair of shriveled-up old grandfathers. That's the rub!' He clapped his paws excitedly.

Teague joined in his best friend's enthusiasm. 'Haha, yes! Wormfood-bound, who would suspect?'

The Stranger looked at the pair like they had lost their minds. 'Not to be incredibly rude, but these barbarians have my family in the castle and time is of the essence. Is this really the best time for riddles and games?'

'But of course,' said Wilding, nonplussed, as he rummaged for his spell book and began thumbing through the worn, leather bound tome. 'I have always found moments of sheer duress to be the perfect time for games — and even better, riddles!'

And with that, Wilding took his staff and tapped it twice on the ground. The ruby at its tip began to glow with an otherworldly light, as Wilding closed his eyes and said:

Mousekin, housekin

Does with pretty blouse pins

Ravages of time,

The great ages past

Make us look like wormfood —

At last!

As the Stranger stared at Wilding and Teague, the air around them suddenly seemed to shimmer, the same way a mirage might shimmer in the desert — a Mousekin might *think* that he sees water off in the distance, but really there is none there. For a second, the Stranger couldn't quite see their faces because of the shimmering effect, but it wasn't just their faces — no, their *whole bodies* had grown blurry. When the shimmery effect faded a few moments later, the Stranger found himself looking at two mice in the exact same clothing as Teague and Wilding had been wearing before — but he was astonished to see that it was being worn by two *different mice*!

Two *very* different mice.

Two *really,* **really OLD** mice.

Wilding and Teague looked at each other for a second and burst out laughing. Teague let out a deep belly laugh and said to his friend, 'Wilding my good mouse, you look like you are about to take a dirt nap!'

'Indeed, Robert!' the sorcerer replied. 'But I feel no different than a moment ago, and I hope you are of the same volition!'

'Absolutely, my friend, as fresh as ever. Well, I think we are prepared now — or as prepared as we could be. Stranger, speak not a word of our disguises, obviously, should the ruse be found out! But this should buy us a little time — and help convince them to let their guard down!'

'I'm not sure anyone would believe me, anyway' muttered the Stranger.

'It's settled then. Let us head towards the western gate and inform the guards there that we have arrived. Stranger, it is fitting that you inform them — as would be traditional protocol — of our Falconrider's sacrifice, so that his bravery will not have been in vain and his body may be properly recovered.' Teague looked at him slyly. 'If this old mouse's memory serves, as a member of the Thief's Guild, you do hold some standing over the rank and file guard of MouseKeep, do you not?'

The Stranger rubbed thoughtfully at his whiskers. 'Well, tradition says so, but I...'

Teague interrupted him before he could finish his thought. 'Indeed! Just as I thought. You thieves are all about secrecy, ritual, the upkeep of traditions, and so forth. So let's not sully the traditions you mice hold so dear now, shall we? Present Wilding and myself to the Mouse Guards and inform them of our arrival. Order them to escort us to our scheduled meeting — make sure to indicate that you wish to accompany us to The King's Pedestal, and make no mention of your family. Remember that it's just another day for you, completing an uneventful mission. Following my instructions to the letter is paramount if you want to save your family.'

With this, the Stranger looked somewhat shaken. Wilding saw his emotion and grasped his paw.

'Have courage, my thieving friend! With a little luck and Her blessing upon us, you will have your family back safely in no time. Just bring us to The King's Pedestal as you were assigned to do. Once you deliver us, ask permission to take your leave and rejoin your family. Assuming this happens, take your family and flee the castle, immediately. You will be safe in Mouseling Hollow at The Sleeping Cat until we return — assuming we do!'

Wilding flashed a reassuring, if geriatric, smile.

The Stranger wondered how these two could be so upbeat in the face of what could be their imminent capture, or worse. But still, he mustered up his courage and said, 'I will do as you ask, but my family's fate rests now on your paws.'

'To the western gate, then. But as disguised, so must we act. Stranger, take my arm!'

The Stranger took Teague's arm, which felt rippled and well-muscled even though the magical aging glamour made his arm appear to be withered and devoid of strength. *How ironic*, he thought to himself, *as a child I loved to listen to the legends of **The Fabled Two**. Now my fate is intertwined with theirs, though I had no idea they truly existed.*

Teague leaned on the Stranger, playing the part of a feeble old man, as Wilding took the lead, supporting himself heavily on his staff and limping with his left paw, as if it pained him from some old war injury. Wilding adjusted his pointy purple hat so that it lay just above his brows and tilted his head downwards, keeping his face somewhat hidden from view so that it was difficult to see his features clearly unless you were standing directly underneath his tall frame.

And it was in this guise that this unlikely party of three — a thief and two mice who looked like they should have been laying on their deathbeds — hobbled and shuffled their final steps to the western gate. Leaving the safety of the grass behind them, they traveled once more from one source of cover to another. Finally, after one last glance to ensure the road was clear of oncoming traffic from carts or humans, they began their final ascent to the western entrance of MouseKeep.

About fifty paces from the hole that served as the western access point for Mouselings seeking admission into the Castle, Teague spotted two guards posted just outside the entrance. Halberdiers, they were called, since they carried the long and deadly halberd of the King's guards of MouseKeep. The gate guards both held their halberds in their paws as they stood at attention — halberds whose blades shone in the noonday sun while the two mice stood watch. Teague could see that though the guards were indeed mice, they wore black tunics trimmed in red, which he found puzzling. Their clothing didn't match the traditional garb of the guardians of MouseKeep — gorgeous Kelly-green tunics with gold trim, mandatory leather doublets for protection, matching boots, and chain head coifs similar to his own.

The guards' clothing did indeed match the uniforms the Stranger had described seeing when he'd been summoned by his superiors. *Either there has been a uniform change in the MouseKeep recently*, Teague thought to himself, *or something is truly amiss here.*

As he tottered forward, keeping up the ruse that he was an elderly mouse trying to navigate the cobblestoned road, Teague quietly said, 'Two mouse guards at the entrance.'

Wilding peered slightly under the brim of his hat.

'Got 'em,' he replied.

The three mice maintained their unhurried, methodical pace as they slowly approached the gate. When the two guards saw them coming towards them, they crossed their halberds together across the entryway, as if to bar the visitors from entering.

'Who approaches The MouseKeep?' rasped the guard on the left, who was slightly larger and appeared more menacing than his smaller counterpart to the right.

'I approach,' the Stranger said confidently, taking on an air of command, 'and bring with me the two who were summoned. My task was given to me by order of the King himself, who required the services of the Thief's Guild. I am to take these two directly to The King's Pedestal, and without delay.'

The gravelly-voiced Halberdier on the left sneered. 'What papers do you have proving that you are on a mission for the King?'

The Stranger's back stiffened and he found himself rearing up even further on his two rear paws, stretching himself to the full extent of his posture. 'You insolent fool! Are you always this insubordinate with your superiors? I told you I've come on a mission for the King. I swear by Her infinite mercy, if we're late to our audience with him because of you...'

With this, the Stranger produced the summons with the broken wax seal of the King Himself on it.

Staring down at the guard imperiously, he said 'What Mouseling who WASN'T on a mission for the King would know about The King's Pedestal? This is highly secret information, you dolt, and if you have any desire to hold onto your rank — or your neck — you will do as I say EXACTLY when I say it! Now uncross those halberds and escort us to The King's Pedestal — ***IMMEDIATELY!***'

Teague and Wilding remained silent, exchanging a barely noticeable glance at each other. Whether the Stranger was venting some of the real anger he felt over his family having been placed in danger or was simply a magnificent actor, he was playing his part to perfection.

The raspy-voiced mouse did move to uncross his halberd, albeit without looking any the less sinister. Swinging around the spiked end of the halberd, he pointed it at Teague and Wilding.

'And who is it you bring to The King's Pedestal, eh? Certainly these old codgers couldn't possibly be ***The Fabled Two?***'

At that moment Teague knew that everything the Stranger had been saying was correct. He'd already suspected that these Halberdiers were imposters, but that proved it — no mere gate guard would ever be entrusted with a secret as tightly kept as the true existence of ***The Fabled Two*** — and certainly wouldn't go blabbing it about to any mouse with an unsealed summons if they had. The castle had been infiltrated by some unknown force...but who were these strange mice who had taken over? And what was the status (and whereabouts) of the King? Why were the Falcon Riders sent on a mission from which they would never return? Did any still remain alive?

But all these questions would have to wait. Teague's racing mind returned to the situation at hand when the Stranger leaned towards the guards conspiratorially and said:

'These...' he lowered his voice to a reverent whisper '...are ***The Fabled Two***. My mission was to bring them to MouseKeep, post-haste, and I have done as I have been tasked.'

The Halberdier on the left hoarsely broke out into an arrogant belly laugh. 'These two mice here? ***The Fabled Two?*** The legendary defenders of Owlhaven?' He continued laughing evilly, his mirth taking on an almost maniacal quality. 'These two couldn't fight a louse from the back of a newborn baby buck! Look how *OLD* they've become...'

He left his posting by the wall and began to circle the three companions, pointing the wooden bottom of his halberd at the two elderly-looking mice. He actually poked Wilding in the chest with it as he continued to cackle, saying:

'I KNEW the legends couldn't be true. Myths...stories! Childish rubbish, all made up, of course. I realize now as I see these two feeble old coots. Oh, it's a bit disappointing, to be sure, seeing these legendary Mouselings looking so...frail, and weak. Poor old buggers probably struggle to gum down their mashed carrots these days, eh? But of course, I know a babe's fairy tale when I hear one.'

'And it was no easy task, either' commiserated the Stranger, quickly switching gears to play this new part. 'I had to practically hand-carry these mice to a squirrel cart and row them across myself. What little speaking they did on the journey over was mostly to grouse and quibble about how their old bones ached, and how much they missed being in the care of their nursemaids!'

'That sounds about right,' said the guard with a chuckle. He seemed to have tired of hurling insults. 'You may proceed into MouseKeep,' he said, affecting a mockingly-gracious tone and gesturing grandly with his halberd. He poked at Wilding once more as he passed by, who let out a loud grunt and leaned even more heavily on his staff as he slowly made his way into the castle.

'One more thing,' said the Stranger, taking an official tone once more. 'While I was in Mouseling Hollow, the gatekeepers there said that some of the harvest workers had found the body of a dead Falconrider somewhere down The Riverpath. They asked me to bring it back across the lake for proper burial and recognition, and to let his next of kin be notified. I would imagine in the hot noonday sun the body isn't getting any...' he paused here for a second and sniffed slightly '...fresher.'

Pointing at the smaller guard on the right, he said 'Luckily, the body is small enough for YOU to handle.' The Halberdier stared back at him, then over at his partner on the left, then back to the Stranger.

The Stranger looked coldly at the gruff mouse on the left, who was obviously in charge.

'Well?' said the Stranger. 'Surely you don't intend to LEAVE A FALCONRIDER TO ROT ON THE SHORE OF THE MIRRORED LAKE, DO YOU???'

The mouse on the left shrugged weakly in capitulation and turned his partner. 'You heard the mouse. Off you go then, go get that body and bring it back here. Quickly now, quickly!' The smaller mouse pulled his hood up over his head to shroud his face, leaned his halberd up inside the entrance of MouseKeep, and scurried down the cobbled path towards the shore.

The three companions, accompanied by the gravelly-voiced Halberdier, now entered the gate of MouseKeep. Due to the darkness of the hollowed-out tunnels, it took their eyes a few moments to adjust from the bright midday sun outside the castle. Small oil lamps provided a degree of light every twenty paces or so, but the effect still made for a dimly lit, somewhat musty-smelling interior.

Teague and Wilding, moving slowly to keep up their ruse, scanned silently for more guards, but did not see any. In fact, as they approached an uphill ascent where another tunnel came and intersected the first, Teague and Wilding could not see any of the usual foot traffic they were used to seeing from the members of the MouseKeep's staff — the behind-the-scenes hustle and bustle of guards, servants, and other mice tending to their duties was noticeably absent.

When they reached the first intersection, Wilding looked around and began to act as if he was barely lucid. 'Aah yes! Aah yes, this is JUST how I remember it! The caverns of the Fischer King!' he said. Then, he turned and started to totter away off of the main path, which was clearly not the right way. The Stranger yanked him back, saying to the mouse guard, 'See what I mean? It's been like this since we left Mouseling Hollow.'

The guard laughed nastily as they resumed their ascent to the chamber containing The King's Pedestal. 'I can only imagine what a hassle that was. Cheer up, friend. Soon we will deliver them to the King and you can be done with the old codgers once and for all.'

Shortly afterwards, they heard paws scurrying up the hall behind them, moving fast. The four turned around to see that it was the other gate guard, the mouse who had been dispatched to retrieve the body of the Falconrider. His cloaked hood was still pulled low over his face, though he had retrieved his halberd.

'Back so soon?' the larger mouse asked his partner. 'That was quick.'

'Sorry sir,' the smaller mouse replied. 'I couldn't make it through the market because there was some sort of calamity down there. Humans everywhere, and many stalls have been overturned, half the market goods spilled this way and that. They're looking for mice who caused some sort of disturbance — something about a frenzied horse being injured. I will have to try to go again before sunset, but until then I wanted to rejoin you promptly.'

'Alright,' said the larger mouse. 'It can wait then, in that case.' Based on his tone, it seemed obvious that he didn't really care if the body was ever retrieved. He continued, saying 'We can't afford to lose good soldiers over the body of one of those mice — erm, I mean, a Falconrider.'

The party, now five strong, turned around and continued its uphill ascent. The Stranger, trying to hide his discomfort after hearing the guard's comment about leaving the Falconrider's body, tried to make casual conversation. 'I have not seen two more vigilant guards in MouseKeep for some time,' he said. 'Remind me to report it to my superiors. Just so I know, Halberdier, what is your name?

'My name...' the gruff guard rasped, after passing an oil lamp and continuing a few paces forward to where the light really dimmed, '...is unimportant. But you may call me Scraptooth.'

'Aah, yes, Scraptooth — fitting name for a mouse of your stature and watchful demeanor. Where do you hail from, Scraptooth?'

The guard looked over at the Stranger, and with an expression of annoyance, said 'Not that it's any of your business, mate, but if you must know, I come from...'

Before he could finish his sentence, all of a sudden there was a loud **WHACK**. The guard mouse fell forward on his snout, unconscious, making an audible **THUMP** as his body hit the smooth, worn dirt floor of the hallway. His halberd clattered forward until it was stopped by the stone wall on one side of the passage.

Startled, the three mice turned to look at Scraptooth's companion, who gripped a small blackjack in his left paw, wooden and menacing looking.

'What just happened?' the Stranger asked, now startled and confused.

'I'd say the cavalry has arrived,' laughed Teague.

The Stranger stared warily at the remaining mouse guard, who was still hooded. The guard took a moment to stow the blackjack in his belt, then gently removed his hood to reveal the face of...none other than Ainsley Hearthseeker.

'Hearthseeker, you rogue!' exclaimed Wilding, 'Well played!'

The bard grinned broadly and said, 'I REALLY wanted to knock that mouse out when he made that comment about the Falconrider, but I thought this looked to be a better spot. Professor, do you have a binding spell? We need to stash his body and ensure that when he wakes up, no alarm is sounded.'

'Yes, of course!' Wilding started thumbing through his spellbook.

'Now,' said Teague, 'While we don't know where our friend Scraptooth is from, we do know his name now. Ainsley, that name suits you pretty well, wouldn't you agree?'

Pulling his cloaked hood up over his snout, in a low and grating voice, he replied 'Aye, sir! Scraptooth here, at the ready!'

Wilding, who had stopped flipping through his spellbook, tapped his staff twice on the ground. The ruby at its tip glowed red and the unconscious Scraptooth's paws suddenly clasped together, hog tied by mystical blue bindings made of magical energies. Ainsley and Teague soon dragged him off to a side passage.

'Sleep well, Scrappytooth!' said Ainsley, with some disdain.

'And now, for the great reveal,' said Teague. They started walking, at a much quicker pace now that they did not have to keep up the guise of being old mice — though their magical disguises still remained in place. 'Soon, we will know who has been playing King in Castle Feldenspar, and to what end. Stranger, when we get to The King's Pedestal, present us as agreed. As soon as you have an opening, get to your family and flee. As for you, Ainsley — ahem, or should I say, *Scraptooth,* — remember, for you, it's just another boring day, escorting two decrepit mice along when you'd rather be at a tavern.'

The bard nodded briskly. 'I *would* rather be at a tavern.'

'As would I,' Teague said. The faces of his family, waiting for him back at The Sleeping Cat flashed quickly before his eyes. But he forced himself to push aside happier thoughts and return to the business at hand. 'At this point, neither Wilding nor I knows what awaits us in there. But if things start to go...downhill, shall we say, I want the two of you to exit the castle.' The Stranger looked relieved at this idea, but Ainsley was about to protest.

'No arguments,' said Teague. 'I mean it.'

'I do so always enjoy a visit to The King's Pedestal,' said Wilding, clapping his paws excitedly. 'Oh, goody!'

'Does he always do that?' asked the Stranger.

'He does clap his paws most of the time,' said Teague. 'But only when he is really, truly excited, does he say 'oh goody.''

'And he is excited for *this?*' asked Hearthseeker.

Teague looked at Wilding for a moment, and eyed his friend up and down.

'Terribly excited,' Teague said expressionlessly, and the party of four began their ascent up the spiral stone stairs that led into The King's Pedestal.

On The Legendary Decoding Stones:

Few items have inspired the imagination like the unearthing of The Decoding Stones. These magical tablets were written to allow the transliteration of interspecies languages. Of course, not all animals have seen or been privy to these — the intrepid Mouselings were the first to lay eyes on these unearthed tablets. When their scholars studied them, they were able, with the help of the tablet's magic, to alter their speech and begin to develop and articulate the phonemes, morphemes, and syntax necessary to emulate other, non-mouse languages. More specifically, their command of the human common language was the first initial breakthrough. However, they are now able to speak with most terrestrial avians and mammals as well.

Beware, though: it has been said that if these artifacts were ever to be destroyed, and the magic within them to perish, interspecies communication across the realm would die with them. It goes without saying what a catastrophic loss this would be! This is why they are kept with a series of curators, under heavy guard, at The Lyceum at Ocean's View — and no one, other than the curators and the King himself, are allowed to view them at present. The secrecy necessary to protect The Decoding Stones is, in large part, why hamlets like Mouseling Hollow have been able to remain such a well-guarded secret from most of the human inhabitants in Castle Feldenspar...

— Taken from **Talking and Listening: The Legend of The Decoding Stones**

Chapter 10

THE KING'S PEDESTAL

With a dizzying quickness, the group ascended the spiral staircase that led to the chamber where the King held his pedestal. The pedestal was built, with the help of the three master masons whom the King hired to construct MouseKeep (and their apprentices), during The First Rat King War. The King needed to be able to communicate with the Mousekin — whose high pitched voices could be difficult for human ears to hear — without having to compromise his posture in an undignified way — i.e., without having to bend over, sit or lie down on the floor, or otherwise do anything not befitting a King's royal manner.

The chamber itself stood adjacent to a small sitting room which formed part of the King's private living chambers on the highest floor of the castle, and was always guarded by human knights twenty-four hours a day. It was a clandestine sanctuary for the King and his family — but just as importantly, it was a secure hideaway where the King could communicate in secret with the Mousekin. The King's Pedestal was where King Teegan could meet with his Mouseling agents in private to discuss their reconnaissance reports and the other intelligence they'd gathered, which he would then present to his human advisers.

Very few of his human counterparts were aware of the Mouselings, their intelligence, and the shared history they'd held with the line of

Teegan throughout its Royal reign — and The King's Pedestal had been designed to keep it that way. The secret field reconnaissance that was gathered and passed along to King Teegan by an army of Mousekin agents appeared to give him, to the outside world, an almost preternatural sense of what was happening within the borders of His Kingdom — an incredibly valuable asset for a King to have, in both peacetime and times of conflict.

Whenever the King needed to communicate with the Mouselings, he would place a tiny note on The King's Pedestal, which was monitored by mouse guards day and night. The King would sit in his wingback chair covered in royal red velvet, the arms of the seat carved of polished mahogany, which sat next to a bedside table and an ink quill with some parchment for writing. He also kept some books on that table, as if for reading.

Yet, when the King would go to sit down in this chair, instead of reading, he would slide a false wall with a gray stone facade into its recessed hollow, which would reveal the small stone anteroom the masons had built into the interior chamber. Inside was a two-foot-tall pedestal made of washed pine, with a small spiral staircase which allowed the summoned Mouselings to ascend easily up to the top. A Mouseling who stood atop the pedestal would find himself at eye level with the King, who remained comfortably seated.

Other mice, be they scouts, Falcon Riders, or even members of the infamous Harrier Legion, could stand at attention at the base of the pedestal, ready to take orders if summoned, witness awards and promotions being issued, or even join in celebrations or feasts for the MouseKeep's ranks, when time (and the King's inclinations) allowed.

As per the King's orders, on the opposite side of the stone wall which graced the King's sitting room stood a mouse-sized oaken door with ornate black wrought-iron, guarded day and night by two more elite MouseKeep guards. And, as Teague's party finished their long ascent up the spiral stone stairs leading to the chamber which held The King's Pedestal, they saw, like clockwork, that there were two Halberdiers dressed in the same garb as the mice at the western entrance.

As the party approached, the Halberdiers crossed their weapons against the door and said, in unison, 'Who approaches The King's Pedestal?'

'It is I,' said the Stranger. 'You saw me leave here several days ago with a mission from the King. My mission, as you may or may not know, was to find and escort these two mice to The King's Pedestal. I arrive now with them in my care, and intend to present them to His Majesty directly, at which point my quest will be completed.' He produced the King's missive with the broken seal of Castle Feldenspar and handed it to one of the guards, who read it over, then looked at his companion, and nodded.

'Very well — let them pass. But I will be taking *this* first.' The guard reached for Wilding's leather bound spell book, which he clutched closely to his chest. Grabbing for it, the guard tried to wrest it away, but Wilding held tight.

'Give me the book, old man...you won't be needing this!' snapped the guard. Wilding relented, releasing his spell book into the paws of the gatekeeper. Once the book had been safely confiscated, the guard's companion produced a small black iron key from his tunic and unlocked the oaken door.

Pushing it forward, he beckoned to the party to enter.

As the party passed through the door, one of the guards looked at the disguised Ainsley Hearthseeker and whispered audibly, 'Well done, Scraptooth.'

'Scraptooth,' still hooded and cloaked, nodded back at his would-be compatriot in silence as the four mice entered The King's Pedestal. Once they'd gone past the door, the two Halberdiers entered the chamber and closed the door behind them, locking it.

The loud **THUNK** the heavy oaken door made as it shut broke the weighty silence and made the Stranger jump. But the Halberdiers remained stationed at the door, their weapons crossed, blocking the exit.

Ahead was The Pedestal.

Slowly, methodically, Teague started the ascent up the spiral staircase which wound from the base of the wooden pedestal, leaning on the Stranger's arm as if he barely had enough strength to make it to the top. Wilding followed, again leaning on his staff. 'Scraptooth' brought up the rear, halberd in hand. Once they had all reached the top of the pedestal, an eerie silence ensued as the four mice looked around.

For a moment, nothing happened.

Then, one of the mouse guards banged loudly on the tiny oaken door three times with his halberd. The loud rapping sound echoed through the silence, until suddenly, the King's false door slid across into its recessed hollow and a human face appeared in it. The mice could see a shock of long, greasy black hair, and a white, sickly-looking face with a two-day growth of black stubble peering in to get a better view of the mice inside. A scurrying of paws could be heard going up the stone staircase, just outside the entrance to the chamber where the mice now stood at the top of the wooden platform.

Teague swiftly got a terrible feeling in his gut.

The Stranger cried out, 'Majesty! I, a member of the Thief's Guild of MouseKeep, was given a mission: to take your sealed message into the woodlands of Mouseling Hollow and return with **The Fabled Two**. I have them with me now, standing here atop your esteemed pedestal. Having completed my appointed task as you've commanded, I will — with your blessing — take my leave to reclaim my family as agreed.'

The human face pressed its eye against the recessed opening, as if to get a better view. He looked Teague and Wilding up and down. Still, he said nothing.

Another silence ensued, this one more uncomfortable than before.

'Majesty, are you able to hear me?' asked the Stranger, somewhat more loudly.

'He hears you fine,' a voice hissed behind them. 'But you will not speak to the King, as you are not worthy. You will speak only — and directly — to ME.'

Both the Stranger and 'Scraptooth' turned around to see that the oaken door had been opened — and that a dozen or so creatures had flooded silently into the room and now stood surrounding the base of the pedestal. Teague and Wilding, in their guise as old men, did not turn around, acting as if they were unable to hear what was going on. The Stranger saw about half a dozen mice — including the two halberdiers — all dressed in the strange black and red garb, as well as the Thief's Guild superior who had given him his mission. The Stranger was also shocked — *shocked* — to see two fischers and a large rat enter the chamber!!!

The human eyeball still peered into the small room unnervingly, saying nothing.

The Stranger saw that it was the large rat who had hissed at them, and the rat continued: 'These two old fools seem to have lost their faculties, starting with their hearing. Could it really be this easy?' He pointed the black claw at the end of a long, crooked finger at Teague and Wilding. 'Make them turn around and FACE ME!'

'Scraptooth' poked Wilding and Teague, then grabbed them by the shoulders and turned them around to face the large rat. The four mice peered down from the top of the pedestal and realized they were outnumbered almost three to one. Any chance of a successful skirmish was rapidly slipping away.

The large rat was clad in chain mail and his dark black fur was oily, having grown slick over the course of interminable years spent living in filth while neglecting his hygiene. *A typical vermin trait for a rat,* Teague thought to himself. Everything about the rat was black except for a small white circle around his eye. Looking more closely, Teague realized the white circle was actually a scar and that the rat's eye was missing.

'A rat in MouseKeep?' blurted the Stranger. 'Impossible!'

'Impossible?' mimicked the rat, flashing his yellow teeth as he smirked. 'No, my gullible friend, my presence here is nothing if not incredibly probable! And here I am, alongside a coterie of my faithful and determined kin, while the last vestige of our resistance stands here before me, feeble and infirm.'

He let out a loud cackle. 'Aah, Professor Wilding and Robert Teague. **The Fabled Two** of Owlhaven. My, how OLD you've grown! You see, thief...'

He pointed to the Stranger, wagging his clawed finger.

'...It really is quite simple. The Rat King, in his infinite brilliance, has decided that Castle Feldenspar is HIS domain — as it always should have been. And since his masterful intellect is far superior to that of you plebeian mousekin, he decided the time was right to foster a takeover of legendary proportions! All it took was a little gold, a few human counterparts who came as 'advisors' bearing 'gifts,' and some key personnel 'changes' amongst the MouseKeep's staff — if you get my meaning. From there, it was mere child's play to mastermind an impossible mission or two for the loyal guardians of MouseKeep, who would do...' his voice took on a condescending tone '...**anything** for their beloved King. And now, with the elimination of these two fools,' he pointed at Teague and Wilding, 'our clandestine takeover of MouseKeep will be complete and we can begin a full scale invasion of The Western Lands. Soon, the royal line of Teegan will be snuffed out, consigned to the dustbin of history where it belongs, and a new era, a better era, a **RATLING** era will begin!'

Cackling wildly, he clasped his claws together, rubbing his palms thoughtfully in his wicked glee.

The Stranger cleared his throat to interrupt the rat's celebration. 'I care nothing for politics, sir. I am but a simple thief. I was given a task, and my family was taken to ensure that I would complete it — which I have. I have no interest in the affairs of men and rats...' he said, pausing to gesture towards Teague and Wilding, '...nor do I care what happens to these two. My only interest is in seeing that my family is released and taking my leave of this place.'

'Oh, yes, yes...' the rat hissed '...you will join them shortly, my Mouseling friend...very shortly, yes!' The rat chuckled evilly. 'It is so interesting to see how quickly you mice collapse when it comes to choosing between the safety of your families versus the betterment of your King and country. We rats are well known for our...*loyalties*. I truly couldn't have fathomed how easy this would all turn out to be. But enough of all this talk. I'll need a good vantage point for what comes next.'

And with that cryptic statement, the rat darted across the stone floor to where a small staircase was hewn into the stone wall — right where it approached the false wall that concealed the MouseKeep from the human side of the castle. Normally, it allowed the Mouselings to ascend up to the stone platform which the false wall rested upon and see the King 'eye to eye,' so to speak. The rat scurried up the stone staircase and, with his back to the King's antechamber — where the human face still pressed its eye into the space for better sight — sat back on his haunches. He yelled to his companions:

'Now is the time my friends! Now is the moment we have all been waiting for. Scraptooth, come now! Your duties escorting these fools to the pedestal are now complete. Come, COME, and see what you have helped us to accomplish!'

With a slightly bent knee, 'Scraptooth' descended the stairs and took a position by the six Mouselings garbed in black and red, all of whom had drawn bows and now stood on their side of the chamber with arrows nocked. The impostor thief 'superior' who had given the Stranger his assignment stood nearby with a hungry look of great anticipation on his face. The two fischers remained by the door, their brown fur looking oily and slick like the rat's. They had drawn their swords from the sheathes which hung from the leather belts tied around their waists, holding them in a ready position at their sides.

The One-Eyed Rat began:

'Robert Teague and Professor Wilding. Corruptors of The Rat King's plans. Murderers of The Rat King's loyal subjects. Befoulers of The Rat King's offensive at Owlhaven, thieves of his rightful property,

The Decoding Stones. Traitors....insurrectionists! I, Cornelius White Eye, Lieutenant of The Rat King's Western Castle — formerly known as Castle Feldenspar — hereby demand that you pay for your foul deeds with your lives. It is only through death that you can earn your redemption in the eyes of his Highness, The Rat King. And I will carry out this sentence in his name on this, the final day of the reign of the Line of Teegan! Kneel, now, and face your doom!'

He cackled threateningly, then continued.

'You feeble, decrepit fools. To think you once stood and challenged the power of the Rat Armies! How ironic, then, to see you as you are now — doddering old simpletons, so silent, so... acquiescent! No fight, no challenge, no defiance! Oh, what lowly depths the once-mighty heroes of the Mouselings have stooped to — it almost pains me to witness your line die like this. Yes...almost.' White Eye shrugged theatrically. 'But, I grow tired of this game. I almost cannot bear to see these once mighty adversaries being laid so low. Why, 'tis nearly a mercy that I grant, putting them out of their misery. The only mercy these geezers will ever receive from his glorious majesty The Rat King...'

The rat raised his clawed paw and screamed, 'Archers at the ready!' Spittle came flying out of his mouth as he yelled.

On command, the six mousekin guards raised their bows and aimed them at the pedestal above, where Teague and Wilding stood helplessly.

'Do you fools have any last words before you go to meet whatever mouse god you think awaits you in the world beyond?' screamed Cornelius White Eye.

The two stood silently, looking old and frail. Trembling. Terrified.

'Well then! Archers, stand ready!' He looked triumphantly at the two mice, knowing their deaths were in his grasp.

Time began to slow down for the two mice as the rat's voice echoed through the chamber.

'Aim!' The pregnant pause continued. But before the rat could say anything else, Wilding raised his paw.

The one-eyed rat looked startled, perhaps even a bit flustered by the gesture, as this was the first time he had seen any sign of life from the two mice. 'Hold!' he cried, after a moment's indecision. The archers lowered their bows as the rat looked at Wilding with a sneer.

'What is it, Mouseling? Do you wish to grovel for mercy?' Spittle ran down his chin and slurred his 's' sounds slightly, as if he had a lisp.

'No, not particularly,' said Wilding, still leaning on his staff. 'Actually, I have a question.'

'Questions? What manner of questions could you possibly have?'

'Not questions. Question. Singular. I just have the one,' Wilding replied mildly. 'Did you say your name was Cornelius?'

'YES!' cried the rat. Upon realizing that the mice had in fact heard what he'd said, and would know who was the architect of their undoing, his gleeful hand-rubbing intensified and he hopped back and forth slightly in barely contained exhilaration.

'I, Cornelius White Eye, Lieutenant of the...'

'That's what I thought he said,' Teague interrupted. 'Cornelius White Eye,' said Teague to Wilding, and they burst out laughing. 'Don't you mean Cornelius **One** Eye?' asked Teague defiantly.

'You DARE to mock ME? You DARE to mock THE LEGIONS OF THE RAT KING?! This game is OVER!' screamed the rat.

'Yes, yes it is,' Wilding said, nodding in agreement. And with that, Wilding stopped leaning on his staff and, muttering unintelligible words, pointed his staff at the rat. The ruby at its tip blazed suddenly with an otherworldly light, and a massive bolt of electricity shot out of it and flew across the room, striking the rat in the chest with crushing force. The blow was so powerful that it knocked the rat backwards, sending him tumbling over the ledge of the false wall and into the King's wingback chair.

'Now Teague!' yelled Wilding. With the grace of an elf, Teague swiftly nocked an arrow and let it loose. The arrow flew straight and true, directly into the eyeball of the mysterious human who was peering in on the scene. With a scream of pain, the human face fell backwards and out of sight.

In the meantime, during Teague and Wilding's verbal exchange with the rat regarding his unfortunate name, Hearthseeker had noiselessly laid down his halberd and begun silently scattering caltrops from the pouch inside his tunic behind the mice archers. While they stood entranced, watching the drama that unfolded above them on the pedestal, Hearthseeker had stealthily moved to take up a position against the wall behind them.

When Wilding yelled 'Now!' Hearthseeker ran behind the archers, shouting a battle cry of 'AAAARRRRGGHHH!' while swinging his sword wildly, looking to chop away at the rear of their legs.

Blood was flying everywhere as Hearthseeker began lopping off paws and slicing calves and hamstrings — and with each stroke, with each thrust which struck deep and on point, Hearthseeker grew more frenzied with bloodlust. The crimson red of spurting blood reminded him of the crimson trim on the garb worn by the infiltrator mice — and what they had done to the loyal servants of the MouseKeep. With every swing of his sword his anger grew greater and he became all the more determined to strike down the infiltrators, sending him spinning into a barbarian fury.

He was like a hurricane of destruction, a whirlwind of steel and rage. The mice archers, having thought he was one of their own, had been caught totally off guard by his attack. They screamed in agony as he spun and danced, chopping off legs and severing quadriceps. The ones who were not immediately cut down by the bard's sword had been immobilized by his caltrop traps, only to fall his sword shortly thereafter. In a matter of mere seconds, Ainsley Hearthseeker's attack had made the odds inexorably much more even.

Seeing his onslaught among the archer mice, the two fischers had sprung into action, intending to attack Hearthseeker. One was dropped immediately by a well-placed arrow to the skull by Teague, who held the high ground from the pedestal. Wilding dispatched the other with a freeze spell. Pointing his staff at the fischer who was about to barrel into Ainsley, he muttered a few words and a bolt of ice shot out of the staff. It flew down from the pedestal, looking almost like an especially icy snowball, and struck the fischer squarely in the chest. He dropped to the floor, shivering uncontrollably.

'Roll, Hearthseeker!' yelled Wilding as the Stranger's imposter superior rushed in from behind him. The imposter thief swung his short sword at the bard's head, looking for a clean removal.

Deftly, Hearthseeker tucked forward into a diving roll. When he sprang smoothly to his feet he looked up towards the pedestal, and time seemed to slow to a crawl.

He saw Robert Teague, kneeling calmly on one knee, drawing and loosing arrow after arrow. He saw the Stranger standing behind him, seemingly frozen in shock — either by the speed with which the battle had erupted, the ferocity with which it was contended, or some combination of the two. And he saw Wilding, a look of anger appearing on his normally easygoing face, as he slammed his staff onto the ground.

Time seemed to resume its normal speed, and Hearthseeker saw a burst of burning embers — a literal rain of fire — erupt in a concentrated area directly above the six mouse archers and the traitor thief, right where he'd been standing just moments before. He watched as the embers descended like fiery snowflakes, setting them all alight.

The traitor thief was soon engulfed in flames. He screamed and ran wildly, his clothing ablaze, straight into a side wall. The blow must have knocked him unconscious because he collapsed from the impact and lay where he fell, smoldering in a heap. The magical flames crackled and danced as they consumed his motionless form.

Wilding pointed his staff towards the false door and it slid closed magically.

'That won't hold long,' said Wilding flatly. He placed a hand on the Stranger's shoulder to shake him from his frozen reverie, and the three mice descended from the pedestal to meet Hearthseeker.

Wilding went up to the fischer who had been paralyzed with a freeze spell and prodded it with his staff.

'Give me a full accounting of how many mice and vermin in the castle. NOW!'

'You...***ch ch ch***...' the fischer said, his teeth chattering from the cold, '...you...***ch ch ch***...can take your staff and your spells, and stick them in...***ch ch ch***...your hat, Mouseling scum!'

Wilding glared and pointed the ruby-tipped end of his staff at the fischer, whose tone immediately changed.

'There are more mice...***ch ch ch***....more mice, down near the basement. White Eye...***ch ch ch***...was the only rat, and there is...***ch ch ch***....another fischer down in the dungeon, keeping watch.'

'White Eye? You mean One Eye?' said Wilding. Having gotten the information he needed, he twirled his staff around and knocked the fischer out with a hard blow from its butt end.

Wilding's three mouse companions looked at him for a moment, incredulously.

'That was for the King,' he said, and grinned.

The Stranger was only just then beginning to fully rouse himself from his dazed state. He looked at the body of the traitor thief (the flames around him still blazing away in the corner) and the charred remains of the mouse archers. The smell of burning mouse hair wafted through the chamber, and he was nearly sick to his stomach. He looked at the one dead fischer with the arrow protruding from his skull, and the other, who lay twitching slightly in his sleep after Wilding's blow, then turned back to Teague and Wilding.

'I never...' he started.

'No time now,' said Teague. 'Our buddy Ratty Rattus, a.k.a. Lieutenant One Eye, is likely racing off to sound the alarm right now. He said the line of Teegan would die today — that must mean that the King remains alive. But where?'

'Where else?' said Wilding. 'The dungeons! The King is far too valuable an asset to put to death. Whatever human faction orchestrated this would want to keep him drawing breath until it determines its next move.'

'It's a good bet that the King's human guards, and possibly even some of MouseKeep's loyal staff are being held there too,' interjected Teague. 'Probably your family as well, Stranger.'

'Well what are we waiting for? Let's be off, then!' he cried impatiently.

'Hearthseeker, you, Wilding, and the Stranger head down to the dungeons and see if you can start freeing some captives. Be prepared for anything.' Teague picked up a sword from one of the fallen archers that had escaped the worst of the flames and handed it to the thief. 'Do you remember how to use this?'

The Stranger smirked and nodded.

'Well, you are going to have to,' said Teague.

Hearthseeker reached down to retrieve a halberd, which he held in his right paw. His short sword, still bloody, was gripped firmly in his left paw.

'No doubt there are more of those imposter mice down there,' Teague said. 'Stay stealthy if possible.'

'What about you?' said Ainsley. He was worried for his friend, who would obviously not be joining them in their descent into the dungeons.

Teague unsheathed the two hand axes from his back and held them lightly in both paws. Watching the deftness with which he produced the weapons, Hearthseeker understood in that moment that Teague truly was as the bard songs described in tales of **The Fabled Two:** a legendary master axe wielder — a Specialist, as the legends of MouseKeep called it. He was a killing machine trained to dispatch foes in hand to hand combat with swift and deadly precision.

'I need to go after One Eye,' Teague said. 'He has answers, and I have...questions. Besides which, if he were to escape, Mouseling Hollow could be in even greater danger. We need to ensure that none of these traitor mice — or other vermin, for that matter — escape the castle to report to whomever their master is. If we are to reclaim Castle Feldenspar and restore the MouseKeep on this day, Ratling reinforcements are the last thing we want to deal with.'

'Very well then. We will meet you down there,' said Wilding, as he bent to retrieve his spellbook from the body of the mouse guard who had wrested it away from him earlier. He gave the flaming body a mild kick of disdain as he picked up the book. Though the guard's body was still aflame, the old leather tome was strangely intact. 'For now, Robert, make sure our rat friend doesn't escape.'

The two friends clasped paws wistfully. Wilding gently tapped his staff twice on the ground and muttered some mystical words, allowing the magic which had disguised them as old mice to fall away — and with just a passing moment, they looked fresh and young again.

Exiting through the oaken door, the party of four descended the stone staircase from The King's Pedestal chamber. Hearthseeker, Wilding, and the Stranger went straight down, following Wilding as he led them down towards the castle's lower levels. Hearthseeker couldn't help but look back, but the other half of **The Fabled Two** had already disappeared behind them, veering off onto a side passage in pursuit of his one-eyed quarry.

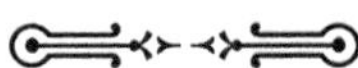

The four siblings stood in the garden room while the thunderous rainstorm continued to roar outside. All eyes remained fixed on the detective in his tweed cloak and deerstalker cap while his butler assistant, Alfred, stood waiting patiently behind him. They were all waiting for him to speak.

But the detective would not take his eyes off the dead mouse lying on the floor.

'It is easy to solve a crime when the killer leaves a signature calling card, Alfred. As I have often told you...'

'Well, my good man, who did it?' interrupted an angry Lord Blackthorne. 'Don't keep us in suspense any longer — our very lives could be at risk! We need to get the constable out here immediately or there could be more killings!'

The detective chuckled out loud, then went and poured himself a glass of whiskey from the half-full decanter sitting on the fireside table. Draining the drink in one deep draught, he put the empty glass back down and looked back at the body, then peered curiously at Lord Blackthorne.

'Lord Blackthorne, you certainly have nothing to fear on that count. The killer is here right now, among us, hiding in plain sight. And as far as the constable goes, well — let's just say that he should be here momentarily, assuming he received the telegraph I sent him last night.'

Shocked looks spread across their faces as the four siblings eyed each other with disbelief.

'Of course, I knew all along who the killer was. But just to be certain, we had to allow that person to strike again. And when thieves — well, more than thieves, actually — betray each other's trust, it is really only but a matter of time before one of them shows up dead. And thus, ironically, here we are. The deal went south quicker than you thought it would — didn't it, Lady Blackthorne? It must have, since it is your presumed lover who now lies here dead on the floor. My my, those jewels must have been far more difficult to pawn than you two anticipated.'

Just at that moment, the constable came bursting through the door. Stormsnout pointed to Lady Blackthorne and said to the constable, 'I think you will find your killer right here, sir.'

Lady Blackthorne lunged with murderous intent towards the detective, but was nimbly restrained by the strong paws of the constable. 'HOW, YOU SCALAWAG? HOW DID YOU KNOW IT WAS ME?!'

Stormsnout looked at Lady Blackthorne and shook his head slowly.

'How did I know it was you? Because, milady, **it is my JOB to know such things!** Besides which, you couldn't have made it any easier for me if you'd tried. You are the only left-pawed 'mouse in the room...the jagged angle of the crosscuts on your lace bodice indicated that they were made with left-pawed scissors, which could only be in the possession of a professional seamstress. And voila, who stands before us? A professional seamstress to royalty, who *just so happens to be one of the few who would have had access to the jewels the night they were stolen...and, of course, the body here...'*

The detective gestured to the corpse on the floor.

'...Of your lover...well, now former lover, it would seem...killed by the stab wounds of left-pawed scissors. It was elementary, Alfred, as I've been saying all along...now be a good man and call the carriage for me! Our work here is done...with any luck, we can be home by sunset. Mistress McGrath said it's Beef Teegan in Puff Pastry with a decadent red wine sauce for supper this evening — and a I have a fine bottle of **Leomar's Undermountain Red Vintage 227** *I fully plan on decanting to enjoy with it. You know how putting criminals behind bars works up my appetite!'*

— Taken from **The Chronicles Of Sir Pendleton Stormsnout, Book II: The Case of the Left-Pawed Jewel Thief**

Chapter 11

PURSUIT THROUGH THE CASTLE

Teague dodged and darted through the chambers of MouseKeep, sniffing the air and working up a sweat as he counted on his intuition to lead him in the correct direction to successfully catch up to One Eye.

He had swiftly descended the spiral staircase from The King's Pedestal chamber at the uppermost floor of the Castle. Leaving his companions behind, he'd exited the sanctum of MouseKeep and crossed into the castle's human halls, then taken a passage he remembered as leading into the Great Hall where feasts were held for the King and his court. Just off of the great feasting hall was a staircase that should (if his memory was correct) let him descend directly into the kitchen on the main floor.

In his gut, Teague was certain that One Eye, like all rats, was mostly interested in saving his own skin. He was sure that One Eye's top priority would be slinking away to safety — wherever that may be — and reporting (in Teague's mind, he knew this really meant groveling) to his superiors about how it was another rat's fault that his mission had encountered unforeseen obstacles that couldn't be mitigated, even if it had been meticulously planned and the odds had originally been in his favor.

Standard rat tactics, Teague thought to himself as he raced down a corridor. *Deflect blame and avoid taking responsibility for one's failures at all costs.*

The shocking bolt that Wilding had blasted One Eye with at the start of the skirmish in The King's Pedestal chamber had had an unexpected downside: when the force of the blow had sent the rat sailing over the edge of the false wall and into the King's wingback chair, his removal from the melee had inadvertently given One Eye a brief window in which to grab a head start in making his escape from the castle.

Of course, One Eye would have to risk moving openly throughout the halls of Castle Feldenspar, where humans roamed freely...as would Teague, if he hoped to have any chance at catching up to him.

Leaving the safety of MouseKeep for the human halls within the castle brought with it its own unique set of problems. But Robert Teague, mouse captain, was fully aware of the...obstacles...that a Mouseling faced when he or she entered into human areas — those wide open, unprotected spaces filled to the brim with a nearly unlimited supply of implements which could lead to a mouse's demise: brooms, mops, traps, thrown books, stamping feet, or poisoned food, just for starters.

Teague surmised that since One Eye (presumably) had only a limited knowledge of the passageways within the MouseKeep itself, that he was likelier to try to make a hasty beeline towards the ground floor exit, rather than seeking to retreat behind the safety of the MouseKeep's walls through one of the many hidden entrances secreted within the mazelike stone corridors of the castle.

He imagined the rat now, hurrying and scurrying from hiding spot to hiding spot within the Castle itself, sneaking behind barrels and skulking behind chamberpots and the like as he made his way down to the first level in search of his escape.

Teague knew that if his rat quarry were to escape that it could only be a harbinger of bad tidings to come for the ranks of MouseKeep —

not to mention for his family and friends back in Mouseling Hollow. *As if the current insurrection wasn't bad enough,* he thought to himself.

Robert Teague was willing to do anything to prevent that — **anything.**

That is, *IF* he could find the rat first.

Even for an experienced Mouseling of action like Robert Teague, traversing the human spaces of Castle Feldenspar was a task as difficult as it was dangerous. If the MouseKeep represented a safe haven for moving about within the castle, the open spaces and halls of the King's palace were anything but. Humans strode about in their daily tasks of minutiae — Teague could see kitchen servants bringing in barrels and baskets of all manner of foodstuffs, as well as squires carrying various pieces of their knight's arms and armor to and fro.

Barely a minute after Teague stealthily exited the MouseKeep and crept out into the Great Hall, he had to scurry to avoid a cobbler carrying a pair of broken shoes up a staircase. He managed to duck under a velvet tablecloth covering a small side table just before the cobbler dropped one of his shoes. The heavy wooden clog bounced once and narrowly missed crushing Teague, who was forced to press himself even further back into the dark corner crevice hidden behind the table legs. Teague held his breath as the cobbler bent to retrieve the clog, lest his presence be revealed and the cobbler start shouting about a mouse in the castle. But his luck held true, and the cobbler picked up the shoe and continued down the corridor without seeing him. In the eyes of most humans, they were all vermin, even though rats and Mousekin certainly could not be more different.

As he continued moving down the staircase which led to the kitchen, Teague heard the hiss and screech of a cat up ahead. In that moment, he knew One Eye had reached the cooking area and was trying to make his escape.

Cats were bad business, to be sure. But if the animal was forcing the rat to take refuge under some dusty pantry or sack of flour and wait it out until the feline lost interest, that might just buy the mouse captain some precious time to make up ground in his pursuit.

Teague quickened his pace but, upon hearing the cat hiss a second time, he paused for a moment to peer down the large, darkened spiral staircase which led to the kitchen. Each step alone had quite a drop for such a small mouse, although it was easier going down them than climbing up them. Realizing that there was no accessible MouseKeep passage nearby that could help him safely descend, the mouse captain steeled himself for what he knew needed to do: leap down each step and hope he didn't get injured. One hard tumble on a stone step, one single misstep, could result in a broken bone — or worse!

He heard the cat screech again, somewhere down by the bottom of the staircase, and felt that his window of opportunity to successfully complete his pursuit of One Eye may be growing short — but froze when he heard footsteps coming up the stairs, ascending at a rapid pace.

Teague squeezed into a small crack in the stone masonry of the staircase for safety, and watched a young maiden carrying a fruit basket and fresh flowers in the crook of her arm climb up the staircase. She held the smooth spiral railing with her free hand, using it to pull her weight up with each step as she rose up the incline.

Seeing the railing got Teague thinking. Was there an easier way to get to the bottom of the staircase than tumbling down dozens of huge steps?

Teague sheathed his twin axes and grabbed the short bow off his back. Nocking the roped arrow that he'd used in the marketplace, Teague waited for the maiden to pass, then shot his arrow up at the railing once the coast was clear.

It struck the soft, polished wood on the underside of the railing with a loud **THUNK** sound. After a quick tug to make sure it would support his weight, Teague then shimmied his way up the rope. When he reached the underside of the railing, he swung himself back and forth a few times to build up momentum, and then with great dexterity, he threw his legs over the top of the railing, being mindful to keep a firm hold on the rope so he could retrieve his arrow after he found his footing on the railing. After finishing his ascent and coiling his rope, he now stood perched atop the smooth, polished surface, ready to descend. Teague tested his footing and decided to shuck off his woodland tunic, placing it under his feet to make it easier to slide and positioning his paws shoulder-width apart for balance.

'Time to ride!' yelled Teague. As he stood on his soft tunic, he shifted his center of gravity and began to surf downwards. Letting his body weight carry him forward, he began gliding along the smooth, glossy railing as gravity took over.

He started out slowly before beginning to go a little faster, and, picking up speed, began to zoom along even faster still. He hit his first curve and had to adjust the position of his lower paws on his tunic to stay on the railing, while his speed and momentum ever quickened.

Curving and twisting, the tiny Mouseling rode the staircase, whipping around turns while constantly accelerating, feeling the wind rippling in his whiskers as he reached a critical speed. It was exhilarating.

As he came speeding around the final curve, ahead of him he could see the kitchen suddenly come into view. In it, he saw humans at work, cooking feverishly and rushing about on any number of human errands. A fire raged away within a large stone hearth, with simmering stockpots suspended over the flames bubbling away with what was presumably going to be the humans' evening meal. An ancient human woman in some sort of blue velvet religious garb had a dead chicken up on a butcher block and was removing the feathers from the carcass. Teague could smell delicious smells wafting up from the kitchen — though this was certainly no time to be thinking about food! All of this Teague saw out of the corner of his eye, in an instant, as he hurtled down towards the bottom of the staircase with breakneck speed.

Then Teague spied him — One Eye! He caught a glimpse of his tail sticking out and looping around the back leg of a pantry table. The rat must have been hiding there from the cat, although the feline's whereabouts were still unknown — at least from Robert Teague's vantage point. The mouse captain felt his anger rise at the sight of the rat's coiled tale. As he glided smoothly along, he prepared to disembark from his improvised slide by once more nocking his roped arrow to his bow. With a mighty roar, he yelled, 'ONE EYE!!! COME GET WHAT YOU DESERVE, YOU RATLING TRAITOR!'

And with that, Teague let his arrow loose. It flew straight and true until it struck Teague's target — a piece of hanging rib roast suspended over the side of the pantry table One Eye had chosen to hide under. The mouse captain used the terminus of the railing as a launch point for his rope swing, propelling himself off the railing with a mighty leap, then hanging onto the rope for dear life, and l etting the centrifugal force swing him towards the table where the traitor rat awaited.

On Rooting:

The intelligence of the Mouseling intellect has allowed them to live a lifestyle quite unlike their distant non-speaking cousins. While their far-off relatives have, historically, fed themselves on the scraps that have fallen from tables and slops that have fallen from pig troughs, modern Mouselings have amassed a resource known as The Rooters. Rooting, as it is known, occurs when the most skilled of Mouselings steal into human pantries and homesteads (generally in the dead of night) and 'borrow' whatever items they decide they have need of. In this way, fine — and necessary — foodstuffs are procured: the most decadent cuts of meats and roasts, chicken, eggs, flour, and of course, a myriad of extravagant cheeses and spices. Thanks to the light-fingered efforts of The Rooters, the caloric intake of the average Mouseling has been allowed to grow, helping them to accelerate in strength, stature, and of course, cognizance. Mouselings now function at the highest cognitive levels — equal to any human, and far surpassing the duller specimens — and their speaking abilities and command of both animal and human languages has made them an invaluable asset to the crown.

Other items of value are frequently 'borrowed' by the Rooters as well: recipes for fine meals, guidelines for brewing and fermentation processes, as well as scrolls and spells of an arcane nature. Once scribed properly, they become an integral part of the Mouseling knowledge base, to be implemented in inns, breweries, taverns, and libraries across the land...

— TAKEN FROM **HOW TO STEAL AN EGG: CHRONICLES AND LEGENDS OF THE ROOTERS**

•••••••••••••

Chapter 12

DESCENT INTO
THE ABYSS

••••••••••••••••••••••••

It was about the same time that Robert Teague went surfing down the spiral staircase railing into the King's kitchen that Wilding, Hearthseeker, and the Stranger finished their descent from MouseKeep and emerged into the cellars of Castle Feldenspar, where the stockades lay.

Easing out of a tiny wooden door, whose exterior was encrusted with small gray cobblestones to emulate the Castle's walls, Wilding, Ainsley, and the Stranger paused a moment to peer around the dank passage. Ahead of them lay the guard's chamber, where a sturdy set of wrought-iron black bars was locked, forbidding entry to the inner cells where prisoners of all sorts were held in detention. Without the key, no human could pass.

Mice, on the other hand — now *that* was quite a different story.

The trio eased slowly up the passageway. Silently they padded, paw over paw, hiding in the shadows, keeping their backs to the wall, using any objects they could find for concealment. An errant mop, a wash bucket, discarded bloody rags — all of the items which littered the rarely-used hallway provided convenient cover for the three tiny Mouselings. In the shadows of the torchlight which flickered at the

163

end of the corridor leading into the guard's chamber, they were practically invisible.

Up ahead, the three mice could hear the frantic voices of humans conversing in the guard's chamber — not quite yelling, but speaking with a feverish degree of urgency. They could also hear a distant clanging sound from their hallway hiding spot — it might have been metal on wood, but they couldn't quite make it out.

Continuing to take the lead, Wilding eased his way down the passageway, stopping in the shadows outside the dim, flickering light the torchlit sconces provided. He held up a paw and bade his companions to halt. Silently, amidst the darkness, he listened to the humans as they continued to argue about something. From his vantage point, Wilding could see the shadowed forms of three humans moving about in the dim illumination of the torchlight, but could not make out who they were or what they looked like.

'Hold still, will you? I can't get it out if you keep moving like that.'

'Get it out! GET IT OUT! Aargh!' another human cried. 'I can't see!'

Wilding heard laughter from a third member of the conversation. 'You said a mouse did this to you, eh?'

Crying in agony, the second voice responded, 'That was no ordinary mouse! It was one of the two we were sent to eliminate.'

Wilding knew that one of these humans had to be the same one who was present at The King's Pedestal, pressing his eye into the chamber where their execution was to have taken place. *It seems Teague's well timed arrow has struck a deep wound*, the Professor thought to himself. As he listened, Wilding got the distinct sense that this wounded human was important somehow. He suspected that this one was colluding directly with The Rat King, for reasons yet unknown.

Since the other humans seemed preoccupied with tending to the one who had an injured eye, Wilding felt empowered to continue creeping towards the prison jailer's annex.

With a silent wave of his paw, he motioned to his two companions to follow him.

As they approached closer, the dancing flames of the torchlight revealed the scene that was unfolding in the quarters where the jailer traditionally held his post.

One human was laying on a rickety wooden table, trying to hold the eyelid open on his injured eye. He was dressed in black leathery rags that had an oily sheen to them. Towering over him was a pale human wearing a greasy black skullcap and holding a rusty pair of pliers. The pliers looked like they were normally used for purposes of torture, but the human was now using them to try to free his companion's injured eye of Teague's arrow. The one with the pliers looked extremely pale, and his face was covered with a three-day beard growth of black stubble.

A third human rested his unusually large arse on a small stool underneath a torch which provided the last light before the prison cells began, drinking some type of alcohol from a flask. This one periodically let out a poorly-stifled giggle as his two companions wrestled to remove the arrow deeply embedded in the injured human's eye. He was obviously quite drunk.

'A Mouseling!' he stumbled with his words. 'A Mouseling shot your eye!' He giggled again.

'Shut up, you fool,' cried the human who was laying on the table. 'I told you these were no ordinary mice! These Mouselings were...special.'

'Special!' tittered the drunk man on the stool. He snickered once again.

'There,' said the one holding the pliers. 'I think I got it out.'

The human laying on the table sat up and clasped a hand to his eye. 'Hmmm — it does feel better, but I still can't see out of it.'

'Let's go upstairs and see if we can get some medicine — or healing herbs, at least,' said the one with the pliers.

'*Hic.* Medicine!' giggled the one on the stool. 'I could — *hic* — stand a bit more medicine myself. Bring me back some, would you?'

'What are we, your servants?' said the one with the pliers. 'Get your own.'

The two humans started down the hallway towards the three mice, the one with the pliers holding out an arm to steady the injured one. With great stealth and stillness, the three mice hid behind chattel in the hallway, holding their breath and praying they would not be discovered. Their ploy worked, and they watched the humans plod off down the hall in search of an ocular remedy. The echoes of their voices faded as they disappeared down the long stone corridor.

There was only one human that remained now, the fat drunk one on the stool. The three companions looked at him and discussed their strategy. Hearthseeker blurted out 'Should we just run past him?'

'Just wait a few moments,' Wilding whispered back. 'We may have time on our side here.'

Silently, the three mice watched the man continue to sip drinks from his flask. Leaning back on the stool, he laid his head against the prison bars as a headrest. In a few moments, he was snoring loudly.

'The coast is clear now,' said Wilding. 'But be on your guard.'

With careful deliberation, the three mice proceeded forward. As they came near the sleeping Jailer they were cautious not to do anything that could awaken him. Behind him lay the barred door to the prison cells. Mice could sneak in below the bars where humans could not, but even so — if they were to encounter prisoners who needed to be freed, the set of keys hanging from the Jailer's oiled leather belt could prove useful. There was also a jeweled dagger on his belt which Wilding thought looked very familiar — but he didn't have time to think about where he might have seen it before right at that moment.

'Wilding,' Hearthseeker whispered, and pointed to the lanyard hanging off the human's belt. 'The keys! We need the keys!'

'Hang on my friend,' the wizard whispered back. He pointed his staff towards the keys and muttered some unintelligible words. Soon, a thin blue light shot from the staff's ruby up at the keys, and they started to levitate off the Jailer's belt. But, as Wilding tried to guide the keys down noiselessly to the stone floor, the Jailer snorted awake for a second, and the wizard mouse saw that the keys were secured to his belt by a thin silver chain.

'They're stuck!' mouthed the Stranger. 'What are we going to do?'

Wilding pointed to the Stranger with his free paw. 'Get under the keys, now! Get ready to catch them.'

The Stranger ran under the keys and sheathed his sword, holding both his paws outstretched. 'Ready!' he whispered.

Wilding let loose a muttered incantation, and from his staff's ruby a yellow star of energy pulsed out. It flew unerringly towards the chain and scored a direct hit, snapping it in two. The three companions held their breath as the keys fell to the stone floor, but were caught — with minimal noise — by the Stranger, though he rolled back on the ground, crumpling under the weight of the falling metal mass.

'I'm ok!' he said with a weak smile, as he struggled to get up with the encumbrance of the keys on his chest. Hearthseeker and Wilding hurried over to help him up and relieve him of the weight. Ainsley took the keys and threw them over his back, tying them together with a length of twine he produced from inside a leather satchel on his belt to prevent them from making noise as the companions proceeded down the hall and deeper into the dungeons.

'Well done, thief!' said Wilding. 'Now, let's proceed for what we came for.'

Leaving the sleeping Jailer behind them, with the keyset firmly secured to Hearthseeker's back, the trio advanced down the hallway. Darkness and dank, moist air surrounded them, the air growing damper and more oppressive with each step. Wilding whispered into his staff and its ruby tip flared and lit a tiny magic flame, which shed a small amount of light in the seemingly impenetrable darkness.

The companions tiptoed forward, darting under the Jailer's stool while he slept. The mice were able to slink under the bars of the entrance door without any difficulty. Its wooden inserts had been designed to keep human hands from prying behind it, but mice were immune to its effects.

As they crept deeper into the dungeon, they could see an entirely different set of doors — cages, really — with wooden outcroppings designed for animals, in addition to the human-sized cells. It was a treacherous corridor to be in — especially if you were on the wrong side of the barred cage doors.

A hush fell across them as they carefully hurried forward, footpad by footpad, not daring to make a sound. It was silent now, as the light from the Jailer's nook faded behind them.

'This way,' beckoned Wilding, leading the trio forward into the oppressive darkness.

Out of one of the human cells, deep down the corridor, they could see a flickering light. It was faint, but the shadows it cast across the bars upon the wooden door which kept its prisoner contained were unmistakable.

Hearthseeker saw it first, picking out the dancing shadows among the darkness; his keen eyes were those of an accomplished bard who occasionally moonlighted as a thief.

'Milord, a shadow dances on the door of the cell up ahead, on our right.'

Wilding saw it too, and paused. 'Let us see who has gained the King's hospitality.'

Crime was generally low in The Western Lands, but even so, the Castle had been built with the capacity to imprison those citizens who chose to commit crimes against the crown or against the citizenry. Murderers, thieves, and traitors to the crown had all seen the inside of this basement prison and experienced its damp walls, constantly dripping with condensate.

Few lived to tell the tale.

The musky, dank air was known to cause sickness. Captives often fell victim to sicknesses of the lungs, which made it difficult for them to breathe. As their stays lengthened, their condition usually worsened with each passing day. It was well known that a few days in the catacombs of the Castle's prison would likely leave a prisoner ill with the flu — at best. A month or more down there was, in all likelihood, a death sentence.

During the First Rat King War, King Teegan's father, The Heaven's King, had expanded the stockades for additional wartime necessities. Interrogation rooms with certain implements of...'persuasion' had been added to loosen the tongues of those human captives who crossed or challenged the crown. Over time, as the King engaged the Mousekin on wartime missions of intelligence gathering, it became necessary to build a MouseKeep version of the stockades, in miniatures of various sizes, so animals who chose to do the bidding of The Rat King could be detained...

— TAKEN FROM **SIR PENDLETON STORMSNOUT'S BOOK OF RIVER TRAVELS, VOLUME 1: FELDENSPAR CASTLE TO MOUSELING HOLLOW**

Chapter 13

A CRUCIBLE OF COMBAT

Their eyes locked as Teague, suspended in midair from his roped arrow, plunged down towards One Eye. The mouse captain was coming in hot, focused solely on attacking his nemesis. One Eye's only eye widened — first with fear, and then with scorn — and he drew the short sword from the sheath that hung at his side. Sensing the predicament he was caught up in, he broke cover and tried to bolt away from his foe. The rat dashed out from under the pantry table, his oily fur now covered in cobwebs and dust, his short sword clutched tightly between his clawed fingers, but it was too late. Teague's aerial assault had been perfectly timed, his aim calculated too precisely. Invigorated by the ride he just took, the veteran Mouseling landed squarely on top of his foe, tackling the rat as he tried to flee. For the first time in nearly twenty seasons, Robert Teague began to feel the delicious rage of a battle frenzy descend upon him once more.

The two creatures went rolling and tumbling across the stone floor, and One Eye's sword clattered away from him. Breathless, the rat tried to scamper towards his weapon, but was unable to gain traction as Teague had grabbed a firm hold of his tunic. Catching the rat's single eye, Teague smiled coldly, then started to reel in his catch as if he was pulling in a net full of silverback from the Mirror Lake.

Teague was forced to let go, however, when the rat turned around and swiped at him with a small, wicked-looking jeweled dagger he produced from somewhere within his cloak. One Eye regained his footing and turned to face his adversary, the polished blade of the dagger creating a sinister glint in the firelight of the hearth. The rat brandished it in a 'Heaven's Grip,' in which the point of the dagger was turned down towards the floor while the pommel faced up towards the sky. The grip, as well as the stance that One Eye now assumed, was customarily taught to Ratling assassins; noting the confidence in the rat's form, Teague could tell that he was a highly trained one.

But then again, Teague was no stranger to combat against highly trained adversaries.

One Eye looked at Teague and said:

'I will take your life now, Robert Teague, and then go to finish off your little friends. After that, your wife and children, and ALL of Mouseling Hollow, will burn!' Spittle flew from his mouth as he hissed at his opponent, his lips curled in hatred and contempt.

Teague was unfazed.

In an even tone, he said, 'If I have to, I will take you apart, piece by piece, until you've answered my questions in full. But let us be sure we understand each other, vermin — you **will** pay for the crimes you have committed here against MouseKeep, and I **will** place your head on a pike at the base of the Early Spires as a warning to the next rat who even **thinks** about daring entry into this domain. On this day, One Eye, I will see a lieutenant of The Rat King laid low. If we are truly about to embark on a new war, I will strike the first blow here in Feldenspar Castle for all to remember.'

Teague drew his twin hand axes out, giving each axe a single twirl in a smoothly practiced motion as they cleared the sheath without even being consciously aware of it. He held them lightly, gently, as he centered himself. He was the calm before the storm, the water before the fall, the spark before the flame — his entire being was now singly focused on subduing his adversary. Teague closed his eyes momentarily and saw the entirety of the fight unfold before him in his mind's vision.

Then he opened his eyes, which shone with an even greater resolve.

The two creatures began to encircle each other, each one scrutinizing his opponent for the slightest hint of an opening — or a weakness — to be exploited. The rat was heavier, having accumulated more fat over the years. His somewhat bulbous body may have moved awkwardly, but his smooth footwork belied his background as a deadly rat assassin who had not forgotten his training. Teague could not see the pointed tip of the dagger in the 'Heaven's Grip,' only the pommel. He knew a slashing crossbody strike was coming — most likely an entry strike which would soon be followed by a flurry of attacks designed to open a critical, mortal wound.

Teague stayed light on his feet. He brandished his axes, one in each paw, slicing through the air to create a 'Z' pattern. The two animals locked eyes for a moment — and then the rat thrust in, slashing at Teague's midsection, hoping to end the contest with a single mortal blow.

Steel met steel as Teague parried the attack. Quicker than he would have thought possible, the rat's daggered paw slashed back in the direction from which it came and opened a gash in the mouse captain's bicep. Blood seeped out and began to darken the fur on Teague's arm. He felt the searing pain, but kept his focus as the two continued to circle each other without disengaging.

Slash, parry, slash, parry — the fight grew more intense now as it was apparent that each meant to take his opponent's life. The cold knocking of steel on steel rung throughout the kitchen.

The two creatures moved together in a macabre dance, neither wanting to overextend himself. Teague blocked an incoming thrust with the wooden handle of his right axe, which he held now in an inverted grip. The rat lunged in again, but this time Teague spun and avoided the blow, then spun back again in the opposite direction, sending his axes in a crescent-shaped arc which came to bear on the rat's shoulder as he completed his spin/dodge, opening a wound as well.

The rat cried in pain, hissing:

'You won't get the best of me, Teague. I will stand today atop of your mutilated corpse — and The Rat King will glorify me for it! All will know my name — Cornelius White Eye, slayer of ***The Fabled Two!***'

The rat and the mouse captain continued their fight. Both were beginning to grow fatigued as the melee took its toll on them. As the two circled each other, the rat began to intentionally move backwards, maneuvering himself towards his discarded sword through a series of circles until he finally drew close enough to retrieve it. He now brandished a sword in one hand and a dagger in the other — 'Assassin's Twinblades,' as the fighting stance was called. It was a deadly combination developed over hundreds of years by Ratling assassins.

A combination designed to kill in an instant.

He pointed his sword at the mouse captain's throat and said:

'Come now, Robert Teague, and feel the agony a skilled rat assassin can inflict at will on his nemesis! Enjoy the suffering that you are about to feel in the next few moments — ***SAVOR*** it, for they shall be your last!'

The melee continued, as One Eye's confidence had clearly been bolstered by the recovery of his sword.

Instead of worrying solely about avoiding strikes from his opponent's dagger, Teague now found himself preoccupied with blocking the long, sweeping, broad-arced attacks from the rat's sword — each followed by the inevitable follow-up thrust from the jeweled dagger.

Parry, dodge, roll, parry, dodge, roll — Teague struggled to break into the rat's stance as the sword attacks kept warding off his entry points of counterattack.

One Eye made a large swing at Teague's head, which Teague blocked with his axe. Catching the tip of the rat's blade, Teague was able to lock it for only the briefest of seconds — and, in a spinning motion, drove the rat's sword into the dirt floor, where the tip lodged itself.

One Eye was forced to pause his attack momentarily as he struggled to get the blade tip out of the ground. Realizing he could not concern himself with this much longer as Teague advanced on him, he dropped the sword and spun forward, launching a vicious dagger thrust at his adversary's midsection.

But it was too late.

Teague stepped inside the incoming strike and brought the flat head of his axe down on his attacker's wrist, *hard* — a blow so forceful that it shattered the lithe bones in the rat's paw. The dagger went flying, rattling away somewhere under the pantry table while One Eye clutched his paw and screamed in pain.

Teague forcefully pushed One Eye towards the back of the pantry wall nearby, reared up, and threw one of his axes at the rat. The axe narrowly missed the chest of his adversary, but struck underneath One Eye's upper forearm as he cradled his wrist in pain, cutting through the rat's black and crimson tunic and pinning him to the wooden cabinet. Teague then reached into his belt and grabbed a small throwing dagger, hurling it straight at the rat's head!

But Teague had missed intentionally. It struck a whisker's breadth away from the rat's face, spearing into the soft wood of the aged cabinet with a **THUNK** and sending a clear message that Teague was done playing around.

One Eye was still yelping in pain as Teague started towards his adversary. Drawing close, the mouse captain pressed his own snout into the rat's face. He then took his axe blade and held it to the rat traitor's throat.

'Now, One Eye — as I was saying before. You will answer my questions. You will tell me all that I ask. I will either be pleased with the thoroughness of your responses, or you will find yourself headless a very short time from now. The next time I put a blade towards your head — I won't miss.'

Though he was clearly in pain and shamed in defeat, the rat still remained defiant.

'You still don't get it, do you, Robert Teague. You think defeating me in this place carries any meaning? That it will bear any weight in the conflict that has already been won?'

'Won? What do you mean, won?' Teague pressed the blade closer to the rat's throat.

'It is too late for you, Teague. Too late for you and your little Mouseling friends. Too late for the humans of Feldenspar. For even as we speak, The Rat King has already begun his invasion of the Western part of The Far Collective. The usurpation and undoing of Castle Feldenspar was but merely a small part of the plan — to remove any vestige of resistance as the *real* infiltration begins.'

Teague wanted to believe the rat was lying, but there was something in his tone which made Teague believe that he was telling the truth. The implications of what One Eye was disclosing were far reaching and nefarious, indeed.

'Keep talking, vermin — I want details. Where? When? What is the size and disposition of the forces?'

'I...I...don't know,' the rat stammered. 'Massive. Unlike The First Great War, The Rat King has unified the Ratling Clans. Where once he had to face resistance from the traitors within his own people who only wanted peace, now he has unified them in a common belief — that they are the rightful denizens of The Far Collective. Any animals who resist are either subjugated or eliminated, as an example to others. Many animals have capitulated and joined his cause under this duress — the fischers, for example. Weasels. Clans of your mouse brethren who stood no chance against the might of his armies or his magic. The list is endless. From his newly rebuilt kingdom in the Darkened Vale, from his city built deep and bulwarked in the Underhill, where you would least expect to find it, he sends his armies forth. High upon his black throne, he commands his minions who obey and kill without question. There is no....there can BE no...stopping them.'

'And what of the humans? The eyeball I saw — and shot at — in The King's Pedestal...who does it belong to? Who are these humans who have joined The Rat King in his crusade? No citizen of Feldenspar would ever rise against the King.'

'Indeed they wouldn't — but these humans aren't from Feldenspar, mouse. They come from far across the Southern Ocean — a faction of humans that know only war and killing. They call themselves the **Wandering Clans**. Brutal. Ruthless. In their wake, they leave only death and subjugation for their adversaries. They are reavers who have no qualms about killing men, women, and children, and they take only female prisoners — to help propagate their ranks. The few they choose to spare either join them and submit to their voracious agenda, or die. And their knowledge of naval warfare is unsurpassed.'

'As we speak, they are sailing at this moment towards the shores of Ocean's View, the gateway to Feldenspar. But even if he were on his throne, your beloved King Teegan would be hard pressed to get troops there to attempt a defense. It's a long way from here to the coastline. Legions of animal armies — and some human resistance, also — now stand in the way. Under the command of The Rat King, they will not hesitate to harass, to infiltrate, to break supply lines, and even to attack humans openly, if The Rat King deems it necessary.'

'The Lyceum at Ocean's View...' trailed Teague, aloud.

'Yesss...' hissed One Eye. 'Yesss...your precious Lyceum and the treasures it holds, not the least of which are The Decoding Stones themselves. The Rat King seeks the stones for...his own purposes. And when he has them, his ability to speak with humans — and bend them to his will — shall be all but complete. That skill, coupled with his mastery of the dark arts, will vanquish the humans and press them into doing his bidding. With control of both the human and animal kingdoms, there will be none left to stop him.'

'But he doesn't have them yet,' said Teague. 'So he must be using a human Speaker to communicate with the humans. We killed his Speaker in the last Rat War. What human has he found that speaks for him now?'

'Not one human, Teague, but three,' One Eye replied. 'Three more has he found who have the gift for speaking with animals. Two are like him, evil in their intent and dealings. One has been enslaved and serves him against her will. This is why the human naval armada has embarked across the ocean — he sent his Speakers as emissaries across the Sea, looking for biddable humans to fill the ranks of his war machine. It is how human agents were able to infiltrate Castle Feldenspar. Three speak for the Rat King. You shot an arrow into the eye of one of them.'

A human speaker for The Rat King? And in the heart of Castle Feldenspar, no less? It was worse than Teague thought. Animal Speakers were rare indeed, and usually had a grasp of powerful magics as part of their talents. When their magical inclinations were drawn to the...darker arts...terrible things could happen. *Like somehow managing to imprison a King in his own castle without the help even knowing*, Teague thought.

'And Teague, there is one more thing you should know — The Rat King has put a bounty on your head, and that of your wizard friend as well. You cannot escape. As we speak, a detachment of The Rat King's forces marches northward up The Riverpath, to burn Mouseling Hollow to the ground.'

The rat was suddenly seized by a coughing fit and spat up some blood. Through bloody, yellow teeth he smiled as he said:

'So you see Teague, you cannot escape. Everything you love will be destroyed. The Rat King will see your family line extinguished, so that he may not be challenged with insurrection by a soft-hearted fool like you — or your squirrel-loving wizard friend.'

At this insult, Teague slapped the rat across the snout with the back of his gloved hand. One Eye stared back at him and spat some more blood, defiantly.

Teague looked at the rat, and his whiskers twitched with disgust.

'We shall see about all this. But for now, it is time for me to put an end to your miserable...'

But before Teague could finish his sentence, a loud hissing sound, followed by a screech, froze the two adversaries in place. A large orange tabby cat emerged from around the corner and crouched down, preparing to pounce. The cat looked at Teague, then the rat, then Teague, and back over to One Eye.

The predator's eyes gleamed. The rat was his quarry — bigger, bolder, a more robust prize than the smaller, skinnier mouse.

Teague started to back away slowly, tugging his axe from its indenture in the wooden wall to free One Eye — if only temporarily — before the rat met his maker between the jaws of the orange cat.

One Eye tried to run towards the spiral staircase that Teague had slid down, but it was too late. The cat had already sprung through the air, past the wooden pantry, and landed a paw on the rat's tail, pinning him solidly and rendering him immobile. Though the tabby cat was blocked from biting at One Eye by the positioning of the table leg, its paw's vise-like grip on One Eye's tail prevented him from moving any further.

'Teague, help me! Help me Teague!' the rat cried out in a piteous wail of fear and despair. He looked up at the cat, which towered over him behind the table leg, in dread.

Teague was about to turn his back on the rat, but something stopped him. Maybe it was mercy, maybe it was compassion, but he couldn't help but think that being torn apart by a cat was a miserable way to die — even if the wicked creature deserved it.

'Teague!' cried the rat again, pleadingly. His tail was pinned at the base, and the feline took a powerful, if playful, swipe at him with its other paw as it prepared to play 'cat and mouse' with its dinner.

Then the rat saw what Teague was about to do and stopped. His face took on a different, far more urgent look of terror.

'No, Teague! Please! No...'

'It's the only way,' said Teague, and he whipped his axe directly at One Eye. Hurtling through the air, the axe whirled with unerring accuracy at Teague's target. With a terrible **THUNK** it landed, severing the rat's tail while freeing him from the cat's deadly grip.

Screaming in agony, One Eye scampered for the nearest safe place. He scurried away under a table, disappearing towards the kitchen's exit. As he made his escape, his tail lay motionless, still pinned under the cat's paw, while a small trail of blood chronicled his path to the outside world — and back to the legions of The Rat King.

On The Black Baron's Arena:

Of all the possible combat rituals an aspiring warrior can choose to engage in, it is common knowledge that the only true proving ground to be found in The Far Collective lies in one place: The Hellion Sands. There, under the gluttonous and indulgent oversight of the animal known only as The Black Baron, animals who have been indentured, enslaved, or come of their own accord seeking fame and fortune may find true redemption — in the dirt-trodden crucible known as The Arena.

Once combatants enter The Arena, they may exit it in only one of two ways: in victory, or in death. Win three fights, and you have not only earned your freedom, but a heavy purse of coin (and a night of indulgence in the excesses that the Denizens of The Arena are known to partake in) along with it. But very few animals have successfully won their three consecutive matches — most are carted out lifelessly by the end of match two. Many second and third matches often consist of an interspecies match — Mouseling versus Feral Cat, or Crested Tarbog Rattlesnake, or somesuch — the odds in which weigh heavily against those brave champions who enter, knowingly and acceptingly, of their own free will — headed to an almost certain, if not entirely guaranteed, death in glorious combat.

— TAKEN FROM **BLOOD AND DUST: THE RISE AND FALL OF LEGENDARY CHAMPIONS IN THE ARENA OF THE BLACK BARON**

Chapter 14

REDEMPTION FOR AN OLD FRIEND

With nary a sound, the three companions slid forward along the wall. As they arrived at the cell door, Wilding peered under it and surveyed the contents of the cell. An aged man, dressed in the undergarments of the King's Knights, read an old book of sacred prayer parchments by the dim candlelight. He recited the antiquated scriptures while he fingered a set of prayer beads in his hand. Though bearded and gray, his powerful muscles rippled and flexed under the shapeless garb of his underclothes. Sweat dripped from his body, drenching his clothing and outlining his impressive physique under the soiled raiment that would have once been gleaming white.

Whoever he was now, once he had most surely been a knight in the King's legion — though as for what crime he had been imprisoned for, that still remained to be seen. Yet through his sweat-soaked garb, Wilding spied an ankh — a cross with a looped oval atop it — tattooed on his left bicep, with the crest of Feldenspar outlined around it on a shield. Clearly, he had once belonged to — or perhaps remained a member of — Castle Feldenspar's 'elite guard.' Or so it seemed. *Assuming he's not another imposter, and this isn't another trap laid by that one-eyed rat and his minions on the expectation of our arrival,* Wilding mused to himself.

Yet something about his figure seemed familiar. Wilding could not see the knight's face as he kneeled, facing away from the barred door in prayerful countenance, but nonetheless — was it something in the shoulders, or the long hair? Wilding couldn't quite place his paw on it, but...whatever it was, Wilding was certain he had seen this man before.

He motioned to Hearthseeker and the Stranger. 'Stay here and keep on your guard. I am going in to talk to this human. Be watchful for imposter animals, or that fischer who is supposedly wandering around down here somewhere about the dungeons. And let's hope those other humans from the jailer's quarters don't come back anytime soon.'

With that, Wilding squeezed under the aged wood of the cell door and scurried under the cell's crude table to where the man remained kneeling, deep in prayer. The cross-bracing on the table's legs formed an 'X' pattern which allowed Wilding to scamper up to the top of the table. Climbing up onto the surface of the tabletop, Wilding paused and studied the wrinkles in the man's face. He listened silently to the prayers the man was saying, with great earnestness and piety, sensing a great deal of trouble and sadness weighing down the prisoner's soul. He heard the prisoner murmuring:

'And though I may never see the Golden Fields, may She know that my gratitude for this life is overflowing. My thanks to Her are eternal, and may my loyalty to my King and Her Dominion be met with favor, though I have failed in my most sacred duty. I failed to see the betrayal coming, and now my King has been imprisoned because of it. I know that because of my failure, I deserve to be given the ultimate sentence — death.'

'That sounds a little harsh, don't you think?' asked Wilding to the Knight on his knees.

The man opened his eyes slowly and looked at the diminutive mouse which had now appeared on the table, dressed in purple robes and carrying a tiny staff in its paws. Droplets of sweat continued to pour off his wrinkled brow. But as he brushed his long greying hair out of his face, the wrinkles of his forehead seemed to clear, and the worried grimace on his face now changed into a broad smile as he discovered in that moment that he was not, truly, alone.

'General Wilding,' the knight bowed in front of the mouse with his arms outstretched, a symbol of reverence and respect by the humans who understood the secret of MouseKeep, and the presence of the unusual, talking mice whose lives were intertwined with Castle Feldenspar. 'I cannot think of a more fitting miracle in this desperate hour than your companionship in my prison cell, with only hours to go before my execution.'

'First off, I told you not to call me General. And secondly, **Commander Gabriel Storm, Sworn Knight to the King and trusted adviser to the throne,** unless you have committed some kind of treason against King Teegan — which by your present situation I am assuming you have not, as it is the traitors who seem to be roaming freely through Castle Feldenspar at this moment — I do not believe that you will be executed on this day. Both men and mice know all must eventually face their doom, though we ne'er may know the hour it shall come upon us. And I, for one, would not presume that you could be so fortunate as to have such knowledge, either.'

Wilding hopped up into the knight's outstretched hand. The knight let out a hearty laugh and reached out his other hand to stroke the Mouseling, but Wilding intercepted his intention with a sharp poke of his staff. 'Do not pet me, Storm! I'm not a dog.'

'My apologies, General!' The knight bowed a second time. 'It's just that my heart is swelling with thanks at your arrival. Bless Her wise counsel and Dominion! I thought I had been forsaken.'

Wilding spoke urgently.

'Forsaken you are not, my friend. But unless you can tell me the status and disposition of the castle's guard, the location of the King, and the current tactical situation, our good fortune may not hold for long. Can you give me an overview of what happened here? My intention is to free the King, if he is still on site.'

Knight Commander Storm understood the urgency of Wilding's request. He spoke briefly and to the point, attempting to provide a summary of what had happened to usurp the King.

'It began when several 'emissaries' arrived at the castle from ships hailing from across the Southern Ocean, offering trade agreements, gifts of gold and other treasures, and magical artifacts which King Teegan believed could be of great use to his Kingdom. He accepted the gifts and invited them to stay, but hidden inside the gifts were animals — rats, fischers, and other mousefolk who did not hail from any of our lands. The emissaries were evidently Speakers for The Rat King, though of course we did not realize that at first. After a day of welcoming feasts put on by the King, the lead emissary — Tempus, he called himself — urged his majesty to dispatch several troop contingents down The Riverpath to The Plains of Andrellion, where they were to escort more shipments of goods and gifts to the bayside port city of Old Town.

'And so the King did, leaving Castle Feldenspar under-defended and ripe for the plucking. After breakfast one morning — it's been hard to keep track of time in here, but I'd estimate it was a week, perhaps a week and a half ago — the King dispatched Falcon Riders at Tempus's urging — for what reason, I do not know. But they never returned.

'When the King asked for a report from MouseKeep on the matter, he found it to be empty. All of the MouseGuard had disappeared, and the chambers of MouseKeep were empty and silent. Surely this had been the doing of the animals who were hidden inside these 'gifts' — oh Wilding, if only we had known! When King Teegan came to me privately to discuss the matter, with a great sense of worry over what had befallen his Mouseling subjects, we were waylaid by Tempus and his men in his private chamber — you know the one, where The King's Pedestal stands.

'The emissaries had somehow dispatched the remainder of Castle Feldenspar's Royal Guard, so we were helpless as newborn babes. Teegan and I were both taken prisoner — though I received a hard blow to my head when I tried to fight back, which rendered me unconscious for what I believe may have been several days. I awoke here, stripped of my weapons and armor. I have received some food and drink, though it is but a meager share — barely enough to keep a man alive.'

He pointed to a crude bedside table where some moldy crusts of bread resided alongside an empty wooden cup.

'I can hear food being shuffled up and down the corridor for other prisoners, and the jailers go back even as far as the cages built for animal prisoners, which leads me to believe the guardians of MouseKeep may still be here — as well as the King himself. I was told by some imposter now masquerading as the castle Jailer, who stank of strong drink, that I am to hang from the gallows tomorrow as a symbol — or perhaps a warning — of treason, for all the citizens of Feldenspar to witness. I overheard him mentioning some plan to take King Teegan away when he thought I was asleep — but to where, I do not know. General Wilding, have you brought a garrison with you to the fight? What resources do we have?'

'Here is your garrison,' said Wilding with a smile. 'Hearthseeker, would you be so good as to slide us the key under this door? I think Knight Commander Storm is ready to take his leave of these accommodations.'

Storm heard the scraping of metal on stone, after which the Knight saw the key to his freedom slide towards him, now only a few feet away.

'At present,' Wilding said, 'our ranks consist of myself, a scalawag Mouseling known as Ainsley Hearthseeker, a strange Mouseling who is a low ranking member of the Thief's Guild, whose family was taken captive by these conspirators, and Robert Teague.'

'General Teague is here?' asked the knight, astonished.

'Yes. And please stop calling us General. We never accepted those promotions, as you well know. We were beckoned to MouseKeep by a summons from the King — we know not if it was a genuine plea for help or a ploy by these conspirators to draw us out — and met a human I can only assume to be one of these 'emissaries' at The King's Pedestal, who was working in concert with a Ratling traitor named One Eye. We had a skirmish at the Pedestal with a large group of these traitorous animals you speak of — where you'll be glad to know Teague 'gifted' The Rat King's emissary with an arrow to the eye. Teague took off in pursuit of that Ratling vermin One Eye, while we made our way here to free what prisoners we might find. Though we know not how our good friend Robert is faring in his pursuit of the rat, we have our own fair share of troubles to worry about at the moment. We must find King Teegan. Open this door, quickly now!'

Wilding hopped out of the knight's hand and back onto the table, after which the knight picked up the key and unlocked the door from the inside. The 'click' of the tumblers turning echoed down the dark corridor.

Hearthseeker and the Stranger rushed to climb up to the table and stood beside Wilding. After opening the cell door just a crack and peeking through to ensure the coast was clear, the knight came back and looked down at the three mice.

'I'll need a weapon, and some clothing.'

Wilding answered him quickly. 'The Jailer who informed you of your pending execution is asleep on a stool not too far away, in the Jailer's Nook. He was sent off to his slumber by a bit of, shall we say.... overindulgence. You may find the jeweled dagger hanging from his belted sheath to be of familiar issue — it was a weapon once gifted to you by King Teegan, I believe?'

'That villainous scum!' hissed the knight.

'Now now, Storm, no time for that now. Go and retrieve your weapon — and make haste. We need to bring that drunken Jailer back here and lock him in this cell in case a watchman comes by. We're going to want him to...stay asleep...if you get my meaning, for a while. A good couple of hours, at the least.'

The knight moved down the hallway with haste. Even starved and dehydrated, and clad in soiled undergarments, the mice could see that he was still an expert warrior who moved like artistry in motion. In the stillness that ensued, they heard a slight moan, a gurgling sound, and a loud **WHACK!** Then silence. A moment later, Commander Storm reemerged carrying the unconscious Jailer over his shoulders. He laid him on the old bed — barely a cot, really — and undressed him, removing his sweat-stained raiment and replacing them on the Jailer, then turning him on his side to face the wall away from the door so it would look like he was asleep. Storm then dressed in the Jailer's clothing. Finally, he held up his stockinged foot to the bottom of the Jailer's boot, then shook his head in irritation.

'I was hoping his boots would fit, but no such luck. This man's feet are tiny — much like his other personal characteristics, I'm sure! At least he is where he belongs now.' He stopped and sniffed the garments he had just put on. 'Ugh, these reek of foulness,' he said, turning his nose up at the smell. 'But in the King's service, we do what we must.'

'We can worry about your hygiene later, I'm afraid. Now, my friend, if you would be so kind as to take those small animal cage keys off the keyring and set them down here...' Wilding pointed to the table with his staff, and Storm did what he asked, setting the keys gently on the tabletop.

'Now, the plan is simple,' said Wilding. 'Hearthseeker and the Stranger will take these keys and unlock any MouseGuards that can be found in the cages. Commander Storm, I will ride on your shoulders as we look for the King, unlocking all human prisoners as we go. Any enemy of my enemy is my friend, or so they say, and that includes whatever prisoners who might have committed crimes before the castle coup that landed them in here. We can use all the help we can, and if they are willing to take the risks of fighting for King and country, perhaps they can find redemption in Teegan's eyes — and earn back their freedom honestly. We will all meet back in the Jailer's Nook, at which point we will prepare for an assault to take back the castle. Assuming we can free MouseKeep and the remaining contingent of the King's knights, we should have a fair fight on our hands. Go now Hearthseeker! And Stranger, if you find your family — send them into MouseKeep for safekeeping. With haste now, GO!'

The two mice scrambled down the tabletop and out the cell door, hurrying down the hall to free any and all animals they could locate.

'Excellent plan, General Wilding!' lauded Commander Storm. 'It's an honor to fight by your side again, sir.'

'Would you *PLEASE* stop calling me general,' Wilding replied as he hopped up on the knight's shoulder. They then started down the corridor, hoping to find the King.

Wilding sensed the King was near, and felt a strong conviction that if they could free the King this day, that Castle Feldenspar, The Western Lands, and Mouseling Hollow may yet survive to fight another day.

But deep within the recesses of his heart, Wilding sensed that war was coming, even if they came out of their current predicament victorious — and he feared that his involvement in it was somehow far, far from being over.

'I'd sooner believe that the Mouse ran down the clock when it struck one. What self-respecting Mouseling runs up a clock, anyways?'

— MOUSELING SLANG MEANING 'YOU'RE A LIAR.'

Chapter 15

DUNGEON DELVING

Silently, furtively, the party advanced down the corridor. Hearthseeker, the Stranger, and Wilding moved as quietly as they could with the visibility afforded by the dim torch in Commander Storm's hand, which he had procured from a wall sconce to light the darkness. Wilding stood perched on Storm's shoulder, while his Mouseling companions sneakily scouted ahead, looking for any signs of fischers, rats, or worse — all could be imagined in the dank darkness of the dungeon's passageways, and the Mouselings knew that any encounter with one of their traditional predators could lead to their demise.

Dealing with humans was always a secondary concern for Mouselings when their mortal enemies — rats and fischers — were about. After the events that had already transpired that day, the party was on *high* alert — unsure of what was to come next, but knowing it would most surely involve battle, deadly traps, or more dangers yet unimagined. While they had gained a victory in their rescue of Gabriel Storm, a Knight Commander of the King's guard, they knew it was but a small victory — the rest of the watch was still unaccounted for, as was the King. There remained an overall sense that they were still in the midst of navigating a dire situation — and only the darkest of tidings lay on the horizon.

Not unlike a game of Root and Field in which your opponent plays Dragon Assault while your own hand remains empty, Wilding thought as he assessed the tactical nature of their situation.

For Hearthseeker and the Stranger, though their hearts were stout, they were unused to this kind of drama — none of them were, in military terms, *battle tested* like Wilding and his friend Teague were. Castle Feldenspar — indeed, The Far Collective as a whole — had been so tranquil for many seasons, so...placid — that feasts, self-study, and many mugs filled with fine ale had been the order of the day for the innumerable, now nearly unthinkable sunny days which had preceded this one. They were scared — and rightly so. For them, nefarious plots and dreadful situations in which life and death rested on the narrowest edge of a blade was totally new — and disconcerting — territory.

But not for Wilding. He *had* been here before.

And, though many seasons had passed since that fateful day long ago, in that moment — down in that particular dungeon, filled with the rank stench of death — the wizard mouse could hardly differentiate between what lay ahead, unseen, in **this** darkness beneath Castle Feldenspar, from the same feelings he had felt back when he and Teague — along with what was left of the First Battalion of Falcon Riders — had supported the Heaven's King's assault upon The Rat King's Black Citadel, infiltrating it via aerial breach back in The First Rat King War.

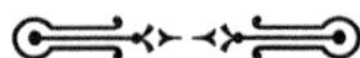

It was such a dark day, that one, Wilding thought, his mind racing immediately to the scene as if it had just happened yesterday. In his mind's eye, he could see it all so clearly: the human and mice battalions trekking across The Hellion Sands, running short on supplies... individual soldiers, and even whole caravans, bogged down by the deadly creatures of the Sands — as well as the unbroken terrain.

The slog of it all.

And that was just the start. There were the scorching temperatures that caused the weaker or less fortified soldiers — and horses — to simply fall by the crusade's wayside, most of them never to rise again. It was so hot during the daytime that even the Falcon Riders had to fly in shifts, the birds and their riders stretched to their very limits after merely an hour in the air. He remembered how they would count each moment until they could return, utterly exhausted and dehydrated, to the safety of a specially designed, covered battle wagon where they could refresh themselves with some water and seek shelter from the unerring and merciless rays of the desert sun. Half of their falcons would become 'sunscorched,' or temporarily blinded, due to a lack of eye protection from the searing light.

The situation that day had grown so desperate, Wilding recalled, that the King himself determined there could be no going back — it was either march to victory or march to their deaths, there in the unending Hellion Sands of lost hope.

No other choice had lain open to them.

The King had decided to lay siege to the Black Citadel in the hopes of ending the destructive conflict once and for all. The ten thousand souls who had suffered the march through the desert, human soldiers and animals alike, were the price to be paid for the citadel's possession — a price that the King had committed to risking in advance though the outcome was yet to be determined.

But the Heaven's King was ever the consummate leader and tactician. He led the march on horseback, his thick grey hair and beard drenched in sweat and glistening in the sun. Though the desert's heat had forced him to stash his legendary golden plate mail in a battle wagon, he still insisted on wearing his first layer of armor, the underlying chainmail, as a sign to his troops that he was willing to share the same discomforts — and face the same dangers — that they did. There was a man who led by example, even under the most intense duress — a man who would not put any soldier's life before his own, nor ask them to bear a risk he was unwilling to share in himself.

Maybe that was why they followed him. Or perhaps they followed him because they knew of The Rat King's sinister nature, and all he had done with such malicious intent to destroy families and townships across The Western Lands. But whatever their reasons may have been, one thing was certain that day: they had all made that fateful choice to leave their families and follow their King into the desert — and would continue to follow him wherever he led.

And there was **no** going back. They knew that ahead of them lay either triumph over The Rat King, or death. There could be no middle ground.

It was on the third day of the death march, as the sunset began to drop in the west, highlighting the eastern horizon, that they saw the tip of The Black Citadel in all its twisted glory. It was a crooked and grotesque architectural marvel, a garrison both intimidating and enviable. Manning their posts upon the high ground that the tall tower provided were both dark human wizards and the animal minions of The Rat King, all fully prepared — and eager — for battle.

And yet, it wasn't the demoralizing visage that the Black Citadel held that day which Wilding could still recall so palpably...so...vividly...

It wasn't his entrance into that keep that Wilding remembered so sharply.

It was being down **in it**, in the very lowest reaches of its depths.

The overpowering stench. The rancid scent of oily, unwashed rats and fischers — the very **filth** associated with them.

Yes, I do believe I've been here before, thought the wizard Mouseling morbidly as he perched on Storm's shoulder — his eyes scanning, peering into the darkness, looking for the most barely perceptible hint of movement, or perhaps a hairline trap.

I had so much to lose back then, he mused to himself. *But now, I don't have anything more to lose.* The scent in the air, as they moved through the corridors underneath Castle Feldenspar, sent him back to that day when the Falcon Riders had made their initial breach on the top of The Black Tower.

The Riders had gone in high, to the very top of the tower where The Rat King's Bat Rider perch was situated, and terrible fighting had ensued. Many brave Mouselings fell that day on the highest tower of The Dark Citadel. Some were shot down in what became known as **The Great Dogfight:** the massive aerial battle of Bat Riders and Falcon Riders, all jockeying to get behind one another in hopes of felling their foe (or his bird) with bow and arrow in flight. Others were killed by the repeating crossbows which had been placed on the parapets dotting the full length of the tower, manned by keen-eyed rats and fischers. They were highly trained, having spent many long, boring days in the desert filled with nothing to do except practice hitting targets launched off the tower.

And, they were very, VERY good at it.

When the fighting was over, a great victory had been attained by The First Battalion, though it carried with it a terrible cost in lives. The Mousekin had ultimately taken control of the spire — a key strategic resource, overwatch point, and resupply hub from within the tower for whatever supplies could be rooted and found. It had been a gloriously valiant moment for the newly commissioned Falcon Riders — yet also a tremendously tragic one — one that would be measured in lost comrades, friends, and loyal birds.

Wilding had been relieved to see that Teague had survived the dogfighting and the murderous crossbow fire. They connected up on top of the tower, with one quick, masculine, hug. But then, it was back to business.

The business of slaying The Rat King.

Wilding remembered the ominous scroll written in black and red parchment which had taunted the victorious detachment of mice as they moved to secure the top of the spire and mop up the remaining crossbow gunners. It had been posted next to the only rat-sized door which led down a spiral staircase into the citadel proper.

Teague and Wilding had approached the parchment and read it together, surrounded by the remaining Falcon Riders who were now encircling them protectively from behind. They awaited their superiors' orders with swords in paw, ready for the inevitable combat which would be shortly forthcoming — paw to paw, melee battle.

When the two friends had finished reading, they looked at each other incredulously. It read:

Captain Wilding —

We have unfinished business, you and I. Assuming, of course, you remain alive to read this missive.

If you are present in any force which tries to occupy my palace, know that I am waiting for you below the first floor, in my personal chambers.

*It's a **long way down**, so you better get going!*

Come find me.

*I have a very...**special**...surprise in store for you.*

One your family would really, really want you to see.

I promise you won't want to miss this!

But your time is running short.

We have something in our culture that we call a 'rat king.'

*Ironic, I know. **Have you ever heard of it?***

It's when many ratling's tails get tangled and intertwined, until there is no way out for any of them.

They all get stuck together and die from starvation. Imprisoned by their own flesh and blood.

*It's something we try to avoid like...hmm...what is your saying? **'Like the plague?'** A phrase that has always puzzled me — we carry plague around with intention, too, as you and your human companions may know.*

Think of it as a puzzle, for which there is no solution...and no escape.

Now that you know what it is, I'll tell you a secret.

You have a 'rat king' on your paws right now.

It's downstairs, waiting for you.

Come see if you can untangle it.

The note was signed with a scribbled drawing of a crown alongside a rat's paw print.

'Teague, do you think this could be related to my family going missing just before we left?' Wilding asked his best friend, somewhat desperately. His mind was going to dark places, catastrophizing and overtaking his thoughts.

'I don't know, my friend. I pray it is not. But if Our Lady is on our side today, then we need to get going immediately...'

Wilding's mind snapped back to the moment at hand. *Where was I?* Yes, back in the dungeon of Castle Feldenspar, where he was still in darkness — albeit a different darkness than in The Rat King's Black Citadel, long ago — riding on the shoulder of Knight Commander Storm, and in the midst of a very real insurrection against the crown.

Still with a terrible smell — a stench of death and decay.

He needed to stay focused.

There is no time to reflect on the past, thought the mouse to himself. He used his military training to calm his breathing and quiet his apprehension, in order to refocus his mental energy upon the task at hand. *I have a duty to see the King rescued, whatever the cost — and get my friends out alive in the process. And I will do whatever it takes to accomplish both these tasks.*

A memory from deep within the recesses of his subconscious suddenly clicked into place. Urgently, he dug his paw into Storm's shoulder and said 'Hold up!'

'What is it?' whispered Storm, who dared not breathe too loudly. The two mice on the ground slunk silently to press themselves against the opposite walls, waiting for direction.

'In the First War, when we infiltrated the castle, they laid traps for humans and Mousekin — 'one steps,' we called them. They were tripwire mechanisms, and when triggered, they would go off, spearing a sharp blade into the offending — or perhaps I should say, unfortunate — victim.'

'Why did they call them 'one steps?'' the Commander asked.

'Because you took one step after getting impaled, and then you died,' answered Wilding, quite matter-of-factly. 'The quick-acting poison on the blades was designed to make sure you were neutralized.'

Storm inhaled deeply and stood motionless.

'My feeling is that as we delve deeper into these tunnels, terrible dangers lie ahead of us,' Wilding said. 'Commander, I see some dungeon doors up ahead. While I know our goal is to find the King and free what prisoners we can find along the way, we must proceed with the greatest of caution. Shine your torch at chest height, then at foot height. Sweep your torch in an arc, and let me and my brothers peer into the light.'

Gingerly, Storm held his torch hand out and started sweeping it in a broad, deliberate arc.

Slowly, slowly.

'I don't see anything,' said the Commander.

'Me neither!' whispered Hearthseeker, nearly inaudible from his position on the floor, so far below where Wilding stood.

'What now?' asked Storm.

'Let's see if a little Mouseling magic can't help us,' said the wizard mouse. Raising his staff in the air, with the ruby at the head of the battle weapon visibly beginning to glow and pulse, he muttered some inaudible words. Suddenly a dim, crimson flash shot into the air like a flare, burst, and a tiny fireworks show glittered down from it. While the display did make a small 'sparkling sound' when cast, the glittering residual effect gently floated down, down — and suddenly, an arms' length in front of of Storm's torch, they all saw it: a wisp-thin string that looked like spider's silk mixed with glass, shimmering slightly in the crimson light.

'There.' Wilding pointed the ruby end of his staff out over the Commander's shoulder toward the trigger mechanism.

Storm breathed an audible sigh of relief.

'Whew!' he started. 'It's a good thing you're here General, or I never would have seen that! Now, how do we disarm it?'

'Let's see what we are disarming first,' Wilding said, 'and stop calling me General. Raise your torch higher — to the right, there, near the wall.'

Storm did as he was bade, revealing a fearsome-looking weapon: a dagger, stained green with a fast-acting poison, balanced atop a torch sconce where the torch had been removed. In the crimson glow the string was still visible, tied in an arc that led from the wall to the hilt.

'That would have most certainly meant my death. Is there a way to dismantle it?'

'This is how we remove it from the field,' said Wilding, making a **Root and Field** reference which Storm would not have understood. He then shot a star bolt from his staff — the same bolt that he had used to dislodge the keys from the Jailer's belt — towards the hilt of the dagger, where the string was tied with great tension. When his bolt sliced through the string, it severed the tension — allowing the string to fall harmlessly to the floor, removing any leverage and rendering the weapon harmless.

'Sir Mouse, I am in your debt! I salute your ingenuity, General!' said Storm, beaming with admiration.

'Storm, would you *please!*' Wilding emphasized, irritated.

Realizing his mistake, the human immediately apologized. 'Forgive me! Once again. I meant, I salute your ingenuity, um...Captain?'

'Just call me Wilding, ok?'

'Ok, Captain. I mean, er, Wilding!'

Wilding sighed, while the two mice on the ground giggled at the exchange. It was a much-needed moment of levity, even though they remained surrounded by the dangers that may have lurked in the dark.

'Up here,' said Hearthseeker, looking to get them back on track. 'On the left, do you see it? Another cell — and it looks like there is a light coming from within. It must have some prisoners in it! I hope, truly, that they are on our side, and this isn't another insidious trap!'

'Indeed, my small Mouseling friend!' said Commander Storm. 'We could certainly use the reinforcements!'

Edging down the corridor, Storm peered into the iron-gated window and saw two humans sitting on the floor. The walls inside were glistening with dampness, reflected from the small glow of the cell's single candle, which had burned down almost to its end. The mice looked under the door and saw nothing else.

Storm looked at Wilding and said, 'What do you think?'

'Talk to them,' Wilding replied. 'See why they are imprisoned.'

Storm pressed his face against the caged opening and whispered into the dungeon cell:

'Hail, prisoners! I am Gabriel Storm, Knight Commander sworn to the service of King Teegan. Tell me quickly, lads, and tell me truthfully — why are you imprisoned here?'

Both prisoners leapt up and rushed eagerly to the cell door. 'Milord!' answered one of them, 'Do you not recognize us? We serve in the King's kitchens sir — I hail from the hamlet of Old Town, my family having sent me here to become a gentleman servant and learn the ways of court, not but two seasons ago. The staff calls me Cullen, my surname.' Though he was bedraggled from his imprisonment in the dank cell, Cullen gave a stiffly proper bow. 'At your service, sir! With me is my cousin, a stout lad from the Rossiter family who comes from the lands of The Black Baron. His given name is Bridie, sir, but Sister Minerva and her staff just calls him The Bird. Me and The Bird was imprisoned here by those emissary folks what took over King Teegan's court several days ago. They said we was traitors to the crown, sir — US! They dragged us from the dog houses without so much as a by-your-leave and put us here. They haven't paid us no never-mind, neither, having brought us little food or water since. I believe they mean to leave us here to die, sir.'

In the little light that Wilding's Mouseling magic provided, he could see the two young men wore green tunics and brown leather breeches, and both had dark, elongated leather caps with straps which hung down below their ears. This was the common dress of those who kept the King's animals, including the dogs.

Still, the Knight Commander wasn't convinced.

'Odd...I don't remember seeing either of you when we did a kitchen inspection two weeks ago,' said Storm suspiciously.

Cullen bobbed his head in agreement. 'Well, milord, y'see, that's because we're the kitchen staff's dog keepers. We live with the King's dogs, y'see, and are given charge of preparing the King's hunted meat, as well as keeping watch over the hounds at night.'

'We help tan the leathers also,' The Bird chimed in excitedly. He then turned his face to the floor bashfully. 'Or at least, we clean and prepare them for the tanner who comes 'round with the ointments to finish the job. But he says in a season or two he might let us start tanning the whole leathers. For true, he did!'

Cullen nodded. 'All of this is done outside the kitchen proper, Milord. Due to the, um...soiling. 'Tis not a bad life, though — we enjoy it quite a bit! The Bird and me, we've had plenty of time to talk over the past few days, and we both agree: it's quite nice living in the kennels. The meals are plentiful and nourishing, and the dogs are most affectionate and warm — they cuddle right up to you at night, especially when it's cold! The previous handlers told us that even in the wintertime, it's warmer in the dog houses than in the castle proper! Can you believe that, sir? Well if you ever wish to spend a night with us in the kennels, you can see it for yourself!'

Cullen suddenly blushed, embarrassed that he might have accidentally offended the knight. Hastily, he added, 'Not that your lordship would ever *wish* to, um, sleep in the dog houses, that is. Plus, we've yet to see how warm the castle is at night ourselves, of course. But winter seems to be upon us, and we'd be more than happy to return to the kennels — if you would free us from this prison, of course, Milord.'

'And I will fight those Ratlicking turncoats, Milord!' chimed in Bird, angrily. 'We have done nothing to dishonor the crown, I swear to you!'

Storm was nearly convinced that the two dog keepers were as they seemed, but he wanted to make sure there could be no doubt of their loyalties.

'You both skin and butcher the animals the King hunts, correct?' he asked. 'Tell me then, what is his favorite cut of meat?'

'Sire, to be clear, we do the initial cleanings and then bring the meat to the butcher for the precise and knowledgeable cuts, those which can only be performed by a master craftsman...' Cullen said.

'However, I will say that I know his favorite meat to be a fatty cut of prime rib, sir' interrupted Bird, cutting his friend off before he could finish answering the question.

'And, he only takes it with a yellow sauce of red wine, tarragon, and egg yolks!' added Cullen cheerfully, eager to show off his knowledge. 'And, when he sups this meal, he insists on having a good quaff of that spicy red wine from across The Sea of Serpents! It is so good, sir, you've got to try some if you've never had it — I even had a wee taste meself, once!'

'Hush your mouth!' Bird whispered sharply to his cousin, for fear of the reprisals he might face for dipping into the King's wine.

In that moment, Storm knew that the two were, in fact, exactly who they appeared to be: two salt-of-the-earth dog keepers, just some of the many servants who had made life in Castle Feldenspar so precious. He knew that they were most certainly on the side of the crown, and had no doubt that, in these most dire of circumstances, they would be much needed friends. Reaching for his keys, he unlocked the door.

'Thank you, Milord!' they chimed in unison.

'There you go lads. Now, can you fight?' asked Storm.

'Sire, we have not been trained in the way of the sword, as such, like you have,' Cullen said. 'But Bird and I both used to wrestle in the village square — sometimes for coin, but mostly for food scraps and pig slop. Back in Old Town, where they hold spectacles for entertainment of all varieties.'

'I have seen these spectacles,' said Hearthseeker from the floor below. 'Back when I was in Old Town, at The Bard's College. They would offer meager scraps of food to the poorest of the townsfolk, and outlying country folk who would fight for the pleasure of the rich — and the hope of a mouthful of food. Disgusting — and brutal. Personally, I couldn't bear to watch.'

The pair looked around fearfully, wondering where the voice was coming from.

'What was that?' said Cullen.

'Never mind that, now, lads.' said Storm. 'We have to find the King. Do you know where those no-good Ratlickers might be holding him?'

'I am unsure, sire,' The Bird said. 'But I saw them drag a hooded man and woman down the hall yesterday. Both were unconscious. I could tell because their toes kept dragging across the floor — it made an awful ugly scraping sound. I heard those treasonous Rat-lovers who are pretending to be jailers say they were heading to the left cell block, which I took to be ahead — down the stairs, on the left. I think it might be something we've heard referred to as 'the lowest cell.'

'Then that is where we are headed,' said Storm. 'I know exactly the cell of which you speak — and we must make haste. But be on your guard, my young companions — and if anything unfriendly moves, at the very least, punch it. Then punch it again. Then keep punching it, until it stops.'

'By your orders, sir!' cheered the two in unison.

I'll bet these two have some great things in store for them, thought Wilding to himself. *If we actually make it out of here alive, of course.*

He watched Cullen and The Bird trail after Knight Commander Storm, playfully tussling with each other behind his back.

If the crown is to survive what lies ahead, it will need honest, loyal men like these — and plenty of them.

The Great Airship Mystery in the Year 199:

*Reports exploded across the land — including many accounts in **The Feldenspar Daily** — of Mouselings in overalls showing up over farms in great airships. Frequently, they would descend down a rope ladder and ask the farmer for something inane — like water, or a watering can, or a frying pan or somesuch. Then, after thanking the farmer, they would climb back up the ladder and depart on the airship, never to be seen again. While there were many accounts of such sightings in the year 199, after that year ended, no one ever saw any of these unusual visitors again...*

— Taken from **Sir Pendleton Stormsnout's Upon the Ancient Days** (Scrolls recovered from ruins found in The Hellion Sands)

• • • • • • • • • • • •

Chapter 16

TRAP DOORS
AND TREASURES

• •

After what had just transpired in the kitchen of Castle Feldenspar, no one needed to tell Robert Teague twice that he had to get out of there — AND FAST.

It had all happened in a split second, really.

Teague's axe remained lodged in the cobblestone floor where it had severed One Eye's tail, and he knew he had to retrieve it. But that simple errand became immensely more complicated once One Eye, now released from the feline's clutches, started to scamper away, maimed but free — and was quickly pursued by the cat, who had been whipped into a wrathful frenzy by the impending loss of its would-be supper.

With a very 'un-catlike' lack of grace, the orange tabby scrambled to race after his fleeing prey, knocking over everything in sight. It was almost like watching dominoes falling, and it would have been comical, if it wasn't such a 'cat'-astrophe.

First, the cat accidentally knocked over a huge crock of cream which was waiting to be churned into butter, sending warm dairy cream splattering everywhere. That created a slick and slippery surface for the cat to slip and stumble along as it tried to sprint towards the pantry table, under which One Eye had temporarily sought refuge. While attempting to pounce for the kill, it slipped and fell again, sliding uncontrollably towards a barrel of milled wheat flour. Though the cat scrambled desperately, it couldn't regain its footing on the slick cobblestone floor, slamming wildly into the barrel with a terrible impact. Both barrel and cat were instantly overturned, sending flour and miscellaneous debris flying everywhere.

POOF! The explosive cloud of flour suddenly made the visibility in the kitchen very, very low. And as it slowly descended onto the stone floor, it mixed with the dairy cream that had already been spilled to form a slick and sticky mess.

To make matters worse, as the human cooks came running to see what all the fuss was about, suddenly the kitchen matron herself — an elderly (and portly) woman dressed in blue velvet — slipped and fell, knocking over the carefully set cheese table which she had been preparing for the evening meal. Cheddar, Gruyere, and aged Feldenspar Blue Cream went flying onto the floor. Some of it even found its way into the cooking fire, melting instantly and sending a choking column of smoke into the kitchen, as well as an acrid, rancid smell.

Teague winced as he watched each event occur in turn. More and more collateral damage kept stacking up, alongside more and more noise being generated, as people kept falling, the cat kept hissing and screeching, and so on — and all of that chaos stemming simply from one Mouseling choosing to save a rat traitor instead of allowing the cat to perform its natural predatory duty.

I should have known better, thought Teague to himself. He quickly retrieved his hand axe under the cover of the flour dust cloud that still lingered in the air and raced back up the spiral staircase.

That was certainly an adventure, Teague thought cheekily, *but one I would rather not repeat.*

Once he was safely out of the kitchen, Teague hid behind a crushed velvet curtain that had been dyed purple and considered his next move. As he collected his thoughts, he started to process the information that One Eye had spilled to him, under an...ahem... *certain* amount of duress. He began to consider all of the information he had been given and ponder its meaning, not only for the King, but for Mouseling Hollow as well. The pending invasion from The Southern Ocean, new human Speakers bent on aiding The Rat King himself, animals swearing fealty to the evil one who had been their archenemy for so many seasons...

Dark tidings, indeed!

But where to, now that One Eye had escaped? What was his next step?

Teague's mind instantly ran to his companions, whom he had last seen running down the spiral staircase of MouseKeep towards the dungeons, bent on trying to unravel the mystery of the King's disappearance and the impostor mice that had infiltrated the castle.

Wilding!

Thinking of his friends and comrades in arms, Teague wondered how they were faring down in the dungeons. Had they found the King? He **had** to get down there, posthaste. Who knew what traps awaited them — or worse, what deadly creatures! The usurpation of Castle Feldenspar and the disappearance of King Teegan had been no meager undertaking. This had all been well-planned, well-manned, well-funded, and well-thought out — not to mention, well-executed.

For a moment he feared his friends had walked into a trap, but then he calmed himself.

No, not Wilding, he reassured himself. *That wizard should be of greater concern for those who would wish **him** harm.*

Teague felt a brief surge of pride at this fleeting thought — but still, he didn't intend to leave his friends' survival to chance. He looked around the great room of the castle, wondering where the next closest access point would be within the walls of MouseKeep that would grant him access to the dungeons — and how quickly he could get there.

He sat rubbing his chin thoughtfully, trying to recall a viable route. It had been a long time since he had been back here — almost twenty seasons!

Suddenly, he heard a slight whisper.

'Psst!'

Teague gripped both battle axes firmly, now on high alert at the potential for further treachery. He cocked his furry ears forward and listened carefully. Silence.

Then he heard it again.

'Psst. Hey, Mister! Over here!'

Teague looked all around him — scanning, scanning — then finally, he saw it: a small, wet, black nose attached to a tiny snout, protruding from the very bottom of one of the hidden hinged doors which served as access points to MouseKeep. If he hadn't spotted the tiny snout poking out from under the false cobblestone exterior of the recessed wall, he would never have seen where the voice was coming from.

But Teague didn't remember there being a hinged door in that spot before. He racked his brain for any hint he might recall as to its purpose. Another trap, perhaps?

'Hurry Mister! Before the mean rats and fischers come back this way!'

Teague could tell this was the voice of a young Mouseling, perhaps seven or eight seasons old. What a youngling that age could possibly be doing on his own in MouseKeep, Teague had no idea. But, given his exposed and vulnerable position in the great room at that moment — not to mention the dangers that Teague had already faced that day — the innkeeper didn't need to be told twice.

He waited behind the curtain until a passing group of servants went hurrying by, bundled down with towels and linens. *Headed to the kitchens, I'd wager,* Teague thought to himself, *to clean up the giant mess I caused.* He grinned at the thought, then sprinted openly across the carpeted floor once the way was clear, crashing through the trapdoor on the opposite side of the hall.

Out of breath, he sat panting on the floor, twin axes still deftly gripped in his paws as he looked around the room. He was in a small niche which had been recessed into the wall, and there was a small stained-glass window of blue, purple and green panes at the top which had light coming through it. The stained-glass window displayed a picture of a wizard with a staff in his hand fighting a black rat with a crown on his head.

A depiction of the final battle of The First Rat King War, as told in the legends, Teague thought to himself. It was an exquisite etching, too. Done by a real artisan.

But for light to be coming in through this window, Teague knew that this had to be an outside wall — and yet MouseKeep, to his recollection, had originally been built adjacent to all *inside* walls. The only outside light which traditionally came into it was through the tiny cracks that served as artfully-designed 'windows,' gaining light from the **inside** of the castle, facing the main human areas of Castle Feldenspar.

'Wow! You run real fast, Mister!' the small mouse in front of him exclaimed.

'That's the fastest I've run in seasons,' Teague admitted, still panting slightly. 'Who might you be, my young friend? And what is this place?'

He looked around in wonderment at the stained-glass window.

'This is an entrance to MouseKeep's library and antiquities wing,' said the small mouse. 'And my name is Finn McGlynn. But the other mice in the castle just call me Squeak.'

'Library and antiquities wing? I don't remember MouseKeep having such a thing,' said Teague flatly.

'King Teegan commissioned it and ordered it built four seasons ago, Mister. That's how me and my family came here. My father is the venerated Mouseling architect and master builder Cathal McGlynn. We came from Old Town at the request of King Teegan, bringing a team of artisan Mousekin with us; stonemasons and skilled laborers and artists — the best that we could find! The King wanted to archive and preserve all of the relics that had been recovered from the fall of the Black Citadel, and he needed a Mouseling curator to take care of the Ratling and Mouseling-sized artifacts. That's where my mom, Dr. Mirade McGlynn, comes in. She is the curator of the library and helps store and organize the antiquities — that's what she calls them. She's really good at it! Spells, scrolls, magical and arcane artifacts, talismans, and all kinds of big fancy books are housed here, on this little-known side of the keep. It's kind of a big secret. They're stored in the central library and, depending on size, what we also call 'The Treasure Chamber.' My family and I have lived here ever since.'

'Where are your father and mother now?' asked Teague.

'The King sent them to Old Town a few weeks ago, to receive a big shipment of antiquities. My mom said that he claimed to have found something important and of great historical value to Mouselings, and the King wanted to make sure it was authentic before paying the large sum the dealer was asking. When they get back, won't they be glad to know that none of those bad mice or rats have come in here, too! I locked all the doors, but I don't think those rats know about this place anyway. I saw some of those creepy mice in the black and red outfits consulting a map of MouseKeep, but they only seemed to know where the military side of the keep was.'

Lady have mercy, where could those impostor mice have gotten a map of MouseKeep? thought Teague to himself. *There must be a traitor inside MouseKeep. I can't think of any other way they could have gotten their grubby paws on such a well-kept secret.*

Looking back at Squeak, Teague continued to question the small mouse.

'And your parents left you alone?' said Teague.

'No, Mister! The wife of one of MouseKeep's soldiers has been looking after me. But when the bad mice came, most of the MouseGuard disappeared. So I hid here. It's the safest place I know.'

'How do you know I am not one of the bad mice?' asked Teague.

'Well, a couple reasons. First, you are dressed like a Falconrider — a high ranking one! But your uniform looks kind of...old. No offense,

Mister. And secondly, I saw you fight that mean rat in the kitchen and cut his tail off. Like this!' The young mouse started making slashing motions in the air with a pretend axe in his paw, suddenly becoming animated. 'When I grow up I want to be a great warrior. Like you!'

'Ok, ok,' laughed Teague. 'Settle down now. With moves like that, I can see you'll make a fine Falconrider one day! Tell me though, does this place lead to the dungeon? And can we get there quickly?'

'Yes, of course! I can show you the way, Mister. I know this place like the back of my paw! But before we get there, we'll have to go through 'The Treasure Chamber.' There is something down there I think you would like to see!'

Teague followed the young mouse through a series of winding passages, all of which were lit by exquisitely crafted stained-glass windows, still shining brightly in the light of the setting sun. Though they were both scampering at a quick pace, he couldn't help but notice the detail on the glass windows, all of them expressing scenes of famous historical battles from Mouseling legend. He saw a depiction of the **Assault on Owlhaven,** a dragon sitting atop his perch at the peak of **The DaggerSpine Ridge, The Black Baron's Arena** portraying scenes of all manner of creatures fighting in front of thousands, and even a picture of a large fish swimming in The Mirrored Lake — presumably, the uncatchable fish known in Mouseling lore as **'The Silverback.'** The artistic design was excellent — unparalleled, really. Teague had never seen such magnificent displays of art.

But there was no time to think about that now.

Finally, they arrived at a larger entranceway that one of the spiraling hallways opened up into. Teague was hit with the musty scent of books — ancient, leather bound, worn tomes in many different languages — all Mouseling sized.

'Is this the library?' asked Teague.

'Yes,' said the diminutive mouse. 'Welcome to The Mouseling Library of Feldenspar Castle!'

He opened his small paws and gestured at the massive freestanding bookshelves which backed up to each other in the large, open space. Ladders on wheels stood like sentinels on each of the walls, which could slide around for easy access to the books recessed in the high, arching nooks that stretched skyward. The architectural design had hollowed out the ceiling in a way that reminded Teague vaguely of a cathedral, with books stacked so high that they reached almost out of Teague's sight (though he craned his neck upwards to see).

'This is amazing,' said Teague with incredulity. He knew in his mind that he needed to get to his friends, but he couldn't believe that such a grand and massive undertaking had been commissioned by the King, or that he had brought in such skilled artisans to complete the task.

'It is pretty impressive,' said Squeak. 'The King wanted to chronicle all Mouseling books that he thought were of importance, historical or otherwise. There are magical tomes here too — spell tomes, tomes of arcana, bestiaries, all kinds of stuff! And, as you probably know, this is not the only library for Mouseling texts. There are six more — one at each of the academies. But this one has very special books. Some of them are in languages which we don't even know how to read, written by Mouselings from eons past.'

'Unknown languages?' asked Teague.

'Yes. There is a race of ancient mice we know only as 'The Lost Ones.' My mom's really interested in them. They were Mousekin of extraordinary skill in mathematics, astronomy, archeology, architecture, even air travel. But one day, they disappeared. It is rumored they have a lost city somewhere east of The Far Collective, off the known maps. But for now, everything we know about them comes through the artifacts and books which have been recovered by treasure seekers, antiquities dealers, archaeologists from The Lyceum, or scholars like my mom. This is the only known collection of artifacts which either come from, or even predate, their existence.'

'I believe I have heard the legends of The Lost Ones. One of my good friends is a Professor...of sorts. There was a rumor that they had mastered air travel, and through that knowledge had been able to gain access to distant lands, even as far as across the oceans. I also heard that they were fond of things like riddles and puzzles. If I recall correctly, the rumors were they would make things like puzzle boxes or unsolvable knots, and create treasure maps to untold riches, some of which may have even been technological in nature. Some thought this was done to test the intellect of their young, which was considered superb to our own — by modern standards.'

'You have done your research, haven't you Mister! Not many mice know about The Lost Ones. Even fewer know about their interesting and fascinating tendencies. By the way, Mister, I didn't catch your name?'

'Teague. Robert Teague, at your service. I am the proprietor and innkeeper of The Sleeping Cat Inn, located on the shores of The Mirrored Lake, in a small hamlet known as Mouseling Hollow.'

'Yes! I know that inn — we passed through there when we came! But we came at night, through the village roads, and my parents said we couldn't stay, because of the King's orders for secrecy in our mission.'

Thinking back, Teague vaguely remembered a mystery in 'the Hollow' about four seasons previous, when a bunch of unknown wagon tracks had rutted the road headed north to the castle, but no one had reported seeing any traffic. Now, it seemed he had solved the mystery. But finding the King was a much bigger mystery at the moment, and he looked back at the young mouse.

'That's fine, lad, that's fine, but we need to get to the dungeons. As quickly as possible!'

'Ok!' said Squeak. 'But before we go, I want you to see something. It'll be really quick!'

Squeak grabbed Teague's paw and led him over to a glass display case. Inside the case was an ancient parchment in the old mouse language, which was indecipherable to Teague — but next to it was a broken slab of granite with legible characters in the modern Mouseling language showcasing the unintelligible characters next to it, acting as a translation tool.

'I told you that The Lost One's language had disappeared in the passage of time — but my mom has been working on translating it. She found this stone in a dig site out in The Hellion Sands, where they believe one of The Lost One's airships crashed. There was a lot of debris buried — technology too. As well as precious magical stones, artifacts, and this strange piece of granite!'

The young Mouseling pointed excitedly at the bottom of the glass case.

'She has worked on this for over two seasons. She thinks it is a riddle, of sorts, which leads to some kind of treasure. The puzzle acts as a treasure map!'

Teague, suddenly intrigued, looked at the glass case more carefully. 'A treasure map...to what?'

'I don't know! My mom says it talks about something called The Lost Treasure of Faronia.'

'Faronia? The legendary city of The Mouseling Old Ones? What was it they called it — 'The Golden City of All Knowledge?''

'Yes!' said the young mouse, excited that his new friend understood the magnitude of what he was talking about. 'And she translated a bit of it at the bottom, there. It's a clue on how to get there. A clue on how to find the Lost City and its treasure!'

Teague slipped his spectacles out of a pouch upon his belt, fixed them on his face, and peered down into the glass case. The day was becoming more and more unreal, that was for sure. Squinting, he struggled to view the writing that had been translated by Squeak's mother. While she was obviously an archaeological expert, her handwriting — if we are telling true tales — needed a bit of work. Practically scribbles, it was almost as indecipherable as the language of The Old Ones.

Almost.

Looking carefully, Teague began to read the translation out loud.

THE FIRST KEY

A Riddle of 7 Cities

In Ancient Days
There were once 7 Cities
Mouseling, Legendary
Ancient, wondrous,
Now lost to Time.
***Mousefather Time** likes sacred numbers.*
He loves games, too.
Did you know,
His favorite number is 7?
Oh, he likes fools, like me and you.
One day he was bored, so he made a choice
To play a game, with the next passerby's voice.
Along came a fool
Who tried and tried
To answer his Riddle.
My wife plays the fiddle.
Do you want to play?

It went like this:

7 into 7
Time then passed
Yet that became 7
Of 7, 1 multiplied thrice
That 1, of fifteen, now by thrice
And find one of those,

Now there you go.
Which one, though?
Two billion years ago
Covered in ice, so many seasons past
Though Melting thaws saw Mountains, at last.
Once I saw Mountains
Empires, too
They rose and fell
Rose again with a view
Great ice became Lakes
Watch out for those snakes
Trees have roots
Rectangles
Aren't square
Playing with numbers is fun, and fair
Let's count down, from ten to 1
Kind of — but fun!
9 7 6 5 6 2 3
Plus six less one, over one
Find one of these
The tiniest, if you please
Where water touches land
Then you'll know where you stand

Two more clues await
And the Mouseling Treasure you will take.

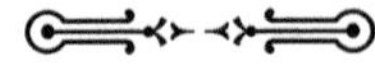

'What does it mean?' Teague asked the young mouse, in wonderment.

The mouse opened his paws wide and started laughing. 'I have absolutely no idea! Isn't that great?'

Teague suddenly became very focused. He had allowed himself to be distracted from the life and death task at hand, but he could not afford to tarry any longer. He meant to rejoin his friends in the dungeons as quickly as possible.

He looked down at Squeak and grasped the young mouse's paws gently in his own.

'Squeak, listen to me — my friends' lives may depend on me getting to the dungeon. The King is missing — kidnapped, I think — and if we don't find him, and fast, who knows what manner of Ratling reinforcements could be on their way to Castle Feldenspar. We must act quickly. Can you take me to the dungeons as fast as possible? When all of this is over, you, me, and my children — who are far cleverer than an old tavernkeep like myself — can all come back here and discuss this amazing mystery you've shared with me.'

The young mouse nodded, then suddenly got very somber. 'Mister Teague, do you think my parents are ok?'

Teague smiled with the wistful, yet understanding glance of a wizened parent.

'Yes, my young friend, I am sure they are fine. And I will keep you safe, too — you have my promise. You can stay with me at Mouseling Hollow until all this blows over, if you like. But for now, we need to get to the lower levels of the castle *immediately.*'

Squeak nodded once more, then squared his tiny shoulders. Teague could see that he didn't need to tell the young mouse twice.

'I will get us there in two shakes of a squirrel's tail — if you can keep up with me!' said Squeak. 'I know a secret passage that runs along the dungeon walls from here. You can even see the bad mice, if they are in there, and still stay safe.'

'Yes, Squeak, that sounds perfect! I knew I could count on a smart and valiant young mouse like yourself!' Teague clapped his new guide on the shoulder. 'I can't wait for you to meet my friends — I suspect one of them will be greatly interested in this riddle you've shown me. But first, we have to find them and make sure they are safe. Then, if She is willing — and I pray that She is...we will find King Teegan.'

With that, the two mice, one young, one older, slipped between the bookshelves and exited the library through another hidden, false door that Squeak opened. In the silence they left behind, the sound of their footsteps faded quickly as they ran down a hollowed-out corridor, searching with expedience for the party Teague so desperately needed to find.

On the Mouseling Gambling Game of 'Flops':

'It's quite a simple game, really,' said the pit boss to the Mouseling who had come to test his fortune at Mousebrook's gaming tables. 'You have different suits, so to speak — Rats, Felines — or 'Cats,' as they are more commonly called — Mouselings, and Serpents. Each of these cards carries a rank as well — 9th, tenth, Knave, Queen, King, and Castle. And, of course, each also has a color — Rats are, of course, red; Felines are green; Mouselings are purple, to represent royalty, and Serpents, as yellow as the desert they hail from. There are also two Fool cards, for a total of 26 cards per deck — sometimes more, depending on the gambling house you are visiting. You get dealt one 'hole' card, which you can use to help make the best paw possible. Of course, the combinations are endless — or are they? And don't forget the ranks — 9th is the lowest, then tenth, Knave, Queen, King, and Castle, of course.

You select a bet amount and place your wager down before the first three cards are dealt. You must bet on the first three cards' outcome — but if you are feeling lucky, you can invest in 'Providence Bets' as well, which are bets on how the cards will fall before they come out. Fortunes have been made and lost at this very table, my son — perhaps you are the next lucky winner!'

— Taken from **Stormsnout's Guide to Gambling** —
A Strategy Guide

Chapter 17

A BATTLE OF WITS

It had been a slog, that was certain, advancing through the dungeon in search of King Teegan.

Though Wilding hadn't had much time to think about it, the fleeting thoughts that kept crossing his mind centered mostly on how well planned the infiltration of Castle Feldenspar had been. Of course, he had only assembled a few pieces of the greater puzzle, as of yet. But something told him that a very slick and intuitive plan must have been implemented — not just to capture Commander Storm and the King, but to do so without raising suspicion, so that the rest of the castle thought that they had merely gone away on a hunt.

In addition, the true MouseGuard remained missing, which added another layer of deception and complexity to the plot. Removing dozens of highly trained mice without raising the alarm...and to where? What about the residents of the castle who acted in service roles — the kitchen staff, the chambermaids, and so on — not a single one of them had been put on alert by the nefarious happenings? Or had the loyal servants all been removed from this Root and Field board as well, like Cullen and The Bird?

Whatever had happened in the castle, it had been executed perfectly. *And that,* thought Wilding, *is an ominous sign of things to come.*

As the party progressed down the hall, they continued to encounter traps. The notorious 'one step' that Wilding had disarmed mere seconds before Storm would have unsuspectingly walked into it had reared its ugly head six more times down the hallway since — always at random intervals. This caused great tumult and anxiety among the humans in the group — though Wilding sat calmly on Storm's shoulder the whole time, coaching him through each area where he suspected a trap was most likely to have been laid and disarming it successfully.

But the traps were only the beginning of their troubles.

Broken glass and shards of ceramic had been strewn about the floor, which was exceedingly problematic because the humans had all been stripped of their footwear. This struck Wilding as not only well thought out, but it suggested to him — with a not-inconsiderable degree of strangeness — that the humans who had infiltrated the castle may have decided that they would have no need to return back down the dungeon hallways. To his mind, it was a sobering indication that perhaps the captors had decided to leave the prisoners to die of sickness and starvation. Bird and Cullen had said as much when they were rescued, and certainly the traps lain were not so easily disarmed, no matter which direction one came upon them from.

But to what end? mused Wilding.

When the party first encountered glass on the floor, after the first 'one step' trap had been disarmed, the Mouselings hadn't even noticed it as they'd crept along the stone wall. It was only when Bird cried out suddenly in pain, hopping and grabbing at his foot, that Storm shined his torch light down close to the floor — and saw, to his dismay, the dazzling reflections of the broken shards all glittering in the light.

'So what now, Gen...err, Wilding?' Storm asked. 'Anyone have a broom handy?'

'Hearthseeker?' Wilding called down to his friend. He had marked that big pack on the bard's back, as well as the utility pouch which had produced caltrops back in the battle at The King's Pedestal. Wilding had the gut sense that if anyone had a quick answer to this latest obstacle, it would be Hearthseeker.

'At your service, milord!' said Hearthseeker, ever cheerful. He reached into his pack and pulled out a length of rope. Running up to the Stranger, he handed the thief one end, and with the other end still held in his paw, scampered ahead, stretching the rope tightly while laying it flush to the stone floor. Gently, but deliberately, he and the Stranger dragged the rope over towards the center of the hallway, clearing a small but hazard-free path upon the left wall — just enough for the humans to pass by without injury.

'Hearthseeker, I do believe you missed your calling as a Tinker Rogue!' said Wilding with a grin. He was referring to a legendary class of Mouseling thieves who used homemade mechanical constructs, weapons, and ingenuity to power all of their...less noble...pursuits.

'Thank you, my good Professor!' said the rascally Hearthseeker. 'But how do you know I wasn't one?'

Hearthseeker shot Wilding a saucy wink. Then, scampering ahead, he and the Stranger repeated the process until at last the hallway was cleared to the stone stairway where the two prisoners that Cullen and The Bird had sighted had, presumably, been taken.

Cautiously they approached the annex, which branched off in all four directions. Lighting the wall sconces with his torch, Storm turned towards Wilding and said, 'What is the plan, Sir Mouse?'

Wilding thought for a moment, his eyes locked straight ahead as he scrutinized the hallway.

'Commander, if I remember correctly, the animal holding cells are straight ahead, is that right?'

'Well, General, um...I mean, Wilding. Yes, as I recall, they are.'

'Give me those tiny keys on the keychain, if you would be so kind.'

Storm produced the keychain that had been taken from the Jailer and detached the smallest set of keys.

'Hearthseeker!' Wilding called. 'You and the Stranger go ahead and see what you can find. If anything moves that isn't in a cell, attack it!'

'Aye, sir!' said the bard. As Storm knelt down, he nimbly jumped into Storm's hand, grabbed the keys, and scurried off with the Stranger in tow behind him.

'I like that mouse,' said Storm. 'He's a cheerful one!'

'Me too,' said the wizard. 'Now, let us go see who earned the honor of being placed into the lowest cell, behind all of these traps and diversions. Proceed carefully.'

With that, Storm, The Bird, and Cullen, with Wilding riding on Storm's shoulder, headed down the stairway to the left, to see if they could solve the mystery of the King's disappearance.

Hearthseeker and the Stranger made good time as they headed straight up the passageway. Without Storm's torch to add radiance to the deep blackness, the two mice relied not only on their sight, but on their noses and whiskers to help compensate for the lack of light as they maneuvered nimbly down the hall.

As they progressed, they spoke in quiet whispers.

'Have courage, Stranger! We will find your family yet — and with Her Grace, the MouseGuard as well!'

'Thank you, Hearthseeker. While I never expected this day to go the way it has — if we're telling true tales, I haven't had an adventure like this in quite some time!'

'Nor have I, my friend. Nor have I. Fortunately, we haven't seen any traps this way, which is a relief. Now, with any luck these keys will work in these cell doors and we can hopefully find some Mousekin...'

But at that moment, Ainsley Hearthseeker was interrupted by a sound that made both him and the Stranger freeze in terror.

A rattle.

They both stood there, frozen in fear. Hearthseeker, who had felt nearly paralyzed in fright for a moment, thought to himself, *Did I actually hear that?*

Then he heard it again.

Another rattle. This time, accompanied by a hiss.

The two Mouselings looked at each other in shared terror, then back down the hallway. They *needed* to free whatever was in those animal cages.

But the bard knew what stood in their way.

It was a crested Tarbog rattlesnake.

And a crested Tarbog rattlesnake was not just any snake.

It was the deadliest snake to Mouselings in all of The Western Collective. Its eyes could hypnotize an unwary mouse, and its venom was so potent that a single bite was enough to kill a Mouseling almost instantly.

Oh, and the crested Tarbog rattlesnake was also very intelligent. So intelligent that over the eons, they had learned to speak Mouseling.

Hearthseeker knew now why there were no traps here in this passageway. This *was* the trap — and it must have been brought, intentionally and at great expense, from The Tarbogs, presumably as part of the conspiracy to usurp Castle Feldenspar and its King.

Perhaps that was where the MouseGuard went — into the snake's stomach? The bard trembled at the thought. His terror grew when he heard a voice — not so distant from where he now stood — call out to him.

'Come to play, my little Moussselingsss?' spat the creature, somewhere in the darkness. The snake spoke the 's' at the beginning and end of 'Mouslings' with an extended hiss, making the sound ugly — and even more ominous.

'Come to play and find your friends? Goooood. Oh, I am so hungry. And bored, terribly booorrreedd! We shall play a game, yesss, shan't we! A fun, fun game! A game...of cat and mouse! Only snake and moussse, yes, yesss, ssssnake and mouse!'

The snake hissed an unhinged and maniacal laugh.

'Don't run now my prettiesss, yesss! I can sssslither faster than you can run, I promissse! So now, we will play our game. After all, I can't eat the mice in those cages, and I have been in thisss damp room for dayssss! Napping, napping, yessssss! And now I am hungry! Yesss, hungry!'

Hearthseeker was relieved to hear that there were mice in cages somewhere nearby — presumably, live mice. The MouseGuard, maybe? But living long enough to get to the dungeon cells was going to prove tricky indeed.

So Hearthseeker mustered up all his courage.

'Back off, snake. I, Ainsley Hearthseeker, am well-known across Old Town as the **Serpent's Scourge.** I have killed many of your kin, and will not hesitate to kill you where you stand. Perhaps you have heard of my magical sword, **Rattlemourne.**'

He drew his sword out. In the silence of the passageway, it made a menacing **shrike** sound of metal running across metal as his paw drew the sword from its scabbard.

Yet the Tarbog rattler seemed unimpressed.

'Kill me, my pretty? Oh, my pretty, tasty Mouseling, that isss no way to greet your hossst. I have never heard of a Moussseling being a 'sssnake ssslayer.' No! I think you tell storiesss to ssscare me, but it is YOU who ssseems to be ssscared, yes! But come now, let's play a game. A little fun before dinner, yes? Yesssss!'

The Stranger whispered to Hearthseeker, 'What kind of game do you suppose the serpent is talking about?'

'I don't know,' replied the bard, 'but I doubt we can 'win' — and even if we do, I suspect we may end up as dinner anyway.'

He pointed the tip of his sword towards the darkness in which the snake was hiding.

'Tell me of this game, snake. I would prefer not to kill you, for my sword arm has grown weary from serpent slaying. But if I must, I will not hesitate to do so.'

The rattle sound started up again, this time, more intensely.

'Yesss, yesss! Joyousss! We will play a game. And I found a treasure! Yesss, yesss, here in this place, I found a treasssure! If you win, you keep the treasure! A chessst with gold and paper!

Snakesss...have no need of these things. And if I win, you ssstay for dinner. Yessss, MY dinner!'

The snake laughed maniacally again, its rattle shaking with an almost deafening sound.

'How do we know we can trust you?' asked Ainsley.

'You don't! That'sss...what makesss it SUCH fun! But I WANT to play...I've been sssooo bored! And YOU...you prettiesss want to play, yesss...play for the treasssure?'

'Very well, snake. For the treasure then — it's been a while since I've won myself a goodly treasure. What is this game?'

'Firssst, it isss not polite for pretty Mouseling to call me sssnake. Call me...Ravenscale. I was the King of the Tarbogs! Then they took me. Yesss! Those humansss. Took me and put me in a bag. Dirty bagsss! And now, I end up here, with no food! No friendsss! And Mouselings ssso close, yet so far, through wooden doorsss!'

He hissed in anger.

'But yesss, the game. Let'sss play! How about a game of riddlesss! The first one who cannot answer the riddle losesss the game! Ravenscale LOVESSS riddles!'

The two mice looked each other, speechless. But Hearthseeker, clever to the last, presented a different solution.

'Ravenscale, I have seen that done too many times, for too long. When I am not killing large snakes — with my magic sword, of course — I go across the land and sing songs in taverns full of Mouselings for coin. And everywhere I go, I see them, always trying to outwit each other with riddles. It's a tired mechanism, a worn-out cliché, and for the cleverest of creatures it has become so...banal. Let's play a game more worthy of the intellect of the King of the Tarbogs.'

The snake suddenly ceased his quiet rattling. When he spoke, he sounded intrigued.

'Yesss! A more bigger challenge! For my ssssooo keen mind! What isss this game you propose, moussse?'

Hearthseeker looked up towards the stone ceiling, deep in thought, then answered.

'We will make a wager — a wager to see who is the smartest at guessing where the treasure is. Do you know what a wager is?'

'Yessss! A wager — where you give sssomething, and I give sssomething! And the winner takesss...all. Yes! Oh, I LOVE the mousy's idea! Then, when I win, I can play with more treasuresss for other mousiesss! Yesss! Ravenscale loves his wagers and bets! Betsss... for treasures! And dinner, yesss!'

Hearthseeker nodded. 'Yes, you get it. I'd expect nothing less from the King of the Tarbogs. I will offer up a wager, and you will offer up a wager. In your case, this treasure you speak of will be your wager. And I will wager this...'

The bard took the golden, polished lute off his back and held it forward towards the still-unseen snake, hidden in the dark recesses of the hallway.

'No, Ainsley!' said the Stranger. 'Your lute!'

'It is wood well-seasoned, Ravenscale,' said Hearthseeker. 'A noble gift, one which will give you many great wagers to come, should you win it.'

'Yesss...I accept your wager. But what are the ssstakes? Oh, that rhymes with snakesss...yes, ssstakes and sssnakes!'

'The stakes are...if we win, we get the treasure and go free. If you win, you keep your treasure and my lute, and you may eat us for dinner. But you cannot cheat! That is the condition of the game.'

'I accept,' said the snake with an evil hiss. 'But what isss thisss game?'

Hearthseeker knew he didn't have much time. 'The game is called...well, let me ask you this first — how many cells are there next to each other, holding mice from the castle?'

'There are four cellsss, and each one holdsss four mice.'

'Just so!' said the bard. 'And this game happens to be called Four Doors. But in order to play, we will have to empty the cells first. I have the key to open them. If you let the mice inside go, I will have my companion here hide your treasure in one cell, and my lute in another cell. We will take turns guessing which cell contains which treasure. If you can guess the right cell with the right treasure in it before I do, you win. And, as an added gesture of goodwill, I will place my sword in the same cell as my lute, so I cannot wield it against you should you win the game. If you guess first, and correctly, you win. If I guess first, and correctly, I win. If I win, we take the treasure, my lute and sword, and will leave peacefully. If you win, you will strike and kill us, and dinner shall be 'on us,' so to speak. What say you?'

'What if you prettiesss...lie...about the treasssure in the cell? Yes, you Mouselingssss are ssso clever, known to deceive, yesss, deceive!'

Hearthseeker replied, 'I've a good mind to take offense at that, you know! But to ensure that our contest remains a square one, you may go into the cell and verify if there is something in there, or nothing — with your own eyes, you can verify. This mouse standing next to me will place the treasures in the corner of two cells, and the other two will remain empty. And, to make it even more fair, you and I will both be blindfolded. Stranger, take off your tunic.'

The thief mouse started to take off his cloak, and Hearthseeker stripped his off also, preparing to blindfold himself. Then, he stopped abruptly.

'But remember, in order for us to play this game, the cells must be empty. I am sure the mice inside have mange and are covered in lice. There is no doubt they have been in here for days, malnourished, growing scrawnier and scrawnier — unlike myself and my companion, who supped this very morning on a huge breakfast of rich, golden eggs, a decadent butter sauce, and bacon to boot! That, of course, makes us a far tastier meal for you than those wretched and pathetic... vermin.'

'Hmmmm,' said Ravenscale, thinking on what the bard had said. 'Yesss, you are right. Thossse mice are ssscrawny and sssmell bad anyway. Not fresh, yes! NOT FRESH! You can let them out.'

'On your honor, as the King of the Tarbogs, do you swear not to eat them?'

'I...sssswear,' said the snake.

Silently, and with haste, Ainsley handed the jail keys to the Stranger, then pointed to the first cell.

'Get them out of there, quickly! I can't wait to play the game — I haven't had such a lively wager in ages!' The Stranger thought the bard actually sounded like he wanted to play this game — which was pure suicide, if you asked him for his thoughts on the matter.

'And I asss well!' said Ravenscale. 'I will play the game, and have dinner, sssoon! Sssooon!'

The Stranger didn't need to be told twice. He rushed to the cell doors, fumbling with the key to unlock them, as the mice inside pressed up against the iron gated cell window at the top of the door.

There were urgent whispers of 'Get us out of here' and 'Hurry, hurry!' — and then, the Stranger heard something that shook him to his bones.

'Daddy?' said a small voice as he struggled with the keys.

'Son?!' he whispered through the first cell door as he continued working on the lock. 'Oh my...may She be praised...hush now, all of you! Son, is your mother with you?'

'Yes, dear, I am here,' said a weak voice from behind the door.

He continued to work the lock on the first door until he finally heard the click of the tumbler.

'Thank you, thank you!' started the mice, as they came tumbling out of the now-opened door. His wife threw her paws around him. He could tell, even in the darkness, that she had grown thin and weak through her ordeal.

He broke off their embrace far sooner than he wished to so that he could continue with the business at hand.

'Hush now, all of you!' said the Stranger. 'There's no time for celebration now — the danger has not yet passed. All of you get to the Jailer's Nook, and posthaste! Watch out for the glass in the hallway back that way — be sure you stick to the center of the passageway.'

He felt a tugging on his pantleg. 'Daddy, I don't want to leave you! I don't want the mean snake to eat you for dinner!'

His heart, which had been stoic and unmoved the past few days, now sank at the thought of reuniting with his family, only to risk never seeing his wife and son again mere moments later. But still, he persevered.

He trusted the bard, and knew he had a plan. That, in itself, was something.

'Courage now, son! Go now, with your mother!' He practically shoved him into his mother's paws, praying to the Lady that they would get to safety.

Suddenly, the snake interrupted, hissing.

'What are all thessse...whissspers? Mouslings, plotting to cheat at the game? Yesss, CHEATERSSSS!'

The rattle became deafening and intense.

Stammering with fear, the Stranger responded quickly.

'N-n-n-no, no milord, these mice have been without food or water for days, and they are bewildered and confused. I was merely trying to send them away in the right direction, so they won't be in our way and we can play the game.'

'Yesss, a good mousy who keepsss his word. Yesss! They are sssick, and sssmells bad! I need a...fresssh dinner!' The rattler seemed satisfied with the explanation — for now.

The Stranger continued to unlock the remaining cell doors as quickly as possible, though it seemed to take forever. Finally, the sixteen mice from MouseKeep, including the Stranger's wife and son, had all been freed and began to make their way down the hall to safety. Some had to help carry others suffering from wounds and sickness, but after a moment, the sounds of their footpads echoing down the hall faded.

Hearthseeker sensed the need to keep the game's momentum going. 'Stranger, open all of those cell doors — nice and wide, so Ravenscale can see they are empty.'

The Stranger opened all four of the doors, their aged and rusted hinges creaking with use.

'Now Ravenscale, as you can see, the cells are clearly empty. You agree there are four empty cells, do you not? I have shown you my wager. Where is your wager?'

'Hmmm...' said the snake, thinking for a bit. Then he slithered away, farther down the hall.

In a moment, Hearthseeker could hear a scuffing sound, which was getting nearer. Peering down the murky hallway, he could just make out the giant outline of the snake as Ravenscale made his return. Suddenly, the snake came closer, closer than it had ever been, its bull-headed snout pushing a Mouseling-sized wooden chest — about as tall as the bard's waist — which was inlaid with golden clasps and binding. It looked luxurious to the bard's eyes — and very valuable.

'Here isss my wager,' said Ravenscale.

'Very good,' the bard said. 'And now, we play. But first, you must cover your eyes, and I will cover my eyes. Only when we have both done so will my companion place the treasures, each in its own cell, leaving the other two cells empty. Then, he will shut all four doors, and only afterwards may the two of us open our eyes. Do you agree, and give your word?'

'Yesss! I will keep my word, asss the King of Snakesss!'

Then, the snake suddenly shot forward, and came so close to Hearthseeker's muzzle that they were nearly touching noses.

'But mousey keepsss hissss word asss well...or else the game isss off.' The bard knew that Ravenscale meant business.

In the ultra-dim light of the passageway, Hearthseeker could now see his adversary — and he was massive, at least three feet long, and with a great girth. *Fattened up on a healthy diet of unwary Mouselings, no doubt,* Hearthseeker thought warily. His black scales were outlined in grey trim, and his green-yellow eyes eyed the Mouseling hungrily through their vertical slits, eager to enjoy his game of 'snake and mouse' — for a bit longer, anyways. His fangs protruded sharply and were almost as long as Hearthseeker's sword. They hung menacingly, glistening with venom. The huge snake, coiled up to his full height, towered over the mouse.

But still, the mouse held steadfast.

'Done,' he said jauntily.

Then, he threw the Stranger's cloak over the snake's eyes, and covered his own eyes with his cloak as well.

'Presss against thisss wall,' said the snake, indicating the wall opposite of the cell doors. 'And I will presss my nossse into your back, so I know neither of usss can sssee. That makesss it...fair, yess?'

'Very much so.' Hearthseeker knew his options were limited — but the fact that he was still alive and hadn't yet found his way into the crested Tarbog's belly was at least somewhat promising. He pressed himself against the wall willingly, and soon felt the sickening press of the snake's snout — and teeth — against his back. The snake leaned its foul mouth in to put pressure on the bard's back, but not too much — just enough to keep him in place.

'Mouseey, you sssmell gooood!' said Ravenscale. 'Sssoft fur, and squissshy insides, yesss! Sssoon I win the game and you become my dinner, yesss?!'

'Focus on the game, my good snake, and we will see who wins this battle of wits! Stranger, go and hide the treasures.'

The two adversaries stayed pressed against the wall, listening for clues as the Stranger shuffled the chest into one cell, and then walked with the lute into another cell. The echoes of his footsteps became confusing as they rang percussively across the chamber — near, then far, near, far. After a few moments, he closed all four doors and locked them.

Removing the cloaks from around both his eyes and the snake's, the bard looked at his coiled adversary and smiled.

'And now the game begins!' said Ainsley. 'Only the Stranger knows for sure where the treasures lie, and he holds the key. Let's see if you truly are King of the Snakes, with the great intellect to match the title. Do you wish to go first, or would you rather I go first?'

'I ssshaall go firssst, for I am the King! I will win thissss game, and win thisss treasssure — and then, win my reward of a tasssty mousssey dinner! Yes, sssnake and mouse game isss fun, yesss!'

His tail began to rattle again with excitement.

'Ok Ravenscale, you're up then. It's your turn to pick. Which treasure is behind which door?'

The snake eyed all four of the doors, and sniffed the air carefully. His tongue slid out of his mouth and flicked about, as if to feel the air's currents.

'Mousey hid the treasssure weell, yes! I cannot sssmell! A good game, yess!'

'Go on and choose now,' said Hearthseeker.

'I choossse...cccell number...three.'

'And, what treasure do you think is in there?'

'I think moussey's songbox and magic sssword are in there! Yesss, I am cccertain of it!!'

'I hope you are wrong, master snake, or else I shall swiftly become your dinner. Are you sure? Are you absolutely sure? I will let you change your decision, if you wish to.'

'Moussey now try to confussse me? Yesss, CONFUSE! Cchange my chchcoicesss...perhaps door number four then? Or...NO!'

He interrupted himself, clearly confused as he tried to think through his choices.

'Mousssey knows it is behind door number three and doesn't want me to win the game! Yesss, door number three! I choossse door number three!'

The Stranger slowly trudged over to the third cell door, head down as though a weighty sadness had swept over him. Slowly, he approached cell number three, and even more slowly, he unlocked the door, opening it wide.

He shook his head and looked at the bard.

Ainsley looked back at the Stranger. 'Tell us, thief. On my life, is it door number three with my sword and lute in it? If it is, I'll lay down, right here and now, and become this snake's...'

Ravenscale interrupted him angrily.

'NOOOO moussey! You try to deccceive the King of Snakes, yesss. You want your friend to lie for you, to ssssave your...ssskin. He even looksss sssad, because he knows Ravenscale won, yesss? I will sssee for myssself!'

The snake slithered forward in eagerness and dove into the cell, to see if he had been right.

But once he was inside the cell, searching the corners for his treasure, Ainsley shouted 'NOW, STRANGER!'

And with that, the Stranger slammed the cell door as hard as he could and relocked it.

Realizing he had been tricked, Ravenscale flew into a rage.

'NOOOOOO! Mousssies trap me and deccceive me...I will kill you mousies! Ravenscale ssswearsss! Kill, yes, KILL!'

The snake reared back and repeatedly struck at the door with its fangs bared. The hollow clang of his venomous teeth striking the narrow metal bars reverberated through the cell chamber, echoing down the empty hall. His screeches soon turned to screams of 'Let me out!' — but Hearthseeker only peered into the cell door window, where he saw the snake's eerie eyeball looking back, staring at him with very sinister intent.

Hearthseeker said calmly:

'Be thankful, snake, that I did not kill you on sight. I will inform the King that you are here, and arrange to have you released once our work here is done. I will not leave you to die, the way you would have killed me and my companion.'

But Ravenscale was in no mood for compassion or professional courtesy.

'You better leave me in thisss...thissss...cage, mousssey! Becaussse if I get out, I will find you, and then I will KILL YOU. No matter where you go, Ravenscale will kill mousssey, and make you my sssupper!'

'I'll look forward to you trying, Ravenscale. If you really want to make a spectacle of it, we can meet in The Arena of The Black Baron and settle our differences in front of thousands of other creatures. I'll give you the chance to taste Rattlemourne's blade, if you insist upon it. Think about *that* for a while. Perhaps if you kill me, you can go back to being King of the Tarbogs. But today, well — today was just not your day.'

'Yesss!!! I will kill the mousssey in The Arena! For aaalll to ssseee!'

While the snake was mesmerized by the sweet thought of revenge, the bard donned his cloak and headed over to the Stranger, returning his cloak to him as well.

'This smells like nasty snake now,' the Stranger said after a quick sniff.

'Better than having to smell the insides of his belly, if you get my meaning. Now, PLEASE tell me that my lute and sword are not in cell number three.'

'Of course not!' smiled the Stranger. 'The truth is, it was impossible for him to win your little game.'

'How so?' asked the bard.

'Because, when both your eyes were closed, I hid both treasures behind a rock near door number four, down the hall and out of sight. But I scuffled back and forth through the cells a few times to make it convincing.' The Stranger gave Hearthseeker a jaunty wink. 'I am still a member of the Thief's Guild, you know. Learning how to cheat at games of chance is a basic prerequisite to becoming a journeyman thief!'

'You sneaky rogue!' said the bard, giving the Stranger a tight hug. 'When you trudged over so sadly towards that third cell, I was sure I was done for. Now, let's retrieve our belongings and get out of here. I wonder what could be in that chest? I suppose we will have to wait until we get back to Mouseling Hollow to find out.'

The two companions headed over towards where the Stranger had hidden Ainsley's possessions. Hearthseeker grabbed his sword and lute, and then they each grabbed a handle on either side of the chest. Then, they started back down the hall to rejoin their companions.

As they proceeded down the corridor, the Stranger asked the bard:

'Do they really call you **The Serpent's Scourge?** And is your sword truly a magical named blade called **Rattlemourne?** I didn't suspect I was in the presence of a true hero!'

'Nah,' Hearthseeker answered. 'I just made all that stuff up to try to bluff the snake and buy us some time.'

There was a momentary silence between them as they both considered what they had just accomplished — and then the two mice burst out into laughter. Their laughter echoed as they made their way back down the hall — with a golden treasure chest in their paws, a near death experience under their belts, and a new and valuable friendship found between them.

'I'll hit you so hard, when you wake up,
*your clothes will be back **IN** style...'*

— MOUSELING HOLLOW BAR INSULT INDICATING
THAT THE MOUSELING IN QUESTION IS A POOR DRESSER.

Chapter 18

RESCUING THE LION

In the forlorn darkness of his prison cell, King Teegan sat in silence, his hands bound above his head. The dampness of the wall had seeped through his clothing, giving him quite the chill. More disturbingly, he was starting to develop a nasty cough from the deplorable conditions in the dungeon — conditions that had not been helped by the fact that he had not had food or water in two days. His thoughts had started to become incoherent as he grew weaker.

And of the clear thoughts he could muster, most centered on the severe gravity of the predicament that he, and his kingdom, had landed in.

His captors had shackled him to the walls. His wife, while unshackled, had been stunned and left unconscious by such a savage blow to her head that she hadn't awoken since their captors had left them there. He knew that his Queen's head injury was far beyond a mere concussion, and that she needed a healer — quickly. But all the King could do was watch her laying on the floor of her cell, moaning in pain as she drifted in and out of semi-consciousness, unable to lift so much as a finger to help her. In all his years, Teegan had never felt more inept, more impotent, more helpless, than he did in the few days that had just passed.

And in his imprisonment, he had had nothing but time to think.

Foremost on his mind was the now utterly precarious situation his castle had fallen into: usurped by intruders who had not only subjugated or replaced the human garrison of his castle, but who had been instrumental in the plotting and downfall of MouseKeep as well. Before their captors had extinguished the dungeon torches, he had seen his beloved mice in captivity, being marched down the hallway towards the animal cages — Finnegan Willowtail, the Falcon Riders' FlightMaster at Arms among them — at the paws of rats, fischers, and strange mice. Teegan didn't know where those mice had come from, but he was certain they were not from his lands. After seeing this sad parade, he heard the slamming of cell doors, the spreading of the broken glass and pottery shards along the dungeon's corridors — and his jailer's boastful chatter about 'no person or animal getting out of this dungeon alive.'

After the jailer's echoing footsteps faded down the hall, he heard... nothing — nothing save an occasional moan from his beautiful queen, who, like him, had been knocked out from behind and dragged to this cell unceremoniously.

The cell, where, presumably, he would die.

Was there any hope at all remaining to him? All seemed lost. The Western Lands had known naught but peace for so long, and now this?

Was it his own fault? Had he failed as ruler? Had he become complacent?

The answer, he knew, could be nothing other than a resounding 'yes.' He and his staff, human and Mousekin alike, had all become complacent. And if he ever got out of this prison cell, that was all going to change, ***posthaste***.

But for now, all he could do was sit, and think — and even that was becoming difficult, as increasingly all he could think about was the burning thirst that consumed him.

As he sat there immobilized in the demoralizing blackness, his mind wandered, crossing over the span of his life. He thought fondly, with great nostalgia, of the good days of his life: his wedding day, the day his daughter Imogen had been born, and especially, the day he had defeated The Rat King in the deserts of The Hellion Sands. There had been feasts, festivals, jousts, music, fanfare — all of the perks of being a King. Fantastic meals every day. Soft feather beds to sleep upon. Days of sailing on The Mirrored Lake with his father, who was King before him, and the lessons he had been taught by that proud yet stern man to prepare him to rule one day. Commander Storm and his staff, loyal to the end — all dead now, he could only presume. His beloved Mouselings: those tiny, furry mice who were so smart they could talk to humans, and who had great athletic and magical talents — not to mention their keen and insightful intellect. His Falcon Riders, who had saved the day at The Rat King's Citadel.

Of course, there had been bad days too, but now wasn't the time to dwell on them.

He struggled in vain against the chains which bound him, trying as hard as he could to pull them free from their wall mountings, but they held fast. His arms were weak and numb from hanging above his head for two days, and he sagged against the wall, trying to muster the strength to try again. He knew in his heart that there was no hope of escape — but, still intransigent, he refused to believe it.

Resting his now crownless head against the wall, as he had done so many times previously in the past few days, he shut his eyes and squeezed them tightly.

Think, he urged himself. *Think of a way to escape!*

But no useful thoughts came to the desperate King, there in the darkness. His stoicism and defiance were met with silence as time passed. Weak with fatigue and nausea, The Lionsmane, King of Feldenspar Castle, nodded off fitfully and dreamed of a way out of this mess.

He awakened a short time later, however, to the sound of scuffling, muffled voices, and scratching paws. Opening his eyes, he saw some light shining through the cell window.

Was he asleep? *Yes, I must be...it has been dark for two days,* he thought. Listening intently, he heard something now scampering around his cell. Some kind of animal. He looked down, and saw...a rat? Yes, a tiny rat, in purple robes, holding a wooden battle staff. A battle rat! *What a delightful delusion*, thought the King, and soon burst out laughing. He knew he must be dreaming.

Battle rat, that rhymes! he thought, and burst into delirious laughter again.

The rat walked purposefully towards the King. He watched it hop up on his leg, and then, as if in slow motion, he felt the rat poking his staff into his ribs.

'Majesty?' said the rat.

The King kept on laughing, until he felt another poke in his ribs — this time much harder.

'Ouch!' said the King. 'Don't you know who you are poking, Mister Rat?'

The rat looked at him once more and they locked eyes. Then he scurried off towards the door, and slid under it.

'Please, don't go — forgive me, Sir Rat. I need all the friends I can get right now! Come back! COME BACK!'

Not even the vermin want to be near me, he thought forlornly. *Not even the rats!*

But then, he heard, **click clackety clack,** the sound of a key operating in the tumblers of the door. With one loud and final **thunk**, the bolt was released and the cell door pushed open, allowing light from a torch sconce to wash over his face, blinding him.

The King was forced to squint so tightly that he could not see who stood in front of him.

'My liege!' Commander Storm shouted. Upon seeing his King, he rushed quickly to his side and started unlocking the manacles that held the King fast.

'Storm! I just saw a rat!' The King looked at his most steadfast knight, and noticed without emotion that the 'rat' was now sitting on his Knight Commander's shoulder.

With a nimble skill, Storm finished unlocking the manacles which bound the King's wrists, and his arms fell back into his lap like loose noodles.

'Sire, the feeling in your arms and hands will return in a few minutes.' Storm rubbed his master's wrists thoughtfully.

'Storm, look! The rat!' The King pointed deliriously at Wilding.

'Sire, this is no rat. It is Commander Wilding, friend to Robert Teague and member of ***The Fabled Two***. Do you not remember the Mouselings who served your father so valiantly in The First Rat King War?'

The King paused, lost in confused thought.

'Wilding...Teague...Fabled Two...the mice who disappeared into legend...'

Suddenly, the King's eyes became clear and focused.

'You're right, Storm. That's no rat. It's General Wilding, Mouseling Battlemage!'

'Aye, my liege, 'tis he,' said Storm, understanding that the King was bravely struggling to shake off his state of delirium.

Wilding bowed graciously. 'At your service once more, my King. But Sire, if I may offer my counsel, we need to get you on your feet and your Queen out of this dungeon and to a healer, posthaste. All of that is predicated upon the notion that we will be able to retake the castle.'

The King looked at the mouse as if he had just been hit in the face with a brick.

'Retake the castle...my Queen...the emissaries who stole the castle, yes...'

He struggled with his thoughts, his senses finally clearing and his memories beginning to flood back to him. He tried to stand up, and then, with an emotional veracity that shocked them all, he screamed out:

'Commander Storm. The castle has been LOST!'

Though he tried desperately to regain his footing, he stumbled and fell towards the stone cell floor. Storm grabbed him before he could hit the ground, and Cullen and The Bird rushed over to help hoist the King back up.

'On your feet, Sire!' said Storm. 'There you are. We have quite a battle ahead of us.'

The King sighed weakly. 'Storm, how did this happen? Who are these people that have done this to us? They WILL...come to justice, I swear it on my people. What is the plan? Who do we have left to us? Lady's Mercy, man, I thought you were dead! Do you have any water?'

'A walking dead man, maybe, my King,' said Storm cheerily. 'But I still have enough fight left in me to reclaim the castle. And we will get water for you soon, my liege, and the Queen as well. The hows, whys, and wherefores of this mishap we can sort out once we have you back on your throne — and those interlopers in chains.'

Storm then looked over at Wilding on his shoulder.

'Wilding, what's next?'

'Let's get out of this dark, hellish place, and get safely back to the Jailer's Nook,' the wizard said. 'There the King's eyes can re-acclimate — we will need his vision and fighting skills if we are to make it back upstairs. I have no doubt resistance awaits us above. Have Cullen and The Bird carry the Queen, while you assist the King. Remember to avoid the glass in the middle of the hall.'

Wilding looked at the King's tattered undergarments and bare feet, then hopped off of Storm's shoulder, scurrying back down to the floor.

'We shall need every fighter we have — intact, preferably — if my plan is going to work.'

Then, the party proceeded out of the cell and began to head back up — back towards the surface, the light, and the cataclysmic fight ahead of them.

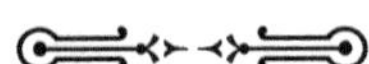

As the King's party made its way up the hall from the lowest cell, they were surprised to see a coterie of Mouselings running past them at the four way dungeon intersection. Wilding sensed them more than he saw them, but heard the scampering of footpads on the stone floor coming nearer towards him.

Finally, as some came solidly into view, running past the human party, Wilding told Storm to stop walking.

Squinting his eyes and pricking his ears forward, trying to make out the details of who was in this procession emerging out from the blackness, Wilding suddenly yelled out a loud and forceful 'HALT!'

As if on command, the Mouselings all stopped, frozen in place, after hearing the deep and commanding voice of another Mouseling. Looking up at the humans, they spied a mouse in purple battlerobes, waving a staff, standing on the shoulder of a tall human clad only in filthy jailer's rags.

'Hail, mousekin. I am Commander Wilding, Mouseling battlemage, who fought in The First Rat King War in service to King Teegan. As you can see, we have freed him from his prison cell and he is now safely with us, though the Castle has been infiltrated by the same nefarious group who, I can only assume, imprisoned you as well. We are preparing to retake Castle Feldenspar. It was not but an hour ago that I sent two mouse companions of mine down that way, into dangers unknown, to search for imprisoned members of MouseKeep. Did you see these mice? Is this how you were freed? Speak, quickly!'

The mice looked at him mutedly, reluctant to speak — but he knew where their thoughts were, trying to absorb the information he'd just given them. Commander Wilding? One half of the legendary **Fabled Two?** Was this another trick?

Finally, their leader, an older mouse with greying whiskers, spoke up.

'Hail, Commander Wilding. My name is Finnegan Willowtail. I am the FlightMaster of the Falcon Riders of Feldenspar. We did indeed see your two friends, a bard and a thief, and it was they who valiantly freed us. And cleverly, too! But sir, I must inform you, with regret, that your friends are almost certainly dead — dead at the maw of a crested Tarbog rattlesnake who goes by the name of Ravenscale, King of Snakes. The infiltrators who imprisoned us brought him in a sack and left him outside our cages to ensure that we did not escape. But your friends cleverly convinced him to play a game of wagers, and the ante for the game was our lives. So now we are free, with your thief's wife and son are among us.'

Wilding heard the sobbing of a young buck, and looked down to see him clinging to his mother, who held him tightly in her paws.

The Stranger's family, thought the wizard.

His voice trembled slightly as he tried to process and interpret the news he was getting. 'Dead? Are you certain? Those two mice were highly skilled and resourceful, not to mention battle hardened.'

'Most assuredly, milord. As they were playing a game for their lives, I do not doubt it. They had agreed to gamble on a wager and, should they lose, become the snake's dinner.' Willowtail sighed resignedly. 'If we are telling true tales, Commander, I see no way that they could have escaped, even if they had won their 'game.' The snake was many feet long, sir, ravenous in appetite, and one venomous bite from its treacherous mouth would mean their death. I have no doubt that their souls have gone to Her embrace. Though I wish it was different, on my heart as a Falconrider, because the thief's family watched them parlay for our freedom. No youth should have to watch his father willingly sacrifice his life for his family's freedom. But that is exactly what the thief did, with great and steadfast courage. Their bravery is a testament to their character, and saved our sixteen souls.'

He pointed a paw at the Stranger's family.

'They made a sacrifice for our lives, but the snake is still down here, which means we all remain in imminent danger. We must depart, sir, and soon!'

Wilding whispered in Storm's ear. 'Storm, do you know this Finnegan Willowtail customer?'

'Aye General — err, Wilding. He is one of us, a Captain and Commander of the Falcon Riders. A strong leader, and a faithful one, too. I believe these mice, and can only presume that they are what is left of the MouseGuard — though the number should easily be double or triple what is here. I wonder what has befallen the others, but I would not be surprised if the rest now lie with Her, given the dire circumstance.'

Wilding, now wary of tricks and troubled at the thought of his friends' deaths, was still unconvinced. He looked sternly at the Falcon Rider Captain.

'And, Captain Willowtail, where is the rest of the MouseGuard?'

The Falconrider looked at his lower paws forlornly. 'Dead, milord. Or missing in action. I saw many brave mice fall when the rats and fischers laid siege to MouseKeep, defending it to the last. The enemy was somehow able to access our secret walls and doors, almost as if they knew exactly where to look to hit us at our most vulnerable — and in doing so, they ambushed us in our own fortified garrison. We were taken by surprise, and woefully unprepared to fend off such a surprise assault in our own Keep. I believe that should we ascend and attempt to retake MouseKeep, we will find many bodies of the fallen MouseGuard littering the corridors and chambers of our hallowed hallways.'

The wizard weighed his options, and was reminded of a saying his old battle master had given him atop a desolate place called Winterblossom Mesa.

It went something like this:

The mind of the beginner holds so many possibilities
Yet, the mind of the expert holds so few.

Hearthseeker and the Stranger, killed? thought the wizard. *And, by a snake...what a terrible death!*

It couldn't be. Those two, dead?

But then again, thought Wilding, *a crested Tarbog rattlesnake...*

Wilding shivered at the thought of the venom — painful, excruciating...and as most Mousekin knew, you *usually* weren't dead by the time that you reached the snake's stomach. Asphyxiation and digestive acids generally handled the remainder of the job, but slowly...so, so slowly.

His mind snapped back to the situation at hand. There was a castle to retake, and time was of the essence. He regained his role as commander, forcing himself to put the thoughts of his companions aside in the higher interests of the group — and the King.

But should he at least go back, to check?

He looked forlornly down the hallway, into the blackness, towards the certain death he had sent his friends off to face. Opening his mouth to speak, he caught himself, stopped, and recollected his composure.

'Commander Willowtail, take these mice to the Jailer's Nook, if you'd be so kind. Watch out for the glass in the middle of the corridor this way.' He pointed with his staff in the direction of the exit. 'We will meet you there and regroup to form a plan to take back control of the castle. Prepare yourselves for battle, for we shall soon meet our foes head on.'

Willowtail saluted and scampered down the hallway, fifteen mice in tow behind him. The procession went into the distance and disappeared out of sight.

'Shall we follow them, Commander?' asked Storm. He glanced at the Queen, still unconscious, being gingerly held up by Cullen and The Bird. King Teegan rested on his shoulder, one arm around his neck, though he seemed to be gradually regaining his footing. Still, it was a ragtag crew, and not one that was really fit for combat of any sort — especially in the condition they were in.

Wilding looked at the knight, and then looked back down the hallway in the opposite direction of the Jailer's Nook, which led into the encroaching blackness — and somewhere, towards a crested Tarbog rattlesnake.

Was that how it went? he thought to himself. Dispatch two highly qualified mice to their deaths — their lives, their blood, now on his paws?

He hesitated again, anger welling up inside him. He tried — and failed — to keep it from turning to rage. He desperately wanted to go back down the corridor and see the snake for himself, to exact vengeance...but, glancing back at the King, he knew his personal priorities had to be set aside — at least for the moment.

And what about Robert Teague? Was he dead, too?

Considering this troubling notion for a thoughtful moment, the answer was clear: never. *If there's one thing I can trust to,* Wilding thought, *it's that Robert Teague would never fall. Not in battle with rats or fischers, that's a certainty.*

He smiled to himself, reassured at the thought of his best friend.

Now isn't the time for any of this though, thought the mouse. Shaking the thoughts out of his head and regaining his resolve, the wizard looked at Storm. Once more, he was the very picture of command. 'Let us head to the Jailer's Nook,' he said firmly. 'There, we can reassess our strength, come up with a tactical plan, and prepare for a counterattack. We will make these ratlickers pay for what they have done, Knight Commander. You can count on that.'

'Aye, Commander,' said Storm. But as the party started to proceed down the corridor, Wilding's heart sank at the thought of his two new friends having become a meal for one of the deadliest snakes in existence. Pain, sorrow, and a deep aching in his heart all washed over him. He hadn't felt this kind of loss since, since...

Suddenly, he whispered to Storm, **'STOP!'**

Had he heard something?

The snake perhaps, slithering towards its next victims?

But there will be no more victims for that serpent today, Wilding resolved to himself.

Scrambling down off of Storm's shoulder, with his battlemage staff pointed towards the darkened corridor, the Mouseling wizard muttered some unintelligible incantations. The ruby on his staff began to glow, and soon, a dim light shot up out of his staff and hovered, suspended magically in midair, providing some additional illumination to supplement the weak light given off by the torch sconces.

He stood there, ears perked forward, battle staff in his paw, waiting, waiting, waiting...for his adversary to appear.

'Wait here Storm,' said the wizard. And then, pressing himself against the right side of the stone wall, he crept cautiously forward.

But what was that sound he had heard...was it slithering? Rattling? Yes, yes...hissing, that was what heard.

This will be the last time this snake hisses today, thought the wizard to himself, gripping his battle staff more closely. *Or ever. I will teach this serpent a lesson he will never forget.*

He waited in the blackness, on the outside edge of the light cast off by his magical orb. Ears outstretched, he listened. The hissing got closer, but then it started to change pitch. Was it hissing? Or was it singing? Yes, singing — the snake was *singing* as it came down the hallway! And speaking the Mouseling language, no less.

What nerve!

He must be in a jolly mood after his big meal, thought Wilding. He listened intently, and heard this:

Snakes in cells

Cockleshells

Rattlemourne and Serpent Scourge

All in a death's dirge!

That selfish snake, he was singing a joyous song about his friends being killed! And as the wizard Mouseling listened, he heard a new sound — *scuffle scrape, scuffle scrape.* It was getting closer! He pressed his back even more firmly against the wall, by the corner of the four chambered intersection. Staff ready, he waited for his prey to come — and be taught a vindictive lesson. By The Lady, was he ever going to teach this snake a lesson!

A lesson for the ages, he thought to himself, struggling to keep the rage from overcoming him.

In the shadows, he prepared with a quiet focus. Spells, yes! *Flame Lick, Freezing Rain, Death Cloud.* All spells which would stun the snake, so he could deliver the final justice with his battle staff, looking it straight in its eyes as he dealt the death blow.

He had fought snakes before, and he knew how this went.

But I have to be quick, he thought. *It's vital that I make the first strike...*

Silently, he waited...waited. Soon, he could see it...it was huge! Out of the shadows it approached — yet still, he forced himself to wait, sizing up the massive shadow it cast on the wall in the flickering torchlight. He saw the reflection of its shadow on the cold stone growing larger, and ever more intimidating — easily four or five times his size. But still, he steeled his nerve. He would avenge his friends and protect the King at the same time. Without ceasing, it drew closer, ever closer.

Soon the shadow was so large that Wilding found himself swallowing a huge lump in his throat.

He could see now why his friends were overcome.

The scuffling was so close now, he could see the shadow of the snake amidst the darkness. *Patience,* he thought to himself. *Patience.... soon now, wait for it, wait...wait...NOW!*

And with that, he struck.

Out of the darkness he leapt, from the recessed corner of the wall, wielding the staff above his head, striking with all his might and delivering his death blow to...a treasure chest?

Two shadows rolled out of the way as he was in midair, and then burst into laughter.

Wilding looked around, unsure of what had happened. This was no snake, but a golden treasure chest! As he stood there looking at it, rubbing his sore paws from the vibration of the strike, two shadows emerged.

It was Hearthseeker! And the Stranger!

'You vile rogues!' spat Wilding, embarrassed and utterly filled with relief at the same time. Then, seeing that they were both hale and hearty, he got even more angry — even as he was more relieved as well. Unsure of what to say, he sputtered 'VILE ROGUES!' a second time. Then the words began to pour out of him. 'What happened to the snake? I was told you were both DEAD! And sneaking up like that. The nerve of you both! You, you...VILE ROGUES!'

'It's good to see you too, Professor,' started the Stranger, clapping Wilding on the shoulder. 'Ainsley tricked the serpent into playing a game — and in doing so, managed to free the hostages. And I...'

'He helped us win the game, milord!' said Hearthseeeker. He looked at the Stranger and they both burst into laughter, thinking about how Wilding had just attacked their hard-won treasure. The Stranger went over to the chest and began to rub at the sizable dent that Wilding's staff had put into the wood. He began laughing again while pointing it out to the bard, who laughed in tandem with him.

'Well, I...I mean, you two...freed the MouseGuard...and played a... game...with a Tarbog rattlesnake? Well, I never, in a million seasons...'

And with that, Hearthseeker came up to Wilding and gave him the biggest hug.

'We will tell you all about it later, my wizardly friend! But for now, we need to focus on bringing justice to those imposters in the castle. And let's make it quick, eh? Because I missed my proper lunch time, and I am dying to have you open this chest — which, I am hoping, is full of treasure! Oh, and also, I need an ale — I don't *want* an ale, mind you, I *NEED* one.'

With that, Wilding's jaw dropped. Hearthseeker had just fought a rattlesnake, and not only had he lived to tell about it, but he was talking about food!

Unsure of what to say, he just looked at the two mice and thought, *These two make a pretty good pair. Perhaps I needn't worry about them so much after all.*

Then he got an idea.

'Hearthseeker, do you have more tricks in that utility belt and pack of yours?'

'Aye, milord! Many tricks, still to be revealed!'

'That's good,' said Wilding, 'because we are going to need them, if we are to retake this castle by dinner time and get you your ale.'

The Legend of The Crows' Court:

It is true that Mouselings developed synergistic relationships with other mammals and avians, to their great utility and companionship. Stories and examples abound of Mouselings using squirrels and other small mammals as beasts of burden, and even as pets. And of course, it is well known that falcons, ravens, and other birds have been trained from birth to carry riders upon them in flight, whether for travel or military purposes.

One of the most interesting tales in the world of Mouseling/Avian relationships is the infamous rumor of the 'Crows' Court.' While always thought to be merely a matter of tale and legend, it seems that 'Crows' Courts' are, in fact, real! In a so-called 'Crows' Court,' what usually transpires is that a large gathering of crows forms a ring around one poor and unsuspecting crow who has seemingly committed some kind of ill or wrong. After the mass of crows quiets down, one crow 'prosecutes' it, or seems to make a case for why that unfortunate exile has transgressed the laws of crow-dom. And when he is done, all the crows in the circle descend upon the poor crow in the middle, pecking him unmercifully until he or she departs for the next world.

Interestingly enough, it is said that if any individual — human, Mouseling, or otherwise — interferes with the Crows' Court, and in doing so saves the life of the 'accursed' crow, that crow will become beholden to the individual who prevented his execution. This is a rare gift, indeed, as crows are known without question as the smartest of all birds. Rumors swirl that the famed 'Professor' at FireMaple Abby stumbled onto a Crows' Court one day, and saved the life of the crow who had been scheduled for execution. It is said that he rides that crow to this day, and it can sometimes be seen perching upon the spires of The Abby, keeping a watchful vigil for those who would seek to bring its master harm.

Yet when asked, The Professor feigns ignorance, saying that there are many crows that frequent The Abby to nosh upon its discarded husks of fresh hops after the fermentation process is complete...

— TAKEN FROM **STORMSNOUT'S BESTIARY: BEASTS AND RIVERFOLK OF THE FAR COLLECTIVE, INCLUDING LEGENDARY FIGURES**

Chapter 19

COMPLETING THE JAILBREAK

It was there, in the Jailer's Nook, where the jailer and his staff would normally spend their days, that Storm's party of humans, Wilding, Hearthseeker, the Stranger, and Willowtail's party of Mousekin were finally able to meet up, take a breather, and regroup.

In the soft glow of the torchlight, Cullen and The Bird lay the Queen — still unconscious — gently on the table where the jailer's staff had worked over Tempus the Animal Speaker not so long before. While they attended to the Queen, Storm helped to ease King Teegan into the chair where the drunken Jailer had sat. Teegan, weak and dehydrated from several days without food or water, slumped in the chair, trying to catch his breath. Storm wasn't in much better shape, but, loyal to the last, he refused to show weakness in front of his majesty — especially given the circumstances.

After attending to the Queen, Cullen and The Bird took up positions at the end of the hallway, right at the bottom of the ancillary staircase that led up to the kitchen. They stood there in silence, waiting just outside the light of the torch sconces to ensure that no troublemakers would be coming to 'check on' any of the prisoners — prisoners who, now that they had been emancipated from their cells, were plotting a severe round of revenge on the castle's infiltrators, both human and animal alike.

The freed Mouselings, under the charge of Finnegan Willowtail, all collected under the jailer's table, seeking out the only natural safe harbor in the room. Their spirits and morale had been raised significantly when Wilding, Hearthseeker and the Stranger strolled victoriously into the Jailer's Nook, getting nothing less than a Mouseling hero's reception in joyous thanks for having saved their lives from Ravenscale. And, the proverbial 'icing on the cake' came when the Stranger watched his son's forlorn sorrow turn into unbridled joy as he leapt into his father's arms, with the Stranger's wife right behind him.

It was a magical moment — one of the few truly good things to happen within the castle's walls since the infiltrators had taken over. Though many of the Mouseling prisoners were keen to hear how the great serpent had been defeated, Ainsley Hearthseeker, sensing the critical nature of the moment, parried their questions. He insisted that the mice sit under the table and rest while they could, knowing that a battle would be forthcoming — and more injuries, if not deaths, likely awaited them on the horizon.

After settling the mice down, both Hearthseeker and Finnegan Willowtail scrambled up King Teegan's leg and joined Wilding on the tabletop. The Stranger, naturally, had chosen to stay below, and was busy snuggling his wife and son, resting and saying prayers of great thanksgiving that not only was he still alive, but his family was unharmed as well.

Hearthseeker clasped paws with Wilding, and their eyes locked. The bard smiled at his wizard friend, but he could tell the Professor was deep in thought.

'Milord, what is the plan?'

Storm pulled up a chair and rested his elbows on the table, while the three mice and King Teegan entered a discussion about the size, strength, and disposition of the adversaries who had overtaken the castle.

'Here is what we know,' started Wilding. 'We came to Castle Feldenspar on an official missive brought to Robert Teague by our thieving friend down below. We know that that missive — whether it came from King Teegan or not — was somehow turned into a trap prepared for myself and Robert Teague, to have us executed atop The King's Pedestal. Due to some good fortune and the bravery of our companions...'

Wilding winked at Hearthseeker, then continued, 'We were able to overcome the guards at the Western MouseKeep entrance, and, in the guise of being taken under guard by the enemy, proceed to The King's Pedestal and rout our foes. This included many mice who are impostors to the MouseGuard, dressed in black and crimson battle dress. Additionally, we encountered fischers there, some of whom we subdued, and rats as well.

"The enemy animals' party was led by a rat called One Eye, who fled in the midst of the melee, with Robert Teague giving chase. Lastly, there was an unidentified human — a most unkempt one, if I may be so bold as to say so — whose eyeball could be seen peering out from the King's chair to spy upon the scene. Commander Teague sent an arrow into his very oculus, sending him running. He had long, greasy black hair and a pale complexion, looking unshaven and lacking hygiene. Do you know this man?'

'Aye,' said Storm, 'Unfortunately we do — though I wish we'd never laid eyes on the blighter! That sounds like Tempus you're describing — he was the leader of the emissaries that came 'offering gifts' to King Teegan. He was part and parcel to the infiltration of Castle Feldenspar.'

The King just shook his head weakly.

'Well, this Tempus was instrumental in the infiltration of MouseKeep as well. How do I know this? Because he is what we call an Animal Speaker. He has the ability to speak to all animals, and has obviously been in the employ of The Rat King. Majesty, as you may recall, we killed the only known Animal Speaker — well, the only *previously* known Animal Speaker — in the first Great War. It was a significant blow to The Rat King's communication infrastructure, being unable to communicate with his human cohorts as cleverly as he once did — and some of his animal legions, as well. But now, it appears that he's found another one. My two companions and I saw this man here several hours ago, lying on this very table as a few of his cohorts tried to tend to his wounded eye. It is imperative that we find this man so that he may be interrogated.'

Wilding steepled his paws together, then continued.

'If he were to flee the castle, we would be allowing The Rat King to have access to an incredibly valuable asset — an asset which would undoubtedly be leveraged against us, to our detriment. I cannot stress this point enough: **We must find this man and detain him alive, however possible**. The Rat King **CANNOT** be allowed to have access to another Animal Speaker. His capture is of paramount importance — and, my gut feeling is that the capture of one of The Rat King's lieutenants will most likely bring about the surrender of any remaining forces within the Castle. Tactically, it is both our most logical, and our most surgically effective, objective.'

'Your logic seems sound to me, Commander,' said Storm, 'but how do you recommend we achieve it?'

'Well, Storm,' Wilding said, 'we need to recapture the Castle, as well as MouseKeep — and as the old saying goes, one should never send a human to do a mouse's work. Myself, Hearthseeker, and Willowtail will take whatever MouseGuard survivors who remain combat ready and look to rearm at the MouseKeep Armory. Then we'll go about clearing out each corridor of MouseKeep, engaging in paw to paw combat if we have to. But your job is bigger. You, The Bird, Cullen, and King Teegan must find a way to retake Castle Feldenspar. Which will certainly be an interesting proposition given the current equipment situation: namely, that you are all unarmed — save for that dagger of yours, Commander — and bootless, and the King is still in his undergarments. We will have to be tactical in how we go about getting you all equipped for battle. We can't just have you march upstairs and start a battle of fisticuffs, as you humans call it, weaponless and in your stocking feet. The most logical place to start? The kitchen. There, you will find an assortment of knives, ropes, sacks, and other throwable items which should at least give you a fighting chance. Plus, I suspect the kitchen staff is likely to be more or less intact — meaning unaware of the Castle's infiltration and usurpation — and you should be able to conscript some loyal staff to help you.'

'But those people aren't trained knights or soldiers!' interjected the King. 'It's my sworn duty to protect my Castle servants, not send them running into harm's way!'

'And yet, sire, they are your best and most reasonable option to bolster your forces,' Wilding said mildly. 'Who knows where your knights and soldiers are? Dispatched, as Commander Storm said earlier, to The Plains of Andrellion on some false mission to help transport more 'gifts' to Castle Feldenspar? As the seasons turn, it doesn't really matter. Whether they are indisposed or imprisoned elsewhere, sent away on some dubious mission like the Falconriders were, dead, or off enjoying a Harvest Festival feast and sampling the local ales in the Ferngrove bottoms, it matters not — all that matters is that they are not currently available to aid us. The kitchen staff will fight for their King, however. To the death, if need be.'

'Commander Wilding is right,' said Storm. 'Whether it be by stealth or serendipity, we will take the Castle back by sunset. I swear it, on my life!'

'We are running out of daylight,' said Wilding. 'We'd best get moving if we wish to keep Commander Storm from failing his oath.'

And so the plan was set, if you could call it that, to reclaim both Feldenspar Castle and MouseKeep.

It was determined that Wilding's party of Mouselings would work on retaking MouseKeep, while King Teegan's party of humans would head to the kitchen to reequip themselves, assess the situation, and prepare for combat. Both Mouselings and humans were briefed on 'The Plan,' and soon, both parties were lined up silently at the foot of the staircase which led up to the kitchen.

No one had come down the stairs while Cullen and The Bird had stood their watch at the staircase, which Wilding interpreted as a very good sign. Between the ceramic and glass shards laid so profusely in the dungeon, the 'one step' traps that had been set at key entry points, and the lack of food and water brought down to the dungeons since their residents' first imprisonment, it seemed clear to Wilding that the recently freed prisoners — both Mouseling and human alike — had been written off by their captors. In the eyes of the enemy, their play to overtake Castle Feldenspar must have seemed a resounding success — their nefarious plan having been executed so smashingly and in the face of such little resistance.

And that gives King Teegan's little ragtag team a fighting chance, thought Wilding.

Storm led the party up the stairs. The Queen, carried by Cullen and Bird, was gently brought up, step by step, as the party crept carefully up the staircase. About midway up the stairs, Wilding called to Storm, who bent down and looked at his Mouseling friend.

'Hold, Storm. MouseKeep has an entrance in this wall here.'

He pointed to a crack in the stone stairwell where a false door lay hidden, waiting to be opened.

'We will take our leave here and head into MouseKeep. If I can, I will come back and check on your progress, assuming I am able. It goes without saying that this is our most desperate hour — not just for Feldenspar Castle and MouseKeep, but for all of The Western Lands and its peoples. Good luck, Commander.'

Storm bowed his head, outstretching his hand.

'And to you as well, Commander Wilding. Without you and your party, we would not have had a fighting chance. Thank you, my friend. And should you fall in battle, may you fall mightily.'

'You as well, Storm,' said Wilding. He bowed wistfully, then turned and opened the false wall.

Sliding noiselessly back, the wall receded, opening up into a dark hallway behind it. With that, Wilding beckoned to Finnegan Willowtail, who directed the Mousekin back into MouseKeep to try to reclaim the property that was once theirs. There was a scampering of paws as the surviving Mousekin made their way into the hallway, with the Stranger and Hearthseeker following behind them. Once he'd checked to ensure he was the last one remaining, the wizard mouse slipped quietly into the hidden entrance, then closed the wall of MouseKeep, resigned to head valiantly and selflessly into a fate unknown.

When Widow, Recluse,

Huntress, want to play

Run, Mouseling, run!

And live another day!

— A popular Mouseling nursery rhyme

Chapter 20

A CULINARY RECONNOITER

After the Mouselings departed into MouseKeep to fight their own perilous battle, Commander Storm continued on, leading his party further up the staircase. This dungeon staircase curved up to the kitchen, allowing the kitchen to discreetly dispose of scraps and other undesirable foodstuffs to the inmates in the dungeons below — and to do so in a way which minimized any inconvenience to the kitchen staff. It was a smaller, narrower, and rarely used staircase, unlike the one which Robert Teague had 'surfed' down in his pursuit of One Eye. Highly trafficked, that staircase connected the kitchen to the main floor which lay above it, and was used by the serving staff to bring food, clothing, fresh linens, hot towels, boiling water for baths, herbs, and so forth to all of the Castle's residents. The main kitchen staircase was how the King's meals were brought to the great feasting hall, sometimes called the Great Hall or Grand Hall.

It is good, then, thought Storm as he crept cautiously forward, *that the dungeon staircase is used so rarely — lest our position be given away before we can afford it.*

Inching up towards the crest of the staircase, Storm signaled his companions to 'hold' in the stairwell by raising up his fist and then indicating a quiet finger towards his pursed lips. Continuing forward alone, he climbed up to the top of the steps to observe and reconnoiter the scene in the kitchen.

He half-expected to see his foes in the kitchen, although as he thought upon it further, he realized that with any potential resistance relegated to the dungeons — and therefore, relegated to the backs of the infiltrators' minds — they were more likely to be engaged in other, more nefarious deeds.

Still, he scanned the scene — and surprisingly, all looked quiet.

Staring in, he could see that the kitchen was indeed bustling — but the commotion was more of a quiet, muted bustle. The staff appeared to be engaged in their normal errands, following protocol with a sense of timeliness and duty. The more he watched, the more Storm got the impression that, as far as the kitchen staff was concerned, they were simply following their regular routine — the normal and somewhat monotonous affairs of any given day. He observed some of the kitchen staff rolling in a large feasting cart, on top of which sat an enormous silver platter that they were preparing to place a massive beef roast upon.

To the side of the cart was a large butcher block on an island table, brimming with side dressings for the roast: onions, carrots, tomatoes, heads of lettuce waiting to be turned into a tray liner, as well as artful sprigs of rosemary and thyme. Accompanying all of this was a large dish of salt — the shared dish that was passed around to guests at a feast. Lastly, Storm spied a great big wooden cutting board containing a variety of hard and soft cheeses, as well as a generous (and fine looking) selection of smoked sausages, with some herbed ground mustard in a serving dish alongside them.

The cheese course, thought Storm to himself. As he stared out at the finely prepared courses of food, his mouth started to water of its own accord. In the midst of the jailbreak, he had somehow forgotten that it had been...he tried to think...how long since he had last eaten? Hours? Days? Yes, days! The rumblings in his stomach were a testament to the gnawing sense of hunger that suddenly came rushing back to him. And then it struck him — if he was suffering these torments of hunger pains, the King and the Queen must certainly be suffering from them as well. Perhaps suffering even more than he was, as they would not be as used to privation as a battle-tested knight. He had to get them — the entire party, now that he thought of it — some sustenance, and quickly.

We are not likely to find victory in combat on an empty stomach, he thought.

On the outskirts of the kitchen were the other accoutrements which so frequently accompanied a massive feast...barrels of beer and jugs of young wine, as well as napkins, forks, and wooden plates. Day-old rounds of bread known as trenchers were lined up, ready to be used as edible bowls for meats and stews. There was fruit piled high, too — all kinds of apples, figs, pears, and also some baked desserts. Pies, cakes, and hot apple pies, fresh from the oven! Storm could smell them now, so fresh and delicious — and starting to become a real distraction.

Focus, Storm! he chastised himself silently. *There will be plenty of time for food later!*

Though his belly rumbled, Storm forced himself to think about what was happening in the kitchen — and what it might mean for their attempt to retake the castle from its invaders. *What day was this?* He couldn't remember, though he continued struggling to think, his mind still foggy with hunger and thirst. With the King 'away,' certainly there would be no feast held in the Grand Hall...the servants would eat in the servant wing of the Castle, and the dog keepers, tanners, butchers, and other outdoor staff would receive their meals in their usual places outside of the Castle's walls.

What is going on here, then? thought Storm to himself. *Who could have ordered such a massive feast?*

He continued to survey the scene. It looked like someone had made a dreadful mess of flour and spilled cream over by the fireplace — he saw no less than three girls on their hands and knees working to clean it up, wringing out woolen rags into wooden buckets as they sopped up the mess. He spied an orange tabby cat who kept trying to lick the remainder of the cream off the floor, only to be chastised by the girls as he kept creeping back, obviously getting in their way. Periodically the cat would pounce randomly, jumping and landing in front of the pantry, then peering under it, as if looking for something.

Crazy cat, thought Storm. *What could you possibly think might be under that pantry?*

While the serving girls scrubbed away — evidently with all their might and fervor — a portly older woman bent over them, giving them quite a verbal lashing. She was wearing the monastic robes of the King's order, consisting of a royal blue crushed velvet habit, tied at the waist with a brown roped cord, and a royal blue veil covering her hair, face and ears.

Storm recognized her immediately. Sister Minerva! He would know her shape and voice anywhere. Like most of the monastic sisters, she served wherever the King had need of her — and when Storm was a boy, the King 'needed' her to teach the class of young male children who were being trained to become his venerated knights. Even now Storm winced, thinking about the sting of her rod on his backside when he would not do his schoolwork, or whenever he caused a commotion among the small classes of eight-to-ten boys she taught at a time. To make it even worse, she had insisted on telling his parents that his handwriting was deficient (a 'motor problem,' as she called it) — and forced him to stay after school every day to practice handwriting while the other boys were out practicing swordsmanship with the King's master at arms.

Storm smiled to himself at the sight of her. The memory was sweet, if not fully nostalgic, and since he'd grown to manhood he'd become thankful for what he now realized were Sister Minerva's efforts to help him. Even today, his handwriting was practically illegible to everyone except his wife. *She gave it a great effort though,* thought the knight affectionately.

If Sister Minerva is anything, Storm's thoughts continued, *she is loyal. Loyal to King Teegan. Loyal to me, and the rest of our castle's elite guard. And that loyalty may just give us a chance to gain some footing or advantage. We shall need such loyalty if we are to succeed in this endeavor.*

Quietly, he made his back down the stairs, to where the staircase had begun to curve downward, to rejoin the rest of his group.

'All is quiet in the kitchen,' he reported, 'though they seem to be preparing a large feast of some sort. Sister Minerva is there, and I know her well. Surely, she remains loyal to King Teegan! I spent much of my youth as a schoolboy in her classroom, before she took over the kitchen. I will speak with her and see if I can gain her aid, and requisition us some quick provisions.'

King Teegan looked weakly at Storm, nodding in assent to the quickly hatched plan. 'If Sister Minerva isn't with us, then we are truly lost.'

'We are not lost yet, my liege. I assure you,' said Storm reassuringly.

Cullen cocked an eye at the Knight Commander, and then addressed him.

'Begging your Knightship's pardon, but how do you intend to do that, milord,' he said, looking pointedly at the soiled jailer's garments Storm wore, 'without giving yourself, and us, away to the other staff? Certainly a Knight Commander waltzing into the kitchen all casual-like dressed in the tattered garments that miserable jailkeeper wore would be, well...out of place in the kitchen, to say the least, sire, and certain to raise suspicion given our peculiar circumstance! I'd be ashamed to let me dogs be seen bedding down on those filthy rags, and they smell somewhat...err...ripe, milord. If you don't mind me saying, of course...'

Gabriel Storm looked at the young dog keeper, and considered what he said. It took him a minute, but after some thought, he looked at the young man, dressed in his green tunic, brown leather pants, and distinctive leather dog keeper's cap, and then he responded.

'Cullen, you are absolutely right. We would most certainly raise the alarm if I were to just stroll in there and start asking for help, dressed like a fool of a jailer. We need to be more...discreet. Take your clothes off.'

'Milord?' asked the dog keeper, somewhat shocked and taken aback.

'It's ok, young man, I think I know where the Knight Commander is going with this,' said King Teegan. The King removed the young man's dark brown leather cap, then, with a sudden smile at his commander's ingenuity, placed it atop Storm's head. 'Dog keepers do tend to frequent the kitchen, do they not?'

Both Cullen and The Bird answered the question simultaneously, though their concert was most certainly unintended.

'Yes, Sire!'

Then the King, who had scrapped through the kitchen on a daily basis in his own youth hunting for snacks between mealtimes, laughed at the thought. It was the first time they had heard a hint of happiness in his voice. With any luck, things would come together — and maybe the day which had started out so dismally would end well for them.

Just maybe.

Meanwhile, deep in the hidden recesses of MouseKeep, Wilding and his band of adventurers had taken a pause about halfway on their course to the Armory. Most (if not all) of the imprisoned mice needed a rest, having been deprived of nourishment over the past several days just like King Teegan's party. But even beyond their weakened state, the truth was that a number of Mouselings in the party were noncombatants who needed to be safely released from the besieged MouseKeep — including the Stranger's family. Obviously unfit for combat, they, along with four other mice who were either unfit or enfeebled from their ordeal, had been shown a secret exit from MouseKeep that led straight into the village square.

Naturally, it had been an emotional moment when the Stranger's family prepared to depart, with both his wife and child tearfully throwing their paws around him as they hugged him farewell. They had resigned him to death when they had first been taken hostage, only to see him return gloriously to save their lives. But now, well... now they saw another opportunity for the most important mouse in their lives to die at the hands of keen and clever infiltrators, be they Mousekin, fischers, or Ratlings. Any hopes they had of retaking the MouseKeep were overshadowed by the thought of his death.

Wilding and Hearthseeker were both quite impressed when the Stranger disentangled himself from their embrace and gently shooed them away, overseeing their exit from the castle, only to then turn back steadfastly and return to his companions. Taking a moment to look them each squarely in the eye, he said resolutely:

'I will be accompanying you both, until the end of this.'

Wilding, ever the erudite yet enigmatic mouse, said to the Stranger bluntly:

'You have served your mission as directed and executed it to completion — not only from the missive you were given by your guild, but also from the moment on the wagon in which you swore to assist us, specifically to aid in the rescue of your family. All of this has now been accomplished. Your mission — and your word — have been honorably fulfilled. No one will pass judgment upon you for accompanying your family into the fresh air and daylight.'

'And anyone who did would have to answer to me,' the bard added doggedly.

Yet even Hearthseeker was shocked at the Stranger's response.

'Milord, I am a thief of MouseKeep, and I will not abandon my brethren in their greatest time of need — even if it means my son must grow up without his father. I am as great a patriot as any loyal mouse. I will see this through to the end, and see this vile treachery lain low — upon this day, and with you both, right by your side. I swear to Her, with my own life, upon this pledge. I WILL fight with you until the end, wherever that end may take us.'

Hearthseeker and Wilding surveyed the thief, as a weighty silence suddenly sprung up upon them at the veracity and forceful tone of his oath.

But finally, the wizard broke the abrupt quiet of the moment, saying 'Well met. Then the choice has been made, and we are with you to the very same end. We will ascend this castle until we can reach the FalconKeep intact. No matter the obstacle, whether She should bring us to our deaths or we arrive there victoriously having met with no further resistance, that is our quest upon this day — and we shall not stand idle until we have seen it to the last.'

The Stranger clasped paws with both Wilding and Hearthseeker, and bent to his knee.

'My life is yours now, milords. So I swear.'

With that, he drew his short sword and loped to the front of the hallway, preparing to lead the vanguard of the Mouseling contingent. For a brief moment, Wilding sensed that the Stranger was just as eager to exact some revenge on the infiltrators who had endangered his family as he was willing to swear his life upon an oath of protection to MouseKeep.

Valiant, nonetheless, thought the wizard.

Wilding looked at the bard.

'Ainsley, bring up the rear, if you'd be so kind,' he said to him. 'While I am unsure what enemies might lie ahead of us, I know that no mouse is more capable of protecting our backside than you. Should you see anything suspicious, drop some caltrops, or perhaps one of the flash items that I assume you keep in your tinkering pouch, and give a yell to warn us of an attack from behind.'

Hearthseeker smiled and gave the large leather pouch in his utility belt a hearty pat. Yet after stealing a glance down the empty hallway behind them, he turned back to the wizard and said, 'Milord, with respect, I feel confident the battle lies in front of us, not behind us.'

'I hope so, Ainsley. I hope so,' said Wilding, without emotion. 'Now, just one more order of business to attend to.'

Wilding reached into his robes and pulled out a piece of blank parchment. He used the quill to write a few words in large, bold letters, and then, with a magic incantation, watched the parchment float up to levitate at about mouse eye level.

Hearthseeker went over and read the note, which was now impressively — if not somewhat eerily — floating gently in the air, slowly spinning around as if pushed by some invisible breeze:

Innkeeper

With expedience, make haste to the Armory.

If you are indisposed,

Come all the same.

We expect resistance through the main channels.

With that done, Wilding headed up to join the Stranger at the front of the line of Mouselings. As he passed each mouse, now sitting down for a much-needed rest with their backs against the wall, Wilding bent down and whispered to each one, putting a reassuring paw on each of their shoulders. If their shoulders — and morale — had been sunken and downtrodden before the wizard had crept down the line and given inspiration, by the time he reached the Stranger at the party's front, the Mouseling contingent, small as it was, was on its feet and now looked poised and ready for battle. Though most of them were still weaponless, Hearthseeker could not help but think that they looked quite formidable, indeed. Of course, armed or unarmed, they were still members of King Teegan's handpicked elite Mouseling Guard — and they had been selected for a reason.

Even in their weakest moment, he felt that they would not give up so easily that day. And their will was bolstered even moreso now that General Wilding was in command.

That's true leadership, thought Ainsley. *That's why this General is part of a legendary duo who helped defeat The Rat King in the First Great War.*

'My friends!' started Wilding. 'It's time we move upward, find our footing, and continue on towards the MouseKeep Armory. But first, we will stop at the Quartermaster's Nook, where we can hopefully find some provisions, clothing, and other items which will help us as we ascend up to the FalconKeep. Stay on light paws, my brothers, and if you see something out of place, don't be shy about calling it out. At this time, we know not who is friend or foe within this castle. Any unknown mice we encounter are to be treated as foes until such time as we have identified them as otherwise. For now, our journey takes us higher — so high that our mission shall remain incomplete until we've reached a point from which we can no longer ascend. Steel yourselves for what lies ahead. The Rat King's forces will not so easily relinquish their dirty grip upon our precious MouseKeep.'

And as quickly as he finished his speech, Commander Wilding — wizard and one half of **The Fabled Two**, after innumerable seasons spent hiding and living a dual life, found himself leading a contingent of Mouseling soldiers into battle once more.

Teague and Squeak had exited the library, with Teague following Squeak as he raced down the corridor. As they scampered ever downward, Teague was continually impressed with this part of MouseKeep which he had never seen before. There were more stained-glass etchings depicting figures from Mouseling legends and lore — at least until they finally went below ground, where there was no daylight to illuminate such gorgeous artistic structures.

Squeak scurried forward to a wall and, after pressing a paw against it, a secret door slid back.

'Mister Teague, this is a secret passageway down to the animal dungeons. There is a trapdoor through the ceiling, and you can rope down from there — or, if need be, look upon the scene safely from above.'

Teague drew his hand axes out and brandished them lightly in his paws, giving each one quick twirl in turn.

'Squeak, does anyone know about this part of MouseKeep?'

'Nay, Mister Teague. Like I told you, those rats and bad mice had a map of MouseKeep, but they only stayed on the old side. I haven't seen any of those intruders here on this side of the castle. It hasn't been used in a long time though. And you know that corridors that go unused can sometimes have...bad things in them.' Squeak checked quickly over his shoulder, then whispered '*Monsters*. I saw one once down here, in the darkness!'

'What did this monster look like?' asked the innkeeper. By his tone, he was now in full on Falconrider mode, and was inclined to take the young mouse's report of monsters seriously.

'I...I'm not sure. I saw some eyes in the darkness the last time I had to come down here. But it was a different corridor, though. There is a storage area down this passageway, to the right, where they store old furniture for MouseKeep. Like bookshelves and bed frames and things. Wine barrels...you know, old wooden stuff. My mom sent me down here to get some shelves from one of the bookcases, and on my way out, that's where I saw it! I had a torch in my hand, and suddenly I saw its eyes in the reflection! Green, green eyes. They glowed in the darkness and I knew it was watching me. So I ran away as fast as I could! When I tried to tell my mom about it, she just laughed and said 'I'm sure it was your imagination, dear. I will go with you next time.' And she never sent me down there again!'

'Monsters? Hmmm...' Teague thought for a moment. 'Well, we will see what is down here, since monsters or no, I need to get to the dungeon. Nonetheless, my young mouse, be on your guard. And if you see anything unusual, anything at all, call out to me immediately.'

The young mouse nodded. And with that, Teague shimmied into the secret passageway and proceeded to light a torch sconce.

He gazed down the corridor. It was dusty and filled with cobwebs. Yet, all seemed quiet.

'See? All is well, young Squeak! No monsters down here,' said Teague cheerfully, trying to bring some reassurance to both of them amidst the foreboding darkness.

The pair continued their walk down the corridor, as Teague used his torch probingly at each turn to ascertain which direction was the right one and avoid any potential obstacles. As they descended more deeply, the chamber widened. The cobwebs were getting thicker, and dust seemed to be accumulating more quickly than before. After a certain point, Teague had to sheath his axes and draw his short sword to begin hacking at the cobwebs which had accumulated, coughing through the dust all the while.

'It seems like no one has been down this way in nigh on forever, young Squeak! How long ago did you say it was since you last came down here?'

'Over a season ago, Mister Teague,' said the young mouse. 'Up here on the right is that furniture storeroom that I mentioned! Then, a little farther down is a corridor, a large open chamber with several doors, and beyond that, the last door at the end of the room leads to the dungeon trap door.'

'Ah! We shall be there soon enough, then,' said Teague encouragingly. He continued up the chamber passageway, hacking at cobwebs and dust, and lighting the occasional torch sconce to give some much-needed light, should they have need to return up this way. On the right Teague could see a small doorway, which presumably led into the furniture storage area. Teague pressed forward.

Shining his light into the storage nook, he froze for a moment. Whether it was what he saw in the nook at the moment which gave him pause, the feeling that he was suddenly being watched, or the chill that shot up his spine, the Mouseling Captain suddenly knew that young Squeak had indeed seen a monster.

'Squeak! Stop right there! DO NOT COME ANY CLOSER! Go back up the hallway. Right now.'

'Why, Mister Teague? What's wrong?' asked the young Mouseling, his voice trembling.

Teague didn't answer for a second, he just continued looking into the storage chamber to make sure what he was seeing was real. He blinked his eyes again, hard this time, and refocused. Unfortunately, the image hadn't changed.

The furniture, or at least the overall shape of it, was still there, but he couldn't see any of the details of its woodwork. That was because everything in the storage nook was covered in cobwebs. *No, not cobwebs,* Teague thought to himself. *Spider's Silk. Woven into a HUGE web!*

And in the center of that web lay an **ENORMOUS** spider sac.

It was bigger than Teague, and pulsing with black energy — the black energy of hundreds of young spiders, soon to be brought to life, deep within the very heart of MouseKeep. This sac would be precious to the one who had lain it — and she was obviously close by.

Close by, and ready to spring upon her unsuspecting prey.

And Teague knew that he was too close to the sac. He could feel her eyes on him. Though he hadn't seen her yet, he knew she was there.

There and ready to pounce.

How could I be so stupid! he chastised himself, *those weren't cobwebs at all. They were spider webs! Stupid, Teague, stupid!*

All this happened in a split second, before Teague was roused out of his thoughts by Squeak, who was on the verge of crying.

'Mister Teague, what's wrong?'

Teague started to back up, but paused when he heard **clickety clack clack clackety clack skitter skitter.**

It was the sound of spider legs nimbly coming near him across the stone floor.

Out of the corner of his eye, Teague saw Squeak freeze in terror at the sound, becoming motionless.

Teague thrust his torch ahead, extending his paw as far as he could, and then he saw **the eyes.**

Eight eyes, shining in the darkness — right above his head. Which meant the spider was at least twice his size.

A huntress spider, thought Teague with a shiver. He locked eyes with the spider. After a moment of the torch light reflecting in the glittering green orbs, he heard a very sultry, surprisingly feminine voice call out to him.

'Well now Mouseling, we have ourselves quite a predicament here, do we not?' said the voice. 'You traveled into unfamiliar passages alone, while I have kept to myself all this time, tending to my own business, unmolested. But alas, our paths have now crossed — and here we have the greatest of paradoxes unfolding before my many eyes!'

The spider laughed with a sultry, seductive glee. Then, she climbed up the wall and hung, upside down, off the ceiling stone which was threaded with spider silk — never removing her gaze from the Mouseling Captain. As she displayed herself before him, Teague could see her size. Massive.

For some odd reason, in that moment, he thought of the childhood nursery rhyme all Mouselings are taught in their early youth. He muttered, 'When Widow, Recluse, Huntress, want to play...' under his breath as he took stock of this new threat.

He could not fight her and win — not alone, anyway. He had seen fights like this in The Arena of The Black Baron, spider versus mouse, and he knew how this was likely to go down. In The Arena, a Mouseling would wield dual weapons, and then an orb weaver or huntress spider would lock down two of his paws while the body pincers would attack and crush his midsection. It was a gruesome — and messy — way to die.

The spider continued.

'I am in your domain, the domain of MouseKeep — and yet you are in my domain too, now, aren't you? And so close to my life's work. Of course I cannot let you escape, because we both know that when my egg clutch hatches, there will be more huntress spiders in these chambers than your pitiful MouseGuard could ever hope to deal with. So unfortunately, my furry-pawed new acquaintance, I will just have to kill you in order to keep my secret secure for one season more — you understand, I'm sure. But before I do, I must confess a different secret to you — I have been alone for some time, and have been longing for some company and conversation in my solitude. What is your name, my pretty Mouseling?'

'My name is Commander Robert Teague, Falconrider of MouseKeep. And, what, may I ask, is your name, milady?'

He made a courtly little bow, knowing that he needed to make a play for time. *Think, Teague!* he urged himself. *How are you going to get yourself out of this one?*

Again, the sultry voice spoke.

'Aah, so polite, my little mouse! Yes, you know your manners, don't you. Clearly, you must be a military mouse. Such a pity too, that I cannot keep you longer for more conversation. If you must know, my name is Arachne. And here, in my domain, is where you shall breathe your last. Unless, that is, you can come up with a compelling reason for me not to kill you both, though I'm afraid that I cannot think of any. Can you?'

Teague sheathed his sword and started to speak.

'Mistress Arachne, listen to me. My young friend and I here are on our way to the animal dungeons. The minions of The Rat King have taken over both MouseKeep and Castle Feldenspar, and it is critical that I get through to stop him. As you know from The First Rat King War, his dominion and dark power are a threat to all animals, including your kin. Should his plans come to fruition, darkness will fall over the entirety of The Western Lands. We must stop him — and it would benefit you and your kin to allow me to do so unimpeded. I *need* to get through.'

The spider laughed. Again, that dark, sultry, seductive voice spoke:

'I care not for the affairs of castles and mice, my silly furred friend. If I were to let you through, Mouseling, would you be willing to keep our little secret? The secret that many hundreds of huntress spiders are living beneath your precious MouseKeep, waiting to be born?'

Her tone changed then, becoming more vile and sinister.

'Save your breath, mouse, and I will answer for you. No officer of MouseKeep would allow that to happen in good faith. And besides, how do you think I came to this place? **It was the very Rat King you speak of who sent me here!** Do you honestly think I have any care for mice and their delicate human counterparts? Nay, Mouseling, nay. I have chosen my allegiance wisely. And though you will not get a chance to relay the message, your brothers and sisters would be wise to do the same. Their resistance will be their downfall!'

Teague looked at the huntress spider, stunned. The Rat King had sent her to MouseKeep? One Eye had been right, it seemed, when he had bragged to Teague about the deceit and treachery of the evil king. His nefarious goals had been well planned out, indeed — and even Teague had to admit that sending a pregnant huntress spider into MouseKeep discreetly was a diabolically clever invasion plan. He shuddered at the implications, and suddenly felt extremely and debilitatingly helpless.

Unless...

Teague looked at the spider and addressed her.

'Mistress, before young Squeak and I came here, had anyone else passed through?'

'Nay my tiny Mouseling. The last...visitor I saw was this young... Squeak, as you say, over a season ago. I saw him getting some wood and then running away when I came close to him. I missed an opportunity for a fine meal that day — but now my patience appears to have been rewarded, as I shall be getting two meals which will tide me over quite nicely. I must say, fresh, tender Mouseling shall be a far superior repast to the crawling insects I am forced to subsist on while I am down here. But why do you ask?'

Teague reached into his tunic pocket and drew something out of it. 'Well, Mistress Arachne, if I am to die today, knowing I was the only Mouseling that could have stopped your nefarious plans, I would desire to give milady a gift. In honor of the birth of your babies... simply because I won't be around to see it.'

He thrust his paw out, still tightly closed.

'A gift? For me? You are more well-mannered than I thought,' she said. 'Well, what is it Mouseling? I wish to see your gift now, so that I may decide if it is a worthy concession of your pitiful, lackluster defeat.'

Teague kept his paw closed. 'Can you not see it? It is quite small, I suppose.'

'No, Mouseling, I cannot.'

'Come a little closer, then, Mistress.'

The spider, still inverted and hanging from the ceiling, slid down a thin strand of spider's silk to come closer towards him.

'Can you see it now?' asked Teague.

'No. Open your paw, mouse, so I can see my gift!'

And so, Robert Teague did as the huntress spider asked. He opened his paw to reveal...

A flask of oil.

'For you, milady.'

And with that he threw the flask with great force into the furniture chamber. It landed on the floor below the egg sac where it audibly shattered, spreading oil everywhere.

Suddenly, the spider realized what Teague was about to do.

'Teague, you maleficent Mouseling...YOU WOULDN'T DARE!'

She started to drop down towards him to attack, but it was already too late.

'Oh yes I would, Arachne. Now go tend to your precious 'project' — what's left of it, that is.'

And with that, he cast the torch into the furniture storage room, where the oil erupted into hot searing flame. Within seconds everything was alight, including the wooden furniture — and the intricately woven web which held the egg sac.

'Run Squeak, quickly! Back up the corridor, NOW. RUN!'

They both started to take off, as fast as their paws would carry them. Out of the corner of his eye, Teague could spy that Arachne had thrown herself into the fiery chamber, using all eight legs to try to stamp out the fire which was all too rapidly engulfing her pulsing egg sac — but it was of no use. The egg sac had caught on fire, and the screams of spiders burning alive could be heard echoing down the corridor.

It was an eerie, disturbing sound — an unnerving sound.

The two mice continued their flight down the corridor, finally arriving at the chamber's end. When they got to the secret doorway, he heard Arachne cry out:

'I will find you, Robert Teague! Mark my words. You have not heard the last of Arachne, I swear it! I will have my revenge, a million times over! I SWEAR THIS TO YOU!'

And with that, Teague and Squeak shut the door and disabled the secret opening mechanism.

That was a miracle, thought the panting innkeeper as he meditated briefly on what just transpired.

He was thankful that he and his young companion were still alive. The pair had not only narrowly avoided a nasty death, but helped to avoid a fate far worse than that for the Mouselings of Castle Feldenspar — the fate that would have awaited them all should The Rat King's spider invasion have come to fruition, deep in the recesses of MouseKeep, far below the castle.

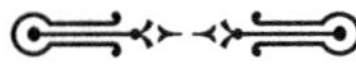

Regarding the Mysterious Circles in the Crops:

Down near Mousebrook, strange runic designs have been spotted by Mouseling farmers in this year's cereal crop. Spied from above, whether on falcon's wing or from a hilltop, they reveal themselves to be intricate patterns indeed — splendid in geometry and mathematical precision. No one knows who makes these strange runes, as they almost appear to arise overnight.

Government officials remain tight-lipped about this strange phenomenon. There have been calls for investigation into the incidents — but as of now, none have answered those calls or risen to the occasion to discover what meaning lies behind the circles in the crops, or who made them...

It is a true mystery.

— TAKEN FROM **THE FELDENSPAR DAILY**, REPORTING
ON A CROP CIRCLE CALLED **THE SYLVIA SET.**

Chapter 21

COOKING UP A COMEBACK

Storm, now dressed in Cullen's dog keeper clothing, crept carefully back up to the crest of the dungeon stairs and entered the kitchen. He kept his head down, skulking in the corner as he tried to gauge the best opportunity to discreetly talk to Sister Minerva.

As he did, he observed her.

She was very focused on her preparation of the evening meal, that was for certain. When not yelling at the dairy maidens (who were still cleaning up the creamy, floury mess on the floor) she was back by the main butcher block, adding decadent herbs and seasonings to the meat which had been removed from the fire and was now resting before being sliced. The butcher had been there by her side, trimming fat and gristle off of the roast, but he soon exited with a burlap bag, holding what Storm assumed were the trimming scraps, which almost certainly would be his family's fare for this evening's supper.

Several of the staff had their arms filled to the brim with dining implements — cups, bowls, and linens, presumably for a grand table setting — which they soon departed with up the main stairwell. The milkmaids, who seemed to have finally finished cleaning up the spill they had been working on for so long, were also preparing to depart. Storm watched as they exited, loaded down with a number of full buckets and soiled linens that had been used to sop up the mess. Sister Minerva, now alone in the kitchen, tended to some biscuit dough with a rolling pin as she prepared to cut the dough into round shapes with a wooden cup.

Storm knew that this would clearly be his best chance to speak with Sister Minerva alone. Keeping his head down to avoid being noticed (just in case any of the staff should happen to reenter the kitchen unexpectedly), he sidled up to Sister Minerva, whose gaze was focused steadily now upon cutting out her biscuits. She was peering down at the dough through her spectacles, intent on cutting out the perfect round shapes.

'Sister Minerva,' Storm said in a gentle voice as he approached up behind her.

'GET AWAY FROM ME, YOU DRUNKEN LOUT! I'VE TOLD YOU FOR THE LAST TIME!' she yelled. And with that, she whirled around and smacked Storm upside the head with the rolling pin, hitting him with such force that his brown leather dog keeper's cap went flying off onto the floor. The impact rocked him, and he saw stars for a moment. Instinctively clasping a hand to his head where the rolling pin had landed and struggling to steady himself, he looked out at her and said 'Sister Minerva, wait!'

But it was too late. He saw that she had reared back her hand again, readying the rolling pin for another vicious attack. But at the very last moment, right as she was winding up her swing, she recognized whom she had just hit, and withheld the blow. Instead of executing another powerful strike, she set the pin down and frantically grabbed for a cool cloth, her face turning red with embarrassment. She started to dab at his head, which was now bruised and beginning to swell up with a noticeable bump on it.

'Why, Gabriel Storm! What are you doing down here, Commander, sneaking up an old woman like that?! And dressed in that silly raiment — have you been demoted?'

Chuckling to herself at her 'joke,' she continued to dab the cloth at his injured head insistently, then continued.

'I am so sorry, my dear! I thought you were that drunken Jailer who has been coming in here lately, trying to grope the girls as they work on preparing his dinners — and that of his boorish and ill-mannered friends! I can't wait until King Teegan returns from his Great Hunt — he would never allow this kind of chicanery if he was around, I can tell you that! Never in all my years have I seen such brutes. Oh, and... why Commander Storm, why are you dressed like a dog keeper?'

'Sister Minerva, you must listen to me. I need your help, and King Teegan does as well. Will you come with me?'

'Come with you? Well of course I will come with you, my dear, but later — I can't just scarper off right when we are about to serve dinner. I don't have time for games right now deary. Maybe afterward, you can come find me...'

'Sister, King Teegan has returned and he needs to see you. He is this way. **Please!'**

When Storm emphasized the word **please**, the monastic sister finally understood that something truly urgent was happening, and that Storm was in need of further guidance. She relented, and Storm took her hand and quickly led her back to the dungeon staircase.

'Come this way, Sister!' said Storm. He guided her downward to the midway point of the rounded staircase, where she saw King Teegan, looking frail, and the unconscious Queen being held up by the two dog keepers, one of whom was stripped down to his underwear.

At the sight of King Teegan, she dropped to her knees and made a religious gesture, almost in shock, as she mouthed, 'My Liege!'

In that moment, she knew something was terribly, terribly wrong.

King Teegan took her hand and said, 'Rise, my Sister! Never has your King been happier to see you — and never has your King needed your aid more than he needs it now, at this moment. Are you loyal to the crown, should your life depend on it?'

'My King, I have served you faithfully since I was a young girl. If I need to give my life in service to the crown, I will gladly do so if it helps to strengthen the kingdom and your reign.'

'Good. I knew I could count on you, Sister,' said Teegan. 'But we don't have much time. Now, listen to what has transpired, and what we must do to fix it.'

King Teegan took Sister Minerva gently by the hand and looked into her eyes. In that moment, she knew that he had been weakened — she had never seen him look so pale, so gaunt. Even his hands were cold to the touch, and they felt somewhat bony — not the rich, warm, robust hand clasp she had become so accustomed to him giving her in greeting over the course of his decade as King.

Finally, after a lengthy pause that seemed like forever, King Teegan began to speak.

'My dear Sister Minerva. The men whom you are about to serve dinner to represent a military invasion force sent to dethrone me as King of Castle Feldenspar and send The Western Lands into turmoil. How, why...that doesn't really matter right now. What matters is that we need to reclaim the Castle as quickly as possible. Only then, when we have regained a position of strength, will we be able to analyze how this was allowed to happen and who is behind it — though I have my suspicions. Storm and I believe that, with the Castle Guard having been sent to Old Town on a fool's errand, there may be a secondary invasion force coming — presumably up The Riverpath. If this is the case, then time is of the essence — and you stand to play a critical role in our attempts to recover Feldenspar Castle.

'First, we have to get the Queen safely out of the Castle. She was given a sharp blow to the head and has lain unconscious for several days. I fear terribly for her safety, and we must get her to a healer, quickly. I am not sure who her assailant was, as I was attacked at the same time, but mark my words this day: when I find the man who struck her, his life shall be forfeit. However, should the Queen be discovered by our enemies, and our prison escape become known before we execute our own plan, all of our lives will be lost.'

'After we secure the Queen, we will need your help to acquire some fighting implements. At this point, anything will do — knives, ropes, even burlap sacks, whatever we can find to help us gain a foothold as we retake the castle. I recall the butcher having an extra stout and sharp cleaver, if you get my meaning. While we arm ourselves for battle, we will also need you to locate any of the staff who can help in this fight — and whom you know, personally, to be loyal to the crown. Lastly, we need to form a plan of attack and neutralize Tempus and whichever of his friends aided him in his bid to take control of the Castle. Can you help us?'

Sister Minerva looked somewhat stunned as she slowly came to the realization that Castle Feldenspar had been torn asunder by a seemingly small and innocuous group of visitors. But as that realization grew, she looked at King Teegan with great resolve, and then began to speak.

'Milord, do you know that these men are upstairs right now, preparing to revel in a grand feast that they said you yourself ordered! They are in the Great Hall as we speak. Close to us— yes, very close! Lady's mercy, if we tip our hand, all will be for naught. Of course, sire, I will gladly help you to punish those insidious fools and traitors to the crown. But I will not, even if it means my neck must stretch for my insolence, have the King's raiding party go into battle malnourished and looking like death twice warmed over, as you do currently — if you will forgive me saying so, my King! I may be old, but I have not yet forgotten the days, not so long ago, when the son of the Heaven's King could be found sneaking in and filching cheese tarts fresh from my ovens — heavens, no! Strength and nourishment go hand in hand, my King, and upon my honor as a monastic sister, I will not have any of you going up there and entering the crucible of battle on an empty stomach. This is one battle we cannot afford to lose, sire   and I won't have us losing it on MY account because the Castle's rightful defenders were weak as newborn babes from hunger!'

Of course, Gabriel Storm was unsurprised at Sister Minerva's unfailing loyalty — and equally impressed at her being so ardently resolute even in the midst of such dire circumstances. Without waiting for the King's reply, she sped hastily back into the kitchen, fetched water and wineskins, filled them, and then busied herself grabbing some soup tureens and a pot of bubbling, buttery beef stew. A few moments later, she'd brought it back quickly down the staircase, and after administering some water to the still-unconscious Queen, King Teegan, the two dog keepers, and Commander Storm were ravenously drinking water, wine, and slurping stew directly out of the bowls.

It was only seconds before they felt a wave of relief wash over them. Storm felt the cool water and spicy wine flow down his throat and into his stomach, parching the burning thirst that had scorched him from days of deprivation. In that moment, hunched over a bowl of stew halfway down the dungeon staircase, Storm thought to himself, *I've had so many meals over the course of my life, but never have I noticed red wine to taste so rich and delicious. Never in all my years has water tasted so sweet and cool, and never have I known stew to be so satisfying.*

Looking in the eyes of King Teegan, he could tell that his King was experiencing the same emotions.

Suddenly, Storm heard a man's voice yelling out in slurred speech. 'Sister! OHHHH SISTER MINEEEERRRVA! WE ARE WAITING FOR OUR DINNER, YOU OLD COOT! WHERE ARE YOU?'

Then Storm heard a crashing sound and the breaking of ceramic pottery — presumably a jug or piece of crockery — as the crashing sounds continued.

Sister Minerva cocked an ear towards the kitchen and blurted in a strained whisper, 'Forgive me my King, but I have to get back upstairs! It's that rapscallion drunkard back in my kitchen, and he is up to no good!'

She raced back up the stairs. Storm saw her pause, wait a beat before entering the kitchen, then watched her skip back in. After a moment, he heard her in the distance saying politely, 'Oh, I beg your pardon milord, your supper will be ready soon. I just sent the dairy maids out for some more buckets and the biscuits will be in the oven shortly. Can I get you some more wine, perhaps, while you wait?'

'Whew, that was a close shave!' said Cullen. 'But Commander Storm, how are we actually going to get upstairs and reclaim the Castle if they are going to have a huge feast? Won't they outnumber us something awful, being all concentrated together and whatnot? Without the element of surprise on our side, surely they'll beat the stuffing out of us and the battle will be lost, milords! After all, between the lot of us, all we have is our bare hands and the Commander's jeweled dagger — and begging the Commander's pardon, but I don't think that'll get us very far against swords, pikes, and halberds!'

Storm rubbed his chin thoughtfully, but his thinking was interrupted by the sound of another ceramic jug crashing to the floor above them and splintering into a thousand pieces.

A second passed, and then Storm lit up, inspired by the catastrophe that was currently transpiring in the kitchen.

'Cullen, you've just given me an idea,' he said. 'I know the perfect way for us to get up there and join the feast unnoticed! We just have to help serve dinner.'

He clapped his hands together and rubbed them with delight and anticipation.

'Let's go lend Sister Minerva a hand, eh? It seems like her plate is a bit full at the moment.'

With that, he beckoned to his companions to join him in stealthily ascending up the stairs, with intent.

But no sooner had Commander Storm gestured towards his companions then he froze and whispered to them, 'STOP! SHHH!'

The party listened quietly. Yes, there was a din in the kitchen, but the sound that Storm heard was not coming from above them, but from downstairs, below their position on the staircase   and it was coming up quickly!

Hearts began racing — had their position been given away?

Silently, the Knight Commander raised a finger to his lips, indicating they should all be quiet. For a moment, the party heard nothing. But then:

Shuffling. Slow shuffling. Cursing. Another human speaking, in low and muted angry tones, growing a little louder with each shuffling step up the stairs.

'I don't know who did this to me, but by Her Magnificent Knickers they will pay. I swear it, I'll crack some skulls this day, I will...'

It was the Jailer! The drunken lout who had been instrumental in imprisoning the King, his Queen, and Commander Storm, as well as the Guardians of MouseKeep.

Storm and the King came to the realization at about the same time and looked at each other. How had he managed to escape the prison cell they'd left him in, they wondered?

But there was no time for answers. Slinking back against the wall, the party was in a precarious position, halfway between the kitchen and the Jailer's Nook, totally out in the open. Should they head up into the kitchen and risk being discovered, or try to ambush the Jailer on the stairwell, while they were still nearly weaponless? Of course, he should be weaponless as well, and they did outnumber him — or so they hoped.

But their hopes were quickly dashed when they saw him come around the bend of the staircase wielding a nasty-looking short sword in his right hand. The Jailer was dressed in his underclothing, yet still wearing his boots — a sight which would have been comical, had the circumstances not been so dire, and the consequences potentially mortal. While Storm had initially taken the Jailer's clothing, it now lay discarded in the stairwell, left in a dirty and rumpled pile at his feet where he'd changed into Cullen's dog keeper clothing.

They saw him before he saw them...he had been distracted for a moment, having spied his clothing on the floor.

'Me clothing! What in the...?'

He went to reach for the pile of clothes, then something made him pause momentarily. He stopped and looked up, only to realize that the source of all his problems was right in front of him.

The shock in his eyes was real, but quickly replaced by rage and enmity.

'Why you lousing scobberlotchers! I'll have all your heads on pikes by the time the sun goes down today! When I'm through with you, you'll wish you had stayed in your cells and died peacefully from starvation, like we intended!'

And with that he started to charge up the stairs, quickly closing the gap between them, brandishing his sword and pointing it straight at King Teegan, clearly intending to run him through.

Gabriel Storm thought fast. With lightning speed, he grabbed the remaining leather cap off the top of The Bird's head and whipped it at the Jailer's face, striking him squarely in the eyes.

'CAP ATTACK!' yelled the Knight Commander.

Taken squarely by surprise and temporarily blinded, the Jailer stumbled backwards, trying to regain his balance as he stepped lightly to the preceding step and worked to avoid slipping and falling down the stairs.

King Teegan saw his moment — and took it. Even in a weakened state, he drew a momentary surge of strength from somewhere deep down within him, and for a few moments, became reinvigorated. He was the King of Feldenspar, after all, and an extremely formidable fighter. Perhaps it was the spark of the great leader inside him, or perhaps it was his recognition that this was the first of several battles — each of which would be instrumental in retaking the castle — that fueled his sudden transformation from weakened monarch to steely-eyed warrior.

As the Jailer was about to slip backwards and fall down the stairs after being hit with the unexpected leather projectile, the King moved in, blocking the Jailer's wild sword swing and trapping his sword hand against the wall. He then spun and gave a hard back elbow to the

Jailer's face, dazing him, then quickly ripped the sword from his hand and held it high over his head in a two-handed grip, ready to strike.

Within seconds, the Jailer had gone from predator to prey. The look in his eyes expressed the incredulity he felt, and almost as quickly an overpowering and unstoppable realization came upon him — that he had been engaged in an unsuccessful coup d'etat to overthrow the King of Feldenspar, who now stood before him, weapon in hand, preparing to render judgment.

His judgment.

And if we are telling true tales, he was, in fact, about to be judged.

'How did you escape your cell?' asked Commander Storm. 'I personally locked you in there after retrieving my dagger from your filthy grasp.'

'You don't know the old key in the boot trick, knight? I was a jailer for The Black Baron's Animals for many years, old man. No jailer worth his salt ever goes to sleep without tucking away a skeleton key for all the prison cells under his minding. It's equally useful for receiving generous bribes to grant a prisoner an 'early release,' or to make sure you can get out of a hairy pickle should you find yourself the target of a jail overthrow — it happens more than you'd think, you know. Standard operating procedure among those of us in the craft, my ancient friend — as is stashing a hidden blade for yourself in case you ever have call for a bit o' steel in your hands. Had you been more skilled, or had a bit of extra knowledge you don't pick up through your fancy-arsed book learnin', you would have thought to check my boot and saved yourself all this trouble. Of course, I thank you for your courtesy — or should I say, ignorance — in failing to do so. Present circumstances excluded, of course.'

The Jailer let out a hollow laugh and then spat towards Storm with intention, but the spittle fell short of meeting its mark, landing idly on the step below him.

'Tell us who sent you, and everything you know. NOW!' said Teegan, his patience wearing thin.

'I'm not telling you insects nothing. No matter what happens to me, your kingdom will soon be in ruins anyways. So go plow yourself, old man! Besides, maybe I never rested my arse on no fancy throne like you, but that don't make me no fool. We both know that you know who sent me — who sent ALL of us. HE is the real King of these lands. Soon his dark plans will swallow you and the entirety of your tiny pissant fiefdom here. There is no stopping the oncoming darkness. The Rat King's forces will reign triumphant before long.'

'We'll see about all that,' said the King. 'As an insurrectionist and agitator, and for your willing participation in a plot to overthrow the rightful King of Feldenspar, I hereby sentence you to death for treason against the crown — sentence to be carried out by beheading. Now go and meet your maker, you vile filth!'

And with that, in a calm and practiced manner, Teegan swung the sword as adeptly as any knight in his kingdom could, sweeping the Jailer's head cleanly off his shoulders. He swung so fiercely that, after decapitating the Jailer, the sword came to a hard stop only after it collided with the stone wall of the staircase, making an eerie, hollow ringing sound that echoed across the stairwell chamber. The body fell backwards, lurching down the stairs, but the now bodiless head preceded it, making an interesting, yet somewhat sickening, bouncing sound as gravity took it back down and around the spiral staircase, occasionally bouncing off a wall before finally settling, with a few final bounces, at the bottom of the staircase in the hallway that led back to the Jailer's Nook.

There was silence as the King wiped the blood off the sword with his bare hands, simply out of habit. He then wiped his bloody hands on his breeches and tossed the sword, its blade now bent irreparably, down the staircase in the direction of the Jailer's head.

'Tis a shame,' said King Teegan with some degree of remorse. 'If ever we could have used a stout blade — or even a pitted and scarred one — it would be now.'

The party looked silently at each other for a moment, until finally Commander Storm broke the silence.

'Speaking of serving dinner, I now know the perfect first course to really get the party started!'

The recovery of Castle Feldenspar had begun in earnest. And King Teegan had struck the first convincing — and decisive — blow.

It was about the same time that Commander Storm and his party were reentering the kitchen that Wilding's party had begun its ascent of MouseKeep.

And, if we are telling true tales, the going was slow.

While most of the time, the doors of MouseKeep were kept open to facilitate the fast passage of the MouseGuard to and fro in their duties, the impostor mice (and their conspiring colleagues) had closed all of the tiny wooden doors. Some were locked and barred from the rear, and some were unlocked — which the party universally agreed meant that there were either traps or sentries behind them. With a diminutive party size and a relatively weak strength against the unknown rogue garrison which now occupied MouseKeep, Wilding and Finnegan Willowtail felt it best to continue their ascent silently. They determined their best course of action was to continue padding and plodding until they could regain the Quartermaster's Nook in hopes of a quick respite and resupply, at which point they would begin the final ascent up to the Armory. If they could reequip themselves at the MouseKeep Armory, they would, at the very least, have a fighting chance against any attackers.

IF they could get there.

After ascending for what seemed like forever, they came to a level juncture where the corridor widened, opening up into a large antechamber which split into three passageways — two on each side, with another corridor continuing straight ahead and beginning a new ascent, presumably up to the next floor. It had been many seasons since Wilding had last been in MouseKeep. Hearthseeker, of course, had never been there, and the Stranger — well, it was understood that at his rank he had never had a reason to spend any real time deep within the sanctuary of the mouse bastion.

Wilding turned to Finnegan Willowtail for counsel and advice.

'Commander, what is this place?' he asked.

Willowtail closed his eyes and sniffed the air for a moment. Then, he opened his eyes and said, 'There used to be signposts here — at all of the passageways, really — to ensure you knew where you were travelling. As far as I recall, if we head east — to the right, that is — that will lead us to the Quartermaster's Nook. Heading west would take us towards the MouseGuard sleeping quarters and family lodgings. Upwards, to the north, would continue our ascent to the Falcon Rider's Perch — and of course, the Armory is right there before you emerge.'

Wilding looked at the party of mice, all of whom were unarmed besides him and his two companions. They had to find some resupply, and quickly, if their mission was to succeed.

'Is there a connecting passageway from the east Quartermaster's Nook which ascends to the Armory?'

A younger mouse, no more than nineteen or twenty seasons, spoke up. He had whitish fur and black markings around his eyebrows and cheekbones.

Well, he is certainly a very handsome one, thought Wilding. You don't see white fur like that too often.

'Commander!' The mouse saluted and addressed the wizard with the proper respect of a MouseKeep soldier.

'What is your name, soldier?' said the wizard.

'Leftenant Snowwillow, sir — son of first officer River Willow, former Commander of the First Rider Legion.'

'Your face seems familiar to me, somehow, though I cannot place my paw on it. What is on your mind?' said Wilding.

'There is a connecting passageway that goes from the Quartermaster's Nook to the Armory, sir. However, it does wind around the castle quite some ways, which raises the possibility we could be seen by the enemy. If we were to take the north passage here, you would find that we could gain access to the Armory more quickly...'

But if Wilding was listening to the young leftenant with his conscious mind, something deep within his subconscious seemed to be called to attention on an instinctual level — something more pressing, deep, deep, down. And right in that moment, time seemed to slow itself down considerably.

Wilding wasn't sure what was happening, but suddenly the leftenant seemed to be speaking slow, garbled gibberish. He heard the scraping of wood on wood, a sliding sound, so soft and quiet he wasn't even sure if he had really heard it. Then, a blast of air roared by his snout — **WHOOSH** — and he felt the arrow fly by his forehead, narrowly missing his temple by a fraction of an inch and slamming into the eastern wall of MouseKeep, sticking there with a slight **TWAANNGG**.

He looked at the arrow protruding out of the wall and turned towards Finnegan Willowtail. But his head seemed to move so slowly, the time running like molasses, as their gazes locked in fear. They were both experienced combat veterans, and through their mutually locked stare they could silently acknowledge to each other what was about to transpire.

Nodding to each other in slow motion, the slowdown of time suddenly shattered and Wilding was able to scream to his fellow mice:

'AMMMBBBUUUSSSHHHH! DEFEND YOURSELVES!'

But it was no sooner than the words had been uttered that all hell broke loose.

Within a fraction of a second, all three doors of the juncture opened, and imposter mice, accompanied by rats, poured in from every direction. Some archers stayed in the doorways, peppering arrows at what MouseGuard they could see — though mercifully, as the narthex became more crowded with bodies, their targets became more elusive.

As he watched the rats pour in, Wilding thought about what that fischer he had blasted with a freeze spell had said to him. *One Eye was the only rat, the fischer said*...either the fischer had lied — or, more probably, he hadn't known about the other contingents of rats that had infiltrated MouseKeep as well.

But the wizard didn't have time to digest and process the meaning of this new information — though he certainly knew it could not be good news for the loyal defenders of MouseKeep — because combat was about to envelop him.

For Wilding, it all happened so fast that pure instinct took over. A Ratling adversary came at him with a sword and a deeply sinister intent, but he parried the incoming blow with his staff, then did the same for the rat's follow-up strikes: **parry parry, dodge, STRIKE!** And with that, he rained a massive, skull-fracturing blow upon the Ratling attacker, who crumpled to the ground instantly like a lifeless rag doll.

Turning, he saw his mouse brothers locked in life and death melee combat.

It was calamity.

Pure chaos.

Young Leftenant Snowwillow, though unarmed, had evidently been trained in some form of martial arts, because Wilding watched him intercept a wild, swinging club attack by an impostor mouse dressed in crimson and black garb. He continued watching with keen interest as, in nearly the blink of an eye, the young Mouseling performed a **Seven Sword Paws** striking combo on the unfortunate attacker: **intercept and disarm club, neck chop, face paw strike, sternum-crushing front paw fist, eye rake, hammer paw to Ratling medulla, ricochet groin strike.**

Snowwillow's attacker fell to the ground with one paw clasping his raked eyes and the other paw holding his groin (which, based on the force of the blow Wilding had observed, had most likely been ruptured). The attacker had been effectively neutralized, and Wilding watched as Snowwillow retrieved the spiked club from his assailant, wielding it deftly with a level of skill Wilding had not seen in years.

Then, almost as quickly, Snowwillow was attacked from behind by an enraged Ratling with a two paw rear choke! But the young leftenant neutralized it just as quickly: **inverted standing paw rising kick to groin, hard rear elbow to snout.**

Wilding watched as the rat, who was almost twice the size of the young mouse, was taken by surprise when his snout exploded with blood. Shortly afterwards, he fell unconscious to the floor.

He's good, thought Wilding.

Then, as if to emphasize Wilding's thought, Snowwillow yelled out:

'Courage, my brothers! Fight to the last mouse—FOR MOUSEKEEP!'

The rallying cry of the young mouse emboldened the MouseGuard. Finnegan Willowtail—who was more of an old school brawling mouse—was busy punching a Ratling attacker in the face with his bare paw, but redoubled his efforts upon hearing Snowwillow's battle shout.

Even the Stranger was swinging his sword wildly, looking frenzied as he attacked a mouse in black and red while cursing under his breath. Wilding heard him say something to the effect of 'and THIS is for the little mouse!' as he cleanly took the head off his opponent. The Stranger watched it roll onto the floor, and then gave it a final, aggressive kick for good measure. The head of the newly decapitated mouse flew and hit another impostor mouse squarely in the snout, knocking him to the floor as well.

Nice move, thought Wilding to himself.

The MouseGuard fought on valiantly.

Out of Wilding's eye he saw Hearthseeker, sword drawn and held menacingly in a combat stance, being accosted by two attackers — a mouse dressed in crimson and black and a rat, both wielding swords.

Above the din of combat, he watched intently as an *extremely* focused Ainsley Hearthseeker pointed his sword at his two assailants as they circled him, then addressed them rebukingly:

'Evil ones, I will warn you both — my name is Ainsley Hearthseeker, and I am known across The Western Lands for my mastery of swordplay. I will tell you truly, and I will tell you simply: I am a legend. You cannot win this engagement. And I would rather not make widows and orphans of your loved ones. Surrender now, and on my honor as a bard of Old Town, I will spare your lives.'

Is he bluffing? Wilding wondered. *That's one intrepid mouse!*

The impostor mouse and the rat looked at each other incredulously, and then charged the bard with renewed anger.

But before they could reach the bard to attack him, they both exploded into fire and fell to the ground, screaming and writhing in pain as the flames consumed their bodies — and their lives.

Ainsley looked over to where the fireballs had come from, only to see Wilding holding his staff, still pointed in the direction of the now-flaming bodies on the ground, with the ruby gem in its hilt glowing brightly red.

Annoyed that his moment for glory had been stolen by the wizard, Hearthseeker yelled out, 'I COULD HAVE HANDLED THEM BOTH, YOU KNOW!'

Wilding yelled back, 'YOU CAN THANK ME LATER!'

The combat continued. But if the tide of combat had been flowing in favor of Wilding's party, their morale began to drop as more and more rats and impostor mice rushed in, flowing over the bodies of their own fallen comrades in an attempt to finish exterminating the remaining guardians of MouseKeep. A few Mouseling heroes were wounded in the melee, and soon both Finnegan Willowtail and Wilding came to the stark realization that the battle for MouseKeep would not — could not — be won in this chamber, where they were vastly outnumbered, outflanked, and out-equipped.

Wilding yelled out:

'Brothers, push upwards. North, through the passageway, to the Armory! Go! Go NOW!'

And with that, the fight continued.

MouseKeep's finest fought their adversaries with great valor, pushing ever forward into the corridor of the northern passageway which went only one direction — upwards. With paw and claw, the warriors pushed into the northern passageway, and one by one, they fought their way in.

Wilding, sensing the need to close this chapter of combat quickly if the war was truly to be won, cast a greater fog spell. And soon, everything was covered in a dense, thick mist.

As the imposter mice and rats choked in the fog and stumbled around blindly, Wilding's party exited the northern passageway, shutting the thick wooden door behind them and barring it from the inside. In the silence that ensued, he took a quick head count: all thirteen had made it through the doorway, including Hearthseeker, the Stranger, Willowtail, and Snowwillow — but it was obvious that three of their number had been seriously wounded and were no longer in any condition to continue fighting.

That was almost thirty percent of their party composition.

'We can't take another skirmish like that,' said Finnegan Willowtail, as he and several other mice tried desperately to attend to the wounded. He was only saying out loud what Wilding had been thinking to himself at exactly the same moment.

'Indeed — another victory like that, and we may be finished,' Wilding replied. 'For now, we must keep moving though, and hope that our luck holds. Courage, my brothers! You must steel yourself for what lies ahead. We WILL end this invasion and reclaim MouseKeep today.'

Wilding had no sooner finished speaking than he regained his position in the front of the line. A true leader and tactician, he led the last guardians of MouseKeep forward — unafraid, and resolutely committed to seeing the invasion forces of their adversaries laid low — even if it meant giving up his life in the process.

A Gambling Mystery:

The Mouseling, impeccably dressed in a tuxedo, placed his bets on the Flops table as all eyes fell upon him; he had bet Castle, Castle, Castle. He also made a pre-bet on Three of a Kind. And then he placed down ten gold!

As everyone finished placing their wagers, the pit boss yelled, 'NO MORE BETS!'

And then, the cards came down —

CASTLE, CASTLE, CASTLE

The crowd erupted into cheers at the gambling acumen and amazing psychic ability the gambler seemed to possess.

'It's a miracle!' I said to Stormsnout, as I watched the unusual gambler get paid 10:1 odds on his impossible bet, and then an additional 10:1 on each individual Castle bet. 'He made 40x his money in one paw, Sir Pendleton! How could he possibly have known the cards would fall like that? Amazing! He truly must have been blessed with a gift from Her Holy Providence!'

'I don't know,' said the detective, looking suspiciously at the gambler's left paw. 'I don't know, Alfred...but, if I have ever made a promise, then I promise you this: I have every intention of finding out.'

— Taken from **The Chronicles Of Sir Pendleton Stormsnout, Book I: The Curious Case of the Gambler Who Couldn't Lose**

Chapter 22

SQUEAK'S GAMBIT

Squeak and Teague hadn't stopped moving since they had left the passageway with Arachne some time ago.

It had occurred to Teague, as they put more distance between themselves and the terrifying event they had just encountered, that the only direction he had known his companions were heading towards was to the dungeons. With no further information available to him, he had to work his way down there to seek their whereabouts and disposition.

Had they found the King? Had they successfully located any of the missing warriors of MouseKeep?

Unfortunately for Robert Teague, all of these questions remained unanswered.

To make matters worse, his encounter with Arachne had presented a huge roadblock to what would have been a quick and efficient route. The trap door Squeak had been guiding him towards would have led directly down to the dungeons, right in front of where the animal cells were. It would have saved them SO much time — but going back to a passage where the now-enraged Arachne awaited was, obviously, not an option.

Though Teague had faced more dangers in his life than he wished to remember, he had never courted them willingly — and only a mouse with a death wish would willingly cross paths with Arachne again.

So, Teague and Squeak found themselves scampering, without a respite, back upwards through the newer side of MouseKeep. After completing that lengthy journey, they would, of course, have to reenter — and cross over — the Great Hall to make it back into the 'traditional' side of MouseKeep. Once there, they would need to head downward again through the Castle's diminutive passages, which would, eventually, lead them to the dungeon's spiral stairwell outside the kitchen.

The very spiral stairwell where, unbeknownst to them, Storm and Wilding had parted ways some time ago.

Teague, of course, had no idea of what his friends' whereabouts were, or what had transpired since they parted ways outside of The King's Pedestal hours before. It was unnerving, not knowing where they were, or if they were well. He knew he had to try to find them — and the most logical place to start looking was their last known whereabouts.

Detective Sir Pendleton Stormsnout would approve of this logic, thought Teague to himself cheekily.

After some time, and a lot of distance covered, they emerged back into the entry chamber where Teague and Squeak had first met. They both sat down on the ground, panting heavily. Peering out of the trap door and into the feasting hall, Teague was taken aback by the sight of a large number of humans engaged in various activities. Some of them — servants, obviously — were making table settings for guests. Some were cleaning, and he could see several humans sitting at the great feasting tables, drinking what Teague assumed must be wine out of golden goblets.

Teague wasn't sure what time it was, but the day was starting to grow long. Everywhere he and Squeak turned, they seemed to hit some new roadblock. If it wasn't pregnant huntress spiders planning a takeover of MouseKeep, then it was the large number of humans that seemed to be everywhere in the Great Hall, evidently preparing for a huge feast at the same time that the two mice desperately needed to cross back over to the traditional side of MouseKeep.

Teague's thoughts focused narrowly on the group now seated at the feasting tables, carousing and having themselves quite a fine time.

Having a party when the King is missing? That's odd, thought Teague. *I wonder if the human whose eyeball I shot is in that room?*

Spying furtively from within the protected confines of the camouflaged door, Teague looked out at the tables and surveyed the towering human faces. Finally, at the head of the grand feasting table — where the King would normally be seated — he spied a pale-faced human with greasy black hair sporting a hastily-crafted black eye patch.

That's him! thought the innkeeper. *Now what in Her name is he doing here, in this hall?*

Teague knew his mission was far too important to stop and try to cause some kind of disruption for these obvious human infiltrators, who Teague knew were most likely pawns in The Rat King's plan to overthrow Castle Feldenspar. Besides, he knew now where the enemy was located (the human ones, anyway), and based on their wine consumption, he figured the odds were good they wouldn't be leaving those feasting tables for some time. *Knowing where they are should give me a tactical advantage,* Teague thought. *To what end, I don't yet know — but an advantage is an advantage, nevertheless.*

Still, crossing the Great Hall was going to be a problem. If we are telling true tales, it can be incredibly difficult for any Mouseling to traverse a room with a lot of humans present, no matter how skilled that Mouseling might be.

Getting spotted is one issue, of course. But getting stepped on accidentally — which would result in an instant, crushing death for an unlucky mouse — is quite another. Teague wasn't sure which was worse: being crushed underfoot, or being spotted — which usually resulted in being chased around by some humans (often with a broom, rake, or some other long-handled instrument), at risk of having your escape routes cut off, or inadvertently running into large, heavy human objects, which could be quite painful and injurious.

Teague had had a cousin who'd died this way. He'd been running as fast as he could, trying to escape from a human with a broom, when he suddenly collided with the leg of a dining table, cracking his skull in the process and resulting in immediate death. Of course, the human (it was reported by his surviving rooting partner) still swatted him with the broom a few dozen times after he'd stopped moving, just for good measure.

I don't know why humans are so scared of mice anyway, thought Teague to himself, annoyed. *If anything, they should be scared of rats! Vile, filthy creatures — they're a far bigger threat. But it's a messy business, I guess.*

Teague's mind snapped back to the matter at hand.

'Squeak, we have to get across this Great Hall, and I doubt if we can make it across undetected without a good plan or a solid disguise. There are just too many humans in there, too much activity. It's extremely dangerous — too dangerous to risk just making a dash for it.'

'Disguise?' said Squeak. 'Like what, Mister Teague?'

'Well, I don't know exactly,' Teague replied. 'I heard a story about two mice who were trapped in a human woman's shoe closet once. They turned the shoes upside down and crept out under them, carrying the shoes on their backs. Whenever the woman came into sight, they would simply 'play dead' under their shoes, and it looked like a pair of shoes had simply been left lying on the floor. Somewhat askew, perhaps, but next to each other. And the ploy worked! They both escaped with their lives — or so the tale went, at least.'

'Is that where **The Old Mouseling Who Lived In a Shoe** comes from?' asked Squeak inquisitively.

'Umm, what?' said Teague.

'Never mind,' Squeak replied. 'That's not really important, I guess. But I do have an idea for a disguise!'

Teague watched Squeak go over to some wooden barrels that were full of archaeological refuse from his mother's work — discarded rocks and dirt and the like. He kicked two of them over and emptied their contents onto the floor. After all of the debris had been removed from them, he rolled them both back over to Teague.

'We found these under some of the feasting tables after a party late one night, lost and forgotten. These aren't barrels — they're wooden drinking cups for humans!'

'Squeak, you are a genius!' said Teague, impressed.

'Now there is just one more thing we need to do...'

With that, Teague lifted up the empty wooden cup, placed it over his head, and squatted down so the cup was flush with the floor.

'Can you see me?' asked a muffled voice from inside the cup.

'No, Mister Teague, I just see a dirty old cup.'

'With a dirty old mouse underneath it!' said Teague as he peeked his whiskers out from under the cup. His face was all smudged, having been covered by the dust and ash left over from the debris that had been in the cup but moments ago. They both started laughing at how ridiculous Teague, a distinguished warrior, looked, his face and fur all covered in dirt as he peered out from beneath a dirty water cup.

And yet, such an audacious and outrageous plan seemed to be just what was needed, given how the events of the day were unfolding.

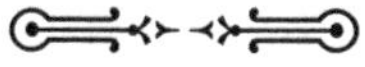

After the Jailer had been dispatched, Storm and the party had quickly ascended up the stairs. There was never going to be a better time to retake the Castle than when its infiltrators were letting their guard down to celebrate with their 'victory feast.' After all, in the minds of their former captors, all had gone perfectly — all, that is, except for that nasty incident at The King's Pedestal. But then again, who REALLY cared about mice? The real mission had been accomplished — from their human perspective, that is. The knights of Feldenspar had been dispatched to Old Town, and the King, Queen, and Knight Commander were locked away in the dungeons, either dying from thirst and starvation with seemingly no chance for escape, or dead already.

Their work was done, and soon the takeover of Castle Feldenspar would be complete. Reinforcements would arrive shortly up The Riverpath to relieve them. But now, in their minds, it was time to celebrate.

It was clear to King Teegan's company that the infiltrators were in an extremely vulnerable position: overconfident, and now swiftly growing complacent. The fact that King Teegan's ragtag company had a legitimate opening to attack and gain the upper hand against their enemies — and to do so with the element of surprise firmly in their favor — was not lost on any of them.

No, not at all. They may have been out-armed and out-manned, but they could all recognize that by Her Holy Providence, they had been gifted a blessed opportunity to strike back — and they needed to capitalize on it before it slipped out of their grasp.

So, in short order, everyone who was 'in the know' snapped to and began working feverishly to prepare for the inevitable conflict that awaited them. Sister Minerva, having deftly intercepted one of Tempus's drunken cohorts, sent him back upstairs with a very generous pitcher of fine red wine and a small cheese board, telling him it had been gifted on behalf of his 'service' to the King. In fact, once she had bestowed this 'gift' on him, she continued the ruse by following him up to the feasting hall with an additional jug of wine in one hand and a loaf of fresh bread in the other. After helping him take his seat, she made a rousing speech to the emissaries' group as they sat at the grand feasting table, which was traditionally occupied by the King.

'Milords, I know that His Majesty is away on The Great Hunt, but in the spirit of his hospitality, we have prepared a grand feast for you. It is almost complete! But I know, through a lifetime of service, that King Teegan himself would not want honored emissaries from distant lands to be left wanting while they await the fine meal that is being prepared on their behalf. Here, lords, please enjoy this jug of wine and fresh baked bread, along with this cheese plate, and rest your weary bones! Unburden yourselves! We will bring the food up shortly. But if it pleases you all, I must have my servants return to the kitchen, as we need as many hands as possible to bring up each and every course of the fine fare you shall soon be dining upon!'

'Hear, hear!' said the emissaries' group, and they all toasted their cups and goblets, drunkenly spilling wine all over the King's table.

Then one of the rabble actually slapped Sister Minerva on the backside as she was leaving!

All the men started laughing, but as poised as ever, the monastic sister continued to walk back to the kitchen — though beneath her veil, her face was red as a beet.

Meanwhile, after listening to Sister Minerva play her role beyond perfection, King Teegan and Storm sent Cullen and The Bird to carry the Queen out to the dog kennels. Climbing inside, they gingerly lifted the King's wife up into the kennels' hay-filled loft and laid her inside. She moaned softly in her still unconscious state, prompting The Bird to ask:

'Cullen, do you think the Queen will be alright?'

Cullen shook his head doubtfully. 'Milady is injured pretty seriously, lad. She needs a healer, and soon — or I fear she may be lost to us. But we have done all that we can for her, and we can't do no more than that. We must now return to protect the King. Bird, grab those two sleakers and that sack of dung the tanner left here when we was working those hides the other day. That'll give them what for!'

The Bird followed his orders, grabbing two long-handled knives that the tanner had brought to trim the uncured leathers which had been left leaning against the dog shack. Then he grabbed the sack of dung and held it up, asking Cullen:

'What's this good for?'

'A dirty surprise, my friend! Special payback to those louts who put us in jail. If I can teach you nothing else, Bird me lad, let me impart to you the greatest piece of wisdom I ever received from me own da: 'Cullen,' he says to me, 'You never know when a sack o' dung might come in handy.' Wise words to live by — and ones that have never let me down in the past. Now, let's get back to the kitchen, shall we?'

No sooner had that pair left the dog shacks then Sister Minerva, at about the same time, had finished ushering all of her servants out of the Great Hall and back down to the kitchen. While the kitchen was empty, the King had put on the bloody apron which the butcher had left hanging by the fireplace. He'd also picked up the butcher's stout steel cleaver as well. Above the roaring fireplace was a black woolen cap, which the King grabbed and placed over his head, pulling it down low over his eyebrows. He leaned against the fireplace, trying to look like the butcher.

'Nice getup, milord,' said Gabriel Storm, still dressed as a dogkeeper.

Truth be told, it actually was difficult to tell the difference between King Teegan and the butcher — there was a more than fair resemblance between the two.

As Sister Minerva brought her servants in, she pulled three of the dairy maids aside, quietly whispering instructions into their ears, then watched as they departed up the stairs, stationing themselves strategically throughout to act as a primitive sentry system: one at the top of the staircase to intercept any of Tempus's men and distract them with conversation, one at the middle of the staircase to help run interference, and one at the bottom to relay a warning back down to the kitchen as needed.

As they took their places, Sister Minerva gathered her staff around her and looked them in their eyes. They surrounded the large butcher block counter where the feast had been prepared. With a serious tone, she said to them:

'I have known each of you for years, and I know that ALL of you are loyal to the King. And if you value your honor and your sense of duty, know that our majesty, King Teegan, needs you now more than he has ever needed you before. I'm not sure how to tell you this, but my monastic Mother taught me that the best way to deal with bad news was to face it head on. So, here it is: the men upstairs — the men who have been terrorizing our kitchen and our staff for days now — are interlopers, infiltrators, and rapscallions. They are guilty of the vilest treason imaginable, and they have somehow succeeded in usurping control of the castle. They have imprisoned our beloved King and Queen without food or water and left them both for dead. Through guile and subterfuge, they have sent away the Castle Guard and sent King Teegan's knights chasing off after a fool's errand, leaving us here undefended.'

She paused to let the veracity and severity of her tone sink in.

There were gasps and looks of shock. Some of the younger women placed their hands over their mouth, and tears filled the eyes of women and men, young and old alike.

The sister waited for a moment more, then continued.

'Fortunately, they did NOT succeed in their evil plans — or perhaps I should say, they have not succeeded yet. Knight Commander Gabriel Storm, who was ALSO imprisoned by these usurpers, was able to escape and rescue the King and Queen. The Queen is injured very badly, but is now safely resting and will be in the hands of a skilled healer soon. The King is safe and very close by, as is Commander Storm. And now, the King desires that we serve the men upstairs a different kind of meal than they were expecting to dine on this evening — rather than roasts and cheese tarts, we will force them to eat blades, and run them through to the last. All of you, save the dairy maids standing guard in the staircase, will be expected to accompany me upstairs, where under the guise of serving dinner, we will attack these imposters at their most vulnerable and reclaim Castle Feldenspar for its rightful — and only — ruler: King Teegan the Lionsmane.'

There was dead silence as the kitchen staff considered what Sister Minerva had said. There were scarcely any men among them — just a few older servants who had served the King for years and settled comfortably into their long-held roles within the Castle's serving staff. Most of the staff was female, and less than twenty years old.

One of the older serving maids stood proudly, though she was clearly scared. Her lip quivered as she said:

'But Sister Minerva, we are not fighters. Who will lead us into battle?'

The monastic sister was silent for a moment, then turned to the figure leaning over the fireplace, dressed in a bloody apron and holding a large cleaver.

'He will,' said Sister Minerva, pointing.

'The butcher?' she asked, her shock betraying a bit of exasperation. 'But he's no fighter!' she stammered, looking at him incredulously. 'You...you only know how to kill helpless animals!'

The figure in the bloody apron walked towards her and she instinctively shrunk back, knowing that she had misjudged her place with the errant comment. The butcher was, traditionally, one of the heads of the kitchen, and from a servitude standpoint, she had lost track of her 'place.'

The tall, imposing figure with the black woolen cap continued to walk towards her, then stopped when he was just a few feet away.

'You are right, milady,' he said. 'The butcher of this kitchen has no fighting experience, and he cannot lead you to victory this day against these vagrants upstairs. But I can.'

And with that, King Teegan took off his cap to reveal his namesake mane of long hair.

'Majesty, Majesty!' they all cried out, and almost in unison, the kitchen staff immediately fell to their knees.

'Arise my friends!' said the King. 'I have known many of you since I was a young man, rifling through the kitchen in search of food to satisfy a growing lad's rumbling belly. And though I am not sure how we fell victim to the predators upstairs, or who they were sent by, I promise you, we *will* reclaim the castle this day. But I need your help — all of you. Every hand counts. We must fight to the last man — and woman — if necessary. Who is with me? Who will fight to save your land, your castle, and your families? Who will fight for Commander Storm?'

Storm came forward from his spot leaning back against the wall and removed his leather cap. He smiled broadly at the kitchen staff.

'Hello, my friends!'

If the kitchen staff were loyal to King Teegan, they *LOVED* Commander Storm. They all rushed up to hug him, asking him if he was well, where he had been, and how had he gotten the huge bruise above his eye.

Sister Minerva, upon hearing the last question, pinched two fingers to her nose and shut her eyes, shaking her head.

'I am fine, my friends, and I thank you for your concern. Time grows short, though. We must prepare for battle.'

He looked around the room at each of the kitchen staff.

'And now, the time for what we call 'head cutting' is upon us. We will need every pair of hands to go upstairs and give these mercenaries exactly what they deserve — a just and violent death. Only when their bodies lay lifeless on the floor of the Great Hall will our task be complete. Once that is done, we will re-secure the castle and close the bridge on Mirrored Lake as we assess the tactical situation. Now, who will fight for your King?'

A moment of silence fell among the kitchen staff. A young girl in a servant's apron raised her hand.

'Commander Storm, if we go upstairs...will we die?'

Storm looked at Teegan, whose stern expression softened as he thought about the question and observed the young girl. No more than fifteen years of age, she was tall, with a lithe and nimble build.

'What is your name, girl?' asked Teegan, gently.

'Cara, milord.'

'Cara, your question is an important one. Will we die if we go upstairs? Yes, it is very possible that we might. Some of us may die, or get terribly hurt. Some of us might lose an arm or a leg, or get wounded and die later from an infection. All of these things are possible. But what you need to know is, I would rather go upstairs, confront the evil that was sent here, and die fighting it in the process, than let my fear get the better of me and run away — knowing that in my lifetime, I was party to letting evil men spread their deeds across The Western Lands from a seat of power within Feldenspar Castle. It is only natural to fear death — but I would rather die knowing that I did so attempting to stop a great evil than to live knowing I could have fought against its spread, but didn't. So I will be going up there to serve dinner, even if it is just Commander Storm and myself who choose to walk into the Great Hall. None of you will be judged if you don't come with me, none will think any the lesser of you, and there will be no repercussions if you choose not to accompany us. I know most of you are not trained fighters, and that you did not choose to serve this Castle expecting you might ever need to go to battle within its walls. With that being said, if enough people do not choose to stand by our side, the battle will surely be lost. How many men are at the feasting tables?'

The King looked around at the kitchen servants. One of the older men raised his hand.

'I counted ten, sire. Plus the one with the eye patch at the head of the table, so eleven men total.'

'Eleven men. Are they armed?'

'Yes, sire. Half wield swords which are in their sheaths by their sides. The other half carry halberds or pikes, which have been set against the western wall in a weapon rack. If you could serve dinner from that side, sire, between the serving carts and the serving staff, we could try to prevent the unarmed mercenaries from gaining access to their weapons. With a mite of luck, sire, perhaps we could hold them off long enough to incapacitate the unarmed attackers whilst your party deals with the armed men.'

'What is your name, my friend?'

'I am called Padraig, sire. I have served in this kitchen for over thirty years, in service both to your father, as well as yourself.'

'Padraig, your keen eye is a tremendous boon to all of us — it may have just saved the castle. Your astute observations will no doubt help us tremendously in the fight that is to come. Now, my friends, eleven men, half of them unarmed, are what currently stand between us spending the rest of our lives as slaves or retaking Castle Feldenspar and becoming free men and women again, as we have always been. On our side, we have myself, Storm, and the two dogkeepers, Cullen and Bird. Who else will stand for their King?'

The staff looked at each other for a moment, in silence.

Finally, the girl Cara raised her hand and grabbed a chef's knife off of the butcher block counter.

'I will fight with you, my King — until we are victorious, or I fall in battle at your side.'

She brandished the knife lightly in her right hand. Her eyes had the look of a woman who had made a firm decision to fight for her freedom and sovereignty.

Padraig stepped forward also. 'I will fight with you, my liege.'

'Good, Padraig, and Cara both. Stout fellow — and stout lady, as well. Your valor will not be forgotten. Who else shall join us?'

Sister Minerva grabbed a large cast iron frying pan from the butcher block table.

'I will fight, and die, by your side, my King.'

Commander Storm looked at her wielding the frying pan, then asked, 'Sister, forgive my impertinence, but you seem equally adept with a rolling pin. Are you sure you wouldn't prefer to bring that along instead?'

Sister Minerva rolled her eyes, and Storm smiled — then they both laughed out loud.

In the end, every member of the kitchen staff stepped up to the challenge their King had issued. Sister Minerva, Cara, Padraig, Cullen, The Bird, Storm, Teegan, and two other older male servants all made a pact to remove the enemy from the castle or die trying. It would be their party of nine versus an armed party of eleven mercenary fighters upstairs. The three dairy maids were sent to tend to the Queen in the dog kennels, with orders to see if they could get her to take small sips of water and tend to her wounds.

'It's an almost fair fight, milord,' remarked Storm to Teegan.

'I'll take these odds. Add in the element of surprise and we'll have a solid fighting chance to give those louts the justice they truly deserve. Now, Gabriel, what's the plan?'

'Everybody gather around!' said Storm commandingly, clearly in his element as a leader of fighters. 'Now, we will need more of these serving aprons, and as many of these serving carts as you can find. Once we have assembled those materials, this is what we are going to do.'

As he listened to Gabriel Storm lay out the battle plan, using kitchen elements like spoons and knives to act as tiny models representing the situation they faced ahead of them in the Great Hall, it occurred to King Teegan that in all his years as prince, and then as King, he had never once thought the day would come when the control — and future — of Feldenspar Castle would come to rest in the hands of untrained kitchen servants, monastic sisters, and dogkeepers.

But be that is it may have been, it was at that moment that the King realized how truly lucky he was to have such good and loyal friends by his side, unflinchingly ready to face what was about to transpire.

Overheard Bar Conversation Between Two Mouselings at The Sleeping Cat:

Mouse 1: *Have you heard about the bard who once fought a Crested Tarbog Rattlesnake — and won?*

Mouse 2: *Bah! Balderdash. No mouse could defeat a Crested Tarbog.*

Mouse 1 (Takes a sip of ale from his wooden mug): *Nay, it's true - I heard it from me cousin himself! Some bard from Old Town did it with a magical sword he called 'Snake Slayer,' or somesuch. He stabbed the snake* right through the heart! And ever since, that's why they call him...*THE HEARTSEEKER!*

Mouse 2: *The Heartseeker?*

Mouse 1: *Aye, the Heartseeker   believe you me! I heard he actually moved TO The Tarbogs because he loves killing snakes so much. Can't get enough of it! Refuses to dine on aught but raw snake meat — or so they say. And it's also said he's been bitten so many times, he is now immune to snake venom...*

Chapter 23

DINNER IS SERVED

Looking out from the trapdoor on the new side of MouseKeep, Teague spied the humans. Both he and Squeak had brought their wooden cups to the door and were preparing to cross the Great Hall. In his heart, Teague felt like he not only was putting his own life, but the life of his new young friend at great risk by attempting to cross over, given the amount of traffic that currently occupied the Great Hall.

Then, a miracle happened.

Teague saw an old woman in blue velvet monastic robes come up the kitchen stairs with some wine and bread in her hands, set them down on the table while addressing the men sitting there, then quickly gather up all the servants and usher them back downstairs. Having done this, the hall was now practically empty, except for the men who were still sitting down at the tables, munching on bread and drinking flagons of wine.

It must be time to serve dinner, thought Teague. *Now is our chance!*

'Is it time, Mister Teague?' asked a nervous Squeak.

Teague looked out the trapdoor, his back against the wall nudging it open. It seemed like the coast was clear — for the moment. If they were going to make an attempt to cross, it was either now or never — they may not get such a window of opportunity again.

But something nagged at Teague. He couldn't put a paw on it exactly, but he felt like maybe he wouldn't make it. A premonition maybe, or perhaps just a dreaded fear of his luck running out. Teague thought pensively that perhaps today was going to be his day to die. He had heard stories of the Eastern Mouseling warriors of old, the ones who had practiced the idea that any day was a good day to die — but for Robert Teague, with his family waiting for him back at The Sleeping Cat, his best friend still somewhere in the Castle lost to a fate unknown, and with a young mouse by his side who would most likely meet his own demise should Teague make an early departure, the sinking feeling in his gut told him he had to make a contingency plan.

So he did.

'Hold on a minute there, Squeak. There is something I have to do before we cross.'

'What is it?' asked the inquisitive young buck.

Teague headed over to one of the tables, found some old parchment, and turned it over so he could write on the back. Taking a pencil in his paw, he wrote a quick note:

Captain Redfur Tumblefox
Feldenspar Tavern and Lodge
23.5 South Main Landing

Honorable Captain Fox —
As you may recall, as The First Rat King War drew to a close, you told me to contact you if I ever needed your service again.

Though it has been many seasons since I have taken up your pledge, King Teegan and myself, plus Commander Wilding, need your help — direly, and with great speed.

MouseKeep has been overrun by forces unknown. As I write this, we are inside the castle, fighting to reclaim it.

Please accept this young buck named Squeak under your care and keep him safe, as a personal favor to me.

If you have any fight left in you, round up the old boys and get them here, posthaste. I'm assuming they are close by — probably at your very bartop as I scribe this.

Rats, fischers, and mice garbed in crimson and black are all enemy combatants and should be treated as such.

Time grows short this day. I am unsure if I will live to see the end of it.

Remember the 59th rule.

Yours Faithfully,
Robert Teague
Falcon Rider Commander, 1st Platoon, Retired - 'Raven's Wing'

Teague rolled up the note and, melting some wax on the table from a nearby candlestick, created a seal upon it, which he then imprinted by taking off his necklace and pressing it against the soft wax as it cooled. When done, it left a striking imprint of a falcon on it, with a hollowed out cavity where the pendant's gem was. He scribbled **23.5 South Main Landing, Innkeeper Tumblefox** on the outside and handed it to Squeak.

Then, he looked the young buck in the eyes and clasped his paws gently.

'Squeak, look at me. Once we cross back into MouseKeep, I need you to take this note into town and ask for an old friend of mine at the address I wrote here.'

He pointed to the rolled-up note, then continued.

'Once you give him this, he will keep you safe at his tavern until I come for you. No matter what happens to me, I need you to get this note to him. You'll have to be careful going through town, but get there as quickly as you can. Do you understand?'

'I...I don't want to be alone, Mister Teague!' said the young Mouseling, now clearly sad and forlorn.

'Courage, young Squeak! This mouse can help keep you out of danger — and with any luck, perhaps send a few mice to help us clean up this mess. But once we've crossed the hall, I want you to get out of your cup and go. No matter what happens to me, you go, and don't stop running until you get there. On your life, now, promise me. Got it?'

The young mouse looked like he was about to cry, though he was bravely trying to hold back his tears.

'I...I promise.'

'Good lad. NOW it is go time! Into your cup with you, my friend, and may She guide us to the safety of Old MouseKeep, free from the sight of humans or the possibility of being caught underfoot!'

And with that, Teague and Squeak, disguised as two old wooden cups, opened the trap door and made their way out into the Great Hall, scrambling for the safety of MouseKeep — which was most certainly in sight, but seemingly still so far away.

Of course, two old wooden cups moving by themselves across the floor of the Great Hall were the last thing on the mind of the men seated at the feasting table. They were focused on enjoying their victory celebration.

Golden goblets of wine had been filled and then refilled, and the men were eagerly devouring both the bread and cheese plates brought up so graciously by Sister Minerva. Ten men were seated at the feasting table, along with Tempus, the Animal Speaking emissary, who sat at the table head in the position normally reserved for King Teegan.

Eleven men had been all it had taken to send Castle Feldenspar into chaos.

And if the men had been successful in their mission, they most certainly were even more garish in their celebration of it.

'I cannot believe how easy this was!' remarked one mercenary, clad in leather armor and sporting a long brown beard, now half-drunk from his cups. 'Those Feldenspar knights were so easily tricked into going on a fool's mission into Old Town, leaving the King and Queen such easy targets. To victory!'

Cups were clashed together in a slovenly toast as wine went flying — though Tempus sat brooding at the head of the table, not drinking, deep in thought.

'Wot's a-wrong with him, ey?' one of the swordsmen whispered to his table companions.

'Awww, he's just sore cuz he got shot in the eye by one of them talking mice,' another swordsman answered him. 'And where's that Jailer? It ain't like him to miss a meal — or a drink!'

'He's probably off chasing and carousing with those dairy maids again,' said a taller man who was seated next to Tempus. They all burst into lascivious laughter at the thought.

'Shut up, you fools!' shouted Tempus. 'Until the reinforcements arrive here, our mission is not truly finished — and that could take days, or even weeks, depending on when our missives arrived and assuming they did as intended. I have no intentions of becoming the messenger who has to return to The Dark One and tell him that we somehow failed him. If we had to do that, your necks would be separated from your bodies as surely as mine.'

One of the men poked his finger towards Tempus and retorted:

'You just sound like you's mad cuz you got shot in the eye by one of them lil' mousies. Them nasty-looking rats and fischies wot came with us will have taken care of them mousies in short order, Tempus, and we won't have to worry about them no more. Quit worryin' and come drink with us!'

Tempus looked around at the mercenary crew that had been assigned to him and shook his head. They were all uneducated, unbathed, and poorly mannered. Had the King of Feldenspar been less trusting, their ruse could have been easily discovered. Yet somehow, it had worked out.

Hadn't it?

He hadn't seen the one-eyed rat since the skirmish at The King's Pedestal — and truth be told, he hadn't seen many other rats, or even had an update on how the MouseKeep operation was progressing since then either. It was unnerving. If there was something happening, it had to be within the walls of MouseKeep, since all was quiet within the Castle. Even though he had the gift of animal speaking, without one nearby to give him an update, he was left just as blind and in the dark as his foul-smelling, illiterate companions.

Out of the corner of his eye he noticed two wooden cups in the middle of the floor, seemingly forgotten and most certainly out of place. He watched them for a moment, idly.

Were they moving?

These thoughts were interrupted by a loud outburst from one of his companions.

'Dinner is served, boys! Prepare to tuck in to a well-earned feast!'

'Hear hear!' the rest yelled. More goblets were slammed together, spilling more wine and making an even grander mess on the table.

Tempus looked around to see what they were cheering for, and soon spotted it. From the crest of the kitchen stairwell poured forth a regal train of kitchen staff bearing all manner of dishes.

It was quite the processional — formal, even ceremonial in nature.

There were older male servants — and a few young ones Tempus had never seen before — dressed in fresh serving aprons, as well as other female staff pushing all manner of carts filled to the brim with gorgeous foodstuffs. On one cart, a cornucopia of fruit, cheeses, and bowls of delicate sauces sat balanced superbly atop a bed of greens. And the piece de resistance was, of course, hidden under a huge, silver-domed platter — presumably, the main course — which was being pushed by two serving maids.

At the head of the procession walked Sister Minerva in her crushed blue velvet robes and a fresh serving apron, carrying something in her hands which was covered with a towel — some kind of carved fruit table centerpiece or some-such, Tempus assumed. With her was a tall butcher, a black woolen cap pulled low over his eyebrows.

What a grand feeling, finally being treated like I deserve...like a King! thought Tempus to himself smugly.

Finally, the procession arrived at one side of the table and the carts pushed until they were set in a way where every man at the table could observe the massive feast they were about to be served. After this was completed, the butcher wheeled the main serving cart with the domed silver top over towards the head of the table, parking it in front of Tempus himself.

Of course, Tempus was in the seat that the King normally occupied — and now that the King was 'away,' he naturally took his rightful place.

I could get used to this, thought Tempus.

Sister Minerva cleared her throat and began to speak:

'Hear ye, hear ye! Lords from afar — though King Teegan is away on The Great Hunt, it is his majesty's will that you receive the same courtesy and hospitality that you were kind enough to show him since you arrived. Though we have not heard from him in several days, he has always had a standing order that any guests of the crown be treated with the utmost gallantry and receive the very best that Castle Feldenspar and its bountiful lands have to offer. And so, with his majesty's blessing, and thanks to the skill of our finest butcher, we have prepared for you this great repast, to thank you for what you have done, and to celebrate the new alliance we have formed with your peoples!'

The men at the table clapped heartily and chortled with laughter at the old woman's obliviousness to the circumstances.

'Hear, hear! Boys, a toast to the King of Feldenspar!' one man said, raising his golden goblet.

'To the King of Feldenspar,' they chorused in unison.

Sister Minerva continued.

'And as we speak the name of the King, may She save him. Our butcher has prepared a special course for the main dish this evening. One which I have no doubt you...gentleman...will find more than memorable. Butcher?'

The tall butcher with the woolen cap eased the cart over even more closely towards where Tempus sat at the head of the table. He then pulled out a huge cleaver and a long knife from underneath the table and scraped them back and forth against each other, sharpening the blades for the coming cut.

'Milords,' said the butcher, nodding and showing respect to the party. He placed his gloved hand on the handle atop the silver dome, and paused momentarily for effect. 'I have prepared a most special meal for you this evening.'

Something about this butcher seems oddly familiar, thought Tempus.

The men all leaned eagerly towards the serving cart to see what was about to be revealed for their dinner. Their bellies rumbled and gurgled, and the men salivated with anticipation.

The butcher paused for one more second, then, with a grand sweeping gesture, pulled off the domed top of the platter to reveal the evening's feast.

'Your dinner is served.'

A moment of deep silence fell over the feasting hall as the men instantly fell silent, trying to comprehend what they were looking at — trying to understand what it meant — because what they were suddenly looking at was no delicious prime rib nor succulent roast of pork.

What the butcher had revealed was something quite different altogether.

It was the head of the drunken Jailer.

With an apple in his mouth.

Meanwhile, the MouseGuard continued their desperate ascent up towards the Armory. After the ambush in the narthex, they remained very much on guard, though for some strange reason they hadn't yet seen any more enemy combatants as they crept upwards through the tunnels of MouseKeep. To make matters worse, they were slowed by the fact that three of their number had been wounded badly enough that they couldn't walk on their own, and each had to be carried by two of their brothers.

Wilding, leading from the front with battle staff in hand, looked back at the three wounded Mouselings and observed the draining strength of the vigilant brothers who labored to carry them. He called for everyone to take a brief rest, then pulled Finnegan Willowtail and Hearthseeker aside so they could hold a brief discussion.

'We can't go on like this,' started Wilding. 'We have six fighters carrying three mice who will probably not last the day if we don't get them to a healer in time. Given the nature of our mission, we cannot afford to go back. We must press forward to the Armory. Ideas, gentlemice? If you have any, now is the time to share them.'

Willowtail looked down at his hindpaws and bit his lip, deep in thought.

'Commander, we can't leave these mice behind. MouseGuard code says 'where we go one, we go all,' and the same applies if a mouse falls in battle. Surely you know this.'

'Indeed, Willowtail, I am quite familiar with the code. One could make an argument, however, that these are somewhat...extenuating circumstances. Hearthseeker?'

The bard reached into his pouch and pulled out a small vial of bright green liquid.

'What is that, ambrosia?' asked Willowtail.

'No, my friend — it's even better. It is a potion of restoration. I was saving it for an emergency, but this seems like emergency enough to warrant its use. Commander Wilding, if we can find a connecting passageway that is safe, we can administer this to each of our wounded comrades. If we are telling true tales, it looks like they will each need a full dose — and I have only the one vial to split between them. But perhaps if She wills it, a third of a dose would provide at least some benefit, and allow them to stabilize long enough to wait for a healer. Depending on how effective it is, they could hide in the safety of a hidden passageway until we return — or, if they recover enough, perhaps even move to flee the castle and make their way directly to a healer. It may not be ideal, but it is, I believe, our most viable option at this juncture.'

Wilding rubbed his chin thoughtfully, then finally spoke. 'Hearthseeker, you never cease to amaze me — you and your bag of tricks. I'm not sure if we would have gotten this far without you. If you are willing to part with it, I say we administer your potion immediately while the rest of our party rests here momentarily, regaining their strength. We can find a suitable place to leave these mice in relative safety and comfort, and come back for them as soon as we have properly equipped ourselves at the Armory and secured the Falcon Rider Perch atop MouseKeep.'

Hearthseeker nodded and headed over to the wounded mice. As he gave them a few words of comfort, he uncorked the vial and began pouring the rich, green liquid into each of their mouths. After a few minutes, he could see that the three wounded mice had some color return to their faces, and their breathing seemed to have slowed and lengthened. It was obvious that the potion was working its magical effects to great benefit. Hearthseeker encouraged each wounded mouse, telling them of the plan to find a safe hiding spot where they could sit and rest. Nodding in assent, all three mice struggled to get to their paws, only this time it took but a single mouse each to help them along, whereas before two had had to help carry each wounded combatant.

'Press onward, my brothers!' said Wilding, and upward they went.

Climbing, climbing — it was all well and good for a human, with their massive height and long legs, to ascend five, six, or seven stories to the top of the castle. But even with the ramps of MouseKeep, going from the ground floor to the top of the Castle was still a lot of hard work for a tired Mouseling!

Nevertheless, they pressed on. Finding a suitable side passage, the party parted ways from the three wounded mice, leaving them safely hidden to continue their recovery.

Still, they pressed higher, Wilding leading them onward and upward. Finally, after what seemed like an endless climb, the floor leveled out and the passage came to a two way split. One way continued forward on the same level, while the other went upwards on a ramp. A small hand-painted sign pointed the way to **ARMORY!** and **FALCON RIDER PERCH!,** respectively.

'Almost there, Commander,' said Finnegan Willowtail. 'And no signs of rats, thank Her mercy.'

He breathed a sigh of relief.

'Stay on guard, my friend,' said Wilding. 'I am sure we have more surprises waiting in store for us.'

The party went forward until finally, Wilding could see a small wooden door up ahead of him. In the door was a sliding wooden panel which served as a window. It was closed, but could be opened from either side.

'Stay here,' he told the mice, then snuck carefully towards the door. Pressing his ear against it, he listened intently.

Nothing...silence.

All he could hear was his own heartbeat, which suddenly seemed to be the loudest thing in the room.

Cautiously, he gripped the handle on the wooden slat which could slide back to allow a viewer to peek into the Armory. He slid the small wooden piece quietly...oh, so quietly...until finally he had a full view of the Armory.

All looked to be in order.

Inside, he saw a grand room — one of the biggest rooms in MouseKeep — and at the outside wall was a large stained-glass window, below which was a wooden ledge with staircases running along both sides. The stained-glass windows let in lots of light, even now as the sun was setting on the western side of Mirror Lake. Draping down along the sides of the stained-glass were crushed velvet curtains which could be closed if it was too bright, or to help keep the warmth in during the chilly months of winter.

As he surveyed the room for any signs of the enemy, he saw weapon racks of all sorts. Bows, quivers chock-full of sleek-looking arrows, halberds, swords, pikes, crescent-bladed knives, daggers. There were throwing weapons, shuriken, caltrops, and even incendiary explosives intended to neutralize larger animals when necessary. Additionally, Wilding saw all kinds of armor sets, from light leather and cloth battle robes up to the sets of full plate mail used by the select mice who had been knighted and trained from a young age in their use.

It was a treasure trove of equipment, and just what they needed right now.

'Come on!' gestured the wizard to his party. 'The coast is clear. Gear up!'

And so, the wizard opened the door and the Mouseling party flooded in. Soon, each mouse was grabbing weapons and armor, whatever their preferred fighting style reflected. Wilding was pleased to see one of the mice grab some white battle robes and a mage staff from a barrel of staves.

A fellow wizard! he thought proudly to himself. But then he realized the mouse had more likely been trained as a monk, and simply preferred to wear simple robes and fight with a staff (or even his bare paws), where he was most adept and skilled.

Even Hearthseeker was in his glory, merrily stuffing his pouches full of caltrops, incendiaries, and shuriken of all sizes and styles. Soon his pouches bulged.

He's ready for war, thought Wilding to himself.

'Ok boys, gather 'round, gather 'round,' started Finnegan Willowtail. 'Now that we are equipped, we will give those rats what for! Here's the plan...'

But if the party's morale had surged to an all-time high as they had been re-equipping themselves, it plummeted sharply as it heard the eerie, piercing laughter that suddenly echoed out and boomed across the chamber.

'Oh, DO tell us the plan, Mouseling,' leered a creepy voice.

All the mice turned and looked towards the stained-glass window, now captivated with fear by the unseen voice.

Then they heard its laughter again. Its maniacal, unnerving laughter.

'HA HA HA! A HA HA HA HA HA! You mice didn't REALLY think we would let you come all the way up here without consequences, did you? You've lost your precious MouseKeep, and you won't be getting it back anytime soon.'

'Show yourself!' shouted Wilding to their unseen tormentor.

'Oh, yes, Commander Wilding. I will show myself...if only to get one more look at your face before you die. When we met at The King's Pedestal, I'll admit, you managed to fool me with your little disguise. But I won't be fooled again by you — or by your little friend Teague, whom I owe quite a repayment to.'

'SHOW YOURSELF, YOU TRAITOR!' yelled Wilding, stepping in front of the group, staff in hand. His rage became palpable at the thought that he had led his brothers into a trap — which grew more and more apparent as he digested the voice and the words that were being spoken to him.

He started trembling with anger.

Still, the Mouselings didn't know who was speaking to them — or more specifically, who was speaking to Wilding, as it seemed.

But Wilding knew who it was.

It was The One-Eyed Rat. AGAIN.

Teague, it seemed, had not been able to dispatch him.

And that worried Wilding — it worried him a great deal.

From above the ledge in front of the stained-glass window, the rat — who was somehow missing his tail — emerged out from behind one of the crushed velvet curtains. The spot where his tail should have been (and where it most certainly HAD been, earlier in the day) had been replaced by a bloody stump which was wrapped haphazardly in a bandage. A large quantity of blood had soaked through the makeshift bandage, staining the cloth brown as it dried. Yet still, he strutted about like an animal who was eager to show off before going in for the kill, gallivanting across the platform almost like he was dancing.

'Well looky here, boys. I, the great Cornelius White Eye, have returned — and I've brought many of my friends with me for you to play with! I thought it only fitting we have a second chance to play Mice and Rats today.'

His prancing would have been almost comical if it hadn't been such a grave situation.

A coterie of a dozen archers followed him out onto the ledge from behind the curtains, bows drawn and arrows nocked. They stood on the high ground, ready to release the arrows into their unprotected quarry standing mere feet below them. Several armed fischers stepped out from behind the curtains as well, and marched down the staircases with pikes in hand, their sharp points aimed menacingly at the now-outnumbered group of Mouseling defenders.

Wilding stood there, staring daggers at the one-eyed rat. Still, seeing that One Eye's tail had been separated from his body gave Wilding hope, knowing that it was most likely Teague who had struck the blow. The two locked gazes, and there was a momentarily silence.

Then Wilding asked him, trying to buy precious time:

'What happened to your tail, vermin?'

The one-eyed rat hissed with rage and spat on the ground.

'You want to know what happened to my tail?! I'll tell you what happened — your honorless, vole-licking weevil of a friend, Robert Teague, snuck up on me while I was right in the middle of fighting a cat and chopped it off from behind! He was too scared to face me, that sniveling coward — he probably soiled his pants when he saw how I was pummeling a monstrous orange tabby cat in the kitchen and just getting ready to hack it to pieces! So while I was occupied in a life and death struggle with a gargantuan giant of a cat, your gutless craven of a friend must have seen some kind of opportunity — because he snuck up behind me, CUT OFF MY TAIL WHILE MY BACK WAS TURNED, then ran away, SCREAMING LIKE A FRIGHTENED DOE! And though I want you to be certain that I WILL make him pay the next time I see his weak, blubbering face — it speaks volumes to the fact that you Mouselings have no honor, and fight like SPINELESS BABY SQUIRRELS!'

Wilding, hearing this story, knew the only truth that was likely to be found in it was that Robert Teague had cut off the rat's tail — probably in combat. Everything else sounded like a rat's typical self-serving fabrication — but still, the wizard was relieved to hear the rat discuss the future possibility of seeing Teague after he 'ran away.'

Considering this, Wilding's thoughts were interrupted once more by the rat, as he continued to gleefully gloat about the dangerous position he'd caught the remaining MouseGuard in.

'What's the matter wizard — cat got your tongue? Surprised to see me again? Thought you were headed towards a safe haven, did you? Tsk tsk tsk...oh Wilding, you think in such small parameters. It really is unbecoming of your so-called magical talents. You and I, we have unfinished business together. But the truth is, I just don't have the time to see it through — so, I brought some friends along who will help take care of my business for me. And if we are *'telling true tales,'* as your miserable, sniveling Mouseling expression goes, I'm a bit late for dinner downstairs. Everything has come together quite well, all things considered. And even though you and your little friend Robert Teague have made quite the mess of it, in the end our plan still worked smashingly. King Teegan is gone, his wife too, as well as that pesky Knight Commander — all removed from the game! Too easy, really. And now, with you and your friend's lives soon to be extinguished, there is nothing to stop us from taking over this very Castle! Although again, if we are *telling true tales*, of course, it really is just a *small* piece on the game board. His glorious majesty, The Rat King, has far grander plans in mind than this petty backwater. His alliance with the Animal Speakers and ability to command humans is a gift which cannot be overcome. You, of all Mouselings, should know this.'

The one-eyed rat steepled his paws together, and looking down from the stained-glass ledge at his prey, then continued.

'Where is your little friend, wizard? Do you know? Oh, no matter, I'm sure he is somewhere in the Castle. The fischers and my Ratling colleagues will find him soon enough and snuff out his despicable candle. Your little disturbance at The King's Pedestal threw a wrench into my assignment — a very minor one, all things considered — but I am adaptable, and flexible. Unlike you Mouselings who are so trusting and think so linearly. It's a shame really, that The Rat King has to destroy Mouseling Hollow. Such a pretty and...idyllic place. But, once all Mouselings have been removed from The Western Lands, his task simply becomes so much easier, so sacrifices must be made.'

'He will never get away with it,' spat Wilding, incensed. 'We will fight you to the last mouse, in this place and across the land, I promise you.'

'Oh, I have no doubt of it! If anything, I'm looking *forward* to it! The Rat King told me that you are *good* at keeping promises, wizard.'

The one-eyed rat emphasized the word *good* here, smiling nastily as he did.

'Like the promise you made to save your family? You know the one I'm talking about, so you may save your breath trying to deny it. But as I said, I am *very* late for dinner, so unfortunately, I must be off. Ta ta for now — or I should say, *hehe,* forever! Boys, make quick work of this and try not to destroy *all* this equipment — I'm sure his sovereign majesty The Rat King could make good use of some of it.'

One Eye started to strut back behind the curtains, then paused, and turned back to address the wizard mouse with a sneer. 'On second thought,' he said, 'I am feeling magnanimous today. Wilding, you old bore, you are covered from the high ground, and you know as well as I do what that means. You are outnumbered, out-positioned, and your tactical situation is extremely, well — *poor*, to say the least. I'll give you one chance, and one chance only, to kneel before me and swear allegiance to The Rat King. He himself admitted that he could make use of a Mouseling with your...talents.'

'Never!' hissed Wilding, now enraged.

One Eye shrugged carelessly. 'So be it — die then, as you wish. Oh, and do enjoy meeting my special 'friend' I brought along to help make sure you meddling Mouselings and your little 'rebellion' are put down once and for all. Come on out here, Bruiser!'

From behind the curtain rumbled out a massive striped badger on his hind paws, dressed in full battle armor and wielding an enormous two-handed battle axe. He towered over the diminutive Mouselings.

'HELLO, LITTLE FRIENDS,' he thundered in a very unfriendly way.

And with that, the one-eyed rat strode off the platform, down the stairs, and exited through a back passageway, presumably off to meet his dinner engagement.

Wilding and Hearthseeker looked at each other grimly.

'If ever we needed Robert Teague at our backs, now would be an optimal time...' said Hearthseeker.

'Prepare to fire!' ordered a Ratling captain. The rat archers drew back their bows and took aim, perched high above the surviving MouseGuard who knew there was no chance of escape.

'That's the kind of mouse who could eat peanut butter out of a snaptrap and live to tell if it was creamy or crunchy...'

— MOUSELING SAYING MEANING
'THAT MOUSE IS A FANTASTIC THIEF.'

Chapter 24

ROBERT TEAGUE LENDS A PAW

The few seconds that passed after King Teegan unveiled the evening's main course passed like an eternity. Yet Teegan's gaze was steadfast, focused solely and intently on piercing directly into the center of Tempus's eyes. The Lionsmane watched adroitly as the Animal Speaker's mouth dropped — first in shock, followed swiftly by disgust.

Finally, he looked up from the serving tray and his gaze began to transform — first from stupefaction, then to a dawning realization that Castle Feldenspar, at that moment, might not be fully under his control. Looking up at the 'butcher,' who was in the process of pulling off his cap to reveal his legendary mane of hair, Tempus instantly realized it was the King of Feldenspar himself who now stood before him — a man who, thanks to his own personal actions on behalf of The Rat King, was now his sworn and mortal enemy.

He opened his mouth to speak, but could barely squeeze a word out.

'Why you...'

But before Tempus could finish, Teegan used the dome of the silver serving tray to smash the Animal Speaker squarely and solidly in the face. The King hit him with such driving impact that it snapped Tempus's head back, knocking him over and sending him tumbling backwards out of the heavy wooden chair he had been sitting in, blood spurting from his nose in a crimson fountain.

'Bon appetit, you treasonous scum,' said King Teegan with resolve.

He then eyed the other men seated at the table.

'Now, which of you miserable Ratlickers is next?' Teegan asked with great relish.

The men looked at each other, speechless.

Then, almost at once, all hell broke loose.

While the swordsmen on the right side of the table were able to push their chairs back and draw their swords, jumping up quickly and preparing to fight, the mercenaries on the left side of the table found themselves in quite a precarious situation. The Castle's servants had taken up positions behind their chairs and quietly waited for the King's signal. The moment he bashed Tempus in the face with the serving lid, they pressed themselves up against each of the mercenaries' chairs, using the serving carts — and their bodies — to prevent the men from being able to push themselves away from the table and go to retrieve their halberds, which were resting securely in a weapons rack on the western wall.

Though risky, it was an incredibly effective tactic. Almost as soon as the seated mercenaries began to realize that they could not easily push their chairs back, Sister Minerva — now fighting with the strength of a banshee and the resolve of a highly trained monastic sister — barreled down that side of the table dealing devastating, knockout blows with the huge frying pan which she had kept hidden under a towel since the ceremonial procession into the feast.

The first man, no less than six feet tall, got hit in the side of the face with such blunt force that his jaw was dislocated. He slumped, unconscious, back into his chair. As Sister Minerva hustled to attack the next man down, she saw that she had no easy opening to club him from the side. So, she simply brought the frying pan down from the sky onto the crown of his head, letting gravity make the assist; he dropped as quickly as the first man.

Padraig was busy trying to grapple with the third scalawag to keep him in his seat — a struggle the older man was beginning to lose. Sister Minerva, seeing how he was about to be overpowered, simply shouted 'WATCH OUT!' and then rained down a blow so hard on the mercenary's skull that she was pretty sure she killed him. The man flopped forward bonelessly in his chair, his face slamming into the table and bouncing a few times before coming to rest.

While they were focused on knocking out the man that Padraig had been struggling with, the two men sitting next to him had managed to escape their chairs, and one had successfully retrieved his two-handed weapon from the arms rack.

Seeing Padraig holding down his compatriot in the middle chair, the halberdier charged the older servant from behind. Sister Minerva practically knocked him out of the way as she tried to strike the last seated attacker with her frying pan.

In the midst of the chaos, Padraig — who had been distracted while trying to dodge Sister Minerva's attack — suddenly felt a searing pain in his back and chest. He looked down, only to see the tip of the halberd protruding through the center of his sternum.

'Sister Minerva!' he cried in pain and shock, as the attacker practically lifted him into the air with the halberd out of spite.

'THAT'S WHAT YOU FELDENSPAR FOOLS HAVE TO LOOK FORWARD TO — THE LOT OF YOU!' screamed the halberdier, spittle running down his chin, his face red with rage.

Sister Minerva was aghast.

'Padraig, NOOOO!' she cried.

But it was too late. Blood was pouring out of Padraig's mouth, and it was clear that he was not long for this world. The halberdier shook Padraig's body off the long, pointed spear top of his weapon, and then watched the body topple to the ground with a great degree of satisfaction showing on his smirking, evil face. There, on the floor of the Great Hall, in a pool of blood, Padraig clasped his hands over the massive hole in his chest as it heaved and gasped for air, trying instinctively to staunch the deadly flow of blood.

Hearing Sister Minerva's cry, Storm looked over and saw that the enemy halberdier had turned his nasty-looking weapon towards Sister Minerva.

'You're next, you old coot. You've caused more than enough trouble,' the halberdier spat. 'Now you will get what you deser...'

But his comments were cut short by a gurgling sound, which came from his voicebox when Gabriel Storm's jeweled dagger flew and struck deep into his gullet. Blood exploded from the soldier's Adam's Apple as he stumbled backwards, and he dropped his weapon as his two hands became firmly fixed on the dagger's hilt, trying desperately to remove it. Cara, who had been standing near the weapons rack, drew Sister Minerva's rolling pin from out of its hiding place in her serving apron, and with a firm, two-handed grip, swung it with all her might. She smashed the halberdier in the back of the head so hard that it caved in his skull with a sickening **CRUNCH**. He fell face down to the floor, clearly never to rise again.

Sister Minerva looked over at Storm in admiration and relief, his hand still outstretched from the precise dagger throw that had saved her life. Then Cara interrupted her gaze by calling out:

'Sister Minerva!'

The nun looked at Cara, who was now on her knees, cradling Padraig's head in her lap. She rushed to his side and knelt down, trying to use her blue robes to stop his bleeding.

'Oh Padraig,' she lamented as blood poured over her and Cara's hands.

Though Padraig was grievously wounded, King Teegan, Storm, and the two dog keepers, Cullen and The Bird, had no time to stop and help. They were all still preoccupied dealing with the swordsmen, who were all obviously seasoned warriors — they had clearly become mercenaries-for-hire because of their skill and expertise with a blade.

Cullen and The Bird, dressed as male kitchen servants, had stowed the two sleakers under a rolling cart during the procession.

They had pulled the menacing blades out from under a table cloth when the time was right, and each was doing his best to engage one of the enemy swordsmen. Storm was making due with a push broom (about the best replacement weapon he could scrounge, now that his jeweled dagger was no longer within his reach), while King Teegan was going to town 'weapon and shield' style, brandishing the large butcher cleaver as his weapon and using the silver serving dome as his shield.

Clash! Cring! Bang! The sound of metal on metal echoed throughout the Great Hall as the two sides fought with incredible zeal. The fifth halberdier, having retrieved his weapon with its polished and evil-looking head, came running towards King Teegan, intending to skewer the King — but quick thinking by Cullen, who was still fencing with an enemy swordsman, saved the day. Spying the incoming attacker, Cullen grabbed the bag of dung he'd snuck into his pocket at the kennels with his off hand and whipped it right at the oncoming halberdier, striking him squarely in the face. The force of the blow caused the bag to burst open, spraying the halberdier with animal feces and temporarily blinding him.

'My eyes! My eyes!' cried the offending attacker. Dropping his weapon to rub at his eyes, he slipped in the dung, falling down to the ground. A quick-thinking Sister Minerva — who was still kneeling nearby, trying to assist Padraig — stood up and grabbed the ceramic wine jug she had brought in earlier from its resting place by Tempus's seat. Gripping it firmly with two hands, she hoisted it high above her head and spiked it onto the face of the last, dung-covered halberdier.

'THIS IS FOR KING TEEGAN, YOU LOUT!' shouted Sister Minerva, her face red from anger and exertion.

The jug shattered with a gut-wrenching ***THUNK*** and pieces of it went flying everywhere. The blow was so powerful that in its aftermath, the halberdier lay motionless on the ground, though his left foot kept twitching.

And still, the fighting continued. There remained five of Tempus's swordsmen against the four armed champions of Feldenspar —

Teegan, Storm, The Bird, and Cullen. Storm was being threatened by two attackers, while Teegan, Storm, and The Bird each squared off with a single swordsman each. At one point, Storm and Teegan backed into each other, parrying blows, then fighting in synchrony as they spun together, fending off attackers and looking for strategic openings to strike.

In the rhythmic sequence of attack and riposte, Storm whispered in Teegan's ear:

'I swear milord, if we get out of this alive, I am going to dance a jig!'

A moment later, he felt a terrible, burning pain in his knee. Looking down, he saw an arrow protruding from it. While he'd stayed occupied with one swordsman, the other had drawn a bow and, with his last arrow, shot it squarely into Storm's kneecap in an attempt to cripple him.

'AAAAAHHH!' Storm cried in pain, falling to his (now-injured) knee.

'Get up and fight, old man!' King Teegan yelled. 'Our day's duty is not done yet!'

Of course, the cataclysmic battle taking place in the Great Hall was not lost on innkeeper Robert Teague.

Squeak and Teague had been moving as quickly as they could, crossing the Great Hall in their cups, when Teague suddenly felt someone's eyes upon him.

'Stop, Squeak!' said Teague excitedly, and they both froze and hid in their cups in the middle of the Great Hall's floor. After a few moments, Teague peered out, only to see the human with the black bandage over his eye staring intently in their direction.

'Should we keep going, Mister Teague?' said Squeak, nervous and anxious to complete the crossing.

'No! Stay where you are, Squeak — under your cup!' Teague spied out carefully and looked at the human, whose one visible eye seemed to be tracking him. He was far away — from Teague's perspective — but with a few large strides, any human could be upon them in moments, spelling out doom for a certain Mouseling Captain.

But, just a moment later, when Teague had been sure they had been discovered, from a distance he heard another man at the table yell something about dinner — and motionless, he watched as the whole dinner processional took place. The butcher — tall and oddly graceful for a servant — presented the food, which the party at the table looked on in awe and anticipation. And then suddenly — **WHAP!** — the butcher slammed the silver-domed serving tray into the face of the unsuspecting human with one eye.

Teague watched him as his chair reeled backwards, and then the room descended into chaos. There was fighting everywhere.

'Now is our chance, Mister Teague!' said Squeak. 'Let's go!'

But something in Robert Teague's heart on this strange day, in the Great Hall of Castle Feldenspar, made him pause. He realized that the two sides that were fighting were clearly enemies. The human with the black bandage over one eye had been at The King's Pedestal, and he knew the man was somehow colluding with that despicable one-eyed rat lieutenant whom Teague had saved from the orange tabby cat. Therefore, Teague reasoned — and correctly so — that the butcher who'd slammed the bandaged human in the face with a serving dome must be an ally of Castle Feldenspar. *Any enemy of my enemy is my friend,* Teague figured.

So, he peered out from under his cup and looked over at Squeak.

'Squeak, now is the time for you to go! These humans are fighting and the coast is clear. Go, go go!'

'What about you, Mister Teague?'

'I will meet you at the inn after you have delivered the note. But you MUST go now, before we miss the opportunity!'

Tears began to well up in the eyes of the little mouse under his wooden cup.

'But I…'

Teague knew their window of time was short, and he didn't have time to argue. Speaking emphatically, he said 'Squeak — NOW is the time. The Castle and I need your help. Get to the inn, now!'

'Yes sir!' said the young mouse, and off he scurried with the cup. 'LOSE THE CUP AND RUN AS FAST AS YOU CAN, SQUEAK!' yelled Teague.

He watched as the tiny mouse threw the cup off his back and sped up to a sprint. Closer, ever closer he came to the trap door allowing entrance into the safety of MouseKeep. Once Squeak reached it and disappeared behind the entrance door, Teague threw his own cup off of his back and nocked his roped arrow.

'Time to make a mess of things,' muttered Teague as he scampered as fast as he could towards the large feasting table.

Soon, he was running adroitly at full steam. He saw that several soldiers had fallen. They looked dirty and unkempt, which made Teague think they were minions of the enemy. He also spied Padraig laying inert with Sister Minerva and Cara sobbing over him, and he realized that the tide of battle could clearly still go either way — and he was about to be right in the middle of it.

Yet there were still five men with swords fighting against four men with makeshift weapons. One was the butcher, who fought bravely with a cleaver in one hand and the silver dome in the other. Two looked like servants, and the last was an older man who was fending off two swordsmen with a broom. Somehow, he looked very familiar to Teague, yet the Mouseling Captain couldn't quite place him. He was obviously trained in combat because, simply using the broom alone, he was still managing to deftly parry and dodge the well-placed sword attacks from his two foes.

After a moment, Teague identified his peculiar yet expert fighting style.

'Knight Commander Gabriel Storm!' Teague excitedly whispered to himself. 'I have to get up there and help him, or the Castle could be lost!'

Noticing that the one-eyed human was starting to come back to consciousness, Teague saw his way into the battle and raced forward to seize the moment. As Tempus tried to sit up from his tipped-over chair, Teague leapt onto the Animal Speaker's head and JUMPED off his forehead with all his might, knocking his head back down into the floor with a wallop.

The **THUMP** of Tempus's skull gave Teague sufficient propulsion through the air to land squarely on the table, and Tempus went back to 'sleep' after slamming his head on the floor again.

'Sweet dreams!' yelled a now adrenaline-filled Teague — whom Wilding often teased for his love of making snarky remarks to opponents. He immediately ran over to the edge of the table where Storm was fighting his two opponents, dragging a butter dish with him in his mouth. Turning around, he placed his front paws in the center of the table and allowed his back paws to rest within the soft butter itself. Then, he ran as fast as he could with his powerful hind paws while balancing himself on his front paws, sending bits of warm butter flying like a hose in the direction of one of Storm's attackers. The butter hit the unsuspecting foe in the eyes with a **SPLAT,** covering his eyelids and forehead with the soft, greasy stuff.

'YOU'VE GOT SOME BUTTER ON YOUR FACE, YOU RATLICKER!' yelled Teague.

Then Teague continued to try to add as much chaos to the battle as possible. He went and grabbed some grapes and a few discarded peach pits from the sliced fruit tray which rested on one of the carts. Lining them up next to the butter, he then started kicking them off towards Storm's attackers.

'FANCY A FRUIT SALAD?!' he yelled, unable to think of something more clever in the moment.

And yet, it worked.

Still limping from his knee injury and intently focused on not getting stabbed, Gabriel Storm suddenly noticed that one of his attacker's faces was covered in butter while the other was suddenly distracted, swatting at all manner of fruit flying through the air with his off arm. Out of the corner of his eye, Storm spied a Mouseling on the table — but it wasn't Wilding. This mouse had a bow on his back and was dressed in Falconrider leathers instead of Wilding's battlemage robes.

'ROBERT TEAGUE, YOU MOUSELING!' Storm shouted, as he quickly concluded who the agile mouse flinging fruit must have been. 'It's me, Gabriel Storm! FIGHT NOW! FIGHT FOR YOUR LIFE!'

With that, Storm took advantage of the temporarily blinded attacker, who was trying to remove the butter from his eyes and refocus them. Still leaning heavily on his good leg, he came down hard with a spinning staff attack at neck level. **Strike! Strike! Slash! Spinning head strike!** The first swordsman went down immediately after this flurry and the final blow to the head, crumpling like a tent in the wind and dropping his sword. Glancing at his other attacker, who was still trying to avoid being pelted in the eyes with fruit, Storm grabbed the fallen attacker's sword and weighed it gently in his hand.

'A fine blade,' said Storm seriously, as he locked eyes with his one remaining opponent. 'Now, HAVE AT YOU!'

And within a moment, it was easy to see why Gabriel Storm had risen to become the top knight at Castle Feldenspar. Deftly, and with his confidence surging, he laid into his attacker. His opponent tried to thrust in with a stab to the abdomen, only to have Storm *cut off his attacking hand.* The lifeless hand, still clasping the sword tightly in its fingers, dropped to the ground. Clutching his now-handless wrist and cradling it to his chest, the attacker fell to his knees in pain, screaming and glowering at Storm. The Knight Commander eyed him coldly for a moment, then proceeded to spin 360 degrees and cleanly remove his opponent's head from his shoulders.

The head went rolling across the floor and came to rest near the fireplace.

It didn't take much longer to get the remaining swordsmen to surrender. Watching wrists and heads fly off, the last few mercenaries dropped their swords and surrendered. Cullen, The Bird, and the loyal kitchen staff quickly bound them tightly and gagged them, then lay them in front of the fireplace, face down on their stomachs, to await the King's sentencing at some point in the near future.

After the last mercenary had been trussed by the fireplace, the kitchen staff burst into applause and cheers. Victory!

Wiping the sweat from his brow, Storm limped over to King Teegan and hugged him heartily, the arrow still sticking grotesquely out of his knee. The two old friends locked eyes and smiled at each other. Then Teegan broke the silence.

'So, Knight Commander. Are you going to dance that jig now? A knight's promise is as good as gold — or so you've always said.'

Storm laughed through the pain. 'I'd love to, sire, though I'm not sure my form would be very good with this arrow in my knee.'

Then he limped over to the table where Robert Teague was resting by the butter, with King Teegan lending his shoulder for support. Storm held out his massive hands in a traditional Mouseling greeting and said formally:

'General Robert Teague, Falconrider.'

Teague hopped up into Storm's hand, and Storm brought him up to his face level so they could look in each other's eyes.

'Thank you for your help, my friend. Your *butter in the face* attack may well have saved us this day.'

'Fighting rats is one thing, Commander. But when it comes to fighting humans, my options are pretty limited. That was the best I could come up with in the moment, I'm afraid...'

Storm nodded gravely at him, though his eyes twinkled with merriment. 'I shall have to remember it, in case I ever have cause to execute such a tactic myself.'

King Teegan smiled and chimed in. 'It's moments like that — the most welcome yet unexpected ones — that have saved my kingdom.

If we are telling true tales, my friend, I have no doubt that it's you Mouselings to whom I owe my entire kingdom to.'

It was only at that moment that Teague realized that this was no butcher standing in front of him, but the King of Feldenspar himself — King Teegan!

Lady forgive me! he thought to himself with embarrassment. *But these humans are so hard to tell apart…they all look alike to me. Remember, Teague, King Teegan is the one with the flowing mane…*

Teague bowed gracefully.

'Majesty! Forgive me for my rudeness sire, but MouseKeep has been overrun! I fear for the safety of Commander Wilding and my friends who went into the dungeons to search for you. Have you seen them, by any chance?'

'Yes!' laughed King Teegan and Storm as they echoed the affirmation in unison, still elated from winning the battle.

Storm spoke first. 'They saved us from the dungeons! I don't know if we would have ever escaped if not for Commander Wilding. And the others as well.'

Far from being reassured, Teague instantly became more concerned. Why was Wilding's party not with the very humans they had been sent to save?

'Commander Storm, I need to find my friends. It is of the utmost urgency. Can you tell me where they were headed? I fear the worst for MouseKeep. I have seen terrible and insidious plots within our precious bastion this day!'

'When last we parted ways, they were headed upwards. To reclaim the Falcon Rider Perch, I believe!' Storm answered.

'Then it is there I must go — posthaste!' said Teague with trepidation and a pressing feeling of urgency.

'Shall we go with you?' asked Storm.

Teague looked around at the mess on the floor, the trussed-up bodies of the captured men who had tried to usurp the King's reign, the servants, some of whom were battered and bloody, and the bodies

— of both the loyal men and mercenary usurpers — that would never rise again following the day's battles.

Teague bowed to the King again, reverently.

'Majesty. It seems your work is here. And if I may offer my counsel, it is of paramount importance that you continue securing the Castle and this island. I would welcome your aid, but given these peculiar and unnerving circumstances, I think it would be better if you finished tending to your human affairs while I finished tending to the affairs of Mouselings. I will meet you at The King's Pedestal, once MouseKeep is secured.'

King Teegan nodded his assent, and Teague hopped out of Storm's hand and back onto the table. Then, with a jaunty grin spreading across his face, he spread his arms wide, as if to encompass all the foodstuffs — many of them smashed, mangled, or otherwise disturbed in the course of the battle — and addressed the King once more.

'Although,' Teague said with a wink, 'I do hope you'll forgive me my rudeness — I always hate to have to eat and run.'

And with that, he turned to leap off the table. But, his way was suddenly blocked by Tempus, who stood up unexpectedly to address Teague. Blood was running from his forehead and his nose was obviously broken, but nonetheless, Tempus looked at Teague and started to speak to him.

'Teague? ROBERT Teague? Oh, The Rat King is looking for you, you pathetic little Mouseling.'

Gabriel Storm brandished his sword and pointed it at Tempus. 'SHUT YOUR FILTHY MOUTH, YOU MAGGOT!' he roared. Calming himself slightly, he stared Tempus down and continued through gritted teeth: 'If it were up to me, you'd have your neck stretched before nightfall. It is only by Her will, and the grace of King Teegan, that I restrain myself long enough to see if you can provide us information valuable enough to make it worth the intense discomfort it gives me to watch you continuing to draw breath into your vile body. But I will only suffer you to continue drawing breath so long as you tell us everything we ask you. And you will give us every last piece of information you have about this attack on Castle Feldenspar OR I WILL TAKE YOU APART PIECE BY PIECE! DO WE HAVE AN UNDERSTANDING, FILTH?!'

Teague drew his bow off his back and nocked an arrow, then addressed Tempus.

'Actually, Speaker, The Rat King will not need to look very hard to find me, since it is really I who am looking for him. The fact that you are addressing me so easily tells me you are an Animal Speaker. We killed his last one, and judging by your current situation,' Teague nodded towards the still-fuming Gabriel Storm, 'it looks like we may be killing another one today as well. So, I am unsure if you will be in a position to relay my message to him. But if you ever do happen to make it back to his dark reaches, please be so kind as to make sure that he gets it.'

'What is your message?' asked Tempus. Though he was still somewhat perplexed as to how his tide of fortune had changed so quickly, he was intrigued to find out what message the Mouseling Captain could possibly have for his master.

'Tell him any Animal Speakers he sends to this Castle will return blind — if they return at all.'

'Blind?' asked Tempus incredulously. 'What do you —'

And with that, Teague jumped up onto the flat edge of Storm's sword blade, pulled back his bow, and unleashed an arrow directly into Tempus's OTHER eye — what had been his sole remaining good one. He then did two flips in the air, and, landing deftly on his hind paws, hurried off in the direction of MouseKeep, where he disappeared behind an entryway.

'MY EYE!' screamed Tempus, falling backwards and clutching at his face.

'You have a great deal more to worry about than your eye today, my friend,' King Teegan said as he stood towering over him.

'Those little Mouselings are feisty,' said Storm, leaning on the push-broom as a makeshift crutch.

'That they are,' nodded King Teegan in assent. 'You know, that is the second time that Mousekin have helped to save the kingdom in the last twenty seasons.'

'I know, sire,' said Storm.

'And thank Her merciful will for it,' Teegan continued. 'Now, Knight Commander, we only have two things left to do.'

'What are those, my King?' Storm asked.

Teegan held up his index finger, making the number one.

'First, this...'

And with that, he punched Tempus in the face with a wild left hook. Tempus crumpled backwards, unconscious, onto the hard stone floor.

'Indeed.' Storm said. 'What's the second thing, my King?'

'Lady's Mercy, look over there!' King Teegan shouted, pointing to the fireplace as he knelt down to pick up a fallen sword.

Storm jerked his head around to look, then suddenly screamed out in searing pain.

King Teegan had deftly yanked the arrow out of Storm's knee.

He looked his companion in the eyes, a moment of silence and comradeship passing between them.

'The second thing, Gabriel, is that you have a jig to perform.'

And laughing through the pain, Gabriel Storm began to dance. He danced with all his heart — the dance of a now-crippled old knight who, with a little help from a band of unusual, talking Mouselings, had somehow cheated death and helped to save his kingdom — and his beloved King who ruled it.

Robert Teague's Last Prayer:

LADY HELP ME TO REMEMBER

If I lose my sight
You gave me the opportunity to see Your greatest gifts
In my family.
If I lose my business,
Let me be thankful I was in business at all
When my so-called friends stole everything.
If I lose my legs
You let me walk in Your ways
When so many tried to dissuade me.
If I never see The Early Spires again
Once You let me see Mountains.
If I lose my Vision
It was only You who ever gave me one.
If I lose my mind
You shared with me what a great Gift is.
If I lose my paws
You let me cook and serve others, which brought me to Mouseling Hollow.
If I lose YOU or my Wife and Children
Remind me once I had everything.

Lady
Teach me
Teach me humility.
Give me Wisdom, like The Lionsmane.
Let me be a servant to those around me.
Keep me mindful
Of the ocean
Its waves
And the timelessness and purpose
of Your design.
Amen

· · · · · · · · · · · · ·

Chapter 25

A CAPTAIN
AND HIS CREW

· ·

The sun was setting by the time that Squeak hit the exit of MouseKeep and tumbled into the open streets of the village which surrounds Castle Feldenspar. He ran, and ran, and ran — he had never run so far, nor so fast, in all his life! On all four paws, with Teague's sealed note clutched tightly in his mouth, he scurried, scampered, and sprinted his way. Crescent-shaped streets, winding turns, sharp corners, and human occupants going about their daily affairs — nothing could stop this young, determined mouse who was fearful for his new friend Robert Teague — who, the last he'd checked, was in the middle of the Great Hall when a massive human battle broke out.

He would do anything to save his new friend and his Mouseling family. But first he had to make it to Teague's friend alive.

'Keep going Squeak, you can do it!' he told himself, panting through the sides of his mouth and doing his best not to salivate on the note he kept firmly in his maw. 'Get there, get there, get there!'

His fur was dripping with sweat, glistening in the setting sun, and he was covered in street dust. But still, he pressed on.

Meanwhile, at The Feldenspar Inn and Lodge, the Mouseling patrons inside were having a grand old time. It was the harvest season, after all, and about to be the weekend, too! Ale was flowing freely, and, as per usual, Redfur Tumblefox — whom the patrons of the inn affectionately called 'The Captain' — was tending bar in the underground recesses of the human blacksmith's building. A monster of a Mouseling, though he served in The First Rat King War commanding land scouts on reconnaissance missions, he had the look of a pirate captain. Wearing a black trifold cornice hat, along with a flowing red coat with gold buttons down its center, he looked regal — but also like a mouse who might rob you blind at any moment. He could have easily passed as a pirate on any Mouseling sloop.

And his tavern was just as clever as he was.

Craftily built underneath the wood framing timbers which supported the blacksmith's daily metalworking endeavors, it was the ideal place for a Mouseling pub. In the soft cool earth, the heat of the summertime was negated by the insulating effect of the clay which surrounded the hollowed-out ground, providing a comfortable ambient temperature which, to universal Mouseling agreement, made for one of the most relaxing spots in town. And naturally, in the wintertime, the furnace from the blacksmith's could add some heat to the underground space through a cleverly designed metal grate in the ceiling which allowed the innkeeper to open a hatch, if needed, to act as a fireplace with no ill effects.

Clever mouse, indeed — he had built the inn after he was forced to retire from active service, having shattered his arm so badly at The Battle at The Black Citadel that he could no longer use it effectively in combat. Besides which, his second favorite hobby — drinking ale — had always had a great appeal to him. So, once the war was over, he retired to the village below Castle Feldenspar, hollowed out his inn home without any help from others, and hadn't left since...except for the occasional fishing trip down to Ferngrove Bottoms with the boys, of course.

And on this particular day, The Captain was busy serving cups to the same half dozen friends he had served as commander to back in The First Rat King War. Those old battle friendships never truly died, and on this day at the bar the usual coterie were well into their ales and lagers, watching a few of the younger mice play Root and Field — and of course, giving inaccurate advice to both players trying to see who would lose first (and secretly taking wagers on it).

This was a fantastic source of amusement for these veteran battlemice, who were always trying to give false information to Root and Field players in the hopes of amusing themselves and generating a little profit while they were at it — not to mention a fantastic laugh once the unsuspecting player (or players) realized that they had been duped. But sometimes, a player would win in spite of the bad advice dispensed by Tumblefox's regulars, who would then think they actually had received some 'solid insight' — which was great for The Captain's crew of scalawags, who would simply keep the ruse going.

In this particular case, one young mouse named Skeeve Tenderpaw was getting advice from a battle-hardened Mouseling named Nimsby, who was The Captain's best friend. Nimsby was commanding the crowd that day, with both his garrulous antics, and the fact that he had wagered a hefty sum of gold crowns on the outcome of this particular game.

'Don't do that, Skeeve! What's the matter with you? Haven't you the sense to know that playing a Falcon Attack under these circumstances would be doomed to failure? Here, do this instead!'

Then, with a gruff paw, Nimsby moved Skeeve's cat figure onto one of his opponent's spaces, which was presently occupied by a huge red dragon figure, prompting a battle.

'Wait, what?' said Skeeve, looking confused.

Dice were rolled and his opponent, after easily winning the combat phase of the game, removed Skeeve's cat figure from the board.

'What did you do that for?!' said a now-irritated Skeeve. 'That was obviously a terrible move!'

The Captain, Nimsby, and their four friends at the bar — Ratbane, Old Punchy, Flies With Eagles, and a mouse they called The Bacon Thief — who, as a group, were affectionately referred to locally and colloquially as 'The Wrecking Crew' — all burst into laughter. Kneeslapping and chortles ensued and more coins exchanged paws as poor Skeeve Tenderpaw proceeded to lose the game — and his precious cat figurine — to his now-grinning opponent.

'You guys, come on!' he lamented.

The Captain, coming out from behind the glossed bar top, put his good arm around young Skeeve's shoulders in an effort to comfort him. 'This is exactly why you shouldn't hang out in bars with ill-reputed mice like these, my son!'

Then, he handed him a bill for his tab, which made The Wrecking Crew burst into laughter once more.

Of course, in the midst of all the laughter and commotion, no one could have noticed the sweaty, dirty young Mouseling come tumbling through the door. The filthy mouse scampered to and fro before finally hopping up onto a barstool, and then directly onto the bar. He ran up to the tall Mouseling in a red coat, the note still clutched in his mouth.

'MMMPF FOOKING FIR HPATIN FUMBFOX!' cried the young mouse desperately.

Suddenly, all the laughter died down as the bar patrons noticed the tiny, grimy, homeless-looking mouse with a note in its mouth on the bar top.

Slowly, The Captain walked over to the young mouse, glaring down at him.

'What did you say, mouse?'

'MMMPF FOOKING FIR HPATIN FUMBFOX!' cried the mouse desperately for a second time.

The Captain grabbed the note out of Squeak's mouth.

'Speak clearly, youngin!'

'I AM LOOKING FOR CAPTAIN REDFUR TUMBLEFOX! ROBERT TEAGUE SENT ME HERE WITH THIS URGENT MESSAGE FOR YOU!' he gasped.

'Robert Teague, eh?' said The Captain. 'Well boyo, let me tell you something: whenever Robert Teague sends me a note...we all go scampering and IMMEDIATELY STOP WHAT WE ARE DOING! IN FACT, TIME ITSELF SLOWS DOWN WHEN ROBERT TEAGUE SENDS US A NOTE!'

The bar filled with roaring laughter at The Captain's sense of humor.

'PLEASE SIR! IT'S AN EMERGENCY!' pestered Squeak.

'Oh, very well,' said Redfox, breaking the seal on the note and reading it carefully.

The smile from his face cleared away and was replaced with a look of grave concern. Calling to his barmaid, Blossom, he signaled her over to the bar top, pointed to Squeak, and with a far more serious tone, said, 'Blossom, take care of this young mouse. Give him a bath and a meal, and then place him upstairs in my quarters. Make sure he stays there until I return — and no one is to know that he is here, if possible.'

'Your quarters sir?' she stammered. 'Are you sure?'

'You heard me, girl!' said Tumblefox with some urgency. 'I'm not in the habit of giving orders twice!'

'Yes, sir,' she said, before taking a very dirty Squeak upstairs to get cleaned up.

The Captain looked at his friends for a long, long moment, then sighed.

'Boys, Robert Teague has invoked the 59th rule — and you know what that means. MouseKeep needs us once more, and we need to go there, posthaste. I would tell you that I don't expect any of you to go and you're free to sit out whatever ruckus awaits us there, but I have no doubt you all are with me.'

That was The Captain's way of saying 'none of you will say no to this request,' although he knew his friends, loyal to the end, would of course be with him, and spoiling for a fight — especially if it involved defending MouseKeep, and enemy rats were the target.

'Now, gear up.'

And with that, he cleared the cups off the glossy bar top and lifted it up, revealing a secret, hinged weapon cache lined with red velvet hidden within. All manner of weapons were stashed there: short bows, longbows, repeating crossbows, silver and bronze swords, chainmail coifs and shirts, shields, helmets, pikes, halberds, throwing stars, and a variety of chained weapons.

As Nimsby, Ratbane, Old Punchy, and The Bacon Thief were grabbing their weapons of choice and gearing up, The Captain pulled Flies With Eagles aside. Whispering something in his ear, the older mouse nodded sagely, grabbed a repeating crossbow, and scampered out the front door.

'Where did he go?' Nimsby asked The Captain, who was donning a chain coif and preparing to sharpen a two-handed bastard sword with a whetstone.

'He's grabbing our ride,' said The Captain with a smirk of satisfaction.

Ainsley Hearthseeker knew the end had finally come.

And it was a bitter feeling.

All of the work. All of the sweat, stress, and pain. All of the fighting and bloodshed — from the dying Falconrider at The Sleeping Cat to the near-death scrape with Ravenscale, the rescue of the King from the dungeons, and of course, all that had transpired on the ascent to MouseKeep Armory.

The bard knew they had made a daring attempt in their most desperate hour. Outnumbered, outgunned, and with the enemy having had ample time to put a deeply calculated strategic plan into place, it seemed that, in that moment, Ainsley finally came to understand that though their effort was true, the Mouselings had simply been unprepared and unequipped to deal with this kind of determined, reinforced enemy.

It has been an amazing run, he thought to himself as he heard the rat captain yell, 'Ready!' to his archers.

I couldn't ask to die next to a better group of battle brothers. We did everything possible to save Castle Feldenspar and MouseKeep. Perhaps, in time, with Her blessing, our sacrifices will not have been made in vain.

'Aim!'

He closed his eyes tightly and awaited the inevitable end.

'FIRE!' the rat captain shouted.

But nothing happened.

He kept his eyes tightly closed for another millisecond. Then, still feeling nothing, he dared to open up one furry eye and peer out to see what was happening.

And he couldn't have been more shocked at what was taking place.

Wilding, with his battlemage staff raised in one hand and an empty paw outstretched towards the Ratling minions, was muttering some type of inaudible incantation under his breath. While he was doing so, the bard saw about a dozen arrows still flying towards him in midair — but slowing, slowing, and then finally stopping while still suspended in flight, as if frozen. Finally, after another second, the arrows fell harmlessly to the ground in front of the Mouseling party, making a ***clackety clack*** sound as the wooden shafts bounced on the stone floor before coming to rest.

Hearing that strange clacking noise instead of the expected death cries, any Mouseling eyes that had been closed were now opened, and the two parties simply stared at each other, both sides trying to absorb the miracle that had just taken place. Tense and dramatic, that moment became the eye of the hurricane — the calm before the storm, the darkness that bleeds pitch, the blackest midnight that seems permanently insoluble, just before the dawn's fervent rescue arrives to bring light back into the world.

And in the midst of it, the penetrating silence permeated the Armory as the Ratlings watched Wilding, half spellbound, his eyes closed and still muttering. The message that his magical chants gave off was so clear, Wilding might as well have been holding up an enormous sign: this group of Mouselings would ***not*** be so easily dispatched after all.

Perhaps MouseKeep was not lost, yet, thought Ainsley.

Suddenly, Wilding snapped out of his magical trance and looked at his brothers. Then he looked at the rat usurpers in front of him and clasped his battlemage staff with two paws, pointing it directly at the massive badger.

'What are you waiting for, my brothers?' he said with vigilance and fervor. 'FIGHT! FOR MOUSEKEEP!!!'

The Mouselings all started to yell a rallying battlecry as they shook their swords and weapons. The rat soldiers raised their own yell, and brandishing their weapons in turn, prepared to charge the other side. Soon, a cacophony of voices arose in an asynchronous chorus, and the rage and enmity on both sides was palpable.

'CHARGE!' yelled Wilding as he took the vanguard of the party forward to act as the tip of the spear, hoping to shatter the enemy rat formation. Snowwillow sprinted to the front and charged right by his side, his two paws holding his short sword in a menacing attack stance.

All the Mouselings followed them, running at high speed, and the Ratling garrison met the oncoming charge with their own tidal wave of force. The two sides crashed into each other in a cacophony of sound, fur on fur and skull on skull, brimming with intention — armor clanging, weapons clashing.

It was absolute mayhem.

And no rat or mouse could say, at that precise moment, what the outcome would be.

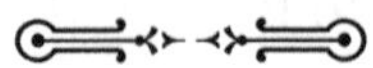

It was about the time the Ratling captain had yelled 'fire' that Robert Teague had scampered his way from the Great Hall into the passageway into MouseKeep, after the humans had finished their battle for control of Castle Feldenspar. He had doubled back towards the kitchen, knowing that one of the main staircases — and the fastest ascent to the Falcon Rider Perch — was midway between the feasting hall and the kitchen. If Wilding and his party had truly intended to make an ascent to the Castle's top floor, that was the way Teague would have gone — and he was confident that Wilding would have taken the same route.

His faith in his friend was rewarded when he got to the annex where a three-way split within MouseKeep occurred: an intersection where one passageway descended down into the dungeon, another exited MouseKeep, and another ramp ascended upwards, farther into the various chambers of MouseKeep. Sprinting upwards from the intersection, Teague noticed a floating note suspended in midair. He had seen these from his friend before — though admittedly, innumerable seasons had transpired since his friend has last left him one.

'I haven't seen one of these since The First Rat King War,' said Teague, not conscious that he was speaking out loud.

He rushed up to the note and glanced at it, hoping it would contain clues into the party's direction.

Scanning it, he read:

Innkeeper

With expedience, make haste to the Armory.

If you are indisposed,

Come all the same.

We expect resistance through the main channels.

Teague smiled at the message, but then gritted his teeth as well.

'It looks like I will have to take an alternate channel then,' said the Mouseling Captain, intent on rejoining his friends with haste.

As fast as he could, Teague ran up the inclined ramp which spiraled into the upper reaches of MouseKeep. At one point he spied a secret side passage that, as best as his memory could serve him, might get him to MouseKeep's upper levels a little bit quicker. He branched off into it, hoping to make up time and avoid any sentries left by the enemy. Should they have the misfortune of running into him, dispatching them would only slow him down, and he knew time was of the essence.

Back in MouseKeep's Armory, all hell was breaking loose.

Snowwillow, charging side by side with Wilding, pulled a great move at the very last second before smashing into the oncoming rat vanguard. Right before impact, he dropped to the floor and slid the last few feet into the oncoming onslaught, ensuring that:

1) He didn't get knocked out by his much larger opponents, which would have meant a certain death, and

2) He would be able to lock in some solid strikes from underneath in a desperate attempt to thin the enemy's numbers.

And it worked.

As he dropped to his haunches and slid along the stone, he used his sword to swing at the feet of the rat attackers. The blows landed quite effectively, too, with two rats falling helplessly to the floor after their ankles had been chopped out from under them. This had a ripple effect on their Ratling compatriots because the now-immobile rats, wriggling on the floor and screaming in pain, acted as a tripping hazard for their fellows. Several more rats went tumbling down over their bodies, becoming an unforeseen obstacle which created new attack opportunities for the charging Mouselings. Multiple Ratlings were dispatched this way, until the rat onslaught regrouped and attackers and defenders began pairing off.

Snowwillow, now behind the rat onslaught, stood up — but a rat pikeman had already turned around, spotted him, and begun charging at him with a spear. The young Falconrider's martial arts training kicked in automatically and he felt time slow down as he entered a *mushin* state — mind like water. He proceeded to parry the incoming strike with his sword, knocking the tip of the pike into the ground and halting the rat's momentum. Sliding down the shaft of the pike as an entry point, he then executed a spinning combination called **Thundering HammerPaws:** *slash to chest with sword, release sword, hammer paw to groin (opponent falls), hammer paw to neck.* And with this combo, his opponent fell face down in agony. Snowwillow then dispatched him with what students of his martial arts school called **Leap of Death**. Snowwillow launched himself high in the air and landed with all his might on the Ratling's back, crushing his spine, rupturing his kidneys, and creating a mortal injury which neutralized his opponent — permanently.

Wow, thought Wilding. *That young mouse shows a great deal of promise!*

Encouraged, Wilding rallied the Mouselings.

'FIGHT! FIGHT FOR YOUR LIVES!' he yelled.

The wizard's body flooded with adrenaline as he faced off with a fischer who had come in to attack him with a spear. Wilding was doing a good job of parrying the thrusting attacks, but his attention was split as he was more worried about how his friends were faring than staying simply focused on saving his own skin. During one moment's pause, he glanced over at Hearthseeker, who was fighting a Ratling who wielded sword and shield against his sword alone. Deftly, he stabbed in — thrust, parry, thrust!

He looks like he knows what he is doing, thought Wilding as he parried an incoming spear thrust, then counterattacked by stabbing the base of his staff into the fischer's paw on the floor.

Screaming in pain, the fischer dropped his spear and started hopping around on one paw, clasping his foot in pain.

Finnegan Willowtail, who had watched the interaction after dispatching a rat archer, yelled at Wilding:

'All that fuss from you poking him with the blunt end of your staff?'

Wilding smiled and lifted his staff up to show Willowtail its underside. At the press of a hidden button, a mean-looking blade had extended from it, which had been the real cause of the fischer's now-incalculable pain. Willowtail looked back at the fischer, who was covering his paw as blood poured out from his foot.

'You are full of tricks, aren't you, wizard,' smiled Willowtail. He went to engage another rat archer with his sword and Wilding smiled back.

However, he was unprepared for the unseen attack that sent him to the floor moments later.

One of the fischers, who had been watching from behind the rat frontlines, had set his sights on Wilding and determined to bring him low. By deftly sneaking around the front line, he now had an open line of attack at the wizard. Seeing him and Willowtail conversing amidst the battle gave him the perfect opportunity. The slender, lithe, and muscular fischer suddenly charged Wilding with a blood-curdling battlecry and crushed into Wilding so forcefully that they both went tumbling across the floor.

From a distance, Ainsley Hearthseeker heard Wilding cry out 'OOOFFFF' as the wind got absolutely knocked out of him by the sheer force of the fischer's blow. Turning to locate Wilding, Hearthseeker saw the fischer climb atop him and take a mounted position.

Baring his teeth and drawing his triangular head back, it was clear the fischer intended to rip out Wilding's jugular vein.

In that moment, something transformed inside Ainsley Hearthseeker. Hearthseeker, the bard from Old Town, changed his profession in that instant to Hearthseeker, Barbarian Berserker of Old Town. With a howling battlecry, he barreled over to the fischer, sweeping Ratlings aside as if they were no more threatening to him than a stiff breeze. The fischer, who was about to impale Wilding's throat with its razor sharp teeth, instead died when Hearthseeker, screaming 'DIE YOU RATLICKING FILTH!' at the top of his lungs, leaped atop him and stabbed his sword deeply into the fischer's spine. The blow was so powerful it severed the spinal column, killing the fischer instantly.

Wilding eyed the victorious Hearthseeker as the fischer slumped over, its tongue lolling out of its mouth and its eyes rolling backward into its head.

'I SAVED YOU, OLD MAN!' shouted Hearthseeker, grinning whisker to whisker with adrenaline-filled glee. 'I SAVED YOU...'

But his words were cut short as a crossbow-wielding rat, who had quietly been taking a steady aim, released a hurtling bolt. It flew through the air and met its target with menacing accuracy, sinking deep into the bard's abdomen — a seemingly mortal blow. The bard flew off the dead fischer's back, driven backwards by the impact of the bolt. Smashing his skull on the stone floor, he was immediately knocked unconscious.

'YOU VILE RAT VERMIN!' Wilding screamed, incensed and scared by what he had just seen happen to his friend. He wriggled out from under the fischer's dead body and grabbed his battle staff, pointing it at the crossbow wielder as the ruby gem at its tip began glowing an ominous midnight black. With a single, unintelligible word, Wilding sent a black ball of rage-filled death magic at the crossbow-wielding rat. The magical orb smashed into the rat, and he disintegrated into a small pile of burnt fur and cracked bones, leaving behind the rank stench of death and rot.

Wilding raced over to the bard.

'Hearthseeker! Ainsley...'

Cradling the bard's head in his arm, frightened and fearful of the crossbow bolt sticking out of his friend's stomach, Wilding shook his friend — gently, but desperately.

'Ainsley, wake up! Wake up, bard! WAKE UP YOU ROGUE! YOU AREN'T GOING OUT THIS WAY — NOT TODAY, YOU...YOU...**SCALAWAG!**'

He slapped Hearthseeker across the snout as hard as he could.

The bard opened his eyes for a moment, jarred awake by the blow, and briefly locked eyes with Wilding. A trickle of blood ran down the side of his mouth and he coughed a few times as he summoned the energy to speak.

'I saved you, old man — I did it! I did something good...something... good...for once...'

And then his eyes rolled back into his head and he went limp in Wilding's arms, slumping onto the floor.

Wilding smiled a bittersweet, soul-crushing smile at Hearthseeker's strange final statement — then looked up at the ceiling of the Armory in absolute agony over his friend. Still cradling the bard's head in his paws and fighting to hold back the hot, bitter tears welling up behind his eyelids, Wilding looked around at the chaos that was ensuing all around him.

The battle was still raging, though several of the MouseGuard survivors had fallen and the tide was clearly turning against them. Finnegan Willowtail had taken a hard slash to the abdomen, and the Stranger — fighting like a wild gazelle trying to fend off a pack of starving lions — was bleeding profusely from the head and swinging his sword at three oncoming attackers in a dazed, but persevering, frenzy. Fatigue was clearly beginning to set in on both sides, and Wilding could see it in the Stranger's sword swings. They were becoming imprecise, almost wild — long, arcing strikes that were more a gamble and less a calculated stroke.

And that is no way to win a sword fight, thought the wizard, *let alone a battle.*

Behind them paced the badger, eagerly searching for a Mouseling he could pair off with — and pummel into oblivion. Wilding saw some of the other MouseGuard that he'd rescued from the dungeons lying on the floor, dead or unconscious — Wilding wasn't sure which. Bodies were everywhere, Mouseling and Ratling alike, but it was growing clear to Wilding that the Mouselings were starting to thin numerically.

Wilding struggled to get his senses back, still weakened from both the fischer's body blow and the death magic spell he had unleashed in its aftermath. But the wizard knew what he had to do.

Rising up to his feet, he slammed his staff on the ground and chanted:

Invaders and garrisons
Rats on the floor
Where you see one Mouseling
Now make it FOUR!

The rat fighters soon paused in confusion since, upon completing the incantation, four times the number of Mouselings suddenly appeared throughout the room, making it appear that reinforcements had just arrived to even the odds.

'FIGHT BROTHERS!' Wilding shouted madly. 'REINFORCE-MENTS ARE HERE!'

But they weren't really reinforcements — only an illusion spell which created a mirror image of each Mouseling in quadruplicate, making each fighter look like he had three identical companions fighting alongside them.

And the effect worked fabulously.

Snowwillow intercepted a dagger-wielding rat attacker using an overhead stab with a technique called **Flashing Wing Paws** — *x-block knife intercept, redirect knife into attacker's lower paw, double bladed neck strike, ricochet groin strike.* But to the rat attackers, it looked like four Mouselings were fighting in perfect harmony, which caused Mouseling morale to rise as much as the rats' morale suddenly began to plummet.

Yet magical trickery aside, the Mouselings were still outnumbered — and though Wilding's spell had bought them a little time, every time a rat attacked an illusion, it would disappear back into the ether from which it had come.

'This spell won't last much longer,' Wilding muttered to himself. 'We shall need a miracle if we are to win this day,' he said forlornly as he watched yet another Mouseling fall in battle.

And then, out of the corner of his eye, Wilding suddenly saw some arrows hurtle out from (what appeared to be) the ceiling. Two rat attackers fell, grabbing at the arrows which were now protruding from their chest. Then the one remaining fischer, who'd been using his spear to get around, suddenly took an arrow through the skull and crumpled to the ground, dead.

Wilding looked up. It was Teague!

'FINALLY!' cried Wilding, both relieved and irritated at the same time by his friend's late arrival.

Wilding watched as Teague shot his roped arrow from a recessed ceiling tile that had been removed, his arrow landing with perfect placement just above the stained-glass window. Teague grasped the rope tightly with his lower paws, then wrapped the rope under his armpit, allowing him to use his two top paws as he swung down through the chamber, sending arrows into Ratling attackers as he flew. Some hit their mark, some missed, but the *piece de resistance* was Teague's proud, boastful shout as he swung through the chamber:

'LOOK WHO'S BACK, YOU RATLING SCUM! IT IS I, ROBERT TEAGUE, MEMBER OF THE FABLED TWO. COME FIGHT ME, IF YOU DARE! COME AND MEET YOUR DOOM!'

And with perfect timing, he lithely landed on the ledge below the stained-glass window, as if he did so every day on his way to work.

'HURRAH!' cried the Mouselings as they battled, their morale bolstered even further to see another hero showed up!

Reinvigorated, the MouseGuard remnants continued to fight. Wilding drug the unconscious Ainsley behind a barrel of weapons and lay him there for safekeeping, then immediately moved to rejoin the battle.

Teague, meanwhile, was sending a barrage of arrows flying across the chamber, though he was beginning to run low on ammunition in his quiver.

'WHAT DO YOU CALL A RAT WITH AN ARROW IN ITS FACE?' Teague yelled to one unfortunate rat archer who was trying to shield himself from the rain of projectiles by hiding in the shadows. His efforts proved futile (though not for a lack of trying) when one of Teague's arrows found its mark, burying itself in the Ratling's skull, and the rat archer crumpled bonelessly to the floor.

Teague laughed out loud at the sight, his timing impeccable. 'A BULLSEYE!' he shouted towards the fallen rat. 'GET IT?'

Teague surveyed the mayhem taking place in the Armory, still smiling at his joke, then let out a powerful rallying cry:

'FIGHT, MY MOUSELING BROTHERS! FIGHT WELL, AND WE WILL WIN THIS DAY!' cried an energized Teague. Running out of arrows, he threw down his bow and drew his dual hand axes, then raced down the staircase from the stained-glass ledge to join in the melee.

'WHERE TO BEGIN?' said Teague, taunting his rat adversaries.

But his taunt was cut short by the badger who was eagerly barreling towards him — so eager to get to his foe that he practically bowled over a half dozen of his own rat companions on his way to get to Teague.

Wielding his massive, two-handed battle axe, he yelled out:

'TEAGUE! ROBERT TEAGUE! THE RAT KING SENT ME HERE TO FIND YOU! COME FORWARD, YOU COWARD, AND FACE ME! IT IS TIME TO SHATTER THE MYTH OF THE FABLED TWO!'

Teague spun towards the booming voice and saw the enormous badger towering above him, with a black and white striped face, dressed in heavy battle armor, and wielding a huge battle axe. Teague had but a moment to size up his opponent before the badger launched a wild, swinging blow with the axe, aimed directly at Teague's neck. Using his twin hand axes in an 'x' formation, he blocked the incoming attack — though it drove him back considerably. Though Teague refused to show it, he was, in fact, shocked by how powerful the huge animal now towering over him really was.

'COME FIGHT ME, TEAGUE!' taunted the badger. 'BRING YOUR LITTLE HAND AXES, AND SEE HOW LITTLE GOOD THEY'LL DO YOU!'

Teague, never one to get tongue-tied, spun his hand axes in both paws with a quick flourish, regripped them in a savage-looking combat stance, and then responded with his famously quick wit. Looking up into the eyes of the massive badger and seemingly feeling no pressure in the moment, he quipped:

'YOU WANT A TASTE OF THESE, SKUNK FACE? YOU WILL SAVOR THEIR FLAVOR EVEN MORE DELICATELY ONCE I GET CLOSE ENOUGH FOR THEM TO SLICE OPEN YOUR GULLET!'

Enraged, the badger raised his huge battle axe high into the air and sent down another chopping blow. Teague dexterously dove out of the way, leaving the blade of the axe to impale itself into the floor, splintering the wood and creating a large divot.

'YOU LIKE THAT, ROBERT TEAGUE? I'VE GOT PLENTY MORE OF THAT WAITING FOR YOU, YOU SCRAWNY MOUSE!' said Bruiser.

Teague responded like clockwork.

'Whatever you say, Rat King's lackey. Can I CALL you lackey? I hope that won't bother you. Here's a question for you, lackey: what kind of real fighter lets his axe get stuck in the floor? You're so clumsy, I could practically take a power nap in between each of your pathetic swings. In fact, your attacks are so slow, are you sure that axe isn't a little too heavy for you? No shame in admitting it, you know!'

Growing even more incensed, the badger placed one of his lower paws on the floor by the head of his axe and pulled with all his might. Finally, the blade released — but Bruiser had been pulling so intently, the inertia sent him stumbling backwards.

Seeing an opportunity, Teague quickly sprinted towards his opponent. Then, launching himself in the air with a flying sidekick, he rammed his paw into the badger's kneecap with near perfect timing. The weight of the mouse impacting the badger's leg sent the huge animal off balance and he fell on his backside, letting out a roar of agony and embarrassment.

Teague burst out laughing at the sight of his opponent struggling to get back up off the ground, weaving and lurching as if he was half disoriented. He couldn't help but taunt him:

'HAHAHAHAHA!' Teague belly-laughed. 'IF YOU ARE THE BEST THE RAT KING HAS TO OFFER, WE CAN ALL TAKE A GOOD LONG VACATION AFTER THIS ONE, MY FRIEND!'

After a moment the badger regained his footing and balance, then stretched himself to his full, towering height above the Mouseling Captain. Now absolutely enraged, he came directly at Teague, swinging his axe with enormous brute force, looking to swipe Teague's head from his shoulders with a single killing blow.

Chop, parry, chop, parry!

Teague blocked a few of the blows that went glancing by him and the badger swung wildly again, getting his axe stuck in the floor for a second time. Teague, watching this spectacle, simply shook his head in disgust.

'Wow...that's just...SAD! I almost feel sorry for you, lackey.'

He continued to shake his head as the display continued.

While Bruiser was busy trying to get his axe out of the floor, another rat charged at Teague with a spear, and the Mouseling made the easy intercept — *inverted axe hilt block, slide down spear shaft, axe hilt strike to throat, rear chopping axe strike to back hamstring.*

The rat attacker dropped the spear and, crying in pain, fell down grasping at his back calf, now crippled.

Teague turned to face the badger once more, but he was no longer in front of him. He scanned the room, searching for his opponent, then called out:

'OK STRIPEY, LET'S FINISH THIS! FUN IS FUN, BUT I'M READY TO GET HOME...'

But before he could complete his sentence, Robert Teague took the blunt side of the badger's massive battle axe from behind. It struck him so viciously on the side of the head and shoulders that he went tumbling across the floor, his body crumpling into a heap and coming to rest by one of the weapon barrels, motionless.

On The Wrecking Crew:

Certainly, there were heroes made through all the sacrifices and endeavors to resist The Rat King during The First Great War. But one of the more colorful tales of heroism to emerge from this dark period concerns the group known as **The Wrecking Crew,** *led by their colorful leader Captain Redfur Tumblefox. How did they get their name* **The Wrecking Crew,** *you ask? The answer is simple: through demolitions and bar fights.*

During the days of The First Rat King War, **The Wrecking Crew** *served at the vanguard of the Mouseling infantry fighting against the insurrectious skirmish groups of the Evil One. Their missions often centered on striving to blow up as much of the enemy war machine as possible. Destroying enemy siege weapons, dams, fortified and walled garrisons, bunkers, treetop perches — to them, it was all the same, and all in great fun. They reveled in demolitions the way an arsonist rejoices in setting fire to homes, or a pyromancer in shooting fireballs at unsuspecting straw targets. And at night, when the explosives were locked away, deep in their cups they would find the 'bad seeds' — as unworthy Mouselings were sometimes called — and fight them in paw to paw melee combat, encircled by a coterie of onlookers.*

It was there, in those nights following the long days of combat, surrounded by their fellow infantry, that they found redemption…taking blow after blow from mice who were bigger than them, or higher in rank, while they stood there — withstanding the punishment, waiting patiently under duress until they could strike a knockout blow. At the end of the war, only five remained, plus their leader, and all were referred to by their nicknames, as their group had grown into something of a legend: The Captain, Nimsby, Ratbane, Old Punchy, Flies With Eagles, and an unusual mouse they called The Bacon Thief.

After their military service ended, they remained ever close, like most brothers-in-arms. These days, they can still be found, deep in their cups (as per usual), at **The Captain's Feldenspar Inn and Tavern** *— a few blocks from the Castle itself, nestled under the old human blacksmith's shop...*

— Taken from **Sir Pendleton Stormsnout's Book of River Travels, Volume 1: Feldenspar Castle to Mouseling Hollow**

Chapter 26

TEAGUE VISITS THE WHITE WEASEL

Bruiser hit Robert Teague's head so hard that he was out cold on the floor. In the center of MouseKeep's Armory, amidst the visceral fighting of the two factions in a quintessential battle of good versus evil, Robert Teague had been removed from the game board.

The badger, after striking the critical blow, had watched his opponent go tumbling across the Armory chamber with a swelling pride — the pride of one whose arrogance and ego needed no more inflation. Yet still, as the biggest adversary on the battlefield, he trumpeted his triumph and called out to the remaining warrior Mouselings in an insulting and diminutive way:

'HAHA, TINY MOUSELINGS! NOW I HAVE DONE WHAT NO ONE ELSE HAS BEEN ABLE TO DO — NOT EVEN THE GREAT RAT KING HIMSELF. I HAVE VANQUISHED THE LEADER OF THE FABLED TWO! I HAVE LAIN YOUR SO-CALLED HERO LOW THIS DAY, FOR ALL TO SEE. COME THEN, MOUSELINGS, AND CHALLENGE ME...IF THERE ARE ANY AMONGST YOU WHO WOULD HAVE THE GUMPTION TO FACE A TRUE HERO! COME AND MEET THE SAME DOOM

ROBERT TEAGUE MET — AND THEN OUR TAKEOVER OF MOUSEKEEP WILL BE COMPLETE!'

The badger's taunting cries of victory resonated throughout the walled chamber of MouseKeep Armory.

But Robert Teague was not present to hear his opponent tout his head-crushing defeat, or to try to cajole his companions into a one-sided fight.

In fact, he was elsewhere.

Where, he didn't know. All he knew was that one moment he had been in the MouseKeep Armory, and the next moment, he...wasn't. He remembered swinging in from the rafters, taking out several Ratlings with arrows, and helping draw fire from the rat archers who had hidden themselves in ambush. And then, an enormous badger in bronzed battle armor, wielding a massive two-handed battle axe, had somehow (he couldn't remember how, exactly, though he knew it must have happened very recently) emerged from the shadows. He vaguely remembered hearing his opponent call out his name with some long winded diatribe, and how he had turned and faced his opponent, parried a few blows, and then...

Nothing.

Still, the nothingness was peaceful, if only just for a moment. Wherever he was, Teague was blind, as the darkness had enveloped him. But soon the darkness subsided — though his vision remained somewhat blurry. He found himself on a mountaintop, surrounded by pink winter blossoms, in the fall.

Without knowing how he knew, he could feel that outside it was cool, and yet slightly balmy.

Peaceful. Tranquil.

So devoid of conflict he almost felt like he could stay here — wherever 'here' was — forever.

The winter blossoms blew silently in the trees, with one occasionally floating down from its branch, as though hinting towards a winter which had not arrived quite yet. Teague found himself sitting under the Winterblossom tree, his paw outstretched, and serendipitously watching a four-leafed winter blossom cascade slowly into it, drifting upon the wind to its final, synchronistic destination.

Suddenly, a voice spoke to him.

'The winter blossom is only the beginning of your journey. How many petals does it hold? Some see four, and yet others see five. How many petals do you see?'

Teague looked down into his paw, and right at that moment, he felt the cool breeze on his face. It distracted him — it was so placid, so… peaceful. Staring out from under the tree he found himself under, he could see a still pond, which evidently was on a mountaintop.

Occasionally, he spied a fish leap out from the water to catch an insect.

For the first time in his life he felt really, truly, at peace.

But every time he tried to stare at the winter blossom in his paw, he could not see it clearly — was it four blossoms, or five? The petals blurred together and Teague could not, for the life of him, ascertain what the answer was.

'And now you have your first lesson,' the voice spoke. 'How many petals on a winter blossom? If you can answer that question, then can you tell me what is the sound of one paw clapping? If you can achieve that, then you will have no more need for training.'

Teague listened carefully to the voice, the sounds. In the moment, it held no meaning for him, but he knew there was a lesson in it to be learned.

Suddenly the scene changed, and Teague found himself dressed in his full battle garb. He was in a dojo of some sort — he felt the wooden floors worn smooth beneath his hindpaws, saw (and somehow felt) the paper and wooden lattice which acted as walls, though they were movable when needed. Outside he could see the top of a mountain, and beyond that, well — nothing. Just a stretch of vast, empty sky.

Across the vista, he saw a black crow flying, calling out for someone — or something.

He could see himself — it was surreal, but seemed very familiar in a way — dressed in the full battle dress of a Falconrider. But here — in this place — his tunic and pants were clean and whole, not ragged and aged the way they were when he took them out of his wine cellar earlier that morning, after so many seasons — first of combat, and then of intentional storage deep within The Sleeping Cat's wine cellars.

Here, his uniform was free of combat or killing. It almost seemed brand new.

He watched himself standing, solitary, as he brandished two hand axes in his hand — not just any hand axes, but the custom-balanced battle axes of the FalconGuard.

In front of him stood a white weasel. He wore a black headband on his head and a crimson tunic around his shoulders, acting as a cloak. The weasel's paws were folded, looking stern and steadfast, but while he stood above the mouse by almost a full body length, he looked down at Teague sympathetically — almost affectionately.

Their gazes locked, and for a time, all was silent.

Then finally, the weasel started to speak.

'When She created the animals, they were all given their own unique and particular weapons. But as time passed, most of them forgot what their weapons were. This is why chickens are now the most hunted food animal. She gave them some of her most devastating weapons as gifts — their claws, their talons, and the precious gift of flight — and yet somehow, over the ages, they forgot these gifts. In doing so, chickens became the most common dinner item on the world's supper table. They refuse to defend themselves simply because the knowledge of their fighting art was lost over time due to complacency. Had they only remembered what they were capable of, chicken would be a rare food item on any dinner table across The Far Collective.

'Do not forget the weapons that She gave to the Mouselings. Do not forget the weapons that She gave to you.'

'What weapons?' Teague asked incredulously.

'These,' said the White Weasel.

And then the scene changed.

Teague and the White Weasel were training together. In Teague's paws were two wooden sticks. Across from him, the White Weasel held the same twin weapons.

Suddenly the Weasel lunged at Teague with strong overhead strikes, and Teague, watching himself, deftly blocked them. High high, side side, low low — and repeat. Wood reverberated on wood, clashing with a thick yet hollow sound as the two animals, intensely focused, fought together in the training exercise.

'Again,' said the Weasel, and they started the exercise over, repeating it over and over again — times too innumerable to count.

'Again,' Teague heard the Weasel's voice echo through his head, over and over and over.

Across Teague's vision, days passed.

Teague saw himself using the **Four Paws Flow** system against a wooden dummy, using skilled footwork to insert himself near the dummy and then chain together complex combinations of strikes with precise execution. Again, and again, he saw himself brandishing combos — punching and striking with forepaws, kicking with hindpaws, spinning and striking both dummy and hanging sandbags with a ferocious and unbridled force he never would have thought himself capable of.

More days passed.

Teague saw himself now at peace, his hindpaws folded into a seated butterfly position upon the mountaintop, eyes closed, sitting in silent meditation. He saw how his body had become muscular, transformed into that of a Mouseling walking the Warrior's Way.

Confident, but humble.

Yet he felt so at peace.

In that moment, he recognized the connection he was forming — how he was becoming one with She Who Created Him, and the spirits and elements of the earth. His training went far beyond merely punches and kicks. He was becoming a warrior whose deepest desire was to walk a peaceful path.

Then, seasons passed.

Teague watched the Winterblossom trees on the mountaintop go from full bloom, to losing their petals, to being barren in the frozen wintertime, to sprouting new buds as springtime once again approached.

How long this took to transpire, he was unsure.

Then the scene changed once more.

Teague saw himself in the dojo again, now far more proficient and skilled, listening intently to the master.

'**Four Paws Flow** can be the most lethal of any combat arts. It is deceptively effective because most animals think of mice as creatures having two paws with which to fight and two that must be on the ground at all times. This is a farce. You must learn to use all four paws effectively at any given time. Should an adversary trap one paw, you must respond with a three paw defense, free the fourth paw, and turn it into an attack.'

The White Weasel looked Teague squarely in the eyes, and then continued:

'Four paws style is a combination of battle techniques gleaned from those who have come before us. Our ancient masters were forced to learn these in the brittle, bare-pawed, life and death situations which came to define their daily existence. This all happened, of course, back when farming was a daily requirement for all families and subsistence was but another name for the game of survival. When raiders came to the hamlets of animals, such as your Mouseling brethren, seeking to pillage, raze, and plunder, your kin defended themselves with simple farm implements: the staff used for walking uneven terrain. The flail used for threshing wheat. Nails, once used for shoeing their squirrel mounts, were twisted into crippling caltrops. Other defenses came in other forms — in the form of stars copied from the shining heavens, thrown at an opponent's eyes as a deterrent. In the form of low stances once used by your seafaring brothers who traversed the oceans, long before your birth. When their ships were boarded, their low stances allowed them to stay nimble and grounded while their opponents lost their footing with each passing wave — making them easy, susceptible prey. This was your ancestors' earliest martial legacy. And, in its quintessential form, is it not still the most powerful? Do you not feel the blood of your ancestors coursing through your veins, mouse?'

Teague closed his eyes for a moment, and felt the wind on his face — on his soft, moist snout.

'Yes, Master. I feel it in me even now. I feel the rolling ocean that moved the ships of my ancestors, and how they fought with the waves, using nature to aid them in neutralizing their enemies. I feel the crush of the wooden flail against the skull of those who would pillage our outposts and take our families as slaves.'

The Weasel looked down at the mouse, and nodded sternly.

'Indeed, mouse. The legacy of the Mouselings that you come from contains a long lineage of proud, ferocious fighters who gave everything to preserve their intellectual secrets — and the gifts that She gave them. They would not bow before any would-be invaders who sought to steal their special knowledge without making them pay the steepest of prices. And now, you must return to where you came from and fulfill the vow you have made in this place, to your ancestors so long ago. Your people need you. Remember, every animal, no matter how large or how ferocious, has a weakness. And sometimes, their greatest weakness is their belief that they have no weakness at all. Do you understand, Mouseling?'

'I think so, Master,' said Teague. He felt puzzled, yet also like he understood perfectly, at the same time — which was quite an unusual feeling.

The White Weasel looked at him once more.

'Consider this story, mouse:

One day, a wandering monk ascended to the top of a mountain to ask the master who lived there a question.

When he arrived, the master looked him over, then simply said, 'What is your question?'

The monk asked the master, 'Once I become a master fighter, how do I ever return to the ordinary world?'

The master replied:

'A broken mirror never reflects again...fallen flowers never go back to the old branches. Crumbling castles don't rebuild themselves, and butterflies never return to being worms once more.'

'Do you understand now?' asked the Weasel.

Teague looked up at the White Weasel, unsure of what to say.

'Now, get back up. Rise, my son, and finish what you started. Call your foe back to you, and make it clear your fight is not yet finished.'

In Robert Teague's mind's eye, at that precise moment, he saw a vision of the badger running towards him in the MouseKeep Armory, an enormous battle axe in his paws. Strangely, though, the badger seemed to be running in slow motion.

Then, the vision was gone.

The White Weasel continued:

'Use the power of your **Four Paws Flow** and bring your opponent to justice. Always remember that weapons are only extensions of your bare paws — nothing more. Your journey ahead is a long one, and filled with adversaries far greater than this one. If you cannot vanquish this foe, how can The Universe expect you to see your quest through until its end?'

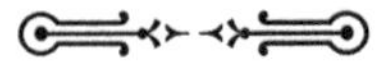

Teague's eyes snapped back open. His head was still spinning, and he stared upwards. What was he looking at? He saw thick wooden beams arching criss-cross across a ceiling before terminating over a stained-glass window.

Teague sat up and looked around. Everywhere around him, Mouselings and Ratlings were fighting, and an enormous badger in bronze armor was parading around triumphantly, yelling:

'I VANQUISHED THE LEADER OF THE FABLED TWO! COME FIGHT ME, YOU MOUSELING FOOLS, IF YOU DARE!'

I'm back in MouseKeep Armory, thought Teague to himself. He scanned around for his hand axes and saw them laying against a weapons barrel. He went to retrieve them and, as he stumbled towards the weapons, still disoriented, he noticed a motionless body behind the barrel itself.

It was Ainsley Hearthseeker, a crossbow bolt sticking out of his abdomen.

'Oh no — Ainsley!' Teague cried out selflessly. 'I've got to get you help!'

With one paw he stroked his friend's face, which was starting to feel cold and clammy. He could see the bard's lips beginning to lose their pink color.

'I know there is still time, my friend. Just hold on!'

In that moment, Robert Teague knew *exactly* what he had to do.

Retrieving his weapons, he looked around him. Wilding was busy fighting two rats, blood pouring through his purple robe from a shoulder wound. Not far away, the Stranger looked like he was about done, having been cornered by two Ratling warriors.

The look on his face showed utter exhaustion.

There isn't much time, my son, he heard the White Weasel's voice in his head ring out.

Shaking his head to clear his vision, he called out to the badger.

'HEY, BRUISER! YES, I AM TALKING TO YOU BIG GUY! OUR FIGHT ISN'T DONE YET!'

Teague held up a paw and made the number 'one' with his first finger, nodding at his foe.

'ONE MORE ROUND, BADGER! JUST YOU AND ME. COME FINISH WHAT THE RAT KING SENT YOU TO DO — IF YOU CAN. I AM STILL BREATHING, SO YOUR JOB ISN'T FINISHED QUITE YET!'

Taken by surprise, and shocked at how Teague had somehow recovered from such a powerful blow, the badger yelled out:

'I SHOULD HAVE BEHEADED YOU WHEN I HAD THE CHANCE, MOUSELING. NOW I WILL SIMPLY CLEAVE YOU IN TWO!'

And with that, the badger came at Teague, wielding his enormous battle axe with two paws.

For Robert Teague, what happened next seemed to happen in slow motion.

Teague's mind became solely focused on the badger, who was sprinting towards him. In that moment, he felt the smooth, worn, polished wood of the twin hand axes in his paws — their balance and grip so perfect. He noticed tiny grey lines around the badger's mouth, a sign that he was no young animal. He noticed the stained-glass window in the MouseKeep Armory, etched so finely in detail, telling the story of how the Mouselings first got the gift of speech from the decoding stones.

He heard the badger yell out to him, his voice now low-pitched and blurred, as he slowly rumbled towards him.

'I'LL KILL YOU, ROBERT TEAGUE!'

And yet Teague stood motionless, watching his opponent running towards him, but slowly — oh so slowly. It felt like being in a dream where you run, and run, and run, but you barely move because you are trapped in quicksand. To Robert Teague, it appeared like Bruiser was stuck — and time itself had somehow slowed to a crawl.

I've seen this exact scene before, Teague thought to himself, strangely. *In a vision, on that mountaintop.*

Silent and focused, Teague stood perfectly still. The White Weasel's face and the image of falling winter blossoms flashed across his mind, and he heard again what the White Weasel had said to him:

'And sometimes, their greatest weakness is their belief that they have no weakness at all.'

Teague was so focused on Bruiser's slow-motion charge that it took him a moment to notice — and pay attention to — the massive, searing pain that suddenly penetrated his right rib cage. He turned to his right to look — still in slow motion — only to see a black rat had crept up next to him — and its two paws were placed firmly on the hilt of a dagger which was now impaled into his side. Teague recognized (ironically, the recognition came to him more as an intellectual thought than a physical feeling or sensation) that the black rat was still firmly pressing the dagger into his midsection — and about to twist the knife to cause more damage.

For a moment, the two locked eyes — the rat's beady black eyes filled with hatred and sinister intent, while Teague's eyes were pools of glassy, placid serenity. Then, Robert Teague, in one effortless and unthinking motion, spun around 360 degrees and cleanly beheaded the rat with the hand axe in his right paw.

The black rat's head went rolling across the floor, making a ***thud thud*** sound and tumbling across the path between Teague and his nemesis — a path that was now clear.

And then Robert Teague, with a dagger in his rib cage and a mind like water, charged directly at his badger foe, who towered over him by four or five body lengths.

Teague raised his voice, his small Mouseling body now filled with adrenaline.

'AHHHHHHHHHHHHHHHHHHHH!'

His voice cascaded as he sprinted towards the massive creature.

'AAAAAAAAAHHHHHHHHH COME GET WHAT YOU HAVE COMING TO YOU, YOU RATLICKING FILTH!'

And with that, all combat in the chamber paused as both Mouselings and minions of The Rat King alike stopped to watch this small mouse charge the colossal, bronze-armored badger while yelling out his ferocious battle cry.

You could have heard a pin drop.

The badger rushed at Teague, and as he approached the lithe brown mouse he raised his battle axe and prepared to cleave Teague in two.

'DIE NOW, MOUSE!' yelled Bruiser.

But Teague had different plans. He didn't veer off or even try to side step the blow.

Instead, he just kept running directly at him.

The badger swung his axe downward at Teague, but Teague was so quick he had already scooted inside the striking area between the badger's legs and his axe head as it cascaded down with the intent to kill.

And then, Robert Teague sprang forward into the air and tucked into a long dive, rolling into a small ball of fur, growing blurry as he tumbled forward towards his foe at great speed, and went spinning, spinning, underneath the belly and midsection of the badger.

There was a flash of glinting steel and the sound of slicing metal that echoed through the air — though the strikes themselves were so fast they were barely visible — as Teague rolled underneath the badger's legs and ended up on the other side. He came to rest in a full split, his right axe held above his head and his left axe held downward at his side in a classic **Four Paws Flow** weapon stance.

His face was expressionless...his mind, the vast ocean, his body, the empty stretch of sky at sunset.

Yet, both axes were now covered in blood.

It was so quiet that, as a tiny drop of blood fell off one of Teague's hand axes and spilled to the floor, it made an audible *drip* sound which could be heard throughout the chamber.

His back was still to the badger, and though he couldn't see his opponent as he remained motionless in his seated split position, Robert Teague still *knew*.

He knew the fight had just ended.

A second after Teague came to a stop on the Armory floor, the badger abruptly dropped his gigantic battle axe and clutched at his belly. Blood was pouring down his legs as he worked to keep his entrails from falling out.

He fell to his knees, calling out with one last breath, his speech already beginning to slur:

'TEAGUE...YOU...SCOUNDREL...'

And then he fell face first onto the Armory floor, dead before he hit the stone.

The eerie silence that permeated the Armory chamber after Bruiser crashed to the floor was so shocking, it felt like it could have lasted a lifetime — but the Mouseling fighters didn't need any further invitation to up the ante after seeing what Robert Teague had just accomplished to turn the tide of battle.

To anyone who knew him, it would have come as no surprise that it was the Stranger who broke that shocked silence first. Noticing that the two rats who'd cornered him were still staring at Bruiser's fallen body with incredulity, he seized the opportunity by kicking one of the rats squarely in the plums. The rat yelped in pain and doubled over, and his companion turned back towards the thief just in time to realize that the Stranger, muttering a string of obscene curses the whole while, had just run him through with his short sword. Pulling the blade back out, the Stranger then beheaded the first rat as it clutched at its groin and kicked its head across the chamber floor as the second rat fell lifelessly to the ground.

Wilding, who had caught the commotion out of the corner of his eye, thought, *I really like that move. I must file that one away, in case I ever have use for it.*

Finnegan Willowtail also saw the spectacle that was transpiring in the corner, and wasted no time regaining the initiative for the surviving members of the MouseGuard.

'FOR MOUSEKEEEEEPPPP!!!!!' he yelled at the top of his lungs, then moved to engage the unfortunate rat foe that happened to be closest to him.

The other Mouseling fighters quickly took up the cry. 'FOR MOUSEKEEP!!!!'

Snowwillow, a precocious fighter and martial arts practitioner in his own right, thought to himself, *If Robert Teague can take down such a gigantic badger with ease, I should easily be able to dispatch what Ratling scum remains against us.* And after hearing Finnegan Willowtail's rallying cry, he proceeded to do just that, moving to engage one of the larger Ratling captains. The rat captain was dual wielding a pair of nasty looking swords, but using his own sword, he swiftly disarmed his opponent, knocking each sword out of the rat's paws with a few short strokes.

Now open-handed, his opponent swiped a massive paw at Snowwillow's face in a powerful haymaker-type swing — but, the young leftenant intercepted it easily with **Snapping the Twig:** *intercept wild hooking swing, spinning opposite elbow to opponent snout, regrip attacking hand with double paw grip, 180 pivot with opponent paw in hand to bring opponent down, rising roundhouse kick to face, step over trapped arm, pin arm between hip bones, shatter elbow joint into compound fracture, rear rising heel kick to face.*

The rat cried out in agony as he felt his elbow shatter in multiple places, his joint making a snapping sound like a dry branch. Mercifully, Snowwillow's rising kick rendered the rat completely inert on the floor, momentarily oblivious to the pain he would be feeling when he awoke.

Of course, while watching your biggest, toughest champion getting eviscerated by a small mouse would be enough to strike fear into the heart of any creature, watching the remaining MouseGuard spring into action after being rallied by Teague's accomplishment

— coupled with the sight of Snowwillow's brutal takedown of the Ratling captain — was enough to ultimately shatter any remaining morale among the Ratling fighters. One rat, seeing that the tide had turned, flung down his weapon and yelled, 'FLEE! FLEE FOR YOUR LIVES!' then sprinted towards the nearest exit, screaming. A second rat soon ran after him, followed by a third. Then, like the rushing of a river after a dam breaks, panic swept through the Ratling fighters.

At the sight of their fleeing comrades, the remaining rats looking around for any semblance of leadership — and not finding any, took a hint from their friends and decided it was not sensible to continue fighting now that the day was irretrievably lost. Dropping their weapons en masse, the Ratling army rushed towards the same exit that Cornelius White Eye had taken (what seemed to them like) such a very long time before.

Stampeding towards the exit and screaming in panic, the rats were so focused on trying to save their own skins that not a single one of them even tried to carry any of their wounded companions away with them. In their rush to escape, they seemed happy to leave their compatriots to the mercy — and judgment — of the Mouselings they had recently left to die in the Castle's dungeons (or more likely, to the now rescued King Teegan).

'So much for no rat left behind,' Wilding remarked to Finnegan Willowtail dryly.

Cheering erupted from the remaining Mouseling brothers as they watched their foes flee, knowing the day had been won and that their deep sacrifices had NOT been made in vain.

'Hurrah! Hurrah for Robert Teague!' they cried as they celebrated and hugged each other.

The battle was finally over. But Wilding looked around the room intently — partly to make sure that no adversaries who might possibly represent a threat remained, and partly to triage the situation and determine what actions they would need to take next.

Snowwillow was helping Finnegan Willowtail, who was bleeding from the abdomen, up to his feet. The Stranger dropped his sword and put his paws on his knees, just trying to catch his breath. Several of the other Mouselings ran over to Hearthseeker and worked on getting a makeshift stretcher together using some halberds and clothing.

Then Wilding spied Teague, who remained motionless — and expressionless — on the floor, in the same split position he'd landed in after taking down Bruiser.

Sprinting over to his friend, he went to hug him tightly, then saw the cruel-looking dagger hilt which still stuck out from Teague's ribcage and refrained from doing so.

Lady, no, thought Wilding to himself with desperation, overtaken by sadness at the sight of his friend's wound. *I can't lose two friends in one day. Please, Dear Goddess, no!*

Instead of hugging him, he knelt down and touched his friend lightly on the cheek with his paw.

'Robert — Robert Teague, you did it! You saved us!'

Teague remained emotionless, expressionless, and did not acknowledge his friend's words.

'Teague!' said Wilding again. 'Robert, I thought I lost you!'

Still, Teague lay unresponsive.

Wilding gently pressed on Teague's paws, which still held his hand axes in a firm **Four Paws Flow** grip. The wizard lowered his friend's paws carefully and gently placed the weapons on the floor.

'Robert — Robert, you don't need these anymore today. Robert, can you hear me?'

A tear started to well up in Wilding's eye, and he brushed it away as his nose began to run from the terrible sadness he was feeling in his heart.

Then, Robert Teague blinked his eyes and slowly came out of whatever trance he had been in, turning his head ever so slightly to meet Wilding's gaze.

'Wilding!' Teague said, motionless except for a single paw he stretched out to clasp his friend's paw — weakly, but with sincere affection. Eyeing his friend up and down, still dazed, he cocked his head to the side and asked:

'MouseKeep…is it safe?'

Wilding couldn't hold back the tears anymore, hearing this and seeing his friend's true colors in the moment. The selflessness of a leader who placed the wellbeing of others ahead of his own concerns — even when mortally wounded and on the brink of death.

Wiping his eyes, the tall mouse replied:

'Yes. It is safe now, Robert.'

The innkeeper stared into space for a moment, then looked back at Wilding, pointing to the exposed wound that showed through his torn battle robes.

'What happened to your shoulder?

Wilding smiled at his friend and replied, 'It's nothing, Robert. Nothing compared with what you just achieved. You saved MouseKeep, Robert Teague! You did what you came here to do, and the forces of The Rat King now lay vanquished. They have been routed from this castle.

Teague was expressionless for a moment, as if he did not hear what his wizard friend had just said.

Then, he blinked his eyes again and looked at Wilding with desperation:

'Ainsley Hearthseeker! Wilding, we have to get to The King's Pedestal and find a healer, before it is too late!'

And with that, as blood poured freely from his rib cage and out onto his pants, Robert Teague slumped to the floor and passed out — having given all he could that day to save his King, his precious MouseKeep, his brothers in arms, and the place he loved the most in the world: his Mouseling Hollow.

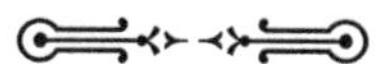

The Legend of The White Weasel:

There is one notable fighter who won his freedom in The Arena of the Black Baron. While none know his true name, they called him The White Weasel. When he won his freedom, after defeating three animals in three separate interspecies matches over a period of three days, he was asked what his fighting secret was...and this is what he said:

> **I breathe in and out.**
>
> **It is a logical, natural, and sequential flow.**
>
> **My heart is like a wildflower**
>
> **Simple and pure**
>
> **And in this calm state**
>
> **I bring those who wish to harm me to the very destruction they themselves seek.**

After that, with a jug of water in his paw and a deep gash across his face (a souvenir from his final match), he walked into the blinding desert sands and was never seen again...

— TAKEN FROM **BLOOD AND DUST: THE RISE AND FALL OF LEGENDARY CHAMPIONS IN THE ARENA OF THE BLACK BARON**

Chapter 27

CHICKEN SOUP FOR THE SOUL...AND BODY

A few days later, Teague awoke on a makeshift cot in The King's Pedestal.

There were rows of similar cots set up on either side of him holding Mouselings who had also been wounded in the battle that had taken place for MouseKeep. Teague tried to sit up, but the searing pain in his side refused to let him do that, so he lay back down immediately. Even the simple act of trying to get up had made him nauseated, so he stared at the ceiling, sweating on the cot from the nausea and pain, trying to figure out how he got there.

'Well, look who's awake,' said a surly voice next to him.

Teague looked over to see Captain Redfur Tumblefox sitting by his bedside, reading a copy of The Feldenspar Daily — a newsprint periodical that was issued in town for Mouselings which detailed gossip, various sordid and sundry affairs, the adventures of a famed Mouseling Hollow detective named Sir Pendleton Stormsnout, and other general hullabaloo that was not considered official news, but that Mouselings across the land loved anyway. It was, of course, considered terrible form to read such a piece of 'yellow journalism,' but Redfur Tumblefox was never one to be dissuaded by public opinion (or encouraged by it, for that matter).

'Back from the dead then, are ye?' said the Captain. 'HEY BOYS, LOOK WHO'S AWAKE! WE GOT US A REAL LIFE HEEE-ROE ON OUR PAWS OVER HERE. RIGHT OVER HERE NOW!' he yelled.

Then he jerked his thumb towards Teague's bed and laughed boisterously.

'You got my note?' asked Robert Teague, breathing a sigh of relief.

'Your note? Aye, I got it — and a dirty little mouse along with it who jumped up on my bar! That scalawag is eating me out of house and home, too. When I find his parents and send the lad back to them, I am going to send YOU the tab! All he wants to eat is the finest Feldenspar Roquefurt — the most expensive cheese we have! And he wants it on EVERYTHING — Roquefurt Sauce on Aged Beef Tenderloin, Roquefurt Parmesan over Guinea eggs with toast points, Roquefurt Feldenspar Rarebit, you name it! He is hungry all the time, Teague — ALL THE TIME! And, he won't stop following me around asking about you. Night and day, it's 'How is Mister Teague? Is Mister Teague going to be ok? Mister Teague this, Mister Teague that.' Won't stop talking about how brilliant he thinks you are, and something about you fighting a huntress spider — which I am sure is a bunch of nonsense. And on top of that, he's started to play Root and Field with my bar patron's game pieces, and is hogging my tables — hogging them right up! Against the rules, of course, but he told me last night 'Mister Teague would probably say it's ok.' Hmph! As if you run MY BAR!'

Teague smiled a weak smile, and reached out for The Captain's paw, who clasped it tightly in his own. The two old veteran friends looked at each other, and when Teague went to release his paw, The Captain held on to it tight.

'You know, Robert Teague, in all seriousness — you saved MouseKeep, and Castle Feldenspar too. If we hadn't gotten that note from you, well...I am not sure what would have happened, but I shudder to even think about it. We had a monster of a time clearing out the lower chambers of MouseKeep, you know. Those rats were fleeing everywhere — many of them still armed and unaware that the

King had been freed and that your friend Bruiser had, thanks to you — how should we say — taken quite a tumble? It was a mess. Those poor falcons atop the riding perch were half starved and terribly dehydrated by the time we made it up to them, and the Mouseling staff that hadn't been imprisoned in the dungeons had been sent home, having been told the King 'no longer needed their services.' There was no way those of us on the outside could have known about the infiltration of MouseKeep and the King's imprisonment. And, Wilding shared with me that you are already aware of the Falcon Rider ambush south of Mouseling Hollow. We lost most of the Riders...it's a bloody mess, and a tragedy at that. But thanks to you, the wizard, and that bard friend of yours, we are picking up the pieces instead of leaving our homes to flee for our lives.'

'Bard...' said Teague, trying hard to think. He knew that something important was associated with that word. 'Bard...BARD! AINSLEY HEARTHSEEKER! IS HE OK?!'

Teague tried to sit up again, but the pain in his ribs held him down, and The Captain placed a reassuring paw on Teague's shoulder until his body relaxed. Still, his eyes held a look of terrible desperation as he hoped for any news of the bard who — at last glance — looked to be not long for the world.

'You are one lucky mouse, Robert Teague. Both you and your friend Hearthseeker would be walking with Her right now had Wilding and the remaining MouseGuard not rushed the two of you straight to The King's Pedestal, where the Queen herself was being worked on by one of the most skilled human healers in The Western Lands — a woman you may have heard of named Sirona. King Teegan had his wife's treatment put on hold when he saw the dire straits you both were in — though Lady help me if I could understand why he'd waste her talents on a washed-up old innkeeper like yourself. The bard I can understand though — I've always been partial to music, meself.'

Tumblefox paused a moment to hum the faint snatches of an old marching tune. Then, turning serious, he continued. 'I'll tell you what, Teague — to Sirona's credit, I have never seen anything like it. Between her healing magic, some medicinal potions she had brought with her, and the skill of Dr. OakenPaw from town, who sutured you two up so's you don't have huge holes in your sides no more, they got both you boys patched up pretty good. In fact, very few Mouselings from Wilding's party escaped from that fracas uninjured — many of them lie here next to you, working towards recovery as you are. Leftenant Snowwillow was one of the few who did not need to seek aid. I have heard he is quite a fighter, that one. Like myself, only not quite as good, of course.'

With that, The Captain cleared his throat deeply and chortled, then burst out laughing.

Teague smiled at the joke, then asked:

'What about the boys? They came with you?'

'Oh, of course Teague, you old rogue, you should know those boys never stray too far from my bar...or their cups! Yes, of course they did. When they heard that MouseKeep had been infiltrated by rats, well, let's just say they were...spoiling...for a good, old-fashioned fight.'

'Is everyone ok?' asked Teague.

'Well...' said The Captain, looking upwards. 'Yes, everyone is fine. Old Punchy took a pike through the back of his shoulder when one rat who was skulking in the shadows came at him — but Punchy just ran backwards with the pike in him as the rat held on, pinned the rat against the wall and slammed into him so hard that the blunt end of the pike handle impaled the rat, too! Just like the old days...you know how Old Punchy is, howling mad as they say...but now, Punchy is walking around with his shoulder in a sling and asking for more of that medicine Lady Sirona was handing out. He says he likes it better than his ale! Tastes of strawberries, he says...but yes, to answer your question, everyone in The Wrecking Crew is fine. Speaking of everyone, looks like you have some visitors incoming. I'll check in with you before you are discharged back to Mouseling Hollow. And Robert Teague...'

The Captain looked Teague in the eye once more firmly.

'Thank you. But now you owe ME one.'

Laughing out loud, the large mouse — still in his tricorne hat and red robe — got up and headed over towards some of the other bedridden Mouselings to check in on them and provide his support.

Not long after, Wilding and Ainsley Hearthseeker, now using a crutch for support, ambled their way over to Teague's bed.

'Well, look who's up,' said Wilding, kneeling down at Teague's bedside and allowing Hearthseeker to take the chair The Captain had just recently vacated. Ainsley Hearthseeker gently eased down in the chair and then saluted Robert Teague.

'Captain!' said Hearthseeker, a huge smile of relief on his face.

Teague looked over at the bard and smiled back.

'Hearthseeker, you look like you're moving about as fast as my old grandmother did — right before she died.'

The two mice burst out laughing, and Wilding smiled.

Then Teague got serious for a second.

'I thought we had lost you, Ainsley. I can't tell you how glad I am you are still with us!'

'Well, sir, the feeling is mutual,' the bard replied with a smile. 'We weren't so sure that you were going to make it, either. Not all of our Mouseling brothers were so lucky.'

Teague paused for a moment to think about what his friend had said, then took his paw and rubbed at his right side, right around his rib cage. He felt pain, but there was a significant layer of cloth bandage between his paw and the wound. Still, he knew it had been a bad injury.

'You know, Robert,' said Wilding, 'by the time we got you onto a stretcher a lot of that badger blood had already spilled out. It made quite a mess all over — including near you, where you were lying.

We are concerned some of it might have gotten mixed in with your blood. You aren't having any strange feelings of aggression, mania, or hatred towards your fellow Mouselings, are you?'

Teague chuckled weakly, then pretended to consider it. 'Well...no more than usual, I would say. Where is the Stranger?'

'Well, he took some wounds in the battle for MouseKeep Armory, but he's up and walking now. He has been recalled for the day to the Thief's Guild to give them a debrief. King Teegan has also asked him — confidentially speaking — to start looking into the issue of which mice in the guild have turned and are now serving The Rat King. There are spies among us in the guild now, that's for certain.

'Bad tidings, indeed,' lamented Teague.

'Indeed,' said Wilding. 'And I have no doubt that, as we pick up the pieces of this nearly-averted catastrophe, we will find more issues of concern. I hope you're ready, Robert — King Teegan has summoned the three of us to meet with him and Commander Gabriel Storm in a few minutes. But for now, since you are finally awake and back from the brink of death, why don't you regale us with some of your stories, and tell us what happened since we first parted ways at The King's Pedestal. We heard you had quite the adventure to share.'

Teague sighed and put both his paws behind his head as he settled back into the makeshift cot. Taking a deep breath, he told his friends the story of all the things that had transpired since they had separated, including meeting Squeak, defeating Arachne, exploring the new and 'undiscovered' side of MouseKeep, and his role in the battle to save Castle Feldenspar that had transpired in the Great Hall.

After he had finished, a few Mouseling orderlies came and politely introduced themselves. Grabbing Teague's makeshift cot, they carried it (very carefully) up a set of recently erected stairs to the edge of the false wall where The King's Pedestal was situated. Wilding and Hearthseeker slowly ascended the stairs behind them, settling into two chairs that had been set out next to where Teague's cot had been lain.

Soon, King Teegan came in and sat in his old wingback chair. Commander Storm, limping in with the use of a cane, followed behind him. A woman in flowing golden robes — who Teague deduced was Sirona the Healer — followed behind them. Sister Minerva came in carrying several trays of food, including a steaming pitcher of what seemed to be some kind of soup. The three Mouselings sat silently as she came in and set down the serving tray on the table next to King Teegan's wingback chair — and then, pouring three bowls of steaming soup onto the tray, she bowed, then left the three humans alone in the King's chambers.

King Teegan then slid the false wall shut so that the three mice were alone with the King, Commander Storm, and the healer.

Without saying a word, Storm drew out three small wooden bowls and three tiny spoons from within his tunic, filled them with hot soup, and using a side dish that Sister Minerva had brought, placed them in front of the three mice. He then grabbed several pieces of fresh toast, still warm from the tray Sister Minerva had left on the table, and slathered them with golden butter topped with a delicate cracked pepper and tarragon spice blend. Carefully cutting one of the toast slices into mouse-sized pieces, he handed several tiny triangles of warm, crusty goodness to each mouse, then cut the remaining slices into quarters for himself and King Teegan.

'Come, heroes.' Storm said, finally breaking the solemn silence. 'Sup with us. King Teegan has longed to speak with you, and been terribly worried for your health and safety.'

Storm pulled up a stool while Lady Sirona came over to the mice, looking at each one carefully in turn.

'How are you feeling, Mouselings?' she said in a low, musical voice. 'King Teegan has asked that I pass another round of healing energy through each of your bodies, to help speed your recovery and aid you in regaining your strength. Will you permit me to do this?'

All three mice nodded. Reaching out a lithe, slender hand, Sirona first touched Wilding's shoulder, then Hearthseeker's side and head, and finally, moved on to Robert Teague. Gently, she removed the cloth covering his wound and touched it with one finger. Teague could feel a warmth — it felt almost like a silvery golden light — shine into his abdomen, causing a flash of pain, but also generating a feeling of utter relief as well.

When she finished, Teague noticed that he was able to take a deeper breath than he had before.

Sirona looked at the mice, and then over at King Teegan and Commander Storm.

'These mice have all suffered significant trauma from the battle and their ordeals, Majesty. It is obvious that these two,' she pointed to Hearthseeker and Teague, 'were in an especially grave situation. They must be monitored, and I will need to check in on them every six hours for the next day or so to ensure they suffer no further complications. Once that time period has passed safely, they should be free to travel back to their homes — where they must continue to rest a few days more. I have never seen animals endure so much violence and pain. It is remarkable — or a sign of Her will perhaps — that they are still alive after what they've endured.'

The healer paused a second, as if debating whether or not to share her next thought, then continued. 'I can't help but wonder if it speaks to a greater destiny — that these incredible Mouselings might have more of a role yet to play. It's just my observation, of course. But it is indeed interesting that these three have survived — especially after what I've heard of their adventures, and all they were forced to endure. Now, sire, if you will excuse me, I must attend to my Queen.'

Teegan bowed his head and grasped Sirona's hand. 'Thank you, milady — thank you for doing all you've done to save her, and them.'

He gestured to the mice as he said this.

Lady Sirona bowed gracefully and turned to exit. As she was leaving, Teague realized that while most humans looked alike to him, this was obviously one very beautiful woman (by human standards, at least).

The mice watched King Teegan dive eagerly into his bowl of hot soup. Large, steaming chunks of hot cooked chicken, fresh carrots and celery, and delectable herbs in a rich, creamy broth smelled heavenly to all in the room, and their stomachs rumbled with anticipation. After a moment, he looked up to see that the Mouselings — as well as Commander Storm — had not yet begun to eat, waiting out of respect for their King.

Laughing out loud, he beckoned to all of them, and said:

'Come, heroes of Feldenspar. Sup with me, and regain your strength. There is much for us to talk about — both of the events that have already transpired, and what is still yet to come.'

When they finally put down their empty bowls, both humans and mice alike were silent for a moment, reflecting. All of them — the King and Storm included — had been through a great deal of pain and agony over the past few days, and knowing what was coming next was on all of their minds.

Finally, King Teegan spoke.

'We have learned much over the past few days. But before I share with you what I know, allow me to thank you for all for your great work and sacrifice. Robert Teague, and Professor Wilding — **The Fabled Two** — I cannot express how glad I am that you got my missive. Although, it is only by Her hand that we are all sitting here now, as my understanding is that my personal, sealed message to you was somehow intercepted by the infiltrators and then twisted to their foul purposes. I understand that some of those responsible were working directly out of the Mouseling Thief's Guild — and THAT, in and of itself, is very disconcerting.'

He paused for a moment, then continued.

'Robert Teague, I consider you and Commander Wilding to be two of my most valuable confidants, even though it has been many seasons since the line of Teegan last had cause to ask your active service. Since you have spent the last few days recovering, let me share with you some of the knowledge we have managed to gain regarding what has taken place since your battle in the MouseKeep Armory — a battle where, I understand, you slew quite a foe.'

The King paused a moment to sip from a cooling mug of tea, then continued:

'Once we had Feldenspar Castle secured, I immediately issued orders to rescind the drawbridge, and to send my fastest messengers to recall the knights who had been dispatched to Old Town under false pretenses. In the days since, we have started a campaign to recruit some of our finest civilian archers and to post them throughout the castle spires, along the town wall, and at hidden spots within The Western Forest. Should there be a garrison en route to Feldenspar with nefarious intentions, they will be our first line of defense while we wait for the return of our Knights Valiant. We have also begun a massive resupply effort seeking to stockpile provisions for the Castle and township in anticipation of a possible siege, and civilians have been instructed not to leave the island — other than to fish The Mirrored Lake, forage, till the fields, or perform other tasks which could directly bolster our food supplies.

'Commander Storm has, under my direction, imposed a curfew on the town. Scouts report no signs of an enemy garrison in sight — at least as far south as the monastic crossing at River's Rest — although we can only assume an enemy force is out there, somewhere, awaiting its moment to strike at The Western Lands. As far as the human side of this conflict goes, this is, on the surface, fairly good news — all things considered. The civilians we have pressed into military service are beginning to bolster our defenses, and just this morning, we've finally begun deploying our anti-siege equipment upon the Castle parapets. I have sent some of our civilian archers — woodsmen and rangers, by trade — out into the woods as skirmish groups to intercept and harass any enemy forces which may be on the march towards the Castle. If they are coming — and we all know they are — this should buy us some time, at the very least. But as of yet, there has been no indication of a force approaching anywhere near the castle. We will continue, of course, to keep a vigilant lookout for any suspicious activity. Our diplomatic ambassadors across The Far Collective's towns and villages have also been notified about the present situation. In terms of our human affairs, it would appear that — thanks to you two, and your brave Mouseling companions — we have avoided losing the Castle and the crown, for now.'

Teegan looked out the window of his chamber for a second, reflecting on the gravity of what he just said.

After a few tense moments, he then resumed speaking.

'When it comes to animal affairs, however, the news is...not good, to say the least. The Animal Speaker we captured, Tempus, was hesitant to speak to us at first. However, with some...encouragement...'

The King paused here a moment, while he and Commander Storm shared an odd glance with each other, then continued.

'He acknowledged what we have all feared. The Rat King has, in fact, returned — and brought a new contingent of Animal Speakers with him.'

'Yes,' said Teague. 'I heard the same news from the One-Eyed Rat'

Wilding leaned over to Teague and quietly whispered, 'Remind me to tell you a story about him.'

'Indeed,' said Teegan. 'According to Tempus, The Rat King's mental power grows and grows, and he has been able to dominate previously uncontrollable members of the animal kingdoms. He has built a new Black Citadel — though we have been unable to ascertain its exact whereabouts, we are fairly certain that it has NOT been rebuilt in The Hellion Sands. He has recruited human mercenaries from beyond the Southern Ocean, and they travel here, to our lands, as we speak. To weaken our alliance with Mouseling Hollow, they have ambushed and killed most of our FalconGuard — as well as many of our trained falcons — and spread skirmish parties of various animal factions from the woods south of Mouseling Hollow all the way down to Ferngrove Bottoms, and possibly beyond. We have received word of strange creatures lurking in The Silent Pines, and of some mysterious darkness stirring at the Haven of MouseBrook. The exact nature of these unusual forces remains unknown to us, and we currently have no remaining resources available to us to dispatch in order to find answers. Commander Teague, Commander Wilding, I will be frank: when it comes to the animal threats facing us all, *we are blind*. All we can surmise is that it has been The Rat King's intention all along to separate and divide us from our most secret, and precious, resource: our loyal Mouseling allies.'

The Mouselings looked at each other and shook their heads. Could it really be this bad?

'Oh, also — there is one more thing you need to know.'

King Teegan looked sternly at the three Mouselings before speaking.

'Tempus indicated to us that The Rat King fully plans to invade Mouseling Hollow and raze it to the ground. Destroying the home of **The Fabled Two** is one of his highest, and most desperately desired, priorities — along, of course, with killing you both.'

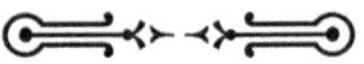

The three mice spoke for almost an hour more with Storm and Teegan. Intelligence was exchanged, as well as stories of everyone's adventures within the Castle. Wilding's rescue of Storm and the King, and Hearthseeker's encounter with Ravenscale were regaled to Robert Teague for the first time, who swelled with pride at what his friend Hearthseeker (and the admittedly unusual Stranger) had been able to accomplish. Teague was especially interested in learning more about the treasure chest that had been 'won' in the exchange.

'Where is this chest now?' asked Teague.

'I gave it to Commander Storm to hide,' the bard replied. 'So we haven't opened it yet. We are waiting to get back to The Sleeping Cat, where Wilding can hopefully lay an eye on its contents and see what treasures, if any, are in there.'

'I hope it's not a dud filled with rocks,' said Teague, and they all laughed at the thought.

'Mc too!' said Hcarthscckcr. 'It was pretty heavy, but sounded like it had some metal or coin in there — or at least it did, before Wilding attacked it!'

Wilding blushed and just shook his head.

'Robert,' Storm chimed in, 'it does feel heavy in my hand, and I can hear its contents rattling around within. I have stashed it safely in my chambers and, when you are ready to depart by falconback, I will bring it and help secure it to your bird.'

'Thank you, Commander Storm. Your help in securing this — treasure chest, or whatever it is, is most valuable to us, and greatly appreciated. What about Ravenscale though?' asked Teague, still focused on the subject. 'Was he still down there in MouseKeep's dungeons?'

'No,' said Commander Storm. 'At least, not that we can confirm. We sent a party down there specifically to retrieve the snake. But when they got there, the cage Hearthseeker spoke about had somehow been opened. We searched all the dungeons, human and animal alike, but unfortunately, we found no sign of the deadly serpent's present location. Just a shed skin, which was...well, unpleasant.'

'And Arachne?'

Wilding looked at Teague.

'The Wrecking Crew went down through the new side of MouseKeep but found no evidence of her — except for the thick cobwebs in the hallway that Squeak told The Captain about. That was in the upper parts of the corridor, near the entrance — just like Squeak described. When they reached the storage area Squeak had told them about, where he said you two...interacted...they said that there had, in fact, been a catastrophic fire, and that all of the stored furniture was destroyed. They found no signs of spider eggs or spider silk anywhere in the chamber. I would like to think that, presumably,

Arachne was killed in the blaze you started. According to The Captain, Squeak has told him the story no less than a hundred times, and he then shared it with us. He and The Wrecking Crew insisted on seeing the crime scene themselves.'

'Hmmm...' said the innkeeper, lost in thought. He shook his head. 'Two bad guys, both now missing in action and unaccounted for. Not good...not good at all.'

'Robert, they did find one thing which I am hesitant to tell you about...' said Wilding.

'Well, what is it?' blurted out the innkeeper.

'They did find some spider silk on the wall in the lower chambers... and it spelled out something.'

A pause filled the room as all eyes focused on the wizard mouse.

'It said...' Wilding cleared his throat.

'Well?' said Teague, obviously growing impatient.

'It said, *TEAGUE WILL DIE. HIS LINE WILL BE SNUFFED OUT — AS MINE WAS AT HIS PAWS.'*

King Teegan looked at the party of Mouselings.

'My friends, the most important fact that we must recognize, and come to terms with, is the fact that we are now at war. How, why, none of that matters right now. Another difficult fact that we must accept is that we are not, at present, in a position to repel the threat effectively. Not with our current situation, at least...and not with the current disposition of our human and animal forces. Here, at Castle Feldenspar, we need to continue to focus on immediate resupply and on consolidating our strength. Getting our troops back, recruiting new forces, and ensuring our alliances across the land are intact. This will be as much a diplomatic mission as it is a martial one. And, on the animal side of things, well...'

Teegan paused for a moment here — a pause which stretched on for a few moments.

Finally, Teague broke the silence.

'Well, what, sire?'

Teegan sighed regretfully. 'Well, Robert Teague...we need ***The Fabled Two*** back. And we need them back as quickly as possible.'

'Did you mean ***The Fabled Three?***' asked Hearthseeker, half jokingly, half hopefully.

'That's a very exclusive club, my tiny friend,' said Teegan, running a hand through his grey mane as he looked kindly down at the bard. 'But if you keep performing the kind of heroics that I have heard you are capable of, mayhaps your friends will let you apply for the position.'

And then he smiled at the three mice, his heart swelling with pride — pride at what they had been able to accomplish, both for him personally and in his name, and pride at the legacy of the secret which had come to define both his, and his father's, reigns.

Robert Teague smiled back the best he could, but noticed he was getting very sleepy and beginning to feel weak again.

'Majesty, I apologize, but I am somehow struggling to keep my eyes open. It must be the chicken soup.'

The King looked at his diminutive, faithful, furry little hero, and smiled a smile at him that was understanding, and yet a little sad.

He reached out and stroked Teague's head gently.

'Rest now, my Mouseling champion. There is much more work that lies ahead, for all of us. Rest, and gather your strength for the coming storm — for when it is upon us, none will be able to hide from it. We will fight to preserve these lands, and its peoples — or we will die in the act of trying.'

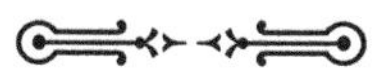

Part III

Returning Home

Chapter 28

FIRESIDE MEDITATIONS

obert Teague sat by the crispy, crackling fire near the hearth in the Teague family quarters above The Sleeping Cat Inn. Nestled in an aged, wingback chair, his hindpaws outstretched on a small wooden stool set out in front of him, he nursed a glass of port.

Silently, he pondered the piece of wedding china he held in his paw as the firelight reflected through it — it was a wine glass, rimmed with golden metal at the top and inscribed with a jade dragonfly on its side. Two of these unique glasses had been gifted to him by his family on the day of his wedding to his lovely Shannon — a day that, to Robert Teague, now seemed to have taken place so many seasons long ago. And though it tended to sit empty and only find use on rare 'special occasions,' at this moment it held what could only be deemed as 'medicine': a tawny port wine from his cellar that had strengthened as it aged and went down silky smooth — so smooth that he could easily drink it in quantity. The delightful port helped to soothe the pain from his injuries, which were still fresh and raw even after the aid of Lady Sirona's healing.

For Teague, who was still only partly mobile after his near-death experience with Bruiser and the dagger-wielding rat captain, alcohol was the most readily available anesthesia that helped reduce the pain of his battle injuries — or at the least, the nerve-crushing sensation he associated with them.

As he sipped his port and watched the twisting, dancing firelight, his mind floated over the events of the past few days — and though he was still in a great degree of pain as he sat recovering from his battle in the MouseKeep Armory, he found himself more troubled by the realization that his days of battle — which he had once thought were left behind him — were now far, far, from over.

Sullenly, silently, darkly, his melancholy mind darted to and fro as the shadows of evening crept in through the last fading light of the setting sun, which bejeweled itself and sparkled in the stained-glass window of his west-facing upstairs apartment. Though his thoughts predominantly focused on his wife and children and what their futures held given the recent turn of events — as his visage was warmed in the soft flames of the hearth, and his insides warmed by the fine aged tawny port — he found himself thinking back on the days of his youth. While he had grown up with next to nothing as just a pup, he remembered with some nostalgia — *nay*, he thought, with a true *emotional fondness* — his days as a whelp in the bottom layer burrow of his babysitter. She was a friend of the family known as Jenny Kahluni, or 'Gentle Jenny' as they called her — a widow who was still somewhat young, but had chosen not to remarry.

He couldn't escape one memory of having been in her burrow and told to take a nap — only to avoid her instruction and, after all the other pups were fast asleep, rise up and travel upwards through her burrow until he'd made his way above ground.

His disobedience was somehow rewarded with the most impressive sight — he had not realized (perhaps because he had never thought to pay attention, at such a young age) that his nanny's burrow was located in the middle of the most decadent of rose gardens, sown with a rich ivy which blossomed among the hedgerows. And when he came above ground that day, he found that he was in the middle of an early Spring rainstorm.

When he emerged out from Gentle Jenny's burrow, his eyes were treated to a gray backdrop silhouetted by the most ravishing dark shades of leafy green rosebushes and ivy, contrasted with crimson roses in full bloom — all while crystal droplets of rain beaded upon their petals, almost as if they were afraid to run down such delicate flowers. A soft golden hue permeated his view of the garden, though the grey background was predominant. It was a moment he would never forget — when the soft dancing drops of rain fell and speckled his soft, moist snout. In that moment, for one young Robert Teague, time seemed to stop and imprint on his mind, refusing to be forgotten even forty seasons later.

It was a decadent moment...one he had been searching to recreate his entire life since in his own garden. There was something so placid about it, so...surreal, about that particular moment. Teague would almost use the word 'heavenly' as he tried to describe it, because that moment in the rose garden had been about the closest to true peace he had ever experienced in his lifetime — so far, at least.

But even as he thought of that cherished childhood memory, sitting in his wingback chair by a cozy fire, he could not recreate that same feeling of peace he'd felt as a young pup. The closest he had come to re-experiencing that feeling as an adult was when he looked at a watercolor above his fireplace by a Mousebrook artist named William 'Two Paws' Neil. It seemed that Two Paws had crept into a similar garden somewhere and somehow managed to capture its unique intersection of colors, time, and space, and impress it all perfectly upon canvas. Though Robert Teague had never actually met him — nor been able to discern where, exactly, the garden depicted in the painting could be found (William 'Two Paws' seemed to be quite evasive when it came to avoiding his fans and well-wishers, to say the least), it was the closest Teague could come to actually possessing a physical impression of that life-changing moment. It was a moment he could never quite articulate to others, even to Shannon, or Wilding — a moment when, as a young mouse entrenched in solitude, an innocent act of disobedience had led to him unexpectedly finding himself in a garden of ivy, roses, and rain.

And then Teague's mind snapped back to the events at hand. While he had given his wife a slight debriefing on what had happened in the Castle, he had been too exhausted, too wounded, and frankly, too protective of her feelings to give her the full debrief when the party had returned, far worse for the wear, on the few falcons that remained in MouseKeep. All he knew at that moment was that his companions were now safely sheltered at The Sleeping Cat as they also recovered from the various wounds they'd suffered at the Castle; that the King, in control of Castle Feldenspar once more, was marshalling what forces remained available to him to go on an (admittedly futile) search and recovery mission of the fallen Falconriders; that spies had been dispatched from the Castle (those who could be trusted, at least — anyone suspecting of colluding with the enemy infiltration had been swiftly imprisoned for safekeeping) to perform recon and gather intelligence on enemy troop formations...but like King Teegan himself had said at their last meeting, **'as far as animal formations and movements, we are currently blind.'**

King Teegan had been bold — and quite direct, as well — in speaking about the importance of ***The Fabled Two*** coming out of retirement to aid The Far Collective once more. Even though he had once hoped his days as a warrior were behind him, with the situation across the land already seeming so dire, Teague couldn't help but agree with him. Even Wilding, who tended to be a little more...contrary...in his opinions, was absolutely in lockstep with Teague's assessment.

They had met once more before they returned to Mouseling Hollow — the three mice, at The King's Pedestal. Teague was still bedridden, Wilding's shoulder still healing, and Hearthseeker was still using his crutch. Teague couldn't remember when, exactly — had it been one day ago, or two? He wasn't sure. But King Teegan had told Teague and company to hitherto depart from MouseKeep, IMMEDIATELY — he'd told them that he needed his party to perform a covert mission — details of which would come to them by courier — and that they needed to rest in Mouseling Hollow and regain their strength quickly while they waited for his orders to arrive. King Teegan and Commander Storm had indicated that they felt that Mouseling Hollow would be safer for the mice — safer even than the once-impregnable sanctuary of MouseKeep. He had also spoken with Teague alone one last time, after dismissing his two other companions, for fear of giving out too much critical intelligence in front of too many ears. It was obvious that, much as he still respected Professor Wilding, King Teegan trusted Teague the most — but even with this honor, Teague didn't much like what the King had to tell him.

As far as going back to Mouseling Hollow went, however, Robert Teague didn't need a written invitation to be eager to return to his beloved home.

In this last meeting with the King, the Lionsmane had spoken directly to his Mouseling companion with great candor. Having recognized that the infiltration and usurpation of Castle Feldenspar had nearly succeeded in claiming all of their lives, his message had been short and straight to the point — Teegan had looked Robert Teague right in the eye, and said simply:

'Commander Teague — Robert, my friend — much as it pains me to say it, The First Rat King War was simply a taste of what we are about to experience. If we cannot quell this darkness, this...' the King paused a second here to search for the right word, 'this... taint...everything we have come to cherish and hold sacred will fall. Our alliance with Mouseling Hollow has never been more precious — or more critical to our survival. I will send you word of our next steps with a trusted courier. Even here, at The King's Pedestal where MouseKeep meets Castle Feldenspar, spies lurk among us — and very few, if any, can be trusted.'

Grave tidings, indeed, thought the innkeeper.

So now, Robert Teague found himself waiting. Waiting in Mouseling Hollow for a King's missive to arrive — but more pressingly, waiting for his wife to come up the stairs and grill him about the events of the past few days...or week? Weeks? How long had he been gone? The innkeeper couldn't remember, or be certain. But he knew that he owed her answers to her questions. And his companions who had served so valiantly, there was no doubt that they also wondered, the way he did, what was going to happen next. But they had been faithful to the last, and all had survived to return to Mouseling Hollow and take up residency there while they awaited the next move — whatever that may be.

As a natural leader, Teague understood that transparency and honesty were the most important qualities that a party could ask for from its commander. He decided it was best to intercept the inevitable and head it off at the pass while he still had the tactical option of doing so.

Spying a small bell on a string that his wife had rigged up to run down to the bar below, he decided to put it to use. After yanking it a few times, he heard the pad of light feet nimbly negotiating the stairs to the Teague family quarters.

Soon, the door opened and Thistlefur appeared.

'Yes, Master Teague?' the young doe asked.

'Thistlefur, dear,' Teague struggled to turn around and face the stairway door due to the pain that still plagued his ribs — 'please rouse my companions and have them meet for supper downstairs at the bar top. Hearthseeker may be in a great deal of pain, so you may have to ask Hawkdodger to assist him. Have Robbie, Kerrigan, and Mrs. Teague come also, if you please. If there are any patrons in the Inn, ask them to finish up quickly and then close up for the evening. I want to speak to all of you, and the best way for us to do this is to have a meal together. I will be down by sunset.'

'Yes, Master Teague!' said the young mouse politely, and she quickly descended the stairs.

Teague turned back to the fire, which was starting to burn down to embers. He reached over by the hearth and threw another log on, before his glance shifted to the west-facing stained-glass window which had an imprint of a rose on it. Outside, the sun was setting — and beyond the trees, though he could not see it, was Castle Feldenspar.

He wondered if King Teegan was struggling with what lay ahead of them as much as he was.

After thinking about it for a few moments, he was sure of it. But what was there to say? His mind raced about, thinking of the whirlwind of events which had transpired since they had first left Mouseling Hollow with the Stranger, heading towards what was most assuredly a trap...but having no option except to go anyway. In retrospect, he was very, *very* glad they had gone — but now, his mind was filled with even more questions than answers.

And answers were what he *really* needed.

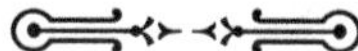

Over the course of his few days of recovery in the makeshift hospital at The King's Pedestal, Wilding, Hearthseeker, and various members of The Wrecking Crew had stopped by to fill Teague in on what they had been up to while Squeak and Teague were having their own 'adventure' through the halls of MouseKeep, so to speak.

But Teague couldn't shake his mind from returning, over and over again, to his fight with the One-Eyed Rat in the kitchen proper. After he had subdued his foe and was interrogating him, the rat had alluded to some intimidating, and potentially dangerous, information.

Teague's mind kept coming back to the dialogue that had taken place between the two of them, down in the kitchen, before the tabby cat had shown up.

The rat had said to him:

'It is too late for you, Teague. Too late for you and your little Mouseling friends. Too late for the humans of Feldenspar. For even as we speak, The Rat King has already begun his invasion of the western part of The Far Collective. The usurpation and undoing of Castle Feldenspar was merely but a small part of the plan — to remove any vestige of resistance as the real infiltration begins.'

I wonder what the rat meant by 'to remove any vestige of resistance as the real infiltration begins,' thought Teague. *What is the 'real' infiltration, and where is it taking place?*

He kept thinking back to the rest of their conversation.

'The Rat King has unified The Ratling Clans...any animals who resist are either subjugated or eliminated as an example to others. Many animals have capitulated and joined his cause under this duress...from his newly rebuilt Kingdom in the Darkened Vale, from his city built deep and bulwarked in the Underhill, where you would least expect to find it, he sends his armies forth...'

Was this place, in the so-called 'Darkened Vale,' the newly rebuilt Black Citadel that King Teegan had alluded to? wondered Teague. *And if so, well...where is it?*

Try as he might, the innkeeper couldn't fathom where to begin a search for the Dominion of The Rat King. It could be in so many places — deep, dark places, where no light shines.

Teague shuddered at the thought.

And what about the Animal Speakers and the garrison sent to Castle Feldenspar? His mind raced as he tried to recall — what had the rat said? Oh, yes...

'But these humans aren't from Feldenspar. They come from far across the Southern Ocean, a faction of humans that know only war and killing. They call themselves the Wandering Clans. Brutal. Ruthless. In their wake, they leave only death and subjugation for their adversaries...

'...as we speak, they are sailing at this moment towards the shores of Ocean's View, the gateway to Feldenspar. But even if he were on his throne, your beloved King Teegan would be hard pressed to get troops there to attempt a defense. It's a long way from here to the coastline. Legions of animal armies, and some human resistance also, now stand in the way. Under the command of The Rat King, they will not hesitate to harass, to infiltrate, to break supply lines, and even to attack humans openly, if The Rat King deems it necessary.'

'The Lyceum at Ocean's View...' Teague remembered himself saying aloud. He spoke it out loud again, as he considered what would happen if The Decoding Stones were taken.

He sat for a moment, gazing at the firelight, and wondered what it all meant.

With the Falcon Riders mostly destroyed, communication — and easy transport — had been cut off from MouseKeep. King Teegan recalling his knights home from Old Town would leave the coastline defenseless, but The Lyceum — and the surrounding cities — had their own garrisons and militias which were still, to Teague's knowledge, faithful to the crown. Many were a formidable force in their own right as well.

And, of course, Mouseling Hollow still stood, which meant that the old animal alliances were, as far as Teague knew, still intact.

Perhaps there is still some hope, thought a now unsettled Robert Teague.

Deep in thought, as he sat mesmerized by the fireplace, Teague heard another knock at the door.

'Come in,' he said, and struggled to turn around. He was taken aback to see a Falconrider with all white fur, in full battledress, at his apartment doorstep.

'General Teague,' said the Falconrider. 'A missive from King Teegan himself.'

Teague reached out for the thick envelope, a large parchment which was sealed with wax. Shaking it, he could hear the *'cling cling'* sound of metal within. He broke the seal, allowing the contents to fall on his lap. He looked down at them, and then opened the enclosed scroll and read it. Looking back up at the Falconrider when he finished, he said 'Thank you, Rider. I hope you can join us for supper downstairs, and stay the night after your weary journey.'

'Thank you, General. It would be my honor, and much appreciated.'

'Go and see Hawkdodger downstairs, behind the bar. He will quench your thirst and set you up with lodging in the Inn. You can clean up and store your equipment as well. Thistlefur will assist you in feeding your falcon, who can stay in the large barn outside. We plan to sup soon, and you are most certainly welcome to join us.'

'Aye, General Teague,' said the Falconrider. But as the Rider was taking his leave, Teague couldn't help but notice that something looked extremely familiar about this young buck.

Just as the Rider was about to close the door, Teague looked at him and said:

'My apologies, soldier. I didn't get your name?'

'Snowwillow, sir,' said the Rider. 'Snowwillow, son of first officer Riverwillow, former commander of the first Rider Legion. My father fought with you, high upon the cliffs at the defense of Owlhaven, and gave his life for King Teegan there, at your side. I am sure he was one of many though, whom you may not remember, who fell in the melee.'

'On the contrary, I remember him well, young Snowwillow,' said Teague. 'All too well. And as I recall it now, I thought you looked familiar — I believe I spied you assisting Commander Wilding in repelling the rat invaders at MouseKeep's Armory.'

'Aye, sir, you are correct. I watched you take down that badger using **Four Paws Flow**. And if I may, sir, if it wouldn't be too much out of line: it was....flawless. I am a student of the art myself, as was my father — though I feel certain you already know this.'

Teague looked back at the fire for a moment, lost in melancholy.

Then he continued speaking to the younger mouse:

'Commander Wilding told me of your bravery and fighting prowess in MouseKeep these past days. Your father was a brave and valiant mouse. A skilled rider, as well. He was a better leader of his brethren than I could ever have hoped to be. As I recall, he had a talent for storytelling, and a preference for the use of clubs on the battlefield as well. I wish even now I could have taken his place. He fell defending his brothers at Owlhaven until the very end, with great valor and honor. And for you and your family, that is a legacy to cherish and be extremely proud of — one that is not so easily forgotten.'

The young Falconrider looked at him silently.

Teague paused another moment, then continued.

'Perhaps someday I can share with you some stories of your father's valiance, and of the things he taught me. He was instrumental in my education of the close quarter wielding of dual combat axes — specifically within the **Four Paws Flow** architecture for weapons training.'

The Rider's visage brightened considerably.

'I would like that sir. I would like that very much — when you have healed and have time to indulge a young buck with tales of history, that is — however much I might desire to hear them sooner.'

'Let's start with supper tonight then,' said Teague with a weak smile on his face. The young Rider, used to military protocol, broke it — and smiled back.

'Until then, Snowwillow. Dismissed.'

Teague pretended to wipe something away from his eye as the buck shut the door softly on his way out.

Looking back again at the missive he had received, Teague read it once more. Glancing at the rose laden stained-glass window, he noticed the fading sunlight was low on The Dagger Spine Ridge across The Western Forest. Turning his gaze back to the fire, he paused for a second, finished his glass of port, and then tossed the note into the fireplace.

Its aged parchment split, cracked, and charred, before finally being consumed by the flames.

No one will be privy to THIS message, Teague thought, *except those who are truly in the service to the King.*

Then, grabbing a small walking stick, he hoisted himself up — though the pain in his ribs was incredibly intense — and headed downstairs to brief his companions, and his family, on the tide of war that was about to crash down upon them all.

Note to Faculty From Headmaster Archmage Blazepaw:

Faculty,

As you all know, we only accept the best and brightest Mouselings here for study at Searing Ridge.

*Part of being the best and brightest is **compliance**.*

*<u>**Compliance, as a reminder, is the ability to understand and do what you are told, whether you want to or not.**</u> We don't need any freethinking mice here in these hallowed halls — that goes for faculty and staff, too.*

*If you see a pupil engaging in free thinking, or questioning their teachings, please bring them to my attention **immediately** for instantaneous expulsion. Magic is difficult enough to learn to control without young people questioning their betters and inquiring as to how and why we do things.*

Your Illustrious Leader,
ARCHMAGE BLAZEPAW

Chapter 29

WHAT THE FUTURE HOLDS

By the time Teague came down the stairs, all of the mice he had wanted to see had been assembled and were waiting for him in The Sleeping Cat's main dining hall. Wilding, a slightly pale but recovering Ainsley Hearthseeker, the Stranger, and Snowwillow were all seated at the bar, engaged in light conversation while drinking mugs of draught. The Professor's Blackhollow stout was long gone, but it seemed Frog Grog was now the drink of choice. Robbie and Kerrigan Teague, his greatest creations (along with the baby Shannon Teague held in her arms, of course) were seated at a small side table, begging Snowwillow to come and regale them with stories of the derring-do that young Falconriders engage in and the trappings of life in MouseKeep, which the youngsters from Mouseling Hollow imagined to be endlessly glamorous and exciting.

Hawkdodger scurried to and fro, happily serving them all. He was eager to have his master Robert Teague at home, as everything seemed to be coming back to normal...excepting, of course, for the party's battle wounds and the strange arrival of the Falconrider.

As he turned past the bottom of the staircase, his companions all looked up at him and started to gleefully call his name: 'Robert,

Robert!' It was a welcome of affection and love that deeply moved Teague's heart. But as a stoic and dignified mouse, he was only able to muster up the following words to express his gratitude at the time:

'Thank you, friends, thank you! We all have much to discuss. The King has sent me a missive that Rider Snowwillow brought to me personally, which is why he has honored us with his presence here. I need to share its contents with all of you — and you alone. But first,' he grabbed his injured side in a dark, though well intended jest, 'I need a drink!'

At which point, his compatriots all burst out laughing and clapped heartily.

Not missing a beat, Wilding yelled out, 'And then, some dinner, Robert! I can't speak for the others here, but I've quite a hunger, and I do believe you've rested from your kitchens long enough!'

Teague nodded and smiled at his friend, saying, 'All in good time! After which, we can discuss the state of the kingdom — perhaps with a good smoke to help soothe our bellies. Professor Wilding, perhaps you can rouse up something after dinner?'

'I don't need magic to do that, Robert,' said Wilding with a chortle. 'Years ago, I hid some special cigars in a waterproof case in your wine cellar — a secret blend of smoking herbs — for just such an occasion as this! I will go and fetch it now.'

Upon hearing this wonderful news, everyone clapped even louder. Shannon Teague scowled at her children, as if to warn them against voicing any notions as to whether they'd be allowed to partake in the smoking herbs, and said, 'In the meantime, Robbie, Kerrigan, you two can make yourselves useful. Go back to the kitchen and help prepare dinner for these guests — on the double!'

As her children proceeded to the kitchen under protest, unhappy about having to leave their father (and the attendant revelry celebrating his return) to resume the monotony of their tavernkeeping duties, Shannon Teague went back behind the bar with Hawkdodger to plan the evening's meal. After some discussion, Hawkdodger went down to the cellar to draw additional drinks and help with preparations, while Shannon Teague climbed up onto the stool before the menu slate and, with a great deal of pride, began writing out that evening's meal:

The Sleeping Cat Inn

Harvest Season Menu

(Today Only, for the Party's Return — A Hero's Welcome!)

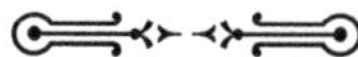

Barbecued, Shredded Beef Pie

Grass fed beef, grass fed butter, chicken stock, herbs of the glade, slow smoked for 12 hours over wood, served in crock. Einkorn cornbread bottom, buttermilk cream topping. Lattice crust, buttered souffle cheese grits on side.

Garlic Tomato Hearth Loaf

Crispy hearth-roasted bread, fresh, with grass fed butter and herbs of the glade. Grated tomato, fine aged parmesan. Fresh garlic shavings.

On Tap (from 'The Professor')

Harvest Berry Wheat Ale

Frog Grog

Lion's Mane Select Rum (from the King's private stock)

Dessert

Gates of Feldenspar Tawny Port (20 Year, special reserve for the harvest)

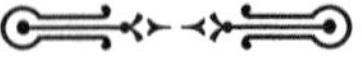

The companions in the Inn watched with fascination as she wrote the menu on the board, their stomachs rumbling in anticipation.

But, despite the pain, the trauma, the shock, and the stress of what had transpired over the past few days, the feeling was overwhelming.

It was a feeling of elation.

Elation and pride at what the party had been able to accomplish together.

It wasn't just elation at having freed the King and saved both MouseKeep and Castle Feldenspar itself, or relief at having thwarted the infiltration forces which had threatened everything that was sacred to The Western Lands — but an overwhelming sense of pride and accomplishment for the synergy and speed at which, against all odds, they had worked together to bring light into darkness. Pride at moments like Hearthseeker's berserker sacrifice in the Armory, the Stranger's sacrificial decision to leave his family after they had been rescued in order to fight by his Mouseling brothers' side, and Wilding's valiant (and dazzling) display of arch magic that saved them from the volley of ratling arrows. And, of course, Robert Teague's epic takedown of Bruiser, which ultimately turned the tide of battle in their favor. It was on all of their minds, both individually and collectively.

It was a feeling that didn't need to be expressed in words, as though words would be unable to truly capture the camaraderie that had taken place and the brotherhood that had formed — and they feared that attempting to articulate it aloud could only tarnish the unspoken bond they had forged.

Nonetheless, light and happy chatter filled the tavern that evening as the mice discussed and lauded all manners of heroic actions that had taken place, praising their companions' actions while sipping from their rustic wooden mugs. An extremely engaging topic which was met with some humor was how Ainsley

Hearthseeker could simultaneously kill a fischer with one blow (an achievement not to be discounted under any circumstances) while almost dying himself. But Wilding's defense of Hearthseeker's actions was met with tremendous respect and quite understood, and no one pressed the subject or teased the bard too hard over it — he had saved the wizard's life, after all.

Even Wilding, not one normally known for being emotional, came up to Ainsley and gave him quite a 'shoulder hug,' promising to teach him how to play a master's level game of Root and Field — a huge honor for a mouse who owned none of the special, extremely rare cards that were most needed in order to play in the game's upper echelons.

Hearthseeker smiled while taking a draught from his mug, and then proceeded to rub the top of his head, which was still recovering from the events that had transpired in the Armory. Still, he was in good spirits — though he had recognized in a private confession to Mrs. Teague that he still needed rest to recover from his significant, near-fatal injuries. Lady Sirona had helped, of course — helped them all greatly — but time was still the greatest healer. Time, and rest.

Hugs and snuggles were freely given as the food was finally served, and even Robert Teague was surprised (and a little taken aback) when his wife and two children doted on him a bit too much, hugging him and thanking him for his 'service' to Mouseling Hollow. It was a touching moment, but Teague was thankful that it didn't last too long, lest he have to pretend to wipe something else from his eye. Hawkdodger and Thistlefur helped to present the dinner plates, a rich and robust sight indeed. Heaping ceramic crocks of shredded beef, overflowing from a freshly baked cornbread muffin which was slathered with butter and a buttermilk herb cream topping as the dressing. On the side, a rich helping of buttery, perfectly cooked cheese grits rounded out the ensemble.

'Well, look at this,' sighed Hearthseeker, pausing a moment and taking a deep inhale of the aromas which wafted from his wooden plate. Finally, after an indulgent sniff, and then a long draught of

Lion's Mane Rum, he tucked in, and his newfound companions of all ages followed suit.

The meal was exquisite.

All the mice lapsed into silence as they supped, the silence between them serving as the perfect assent to the masterfully cooked beef which had arrived on their plates. It was understood among Mouselings that cooking meat low and slow across a wood fire until it reached a perfectly tender and succulent state was an artistic pursuit, and the highest culinary expression of mastery if there ever was one. And when it came to slow roasting barbecue, the Teague family of The Sleeping Cat were known across The Western Lands as some of the truest barbecue masters around.

At least among the animals, anyway — humans (to their great loss) had never been lucky enough to sup upon the Teague family's barbecue.

Hearthseeker looked at his plate after he savored his first bite, transfixed. The wood smoke which had permeated the shredded beef provided a subtle accent to the butter braised roast, rich with its forest herbs and onions from the fertile soil of The Western Forest.

Barbecued perfection.

It was, perhaps, the finest feast the bard had ever known — a celebration for the return of the party which had left mere days before, marching off to fates unknown.

As the party finished their meal, Teague looked at Wilding and gave a slight nod, at which point Wilding began to hand out rich cigars and small self-lighting tinders to light the aged rolled smoking herbs which Wilding had been holding in the basement of The Sleeping Cat for 'safekeeping.' Teague personally went behind the bar and removed the 'No Smoking' slate which normally hung there, placing it discreetly underneath the bar top, and smiled.

In doing so, Hawkdodger and Teague locked eyes, and Teague smiled again. Hawkdodger, no stranger to stories of the Professor's legendary smoking herbs, was ready to indulge and see if they lived up to the legends. And with a wink, Teague imparted his blessing.

Legends, stories, and myths, tales of underhill and over mountain were all told in that warm, inviting space, while the fire roared from the four carved animal hearths which The Sleeping Cat had become known for. In the midst of the reverie, Hearthseeker drew out his lute and began a song:

Lionsmane, and Teegan
Father and Son
Justice and Light
Legacies of Might

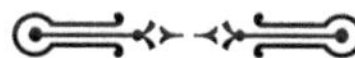

While The Rat King cometh
With One Eye in tow
A Stranger, a bard too
And
The Fabled Two
Smite them
Or Smote them
But oh, what a show!

Hearthseeker paused before the very last line — and when he finished it, an explosion of laughter and applause permeated the inn.

'Well done, Ainsley!' cried Wilding and Shannon Teague, almost in unison.

Eventually, with all parties satisfied and everyone's hunger sated, Teague's wife and children began cleaning up and bussing after the patrons of the Inn. Yet, almost as soon as they had begun, Teague stopped them abruptly.

'Children, pause from your duties awhile and join us. I would like you to sit, and if it pleases you, to have a drink. I need to discuss the events that have occurred with you, as well as what is to come. I promise, it involves ALL of you. And besides...' he stumbled on his words here a bit, 'after you hear what I am about to tell you, you will understand what I mean when I say this: I am not sure when the next time we will all be together like this may be.'

Teague's wife and children stopped and looked at him almost in shock, taken aback both by his bluntness, and the indication that his children — twelve and fourteen seasons, respectively — were now ready for a drink. They wondered, with no small amount of trepidation, what the foreshadowing of his statement could possibly be hinting at.

His wife looked at him and he returned her gaze evenly, simply nodding.

'Shannon, my darling, get one for yourself too, and take a stool at the bar. You all deserve some rest — and, if it would please you, I would have your attention for a short time while you rest from your hard-working duties.' Still eyeing her husband, she nodded, then headed to the bar and filled three cups. She handed two of them to her children, while keeping one for herself, then took a seat at the bar top.

And so it was that Robert Teague's family all gathered mugs of Frog Grog and sat back down at the table where Snowwillow the Falconrider sat. Everyone looked at Teague, who sat nursing a mug of Crab Apple Frost Wine and slowly smoking one of Professor Wilding's select cigars, stuffed full of fine aged smoking herbs which (he reflected upon with some chagrin) had been hidden underneath his feet for Lady-knows how long.

With a captivated audience of his closest friends and companions watching him expectantly, Teague paused a moment to ponder how best to begin telling his loved ones and compatriots something that, three days earlier, he would have never thought would have been possible to mutter. He looked at each member of his party around the Inn, one at a time, and with a deep inhale, began.

'My friends. My beloved wife and children. Companions. Strangers whom I had not known nary a season past. Falconriders, Professors, thieves, and bards. Barkeeps, wives, babies, and hostesses. Scalawags, one and all!'

Saying this word, he pointed his forefinger with intention at all those gathered around the Inn, and all assembled burst into laughter. Teague smiled, his joke having had the intended effect, and continued.

'Children that can hear my words, and my beautiful baby who can hear them, but cannot understand their import yet. First and foremost, I stand before you, thankful for your love and service. For your loyalty. For your faithfulness in service to the King. For your companionship!'

'Hear hear!' yelled the rabble in the Inn.

Teague continued, energized and heartened by his friends' reception to his words.

'Before I speak to you all about what is to come, I have been commanded to first recognize the valiant efforts of those who chose to serve King Teegan, with such faithfulness and in the face of tremendous peril over the previous days, showing great honor and selflessness to a mouse.'

The Inn was suddenly silent, unsure of what was to come next.

'Today, Rider Snowwillow delivered to me a missive from the King himself. In it were instructions I was to follow in a number of matters — which included the awarding of promotions and honors. These medals I hold here,' Teague held up some shining jewelry frocked with colorful ribbons, 'must be given to those who absolutely, and most deservedly, earned them through their valiance, courage, and faithful countenance. Understand that these honors have been conferred on the King's personal command.'

Silence befell the room.

Teague looked at the Stranger.

'To the Strange Mouse of the Thief's Guild, who shall remain nameless,' Teague pointed to the Stranger, 'whose family was taken as ransom to induce him to bring great injury to King Teegan — and who, while under duress, and at great risk to both himself and his captive family, continued to faithfully discharge his duties to King, Guild, and country — I present to you this medal, the King's Service Star, and promote you to the rank of Thief's Guild Captain, so that you may continue to make decisions in the best interest of the Kingdom, and on behalf of the Line of Teegan. May you forever hold truth and justice in your heart and walk in the light, even wherever shadows dwell, should you move among them.'

The Stranger looked a little dazed, like he wasn't sure if this was really happening. Given his puzzled look, Teague bade him to stay seated and reached across the bar top to award him his medal, clasping shut the shining golden star with its royal blue and purple ribbon — the very colors of King Teegan's personal banner — around his greying, bristly neck fur.

Tears filled the Stranger's eyes.

'Tomorrow,' said Teague, 'you will need to return to your family and make sure there is nothing unusual or aberrant happening within the town of Feldenspar. You must now serve — if you are willing — as our sole eyes and ears in the village, in addition to our liaison to the Mouseling Thief's Guild. We do not know many mice we can truly trust at Feldenspar now — save you. You are now within our trusted circle.'

'It might take me a few days to recover, if you will permit me, milord,' said the Stranger weakly, with humility and tears in his eyes. 'But when I am able, I will return and gladly do as you ask. I will not fail to safeguard the trust you have placed in me — upon my family, I swear it.' He clasped his chest and shoulder where he had received multiple stab wounds in the battle for MouseKeep Armory, and where earlier in the day Shannon Teague had applied a poultice of special healing herbs to try to thwart the spread of any potential infection.

'Of course, my friend, of course,' Teague said, clapping him (carefully) upon his good shoulder. 'The Sleeping Cat is yours to stay at as long as you need it, now and in the future.'

The Stranger clasped paws with Teague, nodded, and sat back down.

Teague's gaze shifted to Ainsley Hearthseeker.

'To the bard who saved the life of General Wilding, neutralizing six confirmed infiltrator mice, a fischer, and an enemy captain named Scraptooth — and who, at great personal peril, was instrumental in the investigation and recapture of MouseKeep. For his selfless and valiant efforts, and the vital assistance he provided to **The Fabled Two,** I grant you this medal, and the title of First Bard of MouseKeep, and across The Western Lands.'

Ainsley Hearthseeker was stunned, and it was only after the Inn filled with applause that his eyes welled with tears. Unmoving due to the pain from his stomach wound and concussion, as well as the shock from, well, everything, he remained still as Teague took out a fabulous golden star emblazoned with a lute upon it and wrapped it around his neck. It was trimmed with a Kelly green and gold ribboned clasp — the official colors of MouseKeep — which was of the highest jeweler's quality. Diamonds studded the outline of the lute.

Hearthseeker looked down reverently at the treasure, fingering it with his left paw.

'Milord,' he said softly, looking back and forth between Wilding and Teague. Wilding gave his friend a proud, and slightly amused, smile — it was the first time he could recall seeing the bard at a loss for words!

While Teague leaned across the bar top and reached for Ainsley's paw, Wilding came up and added a bear hug. Teague locked eyes with his new friend, who had proven himself with such faithfulness and valiance, in so many instances, to a group who'd been utter strangers to him mere days before.

'Hearthseeker, you are nothing but a brilliant rogue!' said Wilding approvingly.

And with that, though he sensed that Wilding and Teague were still holding back the full depth of their emotions, deep in his spirit, Hearthseeker felt like he had, for once, finally found acceptance — and the home he'd long sought.

It was an amazing feeling.

Teague took a moment to uncouple his paw from Hearthseeker's and then continued, turning his attention to his oldest friend.

'To Commander Wilding, on the occasion of his reinstatement to the King's Guard at Mousekeep, and the resumption of his legendary valiance in service to the crown. In recognition of his rescue of Knight Commander Storm, and his freeing of the human court of Castle Feldenspar, I present you with this commendation and formal appointment to the rank of Brigadier General of MouseKeep, and to the position of King's Councilor to The Daggerspine Monastic Order — specifically, The Magical Academy at Searing Ridge.'

Wilding bowed his head, torn between accepting his promotion and declining it — but knew his friend Robert Teague would have none of it. Teague clasped a golden chain around his neck, at the end of which hung a small orb. Inside, he saw a tiny sculpture of mountains which were on fire, yet ensconced in a perpetually falling snow which was held in place by magical means. This was truly a magic trinket, if ever there was one.

Teague looked at Wilding and, as they clasped paws, quietly whispered to him, 'the King sent some ancient scrolls along to go with this bauble around your neck. Evidently it can be used in times of peril with great effect — or some such magical nonsense.'

Wilding nodded, but sorcerer that he was, he had already felt its magical energy and knew it must contain significant power. It was a precious gift, and one that he was honored to carry.

The friends clasped paws again, and then Teague took a long draught from his wooden cup. He pondered what his next words should be, but, as always, decided it would be best if he simply went on direct instinct. It was time everybody knew the true nature of the threat they were facing.

'My friends,' he started, 'The Rat King has returned.'

An audible gasp was emitted by the bar patrons — except the companions who had accompanied him on his journey to Castle Feldenspar, of course.

'As you now know, seasons ago when Professor Wilding and I were but young bucks, we chose to enlist in the aid of The Western Lands, in service to the Heaven's King himself. It was through Her grace, and no small lack of good fortune, that we were able to vanquish the armies of The Rat King. That villain, as you can surmise, escaped — though his forces were defeated and his power broken, The Rat King himself was never found. And now he has returned — with a vengeance.'

He took another drink from his mug, giving time to let the effect of his words sink in.

'But as you also now know, the Professor and I retired from the King's service, tired of war and killing, and sought refuge upon the shores of Mouseling Hollow. I, eager to live a peaceful life of family and simple pleasures, met my beloved Shannon and founded The Sleeping Cat. My friend the Professor followed a few seasons later, eventually founding his famed brewery at FireMaple Abby. As the seasons passed, unknown to us in this idyllic glade, The Rat King was obviously growing stronger...silently, and with intention. And now, through his undetected efforts, his armies return to threaten our lives once more, daring to retain Animal Speakers of the human kind bent on twisting the will of animals to his dark and sinister magic. The King's kidnapping, and the usurping of his court, is but a glimmer of what is to come. While we were fortunate enough to turn the tide from the enemy's favor and rescue his majesty, given the dark circumstances, it is possible that without all of our efforts — and the efforts of so many more throughout the entirety of The Far Collective — we may not be as fortunate in the future. The Rat King has used his intellect and cunning with unparalleled wit and resourcefulness. I fear that without our intervention, as well as Her blessed grace, the future tides of battle may well turn easily against us.'

The Inn was silent, waiting for Teague to continue.

'To this end, the King himself has asked, as a personal favor to his majesty, that certain individuals also receive commendations, and immediately depart to begin studying at the Mouseling combat schools of their choice.'

He choked back a tear for a second, and, summoning no minor amount of resolve, continued.

'Given their gifts and skills, as recognized by King Teegan through the seasonal reporting of scouts dispatched to silently frequent The Sleeping Cat Inn, both Robbie Teague and Kerrigan Teague are to be presented the opportunity to select the instructional academy of their choice. And, with the Falconrider's imminent return, they are invited to ride to their respective institutions for the most intense and thorough instruction in their chosen fields. The King further notes that it is expected that, upon graduation, they shall immediately join the war effort as officers under his personal direction.'

Shannon Teague burst into tears at this statement. Wilding went over and put an arm around her to comfort her.

'My dearest Shannon, please don't fret — our children will be in the very safest of places, as you will soon find out. The truth is, the minions of The Rat King are ascending up The Riverpath as we speak — burning and destroying all they encounter and enslaving what is left. Without an organized defense to thwart them, these minions will soon be upon the gates of Mouseling Hollow itself. It is for our family's safety that the King himself has issued these orders — and why I encourage Robbie and Kerrigan to embrace the rare and precious opportunity that has been presented to them. But, if we are telling true tales, we also know very well that the children have earned this privilege on their own merits, and not merely because of who their father happens to be.'

'What privilege do you speak of, father?' asked Kerrigan.

'The privilege of studying at the finest of Mouseling academies, where you will have the chance to learn a skillset which can serve you for a lifetime, while you hone your abilities against your peers.

Professor Wilding himself was a product of this kind of opportunity, and graduated as the salutatorian from The Magical Academy at Searing Ridge. It was there that he fully developed his magical abilities and studied intensely to become the great sorcerer he is now — as well as their newfound ambassador.'

Teague winked at Wilding.

'Who was the valedictorian?' asked Kerrigan, not missing a beat.

'It doesn't matter,' interjected Wilding.

Teague smiled, then continued:

'There are five combat schools you can choose from. You have from this evening until tomorrow morning to think about it and make your decision. No one will judge the choice you make, or force you to embark upon a military career if you have no wish for it. But know that once you select a school, you are committed to following out that path — you will either graduate from it, or else you will fail and be expelled, with orders to join the lines of Teegan's infantry while The Riverpath is under siege. Wilding and I both have fought with the infantry, so I will speak to you frankly: it is a death sentence. To attend a Mouseling combat academy is a great privilege, but one which must be continually earned, both in the classroom and on the practice fields, by proving one is worthy of their place there. I have no doubt, my beloved children, that each of you is most assuredly worthy of such an honor — but it is not a path to be set upon lightly, or with anything less than the full totality of your passion, willpower, and commitment. So, if you don't mind taking an old mouse's advice, I'd suggest that you attend to your studies, respect your professors, and excel in every aspect of your schoolwork, regardless of what school you elect to attend. You are free to choose any of them — or none of them. However, once your decision is made, it is final.'

'Father, what are the five schools?' asked Robbie Teague.

'I'm glad you asked, my son,' said Teague, who took another long draw from his cup.

'I'm glad you asked.'

The Shell Game:

At The Sleeping Cat one night, it is said that a traveling court jester and entertainer was allowed to perform some magic, and then set up a gaming table inside the Inn — much to the delight of its guests. On this table he placed a pea under one of three shells, and then rotated them quickly. The goal of the game was simple: pick the shell the pea was under, and you doubled your money. Pick the wrong shell, and you lose your bet.

Hours later, a few mice who were visiting at the Inn were winning what appeared to be a fortune — and yet the poor unsuspecting mice who resided in Mouseling Hollow seemed to be losing their wages consistently. The legendary detective Sir Pendleton Stormsnout, who was at the bar drinking a voluminous amount of whiskey and enjoying a nice supper of golden fried fish and chips (his housekeeper, Mistress McGrath, having the day off) was asked to play the game while writing in his journal. The Mouselings from The Hollow knew that with his superior intellect, if anyone could figure out the game's secret, it was him.

*'Oh, I've already figured it out,' said the detective. 'I've certainly no need to play it. The mouse at the third table, the last table on the left, and the one by the entrance all came in separately, about fifteen minutes apart, and are all clearly working with the mouse at the shell table. **He lets them win to entice you unsuspecting fools to play**. Then, when you step up, he allows you to track which shell the pea is under...until you pick it. Once you do, by a subtle and practiced sleight of paw, he removes the pea into his paw as he overturns the shell you chose, and then replaces it under another shell that he chooses to 'reveal' as the 'correct' shell. You have been winning all along, but thanks to the magic of a nimble paw, every successful choice is shaped into a losing one.'*

Reportedly, a silence fell across the bar as all eyes turned towards the mouse at the gaming table.

'How would you know such things?' asked the unscrupulous mouse. 'You are just mad because your friends are losing!'

According to eyewitnesses, Sir Pendleton sighed, shook his head, and then looked the mouse in the eye sternly.

'Because, you charlatan, **it is my JOB to know which shell the pea is under at all times.'**

'Well if you know so much, then why don't you come play yourself!' retorted the indignant mouse. 'I've paid the winners fair and square, haven't I?'

'You've paid your hired men out of your own money, yes — that much is true,' said the detective, his gaze unwavering. 'I will play your game, but on one condition — you hide the pea, and Robert Teague here mixes the shells up. Then I will make my selection. If I am right, it proves what I am saying is true — namely, that you are a charlatan, a mountebank, and a scoundrel — and you agree to pay everyone back their losses. If I am wrong, you may keep all the money I have on my person, and I will apologize to you publicly here in this tavern — because you will have represented my first ever failure in logical reasoning.'

Silence loomed as the mouse behind the table considered his options.

Then, in a sudden flurry, he yelled, 'Let's get out of here boys!' And he and his three cohorts overturned their tables and scampered out of the bar. Though several Mouselings pursued them, they escaped, and were never seen again...

....

Chapter 30

THE CHILDREN
CHOOSE THEIR PATHS

....

'You see my son, there are five schools available to Mouselings who excel in their intellectual ability, physical prowess, personal talents, magical adeptness, or other noteworthy abilities. But it is important to know that most mice are unaware of the existence of these schools. Most mice, as they come of age, take up one of the usual Mouseling vocations: fishing, or rooting, or other general labor jobs which help supply Mouseling Hollow with the necessities required to live a rich and full life. A day's toil, rewarded with a day's wage — whether that be a small gold piece, or perhaps a loaf of bread and some sundries. All of these, when accumulated at a month's end, are enough to provide for housing and food, and a few nights' worth of revelry and ale at the Inn. Add in some fishing on weekends with a companion and perhaps a small herb garden, and, for so many mice, it makes for a life well lived.'

Teague looked at his companions, then briefly locked eyes with Wilding. He noticed his companions were transfixed on him, then continued.

'But, after The Heaven's King discovered the existence of The Decoding Stones, and in doing so discovered that Mouselings could speak to him in a language that he personally could understand, he saw the value of investing resources into the Mousekin which would help them to grow their abilities. He found the most intelligent mice, and those who were especially gifted or well versed in the combat arts that humans prized. Upon his command, five schools were formed. And they are:

1) **The Academy at Searing Ridge:** This school, nestled in an eternal winter which is flecked with fire embers from the volcano it is built upon, rests high atop the Daggerspine Mountains in the World Ridge, and it is the home of sorcerers — mages fully devoted to the study and development of magical abilities. Fire and frost mages, as well as those rare and gifted mice known as dragonspeakers, come to study here. However, it is important to know that most are sent home at the end of their first academic semester. It is considered the most difficult of the five schools, and its failure rate shows it. Very few graduate — and those that do become master sorcerers, archmages, and advisers to kings.'

'Dragonspeakers,' Kerrigan whispered incredulously, thinking to herself out loud. 'But father, why is it that so many of the new students are sent home after one semester at the academy?'

'Ask the Professor later,' said Teague, who was thrown off a bit by the interruption. 'He will answer any questions you have regarding Searing Ridge, for he has been there. They asked him to stay on as headmaster upon his graduation, you know — the youngest candidate ever to be extended an invitation to become headmaster, across all Mouseling schools. And yet, he declined.'

Wilding looked down at his drink — unmoving, and lost in thought.

'Forgive me, Professor,' Ainsley suddenly piped in, 'But I thought you were a Battlemage. You wear the robes of Owlhaven, do you not?'

Wilding nodded, impressed by the bard's attention to detail. 'Indeed I do, my friend. Most would not notice the difference between a sorcerer's garb and a Battlemage's. I've come to prefer the extra mobility afforded by the cut of a Battlemage robe. Though I attended the sorcerer's academy at Searing Ridge, I acquired my knowledge of the physical combat arts...elsewhere, shall we say.'

Ainsley nodded, clearly pondering Wilding's words, while Teague cleared his throat and continued:

2) The next academy is the **<u>Ranger School at Canon's Edge.</u>** It is in this rocky mesa where true Rangers are trained, high upon the cliffs, where beyond the straw targets and watermelons placed on pedestals upon which amateurs practice their archery lies only true game — all manner of mountain birds, predator hawks and the like, all poised to take a mouse for his midday meal. It is no small feat for a Mouseling to take down a predator bird by himself, and live to tell about it. And, before graduation, each Mouseling Ranger cadet who has successfully completed his curriculum is sent out on a vision quest — a multi-week solo journey into the wilderness with minimal food and water, seeking for the Great Spirit to come guide and instruct them. Though all 'passed' candidates leave on said quest, many do not return, and their bodies are left in the wilderness to become one with nature and begin the cyclical process of rebirth anew.

It is a hard and dangerous road.

However, those who graduate do so as the finest archers in the land. They serve kings, teach hunters, patrol as bowmen, and — in the case of the most excellent and daring Ranger heroes — are paid handsomely for their ability to neutralize the predators who frequently skirt the edges of Mouseling hamlets. Their lives are ones forged in the crucible of the mountains, scattered among the gentle streams which flow among the woodland — and where, with this knowledge, they can live easily among both, practically unnoticed, supping daily upon plenty of fish and game. They eat well, and are paid well for their skills. Their services are considered invaluable.'

'Father, did you attend the Ranger school?' Robbie asked.

Teague looked at his son, almost feeling as if his next sentence might somehow lower his standing in his eyes.

'No, my son, I did not have the privilege of attending any of the combat academies. As you know, I grew up with nothing. I enlisted to help the King's father, the Heaven's King, during The First Rat King War. I did not have the formal training that so many archers of our kind had received, and displayed so brilliantly, in those terrible battles.'

'And yet, your father was the best of them,' interjected Wilding suddenly. 'He could shoot out a Ratling's eye fifty paces further away than the finest Ranger archer could.'

'Hush,' said Teague gently to his brother in arms. 'A greater threat now lies on the horizon.'

Resettling himself, the mouse continued.

3) Thirdly, we come to the **Monastery at River's Rest**. This is a school where Mousekin forsake the use of all mouse-made battle implements — including armor — except their paws, and the ancient study of the walking staff, sometimes called the *bo* staff. They wear simple robes and study the kinesthetics of the body, while pursuing a daily focus on the intense discipline of the mind. Internal energies, sometimes called *chi*, and the use of this life force in combat and healing are also some of the more esoteric topics which students are taught and expected to master. Yet most mice think of these pursuits as fantasy or legend, tales simply used to keep young bucks and does safely in their beds at night.

However, nothing could be further from the truth.

These mice are rare, and humble — they often disguise themselves as traveling monks, bards, or flower keepers. Their life is one of poverty and service, dedicated to helping alleviate the suffering of others and helping to carry another's burdens. They periodically show up in villages unexpectedly to right the wrongs done by villainous mice or other animals — returning stolen wealth, or avenging family injustices through the use of both honor and reason, for example. Though they are powerful fighters, they rarely, if ever, seek to engage in direct combat — not because they fear it, but because when they do, their enemies often have no prayer of defeating their attacks — though their code of nonviolence dictates that they avoid hurting even an insect. It is highly secretive knowledge which must be earned with humility. Their physical bodies are constantly being tested through fasting, punishment, meditation, and so forth. The King himself considers these mice to be an example to live by, and once camped for several seasons at River's Rest to study with the headmaster there, known as One Who Tunnels Through Mountains. This was when his father, the Heaven's King, was still alive and he was but a prince.

The impact that his study at River's Rest had upon his life, however, is without question.

4)   Our next school is the **Bard's College at Old Town**. The finest bards in the land are taught here — they learn how to read music, music theory, music history, and all the social graces that would be taught at a top-tier charm school. Some of The Far Collective's greatest politicians have studied here, as well as musicians. Hearthseeker himself was a product of this school, is that not correct, Ainsley?'

Teague looked at Ainsley intensely while taking a drink from his mug. Hearthseeker nodded humbly.

'Indeed, milord. Even though I displayed a gift for the lute from a young age, I was still put under the most disciplined regimen of study there, including instructions in the social graces and political discourse. The Bard's College is not for the musician who simply wishes to play songs at the firesides of inns for meager coin. And there was a great, if secretive, focus there on swordplay and combat, as well as subtlety and seduction.'

'I love swordplay!' shouted Robbie Teague. 'But what's subtlety and seduction?'

'Err, well,' started Hearthseeker, 'It's where you...'

'Never mind that, Robbie,' said Teague, cutting off the bard (who looked grateful for the interruption). The innkeeper then continued his instructional discourse.

5)   Lastly, we come to **The Battlemage's Academy at Owlhaven**. This is, of course, where sorcery and combat are combined and Mousekin are taught to use sword and staff with a spellbook to smite their foes. If the Magical Academy at Searing Ridge focuses its curriculum purely on developing its students' magical talents, the Battlemage's Academy at Owlhaven splits its focus equally between developing a student's magical skills alongside their physical combat abilities. It is here that the Battlemages take animal familiars who stay with them for life — like the snowy owls that reside on the clifftop below the academy, among others. It is said the animal comes and finds its Battlemage of its own accord — usually in their quietest moments of study and meditation — looking to bring their magic and spirit to the pairing of the two. Some of the most powerful Mouseling combat mages have come from this school, though magic is a discipline which, while easily learned if one has the innate ability, can be incredibly difficult to master. And, there are both dark and light magics to be considered, as well as other schools to be studied: life and death magic, water, fire, and earth magic, and so on — though dark magic is obviously strictly prohibited at the Battlemage's Academy. It is a lifelong study which tears at the student, who is always looking for a balance, yet rarely finds one.'

'What happens if a student desires to learn, or secretly practices dark magic at the academy, father?' Kerrigan asked.

'They become apostates,' answered Teague flatly, 'and are expelled — forced to wander the land as outcasts and pariahs. There have been rumors that necromancy mages have been sighted entering the Tarbogs, on the edge of The Western Kingdom. These are places no normal human nor mouse would dare enter. And,' he paused a moment here for effect, taking a deep sip from his mug, 'it is said that the apostates most likely find their homes among the legions of The

Rat King — dwelling deep underground with his other dark minions, finding solace in the only company which will ever take them in.'

A silent, yet extremely pregnant, pause filled the room.

Teague looked at Wilding and Wilding looked back at him, then proceeded around the back side of the bar top and joined Teague's side.

Looking sternly at the children, Wilding addressed them directly.

'So, which is it children? Which school do you each choose? The King of Feldenspar has given you a very special commendation indeed, one which should not be squandered or thought lightly upon. Yet, my understanding is Falconrider Snowwillow is here, not only to give your father a dispatch from his majesty, but also to return tomorrow morning with some additional birds, that your travel arrangements may be made, as your departures are imminent — should you choose to depart, of course. The journeys to each academy are made easier by flight, though in the past mice would have to travel along dangerous roads to get to these schools, which are situated in some of the most rugged and remote areas of the world.

Many would have to wait for days outside the walls of each academy, needing to show patience and virtue as well as prowess to gain entrance. In the case of the River's Rest Monastic School, students would often wait three, four, or even five days without food in the scorching summer heat — all while being watched passively by the instructors inside the wall to see who would give up first. It is a rich tradition, attending any of these schools, and one which you should not take lightly.

Yet for you, as the cards have fallen, your admission and instruction will begin once your journey to the school itself is made upon the back of a bird on the wing. So...what say you, children? Listen to your heart and make your decision.'

The eyes of all the elder mice in the room fell squarely on Teague's two children. It was dead silent, as if you could hear a pin drop. Both children looked deep in thought, and then finally, it was Robbie Teague who spoke first to break the dramatic pause.

'Father, I have made my decision. As you know, I have loved my training here at the Inn, and the life you and mother have bestowed to me through the lessons in fishing, hunting, cooking, and botanicals you both have given me. Given my abilities, I believe that I would be an excellent candidate for the **Ranger School at Canon's Edge**. And, by Her will, I pray I can make you and mother proud by walking in the footsteps of my father, a member of *The Fabled Two*. If it is your judgment that this is a good choice, I will begin packing my things immediately.'

Shannon Teague rushed to her son and hugged him tightly — in tears, but with a massive pride swelling deep inside her. 'I know you will do so well there, son!' she blurted out. 'But your father and I WILL miss you!'

'Your mother is right,' said Teague, his tone unchanging. 'I have no doubt that you will be an exemplary student. You have been given a strong foundation to become a Ranger, growing up here on the idyllic shores of The Mirrored Lake, and are well versed in the arts of survival, hunting, fishing, and tracking wild game. Take that foundation, and couple it with the more disciplined studies that you will encounter from your tutors — strengthening of the body, meditation, justice, compassion, animal speaking, and unity with the forest — and you will, I have no doubt, be the best pupil that ever attended their school. With that being said, we have much still to discuss, and you have a grand adventure ahead of you starting tomorrow, so go now, son, and begin packing your things.'

'Aye, father,' said Robbie, obviously excited by his father's use of the words 'grand adventure.' He exited the room, his pawsteps faintly echoing as he darted up the Inn's stairs to the family apartment, taking them two by two, until silence befell them once more.

Wilding sensed what Teague was about to say next and, with the grace and wisdom of a childhood friend, took over once more.

'And so it falls to you, young Kerrigan Teague, to make a decision which will alter the course of your fate for the remainder of your life. As a small circle of us in this tavern know, you have been a prodigy since the day you were born and came out of your mother's womb. You are too much like your father, if I may be honest — and it shows. There is no doubt you carry the gifts that our creator bestowed upon this mouse who came from nothing...'

With this Wilding gestured an earnest paw towards Teague, then continued:

'...his intellect — perhaps his greatest gift — but also so many others: his knowledge and athletic ability when it comes to fighting and the combat arts, languages, storytelling, animal speaking, cooking, business and leadership...the list is extensive, and well proven through the accomplishments in his life. So, what say you, Kerrigan Teague, daughter of Robert Teague...and now that the secret is out, daughter of **The Fabled Two**? What will you do with this King's gift? Will you squander it as so many other mice have done?'

'I will NOT squander it, Professor!' said Kerrigan Teague defiantly, her eyes blazing with fire at the suggestion.

Wilding, unabashed and unabated, held steadfast. 'Then what will you do with it, young mouse?'

'I will...' she stammered for a second, looking down. 'I will...' she looked up again, deep in thought.

'Choose, girl!' Wilding urged intensely, as if to elicit her true heart from the confusion of the moment.

'I will attend **The Battlemage's Academy at Owlhaven**,' she blurted out with intent. 'I will become a Battlemage, like my mouse brethren before me, who have dared the perils of a life of combat and magic — combined, but never in harmony.'

'But of course you will,' said Wilding with a low voice, pacing his words. His dark brown eyes peered out under his bushy, greying eyebrows. 'Of *couurse* you will.'

Almost as if it was expected, as if no other outcome could have ever been possible.

He dragged out his pause a moment longer, then continued. 'It is the most logical fit for someone with your gifts,' he said approvingly.

Teague and his wife remained silent, allowing Wilding to continue to command the conversation.

'But if it is the cliffs at Owlhaven where you plan to study, it is considered customary that your close family give you a magical gift with which to send you on your way. Your parents and I know you have some packing to do, so I will skip the formalities and give you your parting gift here and now.'

All eyes stayed focused on Wilding as he reached underneath his dark robes. From out of a recess in the back of his robes, he pulled out a small golden amulet which was hung on a smooth silver chain. On it was the tiniest outline of a dragon, the detail of which was exquisite — right down to the wings — with the finest miniature scaling and spikes on the dragon's tail. Yet, it was cut in half right down the middle, cleanly and abruptly, so that only half of the dragon was there. The young mouse studied it closely.

'What is it, Professor?' asked young Kerrigan Teague.

'It is the Amulet of the Dragonspeaker,' said Wilding. 'To our knowledge, there are only two artifacts that allow Mousekin to communicate with — and, in some cases, command — dragons. The first one is the Globe of the World Spine, an artifact buried eons ago, deep beneath The Daggerspine Ridge, by small, enigmatic creatures known as frost dwarves. Their magic and knowledge of mountaineering and dragon speaking is legendary — but ages ago, when the humans and the dwarves began feuding over greed and riches, it was an ancient dwarven king by the name of Leomar the Stoic who decided to play a trick on humans. He knew that Mousekin could speak to other races and animals — humans included — through The Decoding Stones, which were artifacts the frost dwarves had originally forged deep within their mines. So, he decided to have his most powerful magicians take any dragon artifacts which could impose speech or command the drakes and refine them, drawing their immense power into one tiny glass globe — where inside, the visage of a red dragon is poised atop The Daggerspines, bathed in perpetual snow and fire.

'But to complete his trick, he made it mouse-sized, placed it in a treasure chamber laden with mouse-sized weapons and valuables, and then, as legend goes, collapsed the passage. Then the dwarves disappeared, heading north into what is now known as the Forsaken Lands. Yet, Leomar's trick was complete. Only Mousekin could wield the Dragonspeaker globe, which is buried deep within the mountain. And of course, this great irony was not lost on the clever king — that one of the smallest animals, with enough courage and determination, might someday command the most ferocious and deadly of all animals. Assuming one was brave enough to venture into the undermountain, and clever and skilled enough to return again.'

'Is that true, General Teague?' asked Snowwillow.

'I have heard the stories,' said Teague, 'though ancient undermountain history is not one of my strengths. Hearthseeker?'

Teague looked at his bard friend knowingly, seeking his opinion.

'I, too, have heard these tales,' said Hearthseeker in an almost comforting way. 'In fact, when I was attending The Bard's College, you were required to learn a song about this very legend.'

He pulled out his lute, whose golden wood shone in the light of the embering hearth, and began to play.

By Leomar's might
And with his tricks played
A dragon in flight
Could be parlayed

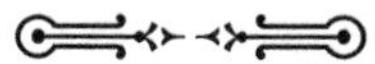

Spoken to or flown
How could humans have known
That creatures so small
Could command them all
Bring peace to a world
Which is always on edge
From the highest of mountains
The Daggerspine Ridge.

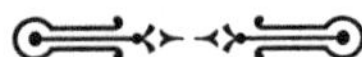

The wonderful tune permeated the Inn as the mice looked into their cups and drank from them with great satisfaction. But Kerrigan Teague was still full of questions.

'Professor, what is the other artifact you mentioned?'

The Professor looked at Teague, who nodded assent.

'You are now holding half of it in your hands. It is, as I stated before, called the Amulet of the Dragonspeaker. The other half — a silver dragon which mirrors your dragon, suspended on a gold chain — is held for safekeeping by...'

Wilding took a deep drink from his mug, then continued.

'...the favorite pet of The Rat King, a puma named Midnight.'

Everyone in the bar gasped, and Thistlefur shouted out, 'A PUMA?!'

'Yes,' Wilding answered, 'the massive mountain cat which has claimed so many of our kin, including some of our bravest warriors. The Rat King was somehow able to tame him — undoubtedly through some form of dark magic — and when he came into possession of the other half of this artifact, he placed it around his 'pet's' neck for safekeeping. After all, what mouse would willingly challenge a puma? We are talking about a cat two or three thousand times the mass of a mouse — more, maybe.'

Wilding felt the trepidation of his companions, and their palpable fear at such an endeavor. He continued speaking in an assuaging tone.

'Kerrigan, The Rat King is looking for your amulet — he has been for many seasons. If he were to find it and take it from you, all would be lost. He could command the pride of red dragons which nests among the highest spines of the mountains, and use their abilities to bring The Western Lands to their knees.

'You must keep its secret. Guard it safely around your neck, deep underneath the mage's robes which you will be given at Owlhaven. Never reveal your secret to anyone, lest he get wind of its location and come looking for you, and then destroy all you hold dear. On your honor as Robert Teague's daughter, keep it safe. And on dark, moonless nights, when you hear the wind blow through the branches — if you hear dragons whispering to you, never tell ANYONE. Listen to their wisdom, but do not speak of it aloud. Ever.'

'I will, Professor,' said Kerrigan soberly.

'And now, bid me goodnight, my young Mouseling, and farewell. I must leave before dawn tomorrow to arrange my own affairs, and there is someone I must see. I expect it will be some seasons before we meet again — though when we do, we shall greet each other as fellow mages.'

With tears in her eyes, Kerrigan hugged the taller, wizened mouse tightly.

'Now, it's time for you to go to bed and finish your preparations for your own grand adventure,' said her father. 'Your mother will help you gather your things.'

With that, Shannon Teague put her arm firmly around her daughter Kerrigan, speaking softly, as Kerrigan gently pawed and clasped tightly the very, *very* special magical gift that Wilding had given her. They disappeared up the stairs together, presumably for a late night of packing and deep discussion.

'You know,' said Wilding after the girls had both disappeared up the Inn's staircase, 'you never told Robbie and Kerrigan about the sixth Mouseling academy — **The Squire's College For Fighters and Knights Valiant**. Did you forget, old friend, in your old age?'

'Of course not, you fool.' Teague looked directly at his friend, incredulous. 'Would you want your children to become arrow fodder? I'd just as soon feather them with bolts or douse them in boiling oil now, and save them the trouble of waiting.'

Taking a final draught from his cup and looking sleepy, Hearthseeker asked *The Fabled Two* the question on all of their minds:

'And what is to become of us, milords? What is our mission now that Feldenspar and MouseKeep have been secured?'

Teague drained his cup also and, slamming it heartily on the counter, looked back at the bard who had shown so much valor over the past few days. He eyed him for a moment, sizing up his impressive resolve.

Then, he said directly:

'The Stranger is returning to the castle village to reunite with his family and assume his observation duties. Snowwillow will return to the castle in the morning at dawn, bringing back whatever Falcon Riders remain to take Robbie and Kerrigan to their schools, respectively. Hawkdodger will handle the duties of the Inn, and Thistlefur — with your parents' permission — you will continue working here, supporting the needs of our fellow mice who seek food and lodging in this sacred log.'

He looked at Thistlefur and Hawkdodger earnestly, knowing that their help — and loyalty — were invaluable commodities at the Inn he had spent so many seasons building.

His glance on the two unwavering, he continued. 'Thistlefur, if you please, I believe that Mrs. Teague and Kerrigan may be in need of your services upstairs. Speaking of which, Hawkdodger, would you be so kind as to check on Robbie while she attends to the ladies?'

The two mice bowed, and up the stairs they went.

'Stranger and Snowwillow, I expect twill be a long day tomorrow for you both. Stranger, return when you are ready, and know you are welcome here at any time, to take advantage of the Inn's services as you require. I bid you both good night.'

The two mice took their leave as well, returning to their lodgings down the first-floor hall.

With only three remaining, Teague looked Wilding and Hearthseeker in the eye and then said.

'And as for us? Well, it's quite simple, really.'

He picked up his empty mug again as if to take a drink, then looked down at it, irritated that it was empty. Glancing back at his companions, he made a brief statement before heading back to his taps for a refill.

'We, my friends...' he said without inflection, pausing momentarily for effect:

'We are going to stop The Rat King.'

On King Leomar's Trick and The Globe of the World Spine:

It is a well-known, but rarely discussed reality: dragons do exist, and have been seen only at the very top of the world, nestled deeply in The Daggerspine mountains, close to the Northernmost known point which is colloquially called **The Dragonspine Tip.**

*King Leomar and his dour band of frost dwarves were quite clever, as they created the only intact talisman known to command dragons, and even allow dragon flight — **The Globe of The World Spine**. They made it Mouseling-sized, and — as the legend goes — left it in a treasure chamber filled with other precious and unique Mouseling-sized artifacts. Then, they destroyed the passageway entrance, and left behind a series of insidious traps to deter all but the most worthy of mice from even attempting to recover such a powerful artifact. It goes without saying that any Mouseling who has a command of interspecies language and the ability to control dragons would be the undisputed ruler of the realm — even over humans.*

This is an irony which was not lost on the frost dwarves, who, after all, did seem to have a sense of humor (albeit a peculiar one).

Those Mousekin who have been intrepid enough to seek out this artifact have never returned, and are presumed to have died in the frozen Northern wastelands somewhere in their ascent to the summit of The Daggerspine Ridge. It has been said The Rat King had lain his eye on this prize as well — but after his defeat in The First Great War, no one ever saw him again...

— Taken from **Are Dragons Real? And Other Questions From Mouseling Bucks and Does**

Chapter 31

TACTICS AND TREASURE CHESTS

Now that the three of them were alone, Teague went and refilled his two companions' cups, as well as his own, then exited from behind the bar.

He looked at his wizard friend and said:

'Wilding, go get your game box for Root and Field.'

Nodding, Wilding padded down the hallway of the Inn's guest quarters to retrieve it.

While they were waiting for him to return, Teague went over and grabbed one of the tables reserved for Root and Field play, complete with its gameboard, and drug it over to the table Hearthseeker was seated at. He pushed the two tables together to make them flush, then set the gameboard neatly on top of the vacant table.

Not long after, Wilding returned carrying with him a weathered, yet smooth and polished, game box. He set it on the table next to the gameboard, and Robert Teague opened it up and began removing the game pieces. Inside were all kinds of ornately sculpted figures, including siege engines, castles, dragons, mice, cats, rats, soldiers, wagons, carts, trebuchets, flags, varied woodland and mountain terrain pieces, and so forth.

The three mice looked at each other for a second, and then Teague began.

'The way I see it...' he started. As he talked, he moved all of Wilding's pieces to the side of the table where their drinks were sitting, leaving the Root and Field gameboard vacant on the adjoining table.

'...there are three questions we must find the answers to. Question Number One is, where is The Rat King's Citadel? The one-eyed rat told me that it was located somewhere he called 'The Darkened Vale.' Personally, I have never heard of such a place before. Hearthseeker?'

The bard was in the midst of taking a drink of ale when Teague surprised him with this question. He lowered the mug down to the table top and glanced at the ceiling thoughtfully for a few moments before responding.

'Well, I have heard songs that speak of a mysterious place referred to either as the 'Wooded Vale' or the 'Darkened Vale,' and such songs always speak to there being some kind of genesis of evil there, or evil creatures which inhabit it. But as for a physical location where such a vale might be found, I would not be in a position to venture a guess. Are you certain it is a physical location that the one-eyed rat spoke of, and not something more...I don't know...metaphorical, for example?'

A look of irritation flashed across Wilding's face at the bard's conjecture, and he quickly inserted himself into the dialogue.

'The Rat King is real, Ainsley, he isn't some...metaphysical spirit who wanders from plane to plane. If the one-eyed rat says he is rebuilding his kingdom, he is most certainly doing it somewhere here — in this world, in these lands — and there is an ascertainable, physical location where we can find him.'

Hearthseeker looked worried that he had inadvertently offended his friend.

'Wilding, forgive me. I only meant to imply that...'

But Teague interrupted him with a pointed good cheer.

'Don't pay him any mind, Ainsley! Our friend the Professor can have a bit of a bad attitude when it comes to matters involving The Rat King. Don't even acknowledge him. Really, Wilding, you're old enough to have learned better manners than that. Stop being rude!'

'Apologies, my roguish friend,' said a rebuked Wilding. 'I meant nothing by it. As Robert said, my patience sometimes grows...strained when it comes to The Rat King.'

Teague, shaking his head at the exchange, continued.

'Anyway, that's question one — where is The Rat King's newly rebuilt Citadel?' He moved a castle piece to the southern side of the board, then positioned a few rat pieces alongside it. A few moments later, though, he moved it to the center of the board and said, 'On second thought, let's leave this piece in the center — because the reality is, this whole discussion truly centers on finding the location of The Rat King and his new Black Citadel. If we knew where he was right now, we would be heading there tomorrow.' After a moment's pause, Teague added, 'But we don't.'

Teague then grabbed a few fischer pieces and moved them near the castle in its central spot on the board.

'Wherever those Ratlings can be found, there'll be fischers there, too. We may as well try to make our game board as real as possible, even though we're playing for far greater stakes than a Root and Field card. Now then, on to Question Number Two, which is clearly...'

Wilding interrupted him.

'Is there an invasion force on its way up The Riverpath as we speak, or preparing to come up The Riverpath in the near future?'

'Exactly,' said Teague, as he moved some rat, badger, and weasel figures down to where The Riverpath started at Rockhollows. He then took a small log sculpture, placed it where Mouseling Hollow would be, and moved some more castle pieces around it to represent towns like Ferngrove Bottoms, Old Town, and so forth.

'We need to know what forces, if any, are coming up The Riverpath — and we need to know it *yesterday.*' Teague paused a moment to emphasize the word *yesterday*, then said 'I continue to hear ominous tidings that Mouseling Hollow remains one of the main targets for enemy attack. If this is in fact the case, we need to discern where this invasion force is, what is its size and disposition, and who is leading it. Notwithstanding, of course, the fact that any invasion force coming north could be comprised of any number of enemy animal combatants — or even worse, human ones. As of now, we've seen no signs of a follow-up human infiltration force since our return from Castle Feldenspar. But as King Teegan himself said, when it comes to the nature of the animal forces arrayed against us, **'we are blind'** — and that, my friends, is an issue in and of itself. Other than Snowwillow, we have had no messengers arrive here since the fallen Falconrider showed up at the Inn the night we met Hearthseeker...'

'...Which would' Ainsley added, 'indicate that the usual communication channels through which you have historically gathered intelligence from may well have been broken. Perhaps they have been attacked?'

'Or perhaps they have changed their allegiance — either under duress, or otherwise,' suggested Wilding, his brow furrowed.

'Both are ominous possibilities, indeed,' Teague agreed. 'It could be that we have friends in trouble. And with our forces so lacking in strength right now, we cannot afford to waste any time pursuing a fool's errand. That being said, it is likely that The Rat King has spies hidden up The Riverpath, and as far down as Mousebrook — perhaps even all the way to Old Town itself.'

Teague took more rat pieces and moved them next to the castle pieces representing Old Town, Mousebrook, and the rest.

'Lastly,' continued Teague, 'there is the issue of these human mercenaries coming across the Southern Ocean from the Unknown Lands. A group of humans that the one-eyed rat referred to as **'The Wandering Clans."**

Teague took several boat pieces and placed them below the game board, where The Southern Ocean would be, then balanced several human figures on top of the boats.

'We know their goal is to destroy The Lyceum at Ocean's View and take The Decoding Stones as their prize. Should that treasure fall into the paws of The Rat King, the tide of war would change dramatically. And I fear that victory for us would, at that point, become...unattainable.'

The three mice looked at each other in silence.

'So, ascertaining the location of this naval armada is an additional task that needs to be addressed. We will also need to warn The Lyceum to prepare for the possibility of an attack as well.'

'Who will handle that?' asked Hearthseeker.

'It's difficult to say — Ocean's View is a LONG trip, even by falcon,' said Teague. 'And we cannot afford to separate at the moment.'

'Speaking of separating,' interjected Wilding, 'there are some rogue elements on the loose that we must also account for.'

Teague nodded at his best friend. 'Yes, Wilding, thank you for reminding me — I nearly forgot.'

He grabbed one snake figure and one spider figure from Wilding's collection and placed them on the board. With a particular interest, he moved the spider figurine close to Mouseling Hollow, placing it on The Riverpath.

'Arachne and Ravenscale. Where are they now? I am not sure, but assuming that Arachne is alive — and it's a pretty good bet that she is — my guess is that she will be fixated on revenge, with Mouseling Hollow as the primary focal point of her ire. As for Ravenscale, who knows what goes through a Tarbog rattlers' mind? But having those two on the loose can only mean trouble.'

Teague took a sip from his cup, and looked at Wilding, who appeared deep in thought. After a moment more of contemplation, Wilding finally said:

'Speaking of Mouseling Hollow — this idyllic glade is ill prepared to repel an attack from any sizable force. We will not be able to gather a sufficient quantity of supplies and gear to repel an invasion from the Old Vole who runs the local sundry shop here, as an example — that's assuming we could get the Mayor to heed a call to action in the first place.'

Teague moved some rat figures towards The Riverpath.

'So in summary, here is what we have: we have no known location for The Rat King, and communication channels among our animal colleagues which have historically withstood the test of time appear to have been severed. We are lacking the supplies and equipment needed to fortify and potentially repel an invasion from The Southern Riverpath, there's a potential naval invasion posing an immediate threat to The Decoding Stones at The Lyceum, and there's two very dangerous bad guys on the loose.'

Pausing a moment to rub at his whiskers, Teague adjusted his spectacles, then continued.

'So, where should we begin gathering answers to these three questions? Well, King Teegan briefed us about two places that were experiencing unusual levels of activity — possibly monster activity. And, taking into account the entirety of the circumstances we have discussed, it seems only logical that we begin our journey by investigating the one which is closest to us — which just so happens to be in the nexus of all of this excitement. I have no doubt it is all related — in one way or another — to this one place.'

Hearthseeker looked at Wilding quizzically for a moment, before the two nodded in understanding.

'Mousebrook,' all three said at the same time.

'Yes, great minds do think alike,' smiled Teague at the synchronicity. 'Mousebrook. Whatever you need to purchase, it can always be found somewhere in Mousebrook: from the seemingly innocuous raw materials needed by Mouseling blacksmiths across the land, to the most rare and enchanted black market weapons and treasures sought after by those who seek glory in the Arena of the Black Baron. Whatever it is you seek, if it exists under the Lady's sun and can be purchased with coin, it can most certainly be found — and bought — in that Mouseling cesspool. Just watch your back and keep a close look out for robbers, cutpurses, and double dealers. There are always eyes and ears everywhere in Mousebrook.'

'Speaking of special treasures and enchanted weapons,' said Hearthseeker, 'don't we have a chest to open?'

An hour later the three sat at the table, where they were still drinking. The effect of the alcohol had long since set in, and the three mice were laughing and telling stories of each other's valor. All the while, Wilding — with a monocle in his left eye and a small jeweler's kit laid out neatly on the table before him — worked the lock on the golden chest that Hearthseeker and The Stranger had 'won' from Ravenscale.

'What is taking you so long, old mouse?' joked Ainsley. 'If this was the lock to the door of a beautiful Mouseling maiden awaiting rescue, I would have had it open twenty minutes ago.'

'That's still forty minutes too long,' retorted Wilding cheerfully, 'for a young Mouseling like yourself. And she most likely would have been saved by someone else while you were still fiddling with the lock, trying to ascertain which tumblers go where and which 'S' hook to use. Besides, this lock is obviously protected with an exceptionally strong enchantment. You can't just bash your way into a lock like this like some common...grave robber.'

The bard furrowed his brows at the insult, and muttered, 'If I ever *did* decide to become a grave robber, I'd be exceptional at it. I'd be anything but common...'

Teague, who was returning from the bar top after refilling his mug (again), noticed that on the top of the hinged lid was some kind of ancient, runic inscription.

It looked like this:

> ᚳᚱᛟᚳᛖᚱᚦᛋ ᛟᚠ ᛚᛖᛟᚨᚠᚱ ᚦᛖ
> ᛋᛈᛟᛇᚲ ᚲᛁᚾᚷ ᚾᛁᛞᛟᛗᚱ ᚦᚢᛖ
> ᚠᚱᛟᛋᛏ ᛗᛟᚾᚾᚦᚠᛁᚾᛋ
>
> ᚠ ᚷᛁᚠᛏ ᚠᚱᛟᛗ ᚾᛁᛋ
> ᛗᚻᛁᚾᛖᚾᚲᛖ ᛏᛟ ᚦᛖ ᛗᛁᚲᛖ ᛟᚾ
> ᚦᛖ ᚳᛚᚠᛇᚾᛋ
>
> ᛗᚻᛋ ᛟᚾᚱ ᚠᛚᛚᛁᚠᚾᚲᛖ
> ᚲᛟᚾᛏᛁᚾᚢᛖ ᛗᚢᛖᚱᛗᛟᚱᛖ ᚠᚾᛞ
> ᛟᚾᚱ ᚠᚱᛁᛖᚾᛞᛋᚾᛁᚳ ᚠᚲᚱᛟᛋᛋ
> ᚦᛖ ᚠᚷᛖᛋ ᚲᛟᛗᛖ ᛏᛟ
> ᛞᛗᚠᛁᚾᛖ ᚾᛋ

Teague ran his fingers over it and felt the inscription etched into the wood. For some reason it shone brightly, even though the wooden chest was obviously very old.

'What is this, Wilding?' asked Teague with a curious eye, still trying to decipher the inscription. 'I have never seen this type of writing before.'

Without looking up, while still fixated on opening the lock, Wilding replied 'I'd be surprised if you had, Robert. No one has seen this kind of writing in ages. I was required to study ancient magical languages at Searing Ridge, and even there, this was considered secretive and advanced knowledge — retained only for upper level students and faculty who demonstrated extreme prowess in sorcery, and a particular facility for enchantment. An honor for any Mouseling student there, to be sure — and somehow, I was one of the lucky few.'

A moment of silence passed as Hearthseeker and Teague exchanged glances. Then Ainsley, unable to contain his curiosity, said:

'And...?'

Wilding looked up at the bard and stared at him through the jeweler's monocle without putting down the small tool in his paw.

'And what?'

Hearthseeker shrugged openly, now animated with excitement from the suspense. 'WELL, WHAT LANGUAGE IS IT? OUT WITH IT, MAN!'

'Oh, that,' said Wilding, somewhat absentmindedly. 'Yes, the language...ahem. Well, this is the language of Leomar, the Stoic, King of the Frost Dwarves — as they are known in legend. Coincidentally, the same one we were talking about with the young Kerrigan Teague earlier in the evening. If we are telling true tales, the only previous examples I'd seen of this language had been in books. I've never actually seen the writing on any real, physical object before — just in old, dusty magical tomes. And even those were just pawscribed facsimiles done by scribes via candlelight.'

'You mean you'd never seen a real example of it before...until now?' said Hearthseeker.

'Yes...until now.'

'So what does it say?' asked Teague.

Wilding looked up and put down his small lockpick. Taking off his monocle for a second, he scrutinized the inscription once more.

'It says...well, if I was going to try to translate it, a similar sentiment in our own tongue would be something like **'DWARVES WERE ONCE ALIVE."**

'Really?' asked the bard, nonplussed. 'That's what it says?'

Wilding laughed out loud. 'No, of course not, you fool. I just made that up. What it really says is **'PROPERTY OF LEOMAR, THE STOIC, KING UNDER THE FROST MOUNTAINS. A GIFT FROM**

HIS EMINENCE TO THE MICE ON THE PLAINS! MAY OUR ALLIANCE CONTINUE EVERMORE, AND OUR FRIENDSHIP ACROSS THE AGES COME TO DEFINE US.'

'The Mice On The Plains?' Teague mused. 'I wonder if they are talking about The Lost Ones?'

Picking his tool back up and placing the monocle back on, Wilding fidgeted with the lock a bit more — and then a click was heard. Wilding uttered a barely audible incantation, a few more clicks were heard, and then a spring mechanism released and the lid pushed itself up automatically.

The three mice stood and stared in awe at what lay before them. A soft glow emanating from the chest fell gently across, and illuminated, their now transfixed faces — it was so radiant it was almost too breathtaking to look at.

'Is that...gold?' asked Hearthseeker in hushed tones.

Teague sat watching in stunned silence.

'Oh, it's much more than gold, I am sure,' said Wilding nonchalantly as he fidgeted with the sides of the chest. 'Usually, as I understand, the Frost Dwarves would put the golden coins on top, to encourage would-be robbers to take the 'easy money' — so to speak — and leave the *really* valuable items that were cleverly hidden in a secret, magic compartment...'

There was another loud click as Wilding loosened the top tray, then he finished his sentence.

'Underneath.'

Wilding removed the top tray, filled with golden coins, and set it aside, gently moving some of his Root and Field figurines so they wouldn't get crushed.

'Now, my adventurous companions, let's see what the legendary King Leomar was *really* sending — and to whom he was sending what I am coming to understand was a *very*, **very** valuable parcel.'

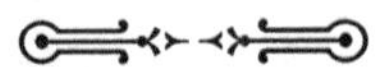

Moments later, the trio was in awe as they pulled item after item out of the chest's secret recessed compartment. Clothing, armor, weapons, and documents were all present in this chest, which had clearly been an especially prestigious gift.

It seemed like there were more items coming *out* of the chest than could actually fit *into* it. The companions tried to take stock of what was present, but the pile seemed to grow ever bigger. There were matching daggers, a cloak, a sword of some kind, and some intricate documents, as well as other pieces of assorted armor — all Mouseling sized.

'What is all this stuff and what does it do?' asked the quizzical bard.

Hearthseeker picked up a gorgeous embroidered cloak which was extremely light, but clearly of finer quality than anything he had ever seen. He gently caressed the cloak in his paws and rubbed it against his muzzle.

'Such fine cloth! I've never felt anything so exquisite — feel how soft it is. And yet so durable!'

He grabbed the cloth with both paws and gave it a hefty pull, to tighten it and test its tensile strength.

It seemed quite strong, indeed.

Teague looked at the daggers, picking them up and balancing them each in his paws, while Wilding studied an unusual-looking robe. All of the mice agreed that the craftsmanship of each item was exquisite, and no such similar items could be found in any store across the land.

A moment of silence passed between them, and then Hearthseeker broke it as he thought aloud:

'Professor, I was under the impression that The Frost Dwarves wove magic into their weapons and armor. That is how the legends always tell it, at least — and you told young Kerrigan the very same thing. Is it possible that these items have enchantments on them, or are ensorcelled in some way?'

'Why ask me, young bard?' retorted Wilding. 'When in doubt, read the instructions.' Wilding pointed his paw to a document he had set carefully aside on the edge of the table.

'Instructions?' said Teague and Ainsley in unison, clearly taken aback with surprise.

'Why yes, of course — they are right here, you know.' Wilding held up the letter in the runic language.

Studying the note, Wilding furrowed his brow for a few moments, before finally breaking out into a big smile.

'Well?' said Hearthseeker.

'Well, what?' replied Wilding.

Hearthseeker looked at the ceiling and rolled his eyes.

'WHAT DOES IT SAY, OLD MOUSE?'

Wilding looked up from the note and stared at the bard, then looked over to Teague, then back to the bard. After that — scanning slowly to ensure an accurate translation — he cleared his throat and finally read the note out loud:

Mouseling Ambassador Drypaws —

Please accept this gift of gold and magical items as a nod to our ongoing alliance, and the deep friendship we have formed with your people. If it wasn't for your recent aerial reconnaissance — which you performed with great valor — we would have had no idea about the brood of black dragons that had hidden themselves among the Early Spires, and the situation could have spiraled out of control far too easily.

It is no small feat for Mouselings to spy upon dragons and live to tell the tale — and we thank you for it.

Speaking of your unusual aerial prowess, I had my top engineer, McKenzie Rustbeard, do some retooling and redesigning of your airship. I think you will find the enclosed blueprints to represent a far superior aircraft — one which is much more suitable to your needs, and which can be easily constructed from common materials, capable of exceeding your current ship's speeds by almost ten leagues for each hour it is in motion. We have also enclosed schematics for some air-to-ground weaponry, should you ever find a need for it — it can be easily mounted on the broadsides of the airship and used with great success against your Ratling enemies.

In addition, please find enclosed the following magic items, that I pray you find a good use for in times of need:

1x Battlemage's Robes — 'Robes of the Fire Drake' *— These robes will increase the efficacy of fire spells for a magic user, while also easing the degree of concentration required to cast them. The wearer can also draw power from the robes to cast* **Fire Inferno** *once daily.* **Remember!** *Extra traits attached to magical items can only be used once per day, as the items require time to recharge their power over one moon cycle.*

1x Mouseling-Sized Enchanted Chain Mail *— Woven from the finest ore found deep underneath the Frost Mountain. It is practically impervious to piercing from sword or bolt. For your Highness' use and protection.*

1x Cloak of the Moon Cycle — 'Her Sacred Grace' *— Will allow you to see evil auras emanating from any creature. Should the wearer choose to draw power from the garment, it will grant a brief invisibility shroud for up to one quarter hour, once per day. Note Well: This is a VERY powerful ability, and should only be gifted upon the most trustworthy of retainers.*

1x Bracers of Rapid Hands *— For your finest rogue, thief, or archer.*

1x Twin Throwing Daggers of Return (with Ambidextrous Leather Sheath) *— Perfect for your top thief or assassin, these daggers will return to the wielder's paw if they miss their target after being thrown. Note Well: They must be retrieved if they strike deep and true.*

1x Enchanted Short Sword - 'Snake's Bane' *— Emits a high-pitched warning sound that only its wielder can hear when serpents are near both those with wings and those who slither. Inscribed with a relic from an ancient Naga king that helps it strike true against snakes that intend to harm the wielder.*

'Holy cheese wheel!' yelled Hearthseeker. 'A sword that is designed to slay snakes! What are the odds that we would find something like that — and in a chest from Ravenscale, no less! At the start of our encounter, I tried to bluff him by claiming I had a magical sword named Rattlemourne, but I had no idea such weapons truly existed. The irony abounds!'

'Well,' said Teague, though not quite soberly, 'if he intends to keep his promise to hunt you down and gut you, then Ainsley, my friend...you are going to need it!'

The smile quickly fell off of the bard's face.

'You are right, Robert. Ravenscale is definitely not a Hearthseeker fan.'

Then he smiled again. 'It'll make it all the more satisfying to see the look on his face when he finds out I now wield Rattlemourne in truth!'

'Are you two done?' asked Wilding. 'I'm translating here!'

Annoyed at the interruption, he continued.

*1x **Partial Map of Directions*** — *Here is our half of the map to The Undermountain. You know where the other half is being held for safekeeping. Please note that while this map will lead you to The Undermountain, once you arrive, there will be additional, coded directions to reach the treasure chamber itself — and only those who are worthy will reach the chamber alive. It is a difficult and dangerous road, and while the rewards are rich, I would discourage you from sending a large party due to the perilous nature of the path.*

*1x **Partial Map of Directions*** — *Here, also, is our half of the map to your Desert City. As with the other map, you know where the other half is being held for safekeeping. This copy should help ensure that our ground shipping routes to you are known and preserved from enemy eyes.*

I hope these gifts find favor with Your Eminence. Know that The Frost Dwarves stand ready to aid you should you need it.

However, you should also remain cognizant of the fact that the day approaches when we will depart from The Undermountain, forevermore. Should you choose to come with us, you need only but ask — and your request shall be granted.

You know where we are going.

We would more than welcome your company.

Yours Faithfully in Friendship,

King Leomar

'The Stoic'

The three mice looked at each other silently.

Hearthseeker fixed his glance on Wilding and said:

'Now THAT...you didn't make that up, right?'

Wilding shook his head, a sober look upon his face despite the many ales he'd consumed that evening.

'I feel confident, my bardish friend, that my translation was reasonably accurate. It does account for each item here on this table, does it not?'

'I can't believe we have the plans to an actual airship!' Hearthseeker shouted, grabbing Teague by the shoulders and shaking him excitedly. 'DO YOU KNOW WHAT THIS MEANS?!'

'By Her hands, we are in a *lot* of trouble,' said Teague with some trepidation, locking eyes with Wilding.

'If the wrong animals find out we possess this technology, our lives may well be forfeit.'

And then he grabbed the magical chainmail off the table and pulled it over his head, straightening it out and admiring the cut of the armor, which fit so snugly across his lithe body.

'But don't she fit perfectly,' he smiled slyly.

The night was winding down, and the candle lanterns which kept the Inn alight after dark were growing short.

It had been a long evening, and Teague's eyes were starting to get heavy — not just from the effects of so many mugs of ale, but from the nature of his wounds, the healing process taking place, the burden of leadership he had been forced to exercise earlier in the evening, the bittersweet experience of finding his children would be unexpectedly dispatched to elite Mouseling academies within a day's span — and of course, his all-consuming thoughts of the party's imminent departure for the insurmountable task which lay ahead of them.

'Soon, my friends, I must retire and get some rest,' started the innkeeper. 'When I got out of bed a few hours ago, I did not realize I would be saying farewell to my children in the morning, and Lady only knows for how long a time. As we finish up tonight, we must make plans for where we need to go next to thwart the threat of evil that has unfortunately been laid upon us.'

Wilding nodded to his friend of so many seasons — his best friend, through thick and thin. It was almost hard to believe all that had transpired in the past few days, and even more difficult to swallow the task that lay ahead of them.

The three friends sat around, nursing what remained of their drinks by the dwindling firelight.

Wilding spoke first.

'I can travel with you as far as Mousebrook, but once safe passage has been reached, there is someone I must go see. I have certain... questions, and I am most decidedly of the opinion that this person will have the...answers...that will help illuminate our way. Robert, with your blessing, I should be able to return to Mousebrook before your work there is done. That is, of course, assuming I don't run into any unforeseen obstacles that may cause a...hindrance. Should Mouseling Hollow be under imminent threat of invasion, I should, at the very least, be able to ascertain a potential timeline for this terrible event and return quickly to assist in the preparations for mounting an appropriate defense. Naturally, we must assume the worst, and your travels to Mousebrook should undoubtedly include ample opportunities for the acquisition of material and defensive weapons which could assist in repelling any invaders who would seek to harm this haven. This dwarven gold should, serendipitously, provide for us in making the necessary payments.'

Teague looked at his friend, and then at the ground for a long, long moment, thinking about who Wilding was likely going to visit. Though Hearthseeker had no idea what Wilding was referring to, Teague knew.

He knew, and was in no position to argue.

'My friend, I will be thankful, as always, for your companionship down the Riverpath. Every moment spent in your presence makes me feel secure, and should we part ways at Mousebrook for a time, I shall be incredibly thankful that you have chosen to delay your...errand... long enough to accompany us there. Your company is as invaluable as it is warmly welcomed.'

Wilding grabbed his friend's shoulder.

'Have no worries, Robert. Assuming my trip to visit him is uneventful, I WILL return to catch up with you in Mousebrook.'

There was a pause, then Teague continued.

'I will, of course, still have need of a good roguish bard who can spin a good tale by the firelight to accompany me to Mousebrook. Hearthseeker, do you know of anyone up for the journey?'

The bard smiled as he pulled out his lute and started fiddling with the tuning, almost absentmindedly.

'You need not ask me, milord, for I am with you both until the end of this — however long it takes, and wherever our path shall take us. Until you ask for my resignation, that is.'

'Indeed,' said Wilding. 'We could not ask for a better companion on this journey. But even with Ainsley's effective presence and vast span of utilitarian skills, one more traveling companion would be advisable, I should think. Someone with a military background, and trained in exceptionally effective close quarters combat.'

Wilding looked at Teague expectantly. Teague quietly laughed and smiled back, once he'd deciphered the hints the wizard had laid out for him.

'Before he departs in the early morning, I will be sure to ask Snowwillow if his interest lies in accompanying us. Will that satisfy you, old friend?'

'I have no doubt he will very much desire to,' replied Wilding. 'He thinks of you as quite the hero, you know — Lady knows where he'd get hold of such a silly notion. And of course, after his father's sacrifice at Owlhaven, well...perhaps a debt is owed, as well. Even if it is only one of mentorship and training. After all, Robert, we won't be around forever, you know. Someone has to train the next generation so we don't disappear into the desert sands like The Lost Ones did.'

The wizard mouse leaned back in his chair, a contemplative look upon his face. 'It's a delicate thing, really, if you think about it. We spent the past twenty seasons trying to hide who we are, only to have the violent and traumatic machinations of fate yank us back into a sacred duty — the sacred duty of protecting the extremely precious things we love. It feels almost like history is repeating itself — though the stakes are so much more dire this time around, and the odds stacked so much more deeply against us. Perhaps hiding who we truly are was but our futile and selfish attempt at coming to terms with who She really meant us to become.'

Wilding took a draught from his mug, then continued.

'It's something to meditate on, anyway. Clearly, all of our destinies — insomuch as we thought of them, at the least — were forever altered the day The Stranger showed up at The Sleeping Cat Inn. Perhaps it is only the wisdom of hindsight, but as we sit together now, I can't help but look back and think it was inevitable our fates should have become intertwined as they have. The fact that the three of us are sitting here, battered and bruised, but ultimately not terribly the worse for wear, after so much collateral fallout from his arrival — I think it speaks loudly to the fact that there is no other way this could have all played out.'

'Hmmm,' said Teague, deeply lost in thought as he pondered the wizard's words.

'Fate and destiny are all well and good — especially in a rousing song,' said Hearthseeker, 'but the fact remains that The Rat King and his minions are very much a threat now, and we must meet that threat head on. First things first, my da always said — so, to Mousebrook we shall go. And, I am assuming — soon?'

'As soon as we can gather supplies and ensure all our affairs are in order,' said Teague. 'Later tomorrow, then? Or perhaps the next day. But quite soon, my friend. Short days, at most.'

The three considered what Teague said, realizing that another adventure was, unexpectedly, so closely upon them.

'Alright then, I'm glad that's settled! Nothing against your Inn, good Sir Robert, but it's just as well — I was beginning to grow a mite bored anyways,' said Ainsley with a jaunty smile. 'So, what shall we do with all of this magical gear, and what about those incredibly valuable airship blueprints?'

Teague took a sip from his wooden mug, then looked back at the bard.

'As far as this gear goes, I am sure we can find the right mice to use them. It appears that some of these items would be a great fit for you rascals right here.'

He threw the fire robes in Wilding's face, and tossed the invisibility cloak and short sword towards Hearthseeker.

He then drew the quickness bracers up over his paws, and set the matching daggers aside — still safely in their sheath — next to the dwarven chest.

'Wilding, I am sure both you and Ainsley would agree that Snowwillow has earned the right to carry these. A gift for him joining us on our next great adventure, I'd call it.'

The two nodded in concert at the idea. Then, Teague added:

'Now, as far as these blueprints go, well...I have a neighbor who I am sure would hold quite an interest in their technical nature. And he is one of the few mice outside of this room that I truly trust.'

Wilding looked at Teague, suddenly alarmed, and shook his head in disbelief.

'Robert, surely you can't mean that whiskey-sodden, red wine-swilling detective that inhabits your southern fenceline?'

'That, Professor,' said Teague, draining his cup and staring his wizard friend right back in the eye, 'is exactly who I mean.'

On FireMaple Abby:

The legendary food and drink which can be found in Mouseling Hollow would not be complete without a mention of where, exactly, the fine ales and spirits found in that village originate from. While the hamlet also stocks generic ales and liquors that come from Old Town, the best — and finest by far in all The Far Collective — come from FireMaple Abby. There, the famous brewmaster known only as 'The Professor' plies his trade, making the most outstanding ales, wines, meads, beer, and fruit liquors of various styles from the fresh fruits and hops he grows on his very own property, nestled upon the banks of The Silver River.

*The rich and fertile soil provides the proper nutrients and **terroir** to create the ideal growing conditions for earthy, fragrant hops — fertilized generously by the rows of bees he also keeps. The Professor brings the harvest in each season with his faithful squirrel, 'Ducky,' and most Mouselings agree — the vintages the old mouse produces get better each year, and most certainly improve with age...*

— TAKEN FROM **WHISKEY IN YOUR WHISKERS - SIR PENDLETON STORMSNOUT'S GUIDE TO FINE WINES AND SPIRITS ACROSS THE FAR COLLECTIVE**

· · · · · · · · · · · · · ·

Chapter 32

THE CHILDREN DEPART

· ·

It had been a hard and difficult morning.

The children had come down the stairs, almost bewildered, looking around the log home they'd grown up in as if to ask 'is this really happening?' and dragging their trunks behind them. Ever in support, Hawkdodger had spent the night down in the cellar, as he sometimes did when he knew that the Inn's next day held tasks which would be stout ones that needed a firm paw — days that he knew would be made all the more difficult (if not altogether untenable) should he choose to return to his burrow home simply for an evening of rest.

Having risen early, Hawkdodger had gone upstairs and guided young Robbie back down, assisting him with his trunk while Shannon Teague helped out Kerrigan, whose trunk seemed impossibly light. After both children, and their belongings, had been successfully navigated to the bottom of the stairs, Hawkdodger ferried the trunks to the Inn's front door and laid them there by the hostess stand.

'Ready for takeoff whenever your flight arrives, milords and miladies!' said Hawkdodger in a coastal accent, bowing his head and doffing his woven cap in a gesture of mock servitude.

Both children giggled at his efforts, as well as his sense of gamesmanship. He was like an uncle to them, having been with the family for so many seasons.

'What advice do you have for us, Sir Hawk?' said young Robbie, playing along.

'Well, young sir, there are only three rules I live by,' said Hawkdodger, clearing his throat.

'First, if you're going to punch your opponent, make sure you punch him squarely in the snout — and always be the first to throw a low blow,' he said.

'Secondly, only date gorgeous does,' he nodded at Robbie Teague with a knowing smirk. 'The ones with lustrous black hair and fair complexions. I've always been partial to tall, absolutely stunning mice named Ashley,' he said, looking off in the distance as if remembering a beautiful mouse that got away.

'And finally...' he looked around the room to see if anyone was truly listening.

'Don't ever, ever venture out for a day of adventuring without eating a hearty, solid breakfast first.'

With that, he headed over to the bar top and sat down where Robert Teague, Shannon Teague, and Thistlefur had been preparing a feast all morning.

And what a feast it was.

Robbie and Kerrigan Teague had grown up having always been taught that breakfast was important. But, on this special day, the day of their departure, the nature and importance of 'breakfast' started to take on an entirely different perspective. After seasons spent working in the kitchen as serving staff and helping to run the family business from the other side of the bar, it finally started to sink in that they were leaving when they were, for once, served their breakfast like royalty — or, in the words of Robert Teague, 'like the royalty that comes in and sits facing us from the bar and pays for all of our bills.'

Though he was generally a late riser, Ainsley Hearthseeker had come down from his quarters to see the children off and provide moral support. Still clad in his nightclothes and wearing his tasseled sleeping cap, with groggy eyes that no doubt owed a significant debt to the many cups of ale he'd quaffed the previous evening, the amiable mouse sat down next to Robbie Teague and beckoned to Shannon Teague for a glass of orange juice.

'Make it three!' said the young Robbie, compassionately ordering one for his sister, who wasn't quite fully awake yet.

'Of course, my Academics!' said Shannon Teague, smiling with pride. Her children had received a dispensation from King Teegan to attend the finest Mouseling academies, after all.

And she intended to celebrate every second of it — right up until the moment she saw their falcons fly out of sight.

Of course, The Sleeping Cat Inn had always been known for its breakfast. To say it was legendary would be an understatement.

It wasn't really a proper start to the day if you hadn't had breakfast — at least not in any way, shape, or form for those who lived, stayed as a guest, or spent a great deal of time at The Sleeping Cat. In many cases, it was the largest meal of the day.

And, quite naturally, the most important.

But on that particular morning, on that very special day — my, what a breakfast it was.

Fresh, golden honey biscuits, just out of the oven, dripping with butter and a honeycomb drizzle...country sausage rooted and brought home from King Teegan's own private stock, chicken eggs scrambled with buttermilk and fresh cracked pepper, country ham slices fried up crisp, piping hot sausage gravy and tender, succulent cheese grits...all served with a side of extra melted glade butter for sopping your biscuits and ham in.

It was a feast fit for kings — or those about to leave their families in the service to one.

One by one, the guests of The Sleeping Cat slowly rolled in, drawn by the succulent smells of breakfast wafting down the Inn's residence hall and up the stairs to the guest quarters — an olfactory invitation to the Inn's residents to come and break bread, take companionship, and sup together, regardless of their status, in a hall where heroes lived.

Teague managed to corner Snowwillow shortly before breakfast started. The Falconrider was expected to fly back to MouseKeep and return with another falcon and rider to help ferry the children to their respective academies.

But, based on his conversation with Wilding and Hearthseeker the previous evening, Teague had other ideas.

'Snowwillow, um...I...um...' he started. He shifted uncomfortably from side to side as they stood looking at one another, and he found himself nervously rubbing at his snout.

'What is it, Commander?' said Snowwillow.

Lady help me, thought Teague. *I didn't think this would be so awkward.* But the awkwardness the innkeeper felt did not stem from some lack of social grace — it came from his very conscious recognition that he was about to ask the son of a deceased friend to accompany him on a journey which could, very possibly, end up being a one-way trip.

'Well, er, Snowwillow, you see...that is, the thing is...Wilding and Hearthseeker and I had a long discussion last evening. As you know, The Rat King has returned, and, well, um...'

'Yes sir?' said the young Falconrider, patiently.

'Well, we all agree...that your prowess has been, um...formidable... and we need to go on a special mission — to Mousebrook, you know. A lot of dangerous stuff happening down there, and we wanted to ask if...'

'It would be an honor to serve by your side, Commander Teague,' said Snowwillow, bowing graciously. 'What do you need from me?'

Teague breathed a sigh of relief. He looked at the frost-white leftenant, noting his youthful features and satiny, moist black snout. *How do you get all white fur like that?* pondered Teague.

'Now Snowwillow, I want you to know that this is going to be dangerous and I can't...well, none of us ever *can*, you know — but in this particular case, I cannot guarantee your safety. I'll confess, I am worried that your mother might have second thoughts if she knew that you would be coming with me and Wilding on an adventure of a...military nature.'

'Milord, I am a soldier of MouseKeep — I will go where I am needed, and with whom. And, my personal feeling is that my father would rather that I be by your side and not anywhere else — especially given the recent circumstances, and their uncertain implications.'

Teague looked squarely into the eyes of the young Leftenant.

'Good. Then the decision is made, and the matter is settled. Now, Wilding and I — and the bard, too — felt that you deserve a special gift, based on your direct contributions in helping to retake and secure MouseKeep.'

Teague produced the twin sheathed daggers, which glinted in the morning sun. The intricate silver and gold filigree on the daggers, along with the rubies which adorned their pommels, made them look truly epic, indeed.

'Believe it or not, these are enchanted daggers that will always return to you if they miss their mark. I believe you will find that they complement your **Four Paws Flow** style of fighting perfectly. And, it goes without saying, these are very, very rare and precious items. An heirloom which, I pray, you will be able to hand down to your children — someday, anyway — when you decide to settle and put down roots.'

The Falconrider drew the daggers out of their nested sheath and balanced them in his paws, then resheathed them and tucked them into his tunic.

He looked at Teague with a mix of admiration and honor.

'Thank you, Commander. I know they will serve me — serve all of us, I mean — well in our upcoming journey. And, if I may say sir — it is a great honor to be serving by your side, as my father did before me.'

Teague pretended to wipe something from his eye and coughed lightly.

'Yes, um, well...it's a pleasure to have you, err, along, Snowwillow. Now...remember to bring back two Falconriders with you when you return, so that when the children leave, you can stay here and begin preparations with us — correct? If you forget to bring a second rider, you will be shoehorned into taking Kerrigan to Owlhaven, and that will cause us delay.'

'Aye, sir!' Snowwillow said smartly. He snapped off a sharp salute and turned to leave, when Teague suddenly blurted out:

'But bring back two of the best riders, please! Umm, Leftenant. I can't afford to have my precious babies falling off from ten thousand feet!'

SnowWillow laughed at the silly notion, and smiled at Teague reassuringly.

'Not to worry, Commander. I will personally make sure they are strapped in tightly, and will not forget to bring back two of the best riders I can find. I will ensure their safety as they travel to the academies at the behest of King Teegan — they will be in good hands. With your permission, I will probably make the first leg of the journey south with them — at least until they split near RockHollows — and then return. It should just be a few hours.'

Teague clasped paws with Snowwillow. 'Well, son, let me be the first to say it then — welcome aboard. We have several objectives that we need to accomplish, the biggest being to find the new Black Citadel of The Rat King. But before we can accomplish that, all signs point to unusual events and unrest in Mousebrook — so we've decided to begin our journey with that destination in mind. Having a Falconrider along to provide air support and reconnaissance on the way there will no doubt prove invaluable.'

'Ah, very good, sir,' said Snowwillow. 'I've heard they have some very fine gambling dens down in Mousebrook. I wouldn't mind trying my paw at a few rounds of cards...err, time permitting, of course, sir.'

Teague smiled at the young Rider.

'Captain, if my feelings are correct, the people we need to find may very well be in those same gambling halls of iniquity. How is your Flops game?'

'Quite good sir! I have been known to win more coin than I lose from my fellow soldiers at MouseKeep, when we have time to play during our downtime.'

'Good,' said Teague, somewhat knowingly. 'Good. Wilding has a penchant for Flops also. As, I don't doubt, does Hearthseeker. It would be good for us all to practice before we leave — perhaps with a few mugs of ale between us. To help keep us hydrated, of course.'

'Using real money?' asked the leftenant excitedly.

Teague cleared his throat at the young mouse's exuberance.

'Maybe with just practice chips to start, I should think. We will set you loose upon the denizens of Mousebrook once we get there.'

Then the two mice laughed out loud. Teague clasped paws again with the Falconrider, and then watched the snow-white Mouseling exit the Inn, knowing that he would soon be on the wing, flying high over Mouseling Hollow on his journey back to Castle Feldenspar.

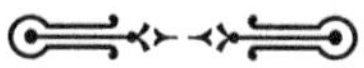

It was much later on that Robert Teague sat across from his wife Shannon at a table in The Sleeping Cat, after what had been a highly emotional morning and afternoon. The children had been whisked off on the backs of falcons to their respective academies, and Ainsley Hearthseeker had been sent into town to buy supplies, taking with him some of the dwarven gold from the treasure chest. Foodstuffs, water and wineskins, fire-making materials, camping gear, and perhaps most importantly, the warm clothing, blankets, bedrolls, and tenting which would be needed to protect them as they traversed their way South. The party would require enough gear that Teague had sent the bard into the village with a squirrel cart to help him haul all of it. Provisions were available — and plentiful — now, but if and when the war reached Mouseling Hollow in earnest, or a critical supply chain was cut off, who knew when supplies would be available next?

Teague's experience in the first war had taught him that preparation was the mother of survival — and when it came to survival, Robert Teague was not inclined to take chances unnecessarily.

Of course, the innkeeper pondered all of these thoughts as they crossed his mind, but soon found himself shooing them away. Where, how, why...none of it mattered now. Based on the King's most recent missive (the one that the innkeeper had burned in the fireplace the day before), their present mission was to identify threats and provide reconnaissance to the crown — starting with Mousebrook, but networking with animals and small villages along the way. They were to look for indications of the whereabouts of The Rat King's skirmish parties that were (allegedly) ascending up The Riverpath, and in doing so, reestablishing the communication chain which had seemed to have disappeared since the attempt to overtake Castle Feldenspar.

Teague already suspected that the recent disruption in communications was likely due to those same skirmish parties, who sought to gain a foothold within the King's lands. And the innkeeper had no doubt that as soon as *that* mission was successfully accomplished, the skirmish parties would be followed by a battalion of animals bent to nefarious purposes, all serving The Rat King and looking to establish garrisons at key choke points. Undesirables of all stripes: fischers and rats, perhaps badgers and coyotes, and who knew how many others. And once they took a territory, it would take nothing less than a massive insurgency to uproot their hold. While a party of human forces to assist in the fight might make a counterattack slightly easier, well...frankly, if they ever found themselves in a situation where they were forced to take back an established garrison through direct combat...they would be facing, at best, a suicide battle.

As wicked as he was, Teague knew that The Rat King was clever in his machinations and made sure to only recruit the deadliest of animals to his cause. Weak, soft animals who hated fighting were simply fodder to him — menial servants if they could be recruited to his ranks, or the next evening's meal if they refused to yield and supplicate themselves to his desires.

The prognosis is bleak indeed, mused Robert Teague.

And winter was coming.

Harsh snowfalls had been expected, as the weather seers had indicated throughout the year. And here was Robert Teague in the middle of all of it, who just a few days ago had been a simple innkeeper preparing for the harvest celebration. But now, quicker than he could have ever imagined, his disguise had been blown, and he had not only been called up to the King's service and reinstated alongside his best friend, but he had watched his children be dispatched to elite academies to get them out of the way of the coming onslaught.

Trying to take this all in, he sat across from his wife. It had all been so emotional, the goodbyes that had taken place just hours previously — Kerrigan crying in her father's arms, and Shannon Teague in tears herself, clutching her firstborn son to her, distraught over his departure and his all too early 'growing up.' The elder Teagues held hands unwaveringly, watching as their children — on the backs of their falcons, and with Snowwillow guiding them on his bird in the lead — departed from Mouseling Hollow.

Robert Teague had hugged his wife tightly as they watched their children fly off into the distance. But if there was a silver lining to be found in all this, it was that he knew that their children would be safe now. But of course, even with the humble reassurance that came from knowing that Snowwillow would be there to guide them on the first leg of their journey, both Teague and his wife knew, with a great sense of melancholy as the grey winter skies set in, that it would be some time before they saw their two children again.

Back inside the comfort of the Inn, where a fire was roaring, Robert and Shannon Teague sat quietly together as evening began to fall, sipping from mugs of steaming coffee. Mrs. Teague held their young baby, gently rocking her as she slept. Lost in thought, they both looked out the window at the crepuscular twilight, then back at each other, finally locking eyes.

His wife was the first to break the silence.

'My love, I must confess: when I heard the legends of **The Fabled Two,** I always knew of their honor and valiance. But I never knew them to be so...quiet. That is something the bards seemed to leave out.'

The ice broken, they both laughed.

Teague replied, 'If we are telling true tales, my love, I always thought those two were absolute fools.'

'Fools maybe,' said Shannon Teague, gently and lovingly. 'But I'm infatuated with one of them.' She reached her paw across the table and clasped his, looking deep into his eyes. 'But what now?'

Teague thought about his next words carefully. Reluctantly, he spoke.

'The package I got from the King last evening included a dispensation for you and the baby to go to MouseKeep. You can fly there as soon as you like and stay under the safe watch of the King and the MouseGuard. If we are telling true tales, it would be an ease upon the burdens of my mind if you accepted the offer.'

'I will do no such thing!' said Shannon Teague, defiantly. 'You would have me see our work together here in Mouseling Hollow go to waste — and,' she added emphatically, 'in such a time of coming need? Mousekin will need shelter, food, camaraderie — everything the Inn has always provided. And will continue to provide! I will not abandon our dreams just because The Rat King has made the ill-fated choice to try once again to do what The Fable Two prevented him from doing twenty seasons ago. And, with you by my side — or without you, should fate dictate otherwise — I will make my stand upon the shores of The Western Forest, here in Mouseling Hollow...at this very Inn, if need be! Any animal foolish enough to set an unwelcome paw here in the Hollow will pay dearly for their treachery!'

Teague saw the hackles of the fur on her back stand up, poking through the blouse she had put on before the evening's meal service.

She's a firecracker, that one, he thought. *I'd marry her all over again.*

'I was afraid you would say that,' he said aloud, looking down at the worn wooden floor. 'You should know, he also offered you your own dispensation to attend The Academy at Searing Ridge — and to bring the baby along with you. While you would be the oldest student there, he has great faith in your ability to become a sorceress who could one day be of great service to the crown — a faith I share quite emphatically, I must add. And, again — you both would be safe.'

'I will remain here in Mouseling Hollow, and my decision is final.' She grabbed his paw even tighter.

'So be it,' said Teague. 'But, before we leave tomorrow, I will instruct Hawkdodger about the passages in the wine cellar — Thistlefur, as well — in case trouble should come to our village home. If it does, I expect you all to flee to the safety of MouseKeep. Taking a stand in this village would be a very foolhardy decision...tactically speaking, that is. You should take as many mice with you as you can, if trouble shows up.'

Shannon Teague looked at her husband.

'I will consider all...'

Suddenly Hearthseeker bullied his way through the Inn's front door and a chill wind followed him, stoking the fire. With his back to the oak door he pushed it closed, then took a deep breath.

'What a day, what day!' he said, somewhat cheerfully. 'You would think that that old ratty vole down on Orchard Lane has missed his last three meals, he was charging so much for a wool blanket! I had some stern words with him, I did — and in return, he threatened to call his friends over to 'teach me a lesson,' if you can believe such nonsense. What lesson, said I? That voles are the weakest fighters around? I'd have a more challenging time fighting a nightcrawler that was half eaten on a hook! After I said that, he blustered and rumbled and squeaked like a rusty old teakettle, and eventually gave me a discount. No one ever accused Ainsley Hearthseeker of being scared of any creature, let alone a vole. Victory!'

The few patrons of the inn, as well as the Teagues and Hawkdodger, who was manning the bar, burst into laughter and applause. They all knew that nasty vole was crotchety on a good day — and downright cantankerous on a bad one. With a smile on his face, the bartender began to fill a wooden mug with some harvest berry ale.

'A drink, master bard?' said the bartender welcomingly. It was hard not to like such an affable mouse — and Hawkdodger, for his part, was always a great fan of characters who held both wit and charm. Obviously, Hearthseeker had more than his fair share of both.

'Bo!' said the mouse, which was slang for 'yes!' in MouseSpeak. He advanced to the bar, grabbed his mug, and took a drink, generously throwing some gold coins on the bar top for Hawkdodger's efforts. Then he made a path straight over to the Teagues' table and sat down. A mustache of foam lay underneath his whiskers, which he quickly added to by taking another big draught of his ale.

'Milords, I believe I have supplied us well for at least a season of travel! Though I hope 'twill not be that long, as I'll admit I've grown fond of this old, weathered log. Tell me, Master Teague, why do they call this Inn The Sleeping Cat?'

'Well, Ainsley, it's because many seasons ago, back when this Hollow was naught but a few straw huts and mushroom houses, I was being pursued by a tabby cat who...'

The door opened again, and an even louder wind whipped through the bar. All the mice turned to see who the offending party was — and in walked Wilding, the Professor, with his hooded traveling cloak drawn tightly over his head.

With Thistlefur's assistance, the two of them closed the door as quickly as they could.

'Professor!' all the mice cheerfully shouted in unison.

'Drink, Professor?' asked Hawkdodger with his same hospitable wit.

'Absolutely,' said Wilding. 'I need something to help warm my bones. Robert Teague! Hearthseeker! It is beginning to get dark.

Robert...' said Wilding, pulling his friend closer. He dropped his voice to a conspiratorial whisper and asked, 'Did you want to visit your friend on the southern fenceline? I would join you, if you don't mind, to make sure that the, um...paperwork...that we found in the chest last evening will remain unmolested once we depart upon our journey to Mousebrook.'

Hearthseeker, who was sitting nearby, suddenly interjected. 'Oh, can I come along too? I've read several of his books, you know. He is quite the legend!'

Teague looked at the bard, sighed, but nodded his head in assent.

'Just make sure you don't start talking with him about his books, or else we will never get out of there. How did you know who we were talking about, anyways?'

'Elementary, my dear Teague! The sign outside of his home is hard to miss, you know. **Sir Pendleton Stormsnout — Legendary Detective and Seeker of Adventure**. Besides which, he is the only one I've noticed who inhabits your southern fenceline.'

Teague shook his head in disbelief as he looked out the window to the south, observing the day's last few fading rays of sunlight.

'He's usually home around this time, so we may as well get to it. Let's crack on over there and give a loud knock. Perhaps the old rascal will turn up.'

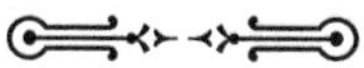

They drew their traveling cloaks up around their heads as they exited The Sleeping Cat. A fine misty rain had started to drizzle, and it was threatening to turn into a storm shortly. The sky was just beginning to turn midnight black from the deep harvest orange of sunset. Autumn was most definitely about to be upon them, and Teague felt a touch of melancholy at the thought of missing his favorite season in Mouseling Hollow. The trees were always so beautiful when they changed colors, and inspired by the sleepy days and crisp autumn nights, he and

Wilding would often head off to go fishing at Wilding's home down at FireMaple Abby. Those long fall days, in particular — after the harvest festival, but before the snows set in — fishing and drinking on the dock at the Abby, or out in a skiff, were some of Teague's favorite — and most restful — times.

But it looked like all of that would have to wait until next year.

Crossing the fenceline, the trio soon approached the neighbor's door. Teague looked up at the hanging sign that said **'Sir Pendleton Stormsnout — Legendary Detective and Seeker of Adventure'** and wondered how the fabled mouse actually made a living. It never seemed like there was much of interest in Mouseling Hollow that would require a keen mind to solve crimes, but there were always fantastic stories in **The Feldenspar Daily** of his astounding feats as a champion of the law. Teague assumed that he must work in other villages and hamlets, whenever his unique services were required. Wilding often grumbled (when the subject of Sir Pendleton Stormsnout came up) that he suspected the 'legendary detective' spent far more time exaggerating his own exploits through quill and ink than actually solving any crimes.

Wilding rapped on the door loudly three times. They were met with silence.

Teague stepped out from under the eaves of the doorway and looked upstairs — unsurprisingly, he could see that candles were aglow in each window, indicating somebody was certainly home.

'Knock again,' said Teague.

Wilding rapped on the door three more times, with a bit more energy, intensity, and sound.

After a minute, the door creaked open and an older mouse, dressed in butler robes of all black, looked out at them.

'Yes?' said the mouse with a huffy, almost aristocratic air.

'Ahem,' Teague cleared his throat. 'Alfred, it's me...Robert Teague...your neighbor. I need to speak with...'

'He has been expecting you,' interrupted the butler mouse. 'Come in, and please remove your wet raingear. You know how he is about such things.'

The party of three came in and took off their footwear and traveling cloaks, while the butler instructed them to wait for his return. Glancing at the grandfather clock in the hallway, they saw the time was 5:43.

They stood there, waiting awkwardly by themselves, until the clock read 5:45.

Then, at the final chime of the grandfather clock, the butler returned to the foyer and said 'You may now proceed upstairs. His study is to the right of the landing.'

Ainsley looked excited, while Wilding rubbed at the bridge of his snout. Teague sighed and said 'We know, Alfred, thank you.' Muttering 'we know' again under his breath, he set off down the hallway.

Upstairs they went, with Teague at the helm and Wilding bringing up the rear. When they crested the stairs, Teague turned right and headed for a room at the end of the hallway, its door left half open. He peered inside and saw a massive collection of books shelved upon the wall, along with some tables which held various medical instruments and an alembic. A roaring fire in the fireplace shone brightly, and a wingback chair was turned towards the fire. Next to it stood a small polished wooden table with a snifter of whiskey on it.

Teague could not see anyone in the room.

'Enter,' said a deep, baritone voice coming from the chair.

The three looked at each other, then started to proceed in.

'Stop right there,' said the voice, after the three of them had barely gained entry into the room. 'Three companions come to see me. Who are they, and what do they want? I wonder...'

The voice paused for a moment, then continued.

'I'll save you all time explaining. Robert Teague, innkeeper and proprietor of The Sleeping Cat Inn, known for its legendary food and hospitality. With him, as always, his heavy-footed wizard friend — I knew it was you when you practically plodded up the stairs with that strange gait of yours — and a third companion. Someone whom I have not yet met, but already know such a great deal about.'

Teague looked at the floor awkwardly.

'Well, Sir Pendleton...'

'I am not finished yet, Teague.'

Teague closed his mouth and shook his head, eying the floor.

'A third companion whom I have not yet met, but who, I am quite certain, was part and parcel to all of the strange rumblings that have been coming from the castle these past few days. What is the word they use when an attack on the crown occurs? Ah, yes — *insurrection*, that is what it is called. An *insurrection* which was, seemingly, thwarted by the three of you.'

A paw shot out suddenly from the wingback chair, grabbed the snifter delicately, and then disappeared with the snifter behind the back of the chair.

A second later, the snifter was returned to the table, now empty.

The deep voice continued.

'And now, at the end of a day with quite a bit of hubbub occurring at that Inn of yours — with falcons and strangers of all kinds coming and going, and squirrel carts full of gear traipsing back to the Inn with enough camping gear to supply nearly the entire village — you show up at my doorstep, of all places, bringing your best friend along. A friend who is not a fan of...how shall I call them...my methods? But he comes nonetheless. What you have brought for me must be very precious, indeed, Robert Teague.'

'Indeed, Sir Pendleton, it is. And on that subject I wanted to ask your opinion...'

'I'm not done yet, Teague,' interjected the voice.

Wilding started to get flustered, and unable to contain himself, blurted out 'See! I told you this was a terrible idea...'

'A TERRIBLE IDEA?' the voice suddenly thundered, undaunted. 'By Her omnipotent and omnipresent paw, wizard, this seems to be the only *sensible* idea you have allowed in Lady knows how long?

Which makes me wonder why, by any stretch of the imagination, you argued with your friend and tried to deter him when he told you he was coming here.'

'I didn't argue with him...' stammered Wilding, 'I asked to join him.'

'Indeed,' said the voice, now annoyed. 'And if you do indeed intend to perform a reconnaissance of Mousebrook, you will need to have more faith in your innkeeping friend than that! Besides, Wilding, you are a terrible liar. I consider it one of your finest traits! It's why you have never been able to win the Root and Field Open Championship. What did you end up placing last season? Aah, let me recall...seventh, I believe it was? And such a poor misplay on your part to give the seemingly clasped victory to your highly unworthy opponent, and snatch ignominious defeat from the jaws of triumph. So close though, tsk tsk.'

A bottle of whiskey was suddenly produced from somewhere, filling the snifter back up. The bottle disappeared again, and the deft paw shot back from the chair, grabbing the glass once more. The paw and glass then promptly disappeared, and when the glass was returned a moment later, it was, again, empty.

How can he drink whiskey like that? wondered Teague.

'But where was I...oh yes...your little trip to Mousebrook,' said the voice.

'That is supposed to be a secret,' said Teague.

'A secret?!' The voice barked a single, sharp laugh. 'If it is secrecy you desire, Teague, perhaps sending your bardish friend parading all over town for supplies, sharing with everyone his undoubtedly embellished tales of your recent adventures, is not the best way to preserve your element of surprise.'

Hearthseeker blushed and looked at the floor. The voice ignored him and continued on, undaunted.

'Not that you should be too hard on the bard, everyone already knows there is trouble brewing down there. It's practically whispered on the wind. It's also your logical next step, you know, in this morass of a quagmire you are probably calling a 'quest,' or some such overromanticized balderdash. They won't admit it openly, of course, but the words they are using to describe the disturbances down there are things like *'Supernatural,'* and *'Monsters.'* You know, the sort of entities that show up when darkness starts to cover the land. A bunch of embarrassing tommyrot, really. Childish oversimplifications. But you aren't here to discuss Mousebrook, are you Teague? No, certainly not. You are here to discuss those ancient parchment papers stowed in Wilding's robes.'

'How do you know they are ancient?' asked Wilding, trying to engage Stormsnout in a battle of wits.

'Oh, please,' said the detective with an abhorrent sigh. 'Let's *try* not to embarrass ourselves too terribly, shall we, wizard? Where should I even start? Naturally, it would be easiest to simply answer that I know all about those ancient parchments you're hiding **because it is my JOB** to know what is in your robe! Or, would you be happier if I were to discuss the unique sound they make, along with the *dreadful* cacophony that awkward gait of yours produced as you trudged disdainfully up the stairs to this meeting — or the unique crinkling that ancient parchment which is not preserved properly makes when it is exposed to air and begins to decay, as it is doing at this very moment. Of course, we could also discuss the unique scent related to that peculiar chemical process — it's quite easy to identify, if you know what it smells like. To save us all some time, why don't I just say that you've found documents that have been lying in a hermetically sealed chest for several centuries — bound closed with magic, no doubt — and based on the timeline of those parchments, and their mouse 'sizability'...I would venture to say — quite confidently, I might add — that you have uncovered one of the legendary missing shipments that King Leomar of the Frost Dwarves sent to The Lost Ones — shipments which famously disappeared before they could arrive at The Lost Ones' city, which supposedly resided somewhere in The Hellion Sands. According to legend, one of those shipments included schematics for a lighter than air ship, which would, it goes without saying — *if it were real, that is* — be a weapon which could theoretically end a Second Rat King War before it had even begun.'

The paw refilled the whiskey glass again, then grabbed the snifter.

'So, I'll ask you again, Wilding: what is it you wanted to ask me?'

'Nothing,' Wilding muttered as he shifted uncomfortably, defeated. *Lady how I hate talking to this guy,* he thought.

'I might be inclined to help you, Teague,' the voice continued. 'If I choose to do so, in return, you will do something for me. But as you well know, the rule that I follow unwaveringly, in all of my dealings, is this: no secrets. When I work with my clients — and keep in mind, I haven't actually agreed to work with you yet, having now been annoyed by Wilding's juvenile — and futile — attempts to disprove my methods and make them look insufficient...'

Teague punched Wilding as hard as he could in the arm, while trying not to make enough noise to disturb the detective.

'...when they are in fact, as I have so neatly demonstrated, *more* than sufficient...well, let's just say you are incapable of keeping anything from me. The truth is, though, I like transparency. I prefer it. I *insist* upon it. If all animals embraced transparency as I do, there would be no need for someone with my particular...talents.'

The paw refilled the whiskey snifter a third time.

'And the final question we should be considering is *not* 'will I keep these blueprints safe?' — for we all know that I will. The *real* question is, or should be, in your minds: 'am I capable of interpreting these blueprints and getting this contraption built?'

The three mice looked at each other with incredulity.

'And the answer of course, is absolutely and unequivocally yes.'

Shannon Teague's Fire Baked Garlic Rosemary Bread

Makes 2 Loaves

Ingredients:

1 Acorn Top yeast

1 Acorn Top sugar

1 Thimble warm water

2 1/2 Thimbles flour

1/2 Acorn Top salt

2 Acorn Tops rosemary

3 Pats butter

(Conversion Key For Humans: 1 Thimble = 1 Cup

1 Acorn Top = 1 Tablespoon

1/2 Acorn Top = 1 Teaspoon

Butter Pats = Tablespoons)

Directions:

Place yeast, sugar and water in large bowl and allow mixture to become bubbly.

Mix in 2 Pats butter, salt, and 2 Thimbles of flour.

Add 1 Acorn Top of the fresh chopped rosemary.

Knead for about 5-ten minutes by paw until smooth and elastic.

Add more flour if necessary.

Oil a bowl, put dough in it, and cover with a towel.

Let dough rise in a warm place for one hour until doubled.

Punch down dough and divide in half.

Let dough rest about 5 minutes.

Grease baking pan or cookie sheet with melted butter.

Shape the dough into 2 small rounded oval loaves.

Sprinkle remaining 1 Acorn Top of rosemary over the loaves and press lightly into the surface.

Let loaves rise again until doubled, about 45 minutes.

Preheat stone hearth to baking temp (375°F).

Bake for fifteen to 20 minutes, until lightly browned.

Carefully remove from hearth, brush with remaining butter (and sea salt, if desired)

Chapter 33

FAREWELL TO MOUSELING HOLLOW

Later that evening, after the trio had concluded their business with Sir Pendleton Stormsnout, Wilding had returned to his riverfront home, which was affectionately called FireMaple Abby by the locals. Though the previous day had been chilly, when the sun arose the following morning, it broke through the clouds and a warm breeze began to blow.

The mice called this strange effect 'Second Summer,' and it was most certainly a tiding of good omens to come.

Wilding had arisen early, well before the sun had come up that morning, and retired to the top of his wizard spire to meditate. He could already tell that it was going to be a gorgeous day — and after the events of the past week, taking a moment alone at his riverfront home was both a blessing, and a much needed pause, indeed.

Of course, it had been so many seasons ago, in the wake of The First Rat King War, that he and Teague had wandered The Western Lands together, trying to find their way. A mentor of his had once advised him to get into the business of brewing, and with what little coin he could scrape together, he had bought this picturesque place at a bend in The Silver River and built his wizard's tower upon it. It served as a combination triple-spired arcane tower, hops farm, and wine cellar, all in one. To the north of the tower were the hops fields, now ripe and ready for harvest. Down below the rock foundation that supported his tower home was a fermentation and storage area that was the perfect year-round temperature in which to keep his concoctions of yeast and mash going — and which, in turn, provided tasty beverages for thirsty Mouselings all across The Far Collective (and allowed the wizard an effective method of generating coin, to boot).

Wilding would have done it all for free if he could have, though. Brewing — and drinking brews — were his real passions.

To the south of his triple-spired tower stood the gorgeous FireMaple tree that had given his riverfront residence its namesake. Even now, from the top of his tower, he could only stare upwards at the crimson red and orange majesty that the old, weathered maple tree held — as if it were a kind of magistrate overseeing nature's own court, which Wilding could only be an outside witness to.

As the seasons had passed, this place had become the erudite Mouseling's hearth and home. He had become so comfortable there, settling into his routine of brewing beer and then delivering it up and down the Riverpath, that the idea of leaving it for an interminable time was a thought so sad, his heart could hardly bear it. Though he knew the tasks that lay ahead of him were necessary ones, something about the thought of leaving this wonderful place behind just didn't sit well with him.

But if you don't stop The Rat King — who will? whispered a small voice inside his head.

Looking up and sighing at the sight of the FireMaple's beauty as the sun rose up above it, he suddenly heard a jovial voice yell out from three stories below.

'Ahoy, Professor! Permission to come aboard?'

It was Ainsley Hearthseeker, accompanied by Robert Teague. They had left to come down The Riverpath before dawn — an early departure for what was certainly going to be a long day, and an even longer journey ahead of them. Wilding, peering off the roof of his tower, spied a squirrel cart laden heavily with stock and provisions. Overhead, out of the corner of his eye, he saw Snowwillow on falconback, with a halberd in his paw and a bow on his back, a quarrel of arrows by its side, gliding in for a landing with great finesse.

'Granted!' said Wilding cheerfully. Though he would miss his beloved home terribly, it was still good to see his companions. Anticipating what was about to befall all of them on the mission they had all signed on for, he could not imagine a group of friends and comrades he would rather have by his side to watch his back. He climbed down the three floors of his tower quickly and met his companions outside. Clasping Teague's paw firmly, the pair locked eyes solemnly for a moment, knowing what lay ahead — and then Wilding took an unsuspecting bear hug from Hearthseeker which almost sent him to the ground.

He's a good egg, that bard, thought Wilding.

In the midst of the unexpected embrace, Snowwillow gracefully landed his falcon by the trio and dismounted.

'Have you taken breakfast, Professor? If not, now is the time to do so! The Riverpath holds unknown adversaries ahead of us, and it may be awhile before we sup again.'

'Indeed, Snowwillow, I had a sausage with my apprentice but naught an hour ago. I am prepared and ready to go.'

The Falconrider nodded back at him briskly, all business.

'Then to the squirrel cart we go — with me in the air as an advance observer, in case trouble should arise. Try to stay on The Riverpath, where there is the least foliage, in case we should encounter an ambush. I will cover you as best as I can.'

Wilding stood unmoving, looking at Teague.

Teague was silent.

'Professor, are you ready?' asked the Falconrider again.

'I am ready, Rider, but I had somewhat of a different idea for how we would approach this journey. Come, follow me.'

The trio followed the wizard to the waterwheel house that was nestled along the banks of the river, where he slid open a secret door, revealing several pole boats and a skiff inside. The craft bobbed and floated in the gentle water which flowed peacefully underneath the waterwheel structure, as if meditating, with eager anticipation, upon the possibility of a journey.

Hearthseeker poked at the craft, enchanted.

'Rivercraft! I frequently sing the legends of the mice who traversed up and down The Silver River, having brilliant adventures while fighting the forces of evil. Are we about to disappear into those legends ourselves?'

Wilding smiled, looking at Teague for approval, and Teague smiled back.

The wizard then said:

'I can think of no better way to begin a reconnaissance mission then to thwart our foe from the start. Whereas they will expect to ambush us easily upon the Southern Riverpath, we will instead float silently and undetected upon these watercraft, heading down the river safely to our destination, wherever that may truly lie. Hearthseeker, grab those fishing poles off the wall of the wheelhouse, if you'd be so kind, so that we may make an adventure of it, eat well, and avoid detection in our disguises. We are but simple fisherman, after all, heading out for a day of peaceful recreation.'

From the wall of the wheelhouse, Wilding grabbed several pairs of fishing trousers and hats and handed them out to the mice, who quickly dressed themselves in the garb of simple fishmongers.

'And now, now, for the piece de resistanc...' Wilding was interrupted suddenly, as a voice called out his name.

'Professor? Young Hopmaster? Is anyone home?'

Wilding listened intently. It was Fyz, the River Otter, delivering the mail! Wilding stepped out from the boathouse and walked onto his dock, where Fyz had swum up, calling out eagerly.

'Oh, hail professor! I thought no one was home. I have no mail for you today, I just wanted you to know!'

'Thank you, Fyz!' said Wilding. 'Tell me, how have your travels been downriver?'

'Uneventful, sir, uneventful. I have delivered mail as far down as Mousebrook, and other than the occasional soggy mail complaint, nothing of interest seems to be happening.'

'And how is the fishing down that way?'

'Why, splendid, of course! The muskie minnows are biting, and the Silverback continue to thrash and jump. I myself had a breakfast of muskie about two hours ago. Fresh as can be, sir!'

'Wonderful, Fyz! I have planned to take some friends downstream for a day's fishing sojourn, so you have given me good news. Should we choose to camp out for a night or two, I expect you can slide my mail through the slot on our front door? My apprentice will remain here, as he has work which calls him to the fields and requires immediate attention.'

'Indeed sir, I shall do as you ask. To good fishing, then!' And with that, the otter leapt from the dock and dove underwater, then began heading upstream towards Mouseling Hollow with a satchel full of the hamlet's mail still waiting to be delivered.

'Wait, wait!' yelled Teague. 'Fyz, I almost forgot — come back!'

The river otter poked his head above water again.

'Did you call me, sirs?'

Teague sighed a breath of relief and reached into his pocket, pulling out a note.

He looked at it one more time. It said:

My Young Friend Squeak,

I have heard that you are doing a fantastic job of keeping The Captain on his toes. Unfortunately, I was...delayed...in being able to come visit you at his inn, and am now about to embark upon another journey.

Know that your aid to me in our recent adventure was invaluable, and instrumental in saving Castle Feldenspar. When I return, I will look forward to us having an extended visit together. We keep plenty of Feldenspar Roquefurt in stock at The Sleeping Cat, as it is one of my wife's favorites.

*Know also that we will look for your parents along our journey. I am sure they
are not far from home now. Keep the faith for their return.*

*Take these gold coins that I've enclosed for you — give two to The Captain
for your upkeep, and use the last to go and buy yourself some new clothes — I'm
sure his assistant will be able to help you with that. Mind your manners with The
Captain, as he is doing both of us a great favor.*

Until the next time we meet.

Yours Faithfully,

Robert Teague

*P.S.: I have found some interesting information on The Lost Ones, which I
look forward to sharing with you when we see each other next. Keep working on
translating that puzzle — I know that treasure is out there somewhere!*

Teague folded over the parchment and stashed three gold coins
in it, then looked at Fyz.

'I'm afraid I don't have an envelope with me, postmaster. Could
you be so kind as to help me?'

Fyz grabbed the note and placed it in a special pouch in his mail
sack, then gave Teague a jaunty salute.

'No problem at all, Master Teague! Where will I be taking this?'

'The Feldenspar Inn — to The Captain, if you will.'

'Ahh, indeed sir. I will have it in his paws by sunset then — you
have my word!'

And with that, the otter dove back underwater and resumed his
swim upstream.

Wilding, meanwhile, had strolled back to the barn. 'Well boys,' he
said, 'all we need to do now is load up, and I believe we can then be
on our way.'

And so they did. After heaving provisions, camping equipment,
and cold weather gear onto the flat skiff, Snowwillow appointed
himself loadmaster and directed the others in how to tie it all
down firmly. Once that task was complete, the party proceeded
to stow the remainder of their gear into the pole boats — fishing
gear, waterskins, snacks and weapons, all cleverly secured beneath

the gunwales. With their gear now stashed safely, they stood in the boathouse silently as Wilding lifted the door which would allow the boats to access The Silver River. With the door open, the balmy breeze and sunshine of Second Summer floated in and warmed their whiskers, and an eager anticipation filled them all. They watched the river meander placidly as it curved around the bend. The sight held such a sense of...tranquility...that it momentarily belied what they knew was to come, and the challenges they would most certainly be facing in the days ahead.

The four mice looked at each other until Robert Teague broke the silence.

'Well,' said Teague 'there is only one thing left for us to do.' They looked at him quizzically until he thrust his paw into the middle of their circle.

'To defeating The Rat King — no matter what the cost.'

The other three thrust their paws in, and with haste, all of the paws were soon stacked on top of each other.

'To defeating The Rat King,' they chimed in unison.

And with that, there was nothing left to say.

Snowwilllow headed back to his falcon and it soon leapt into flight, rising high on a warm updraft to act as an overwatch for the rest of the party. Wilding climbed nimbly onto the gear skiff and pushed it out of the boathouse using a long pole. It quickly caught the downriver current and began gliding away from the riverbank, with Wilding using his pole to deftly navigate the currents. Teague and Hearthseeker settled into the more deeply walled pole boat, which was driven by Teague's careful maneuvering of a long pole. With Teague standing astern and Hearthseeker sitting in the bow, their boat gently eased itself out into the current as well.

As the party floated downstream, taking in the idyllic setting, they heard the chorus of birds and the buzzing of insects as the sun came out over the treeline — and suddenly, things were looking up. Hearthseeker took his golden, polished lute from off his back and began to play a tune, with Teague and Wilding singing along. As they continued their drift downstream, to destinations and adventures unknown, Hearthseeker couldn't help thinking to himself, *The Fabled Two, once written off as legend, now return, ready to thwart the legions of The Rat King — and I will be accompanying them every step of the way. It's true what they say: the Lady does indeed have quite the sense of humor.*

It was going to be a grand tale, to be certain — a song to be sung with equal pride in both royal castles and Mouseling hamlets, throughout the underhill and dales. Brilliant tales of valor and honor — some of which had already transpired, but so many of which remained to be seen and recorded — most certainly awaited them down river.

But for the time being, as the party drifted downstream with the gorgeous melody of Hearthseeker's music to lull them — everything seemed very normal and uneventful. Wilding saluted Snowwillow high in the air and the Falconrider waved back, while Robert Teague baited a line with a lure of grub on it and cast it into the waters behind his boat, allowing it to dance and drift along the river's current. It was there, in the picturesque tranquility of that particular moment, as he breathed in the fresh air and absorbed the enchanting miasma of the headwaters that almost seemed to be alive themselves, that Robert Teague thought to himself, *it is almost too easy to forget what lies ahead and to just be thankful that I'm surrounded by the finest companions one could ask for. Were the circumstances different, this could just as easily be a fishing trip in truth.*

Teague took a moment to breathe in the fresh river air, and to look at each of his companions in turn.

And THAT is an encouraging notion, he thought while he watched the spires of FireMaple Abby slowly disappear out of sight as the river began to bend — though he could still spy the brilliant orange and crimson leaves of the FireMaple tree begin to scatter and drift upon the wind, high above the waterwheel on the riverbank. Suddenly — and quite unexpectedly — the small mouse was overtaken by a deep sense of melancholy, saddened by the thought that he may never see Mouseling Hollow, or his beloved family, again.

Yes, just a simple fishing trip, he reminded himself, *nothing more.* And his heart brightened a little.

A fishing trip which would, no doubt, lead to much more... interesting adventures to come.

And so I chronicled this story by my left paw, and firsthand

Ainsley Hearthseeker,
Bard of The Fabled Two
The Year of Our Lady 250

EPILOGUE

While the winter wind continued to whip outside the log home, inside, the cozy fire had burned down to embers.

With a great stretch and a bear-like yawn, the old mouse in the chair placed a bookmark where the story had stopped and closed the aged leather tome he held in his lap.

Glancing across the carpet, he was surprised to see that of the dozen mice on the carpet, none had fallen asleep. Twelve pairs of eyes remained transfixed on their grandpa, enthralled by the story.

Clearly, they wanted more.

'Come on, Grandpa, read some more of the story!' said one.

'Shhh, shhh!' said some of the other mice, trying to quiet the one Mouseling down and demonstrate to their grandfather that they had behaved well enough to earn the right to hear more of the story.

A moment of silence passed between them all, as the wind continued to whip in a frenzy outside the warmth of the old log house, out in the darkness.

Finally, one inquisitive mouse asked, transfixed, 'What happens next, Grandpa?'

The old storyteller in the chair smiled, and put his legs back up on the figure-8 shaped stool in front of him. He knew the way he had told the story had undoubtedly captured all of their imaginations.

And that's a good thing, the old mouse thought to himself as he took another nip of port, finally draining his once-full glass. *This world needs a great deal more heroes in it — and who better than these mice to start off with, inspiring them to greatness through the deeds of their legendary ancestors? Yes, we need more heroes, that's for certain.*

He looked back at the inquisitive mouse, who was wearing a large pair of spectacles.

'What happens next? Why, you should know the answer to that already...what happens next is you mice going to your bunks and turning in for a good winter's nap!'

At this amusing joke, the old storyteller laughed heartily. The younger mice, however, were *not* amused.

'Nooo, Grandpaaaaa!' the young mouse protested. 'I *mean*, what happens next in the *story*?'

'Aaah, in the story...' The old mouse steepled his paws together and looked up at his wooden ceiling, thinking about how best to answer the question.

'What happens next in the story, you ask...well, my young friend, allow me to answer your question with a question. Do you know where The Silver River ends?'

'Yes, Grandfather. It ends in Pirate's Bay, which then opens into The Southern Ocean.'

'Exactly,' said the old mouse. 'And tell me, my intelligent young Mouseling — does The Silver River run in a straight line, flowing quickly to its end?'

'Nay, Grandfather! It meanders its way south, winding, twisting, and turning along the ports of all the cities poised upon its edge, until it finally reaches The Bay of Pirates after great length.'

'Correct again!' said the wizened old mouse. 'And now, answer my last question — could you run down The Silver River and reach The Bay of Pirates in but a day? Or an evening?'

'Of course not, sir! It would take seasons and seasons to reach the Bay! Or one full season, at least,' said the spectacled mouse, thinking keenly about the size of the undertaking. 'And you cannot run down the whole river anyway! You would have to take The Riverpath, then make the crossing at Mousebrook, and then...'

His grandfather interrupted him.

'Exactly, my lad, exactly! You could not make it in a day — or a night — and you cannot run where the river does not take you. This story, children, is like The Silver River. There is only one way you can get to the end of it — and that is by taking your time, listening to every word, and enjoying it! Have you enjoyed your story this evening, my grandchildren?'

'Yes!' they cheerfully chorused in unison.

'And who is your favorite Mouseling in the story, my young bucks and does?'

The children burst into a choir of shouts, with the old mouse hearing everything from 'Robert Teague' to 'Wilding' to 'Kerrigan Teague!'

'Alright, alright,' laughed the old mouse in the chair. 'I am glad that you have all found that you identify with some of the heroes in the story! And there is still much more to come tomorrow night — as long as you don't pester me all day asking me about it, at least. Now then, off to bed, my grandchildren. Hup to, quick march!'

And with that, the mice scurried off, down through the kitchen to the bedroom wing of the hallway. He could hear the muffled sound of them jumping and crashing into their bunk beds, many doubling up, with echoes of laughter reverberating down the hallway.

Good sounds, those, thought the mouse. *Life has returned to Mouseling Hollow.*

He reached for his glass of port again, only to see, disappointingly, that he had emptied it moments ago.

Well, on that note, perhaps it is time for this old mouse to go to bed as well, he thought.

Getting up out of his chair, he put the old book back upon the shelf and threw a few more logs into the fire. Walking over to the frozen window, he pressed his snout against it and watched the blizzard whip snow gusts into a frenzy. He could see the leafless trees, silhouetted in the backdrop of the purple-black sky, looking crooked and empty.

BRR! It sure looks cold outside, he thought.

Glancing back at the fire, he saw the seasoned wood he had thrown into the fireplace had begun to catch flame.

But it's cozy and warm in here, he thought to himself with a nod of satisfaction.

As his gaze switched from the window back over to the fire, something gleaming above it caught the corner of his eye. He looked above the fireplace mantle and spied a shining sword hanging upon the wall, looking just as valiant and epic as the swords described in the leather tome he had just finished reading to his grandchildren.

That sword looks exactly like Rattlemourne, he thought to himself with a smile.

As the winds continued to whip mercilessly in their nighttime frenzy, the old storyteller exited the library, still fully dressed in his tasseled nightcap and gown, and trundled down the hallway to his own snuggly bed — where his warm wife, warm sheets, and a warm winter's nap awaited him as well. But still, he had quite enjoyed telling the tale of **The Fabled Two** — the first part of it, at least — and knew that the children who had listened to it, who in all likelihood had already drifted off to sleep, were now dreaming of the valiant adventures they had been regaled with. And, perhaps — should the dream fairy be so generous — playing a starring role in those adventures: fighting evil, saving the weak and helpless, and in doing so, becoming heroes themselves.

Even if only in dreams, he thought.

He couldn't wait to tell more of the story tomorrow.

But even in Mouseling Hollow, thought the storyteller to himself, *the best things come to those who wait.*

Stormsnout: By Her holy paw, Alfred, I've done it! I'VE DONE IT!

Alfred (comes running): *Done what, sir?*

Stormsnout: *I have effectively synthesized Element 115 on the Periodic Table into a stable isotope at room temperature — with a half-life of no less than three days! Look at this, it is right here in its physical form! DO YOU HAVE ANY IDEA WHAT THIS MEANS?*

Alfred (flustered, aghast): *What does it mean, sir?!*

Stormsnout: *Holy cheese wheel, my good man, do you not understand the implications? It means that pariah Bobby Lazarus down in Old Town was right all along, you damned fool!* **THEY CRUCIFIED HIM FOR IT**, *but he was telling the truth* **THE WHOLE TIME!** *They live!* **THEY LIVE!**

(Stormsnout runs over and squints, peering through the observatory telescope)

Stormsnout: *AND THEY ARE OUT THERE, WATCHING US, RIGHT NOW...*

— Taken from **The Adapted Plays of The Life of Sir Pendleton Stormsnout: A Mad Genius of The First Age**

AFTERWORD

I'm sitting in my office in Memphis, Tennessee, looking out the window. I've been in the better parts of two states today, dropping my young daughters off at school and buying houses. I just finished buying a home in North Mississippi, and after finishing up the requisite documentation I sent over to my closing attorney, I will resell the home to a client who has been asking me to help them buy some rental property for their child's college fund.

That's what I do — I write about, invest in, and help counsel others to buy real estate. And I've been doing it for fifteen years, full time.

Outside my window though, the temperature is dropping — grey clouds and the scent of an afternoon rain lurk on the horizon. It is the first official day of Autumn. And, due to the fact that the air is becoming chilly and the harvest time is upon us, my mind naturally drifts to the world of **Mouseling Hollow**. As it wanders, I wonder what Robert Teague and his merry band of stalwart, yet diminutive, adventurers are up to.

If I had to guess, they would be getting a late afternoon dinner ready and having some well earned drinks at The Sleeping Cat Inn and Tavern, watching the brilliantly colored leaves change and fall quietly from the trees. Maybe they are sitting around an outdoor fire, sniffing the delectable crisp Autumn air as some Rosemary Garlic Butter Bread rises over the crackling flames. Perhaps Ainsley

Hearthseeker, bard that he is, sits on a nearby log enjoying the smell of the succulent, fire-baked bread. Perhaps he is playing his tiny, golden wood lute as Wilding makes his way up The Riverpath with Ducky for a delicious fall supper by the outdoor firepit with kindred friends. As the sun sets, tiny decorations of hay and mouse-sized baby pumpkins permeate the doorstep of The Sleeping Cat, adding a sweet — but wistful — sense of melancholy to the scene; the unspoken foreboding of the unseen, yet inevitable, touch of coming Winter, close at hand — or should I say, **at paw.**

I haven't always wanted to be a writer. But at some point as a college freshman at Syracuse University, I realized I had a knack — some even dared to say a gift — for two things: writing and speaking. Then one night, in my dorm room, I had a dream about an eleven year old boy named Ragan who lived in an abusive household with a terrible stepdad, and he ended up running away — stowing away on a steamship to Africa. There, he witnessed the poaching of a female elephant who had recently given birth to a baby elephant, whom Ragan helped to escape the poachers' clutches. The two formed an inseparable bond and went on to have adventures across the African continent. That dream became my very first novel, titled **'A Cry For Elephants.'**

But when I sent it to the person who I thought would like it the best, they ripped it apart instead. 'No eleven year old boy would ever stow away to Africa,' they said. When I pointed out that Issac Albeniz, the famous Spanish pianist, did just that, stowing away to South America, it didn't matter. 'Stick to teaching — you can get a safe, secure job that way. You'll never become a great writer.'

And, unfortunately, I listened. And with that, my first novel died, along with any thoughts of becoming a professional writer — as did the eighteen year old kid inside of me. I threw out the manuscript and was really sad afterwards, but life had been like that for me growing up — a lot of hard roadblocks to face, so to speak. I went back to studying, working my bartending job, and trying to graduate, and for three decades afterwards I thought my dreams of writing had been left back in that trash can up in Syracuse.

Years later, when I found out that there was neither 'safety' nor 'security' in the world of public school teaching, I ended up getting into real estate. Fast forward fifteen years, and I am glad to say that my first published book, **The Short Term Retirement Program**, became an international bestseller on Amazon. That's good, because it tells the story of how a schoolteacher became a successful real estate investor, and I designed it to help people who are sick of being broke become financially free through real estate in a reasonably short period of time. I am really proud of that book, even though it took me seven years to complete, simply for this one reason — there is so much baseless fluff in the world of nonfiction real estate that you can buy dozens of books and not really learn anything. I wanted my book to be different — **and it had to be perfect.** I wanted to put a book together that would be a companion, in a sense, for someone starting out — for a $20 investment you could really move forward on solid ground and have a manual by your side to help you stay focused.

But the flipside of getting my first book published was that I learned a LOT about the publishing industry. It is a lot like the radio industry today, and I should know — I spent ten years in radio with the top weekend program in conservative news talk in Memphis. Publishing books and radio programming can both be very predatory — if you have the money, then you can have a radio show, or get a book published, too, regardless of talent — and oftentimes even the best writers don't ever get recognized. Of course, I learned all this the hard way — like so many lessons in the publishing industry.

It was a rough road.

Finally, I just made the decision that moving forward, I would self-publish all my books. It is easier that way, and that way my books will never go out of print. I wanted to write books *my way* — original stories written for readers who don't like conformity. And I *know* there are alot of you out there.

Which brings me to **Mouseling Hollow.**

I've always wanted to write a book about mice. I'm not sure why — maybe it's a compulsion, or maybe it's just destiny — but for twenty years I thought to myself, 'someday, when I have time, I will write a fantasy book about mice.' Last Thanksgiving, with **The Short Term Retirement Program** completed and released, I sat down and composed the first chapter of **Mouseling Hollow** — just to see if I could write fiction. For me, writing nonfiction came easy — it's a lot like teaching, which I had studied and done for years. Each chapter is like a lesson plan. It's very cut and dried.

The original first chapter of **Mouseling Hollow**, however, was a train wreck in slow motion — I realized I had to make up names and places, but more importantly, it all had to be coherent and consistent — not to mention having an engrossing story line. It was WORK. A **LOT** of work. Fiction — especially high quality, high fantasy fiction — is a different bear altogether, and that bear ate my lunch, plus my Thanksgiving dinner that holiday.

But I kept at it.

The thing that makes writing about mice so fascinating to me is that when you reduce the scale of the world from human size to Mouseling size, you get to do so many more descriptive, imaginative, and fun things. Mouselings ride squirrels, ravens, and falcons. They hide under cups. They go fishing in pairs for minnows because one Mouseling alone isn't strong enough — if he or she is lucky enough to get a big bite — to reel a minnow in on their own without the possibility of taking a swim. They live in logs — exquisite, well furnished logs. They cook magnificent meals with ingredients they've 'borrowed' from their human counterparts. They play games and train in physical combat with diminutive weapons. It's fascinating and fun. The hamlet of **Mouseling Hollow** — and its commensurate larger world, which has become known as **The Far Collective** — was a fun place to spend time in. Creating in it, writing in it, adventuring in it, playing in it — these were all terribly fun things to do.

The real problems arrived when I finished the manuscript — or thought I had. I sent it to my editor of **The Short Term Retirement**

Program, who sent it back to me and politely recommended that I hire a developmental editor. She gave me the name of the Editorial Freelance Association (THE-EFA.org), and feeling rejected, but knowing she was giving me sound advice, I put up a post advertising the fact that I was writing 'Mouse Fiction.' I went to bed that night dejected, thinking that no one would want to work on this project.

However, when I woke up, to my surprise and bewilderment, I had received hundreds — yes, hundreds! — of responses. All very qualified editors, of course — but I had to make a selection, and narrowed it down to three super qualified candidates. But what really matters is that I picked the right one from the start — Dr. Matthew Ross.

Dr. Ross and I worked diligently to take **Mouseling Hollow** and mold it into its best possible form. A form which, we both realized, would span multiple books of significant length. I couldn't have done it without him, to be frank — if I was its architect, he was the supervisor of construction who kept giving me honest and critical feedback. It wasn't easy to hear at times, to be sure — but what really kept me going and the thing that made me realize I had selected the right editor was that **MATT LOVED THE BOOK**. He loved the story and its characters, and we would talk for hours on the phone about the antics and personalities of all of these vibrant adventurers that we brought to life, their interweaving stories, and the challenges they faced both individually and as companions.

Sir Pendleton Stormsnout, the legendary Mouseling detective, is just one example — he is so smart, but he comes across as a *total and unadulterated jerk*. Matt and I, in email and phone conversations, discussed how we both loved and are highly approving of his particularly unique qualities — and as I wrote more about this Mouseling and his offensive personality, we decided that he probably deserves his own book. That's the way **Mouseling Hollow** has worked, interestingly enough — it is a world which is openly welcoming and lends itself to any number of a variety of purposes for high entertainment and engagement: the high fantasy reader, the role playing gamer, the board gamer, the collectible card gamer, the lover of detective novels, the film fanatic. It's a world that has its own breath and life — and for that, as its author, I am forever grateful. I can't wait to see what new directions **The Far Collective** finds itself heading in, beyond simply the printed page.

It is its own sandbox — and **that**, my friends, is a very exciting prospect.

It goes without saying, we ran into a lot of obstacles along the way — mainly from the publishing industry itself. I wanted to write a book for both young adults and older adults that focused on mice who 'drink beer and get into fights' — and many editors told me that:

1) I needed to pick a category, so which was it? In their eyes, there are no 'crossover' reading groups — meaning that they don't believe young adults read adult fiction, and vice versa.

2) Any book about mice 'needs to be a children's book' because — according to them — **adults don't want to read books about mice who drink beer and go on adventures,** and,

3) When I told them I wanted to illustrate **Mouseling Hollow,** they told me that no one illustrates books for adults or young adults, because quite simply (in their eyes), 'that's childish.'

As we completed the book, I did get an offer — a few offers, actually — from publishing companies after we sent them the manuscript. One publisher described it as 'absolutely charming' — win! **(insert fist pump here).** But in the end, we both decided to move forward the way we had from the start — which, in a nutshell, meant doing the opposite of what we were told by the dinosaurs in the world of book publishing. That's been the story of my life, really — **see which way the crowd is running, then run the other way as fast as possible.**

So, with that, here is a book about 'mice who fight and drink beer' (alot of beer, actually), with maps and illustrations, for **both** older adults and young adults alike.

It is my fervent prayer that you love **The Far Collective** as much as I do — and, if you do, drop me a line at robertfeol@gmail.com to let me know about it! I will keep writing adventures for Robert Teague and his crew for years to come, if you promise to keep reading and enjoying them.

Lastly, it's important to me to note that this book can be read out loud to your family as a family centered activity — there is no offensive language, nor any racy scenes, contained herein. As a parent with three young children, **The Far Collective** is, and will always be, G-rated. Finally, as a gift to the publishing industry, I created a new name, and a new genre, for this kind of book: **Family Fireside Reading**. That means that this tale is truly meant for the ENTIRE family — both adults and children. It's G-rated, but not intended solely as a children's story. While publishers told me I had to make a critical decision and answer the question: 'is this a story for children or adults?' **I rejected that way of thinking in favor trying to write a story for ALL ages** — the idea being that this is a book written so that children, young adults, and older adults can all read and share it together, taking pleasure in a timeless story while sharing one another's company.

Innovative, I know.

May your journeys through **The Far Collective** be ever amazing, your **Crab Apple Frost Wine** be ice cold, and your **Root and Field** game always be on point.

From my Mississippi Farm to Your Hearth,

Robert C. Feol

Memphis, Tennessee
September 22nd,2020

Pitmaster Robert Feol's Tavern Smoked Meatloaf with Garlic Boursin Mash

A real 'Ratatouille moment,' this will bring you back to dusky, wintry Decembers looking at the barren trees in the crepuscular twilight outside while savoring the warmth and goodness of family inside. Pair with Pinot Noir for an additional layer of decadence.

Seasoning Mix:

2 teaspoons dried mustard

2 teaspoons paprika

1 teaspoon salt

1/2 teaspoon Spanish thyme

2 teaspoons Old Bay

1 teaspoon black pepper

1 teaspoon garlic powder

1 teaspoon onion powder

Several sprigs dried thyme, on stem — the fresher the better

For the Meatloaf:

2 Eggs, fresh

About 25 crackers, crushed (butter style)

⅛ cup milk

1 lb ground chuck, fresh

1 lb ground mild Italian sausage, fresh

Montreal Steak Seasoning

Uncle Feol's Tennessee Style Competition Steak Seasoning System Part I (with garlic butter!)

One yellow onion, sweet, diced

1/4 cup minced garlic

For the Glaze:

Blues Hog 'Feol Style' Sauce (Blues Hog original base, ⅓ can pineapple concentrate, ⅓ cup Cimmaron Doc's sweet chili rub)

⅛ cup Light brown sugar

Worcestershire Sauce, about 5 teaspoons

Dijon mustard (preferably Grey Poupon)

Directions:

In a stainless steel bowl, combine dry ingredients for rub, add two eggs and milk, stir with whisk until well combined. In a separate sauté pan, incorporate diced onions and garlic, sauté until garlic is slightly toasted and onions translucent, then add dash of salt and pepper. Add both beef selections to seasoning bowl, add garlic and onion, add crushed crackers and mix by hand until well combined. Once combined, add fresh or dry thyme springs and incorporate. Form into a loaf and place in meatloaf pan. Top generously with Montreal Steak seasoning. Let sit for fifteen minutes while you make the glaze.

Form the glaze by using a saucepan or small skillet — add the base sauce, mix in the brown sugar, mustard and Worcestershire sauce, bring to a boil and then remove from stove. Allow to cool for a few minutes, then, using a silicone brush, glaze the meatloaf top with the glaze mixture.

Preheat a pellet grill to 350 using apple pellets. Once your smoker has reached 350, put the meatloaf on for about one hour until cooked through. There should be no pink spots in the loaf and the glaze should be very sticky and caramelized.

> **Note:** *You can smoke in a meatloaf double pan (so it does not cook in a pool of fat, which is nasty) OR, leave the loaf on a cooking sheet in the smoker (or foil) and let the smoke penetrate more deeply to get an even more robust smoke flavor.*

For the mashed potatoes:

6 Yukon gold potatoes, scrubbed but unskinned

1/2 tub Alouette boursin (or similar) with garlic and herbs, tub size 5.2 oz.

⅓ stick French salted butter or Kerrygold

Himalayan pink salt

1 tbsp white truffle butter

Heavy whipping cream

Dried paprika and thyme springs (for garnish, optional)

1 head garlic, roasted in oven until softened (395 for 1 hour, in foil with olive oil and salt drizzle)

Directions:

Boil the potatoes for about an hour until a knife can penetrate easily through — do not overcook. Drain potatoes in colander. Using a hand mixer, smash potatoes, add butter, truffle butter, and alouette boursin. Add heavy cream and incorporate. Once potatoes start to smooth with mixing, add roasted garlic and beat until smooth. I used about ¼ quart heavy cream for a very smooth mash. Garnish with paprika and thyme sprigs.

ABOUT THE AUTHOR

Much like Mouseling Robert Teague, International bestselling author **Robert C. Feol** as a testament that if you put your mind to it, you can achieve anything, no matter how hard the task. Among Feol's accomplishments, he triple majored at Syracuse University and obtained a Master's Degree in Deaf Education from The National Technical Institute For The Deaf, where all his classes were taught in American Sign Language.

A modern *renaissance man*, Feol is an eager and accomplished student of many disciplines — real estate, writing, radio, martial arts, classical guitar, fantasy gaming, and competition BBQ. The most important things to him, however, are striving to be a great husband and parent.

He lives on a micro farm with his amazing wife Shannon and three children — Robbie, Kerrigan, and Tennessee…a lot of chickens… and a massive German Shepherd named Ranger who would definitely want to snuggle with you if you came to visit.

They live in Olive Branch, Mississippi.

'Destiny isn't a chance, it's a choice….'

—Robert Feol

*"Winning is not a sometime thing;
it's an all time thing.
You don't win once in a while,
you don't do things right once in a while,
you do them right all the time.
Winning is habit.
Unfortunately, so is losing."*

– VINCE LOMBARDI